'Written with the usual biting wit and a talent to create likeable characters in believable situations, it's another unputdownable Haran masterpiece'
– *What's On*

'Maeve Haran has the great knack of tackling a tough contemporary issue, adding a dollop of warmth and humour and telling her tale at a rollicking pace'
– *Northern Echo*

'Maeve Haran whips up a light and enjoyable read in *It Takes Two*'
– *Woman's Journal*

'She has a feel for the substantial concerns of her readers . . . which is why she has become required reading for modern romantics'
– *The Times*

'The new st

Maeve Haran was editor of LWT's acclaimed Six O'Clock Show where she produced Michael Aspel, Paula Yates, Gloria Hunniford and Chris Tarrant. After the birth of her second child she gave up television to write at home. She lives in London with a large Scotsman and their three children.

Her first novel, *Having it All*, was a massive bestseller in both hardback and paperback and has been sold in twenty-two languages around the world. Both this and her second novel, *Scenes from the Sex War*, are published by Signet and available as Penguin Audiobooks read by the actress Belinda Lang.

MAEVE HARAN

IT TAKES TWO

A SIGNET BOOK

SIGNET

Published by the Penguin Group
Penguin Books Ltd, 27 Wrights Lane, London w8 5tz, England
Penguin Books USA Inc., 375 Hudson Street, New York, New York 10014, USA
Penguin Books Australia Ltd, Ringwood, Victoria, Australia
Penguin Books Canada Ltd, 10 Alcorn Avenue, Toronto, Ontario, Canada m4v 3b2
Penguin Books (NZ) Ltd, 182–190 Wairau Road, Auckland 10, New Zealand

Penguin Books Ltd, Registered Offices: Harmondsworth, Middlesex, England

First published by Michael Joseph 1994
Published in Signet 1994
1 3 5 7 9 10 8 6 4 2

The quotation on page 201 from 'This Be The Verse',
from Philip Larkin's *Collected Poems*, is reproduced
by kind permission of Faber and Faber Ltd

Typeset by Datix International Limited, Bungay, Suffolk
Set in 10/12 pt Monophoto Plantin
Printed in England by Clays Ltd, St Ives plc

To Sweet Baby James –
hoping you grow up to be a New Man

ACKNOWLEDGEMENTS

With thanks to Hugh de Wet, until recently a top PR man, now an even better painter, for advice on art, art school and the joys and perils of changing careers at forty!

And to my brother, Tom Haran, who has also become a talented painter in his forties, for artistic background, for taking me to London's louche haunts at an impressionable age, and for always being such good company.

Also to Timothy Meaden for opening up the mysteries of Nintendo, Sega Megadrive and World Wrestling Federation.

And finally to the very kind divorce lawyers who answered my questions and explained what it's like to work in such an emotional minefield, especially when they are mothers themselves.

CHAPTER ONE

Stephen Gilfillan nuzzled his wife Tess's neck lascivi-
ously as she stood in front of their bedroom mirror
doing up the final button of her navy suit. Career
woman suits had always turned him on. Tess said she
wore them so as not to frighten the judges when she
had a court appearance, but Stephen suspected the
judges were probably more distracted than reassured
by the sight of Tess in strict tailoring, her red hair
tumbling to her shoulders, greeny-blue eyes glinting
with radical passion, reminding them of their lost
youth.

Just watching her Stephen felt himself harden until
his cock popped enthusiastically out from the tartan
boxer shorts she'd bought him for his last birthday.

'I don't suppose you've seen my dinner jacket anywhere?' he asked, turning her round to face him and
trying to undo the button she'd just done up. 'I need it
for tonight.'

'When did you have it last?' Tess enquired briskly,
ignoring the impressive display of ardour poking into
her right thigh.

'About 1973.' Stephen recognized that voice. It
meant Tess was in her Efficient Mode and that he was
doomed to disappointment, but her white neck looked
so inviting he had to kiss it one last time. 'Events like
this aren't really my thing.'

She smiled back, briefly sidetracked by Stephen's
beauty, by his dark curly hair, his eyes the colour of
stonewashed denim, the tautness of his body, still
lightly tanned from last year's holiday. He might be

pushing forty and staring the male menopause in the face but he was certainly in good nick. Just in time she pulled herself together. 'Chop chop. Time you got dressed.' She watched his erection subside in the face of her matronlike tone and pushed it gently but firmly back into his shorts. 'Your dinner jacket's in the wardrobe. I took it to the dry cleaners for you. They said it was very nice. The last one they'd seen like it was on George Raft. And there's a clean white shirt in the top drawer.' She patted him on the bottom in a patronizingly masculine gesture. 'Don't say I don't spoil you!'

'There's nothing wrong with my dinner suit,' Stephen defended it. 'My father wore it to every artistic event for thirty years. And there are better ways of spoiling a man than picking up his dry cleaning.' He made a last defiant lunge for her. 'In fact I can think of one now.'

'After the awards tonight,' Tess promised, squeezing his crotch affectionately, 'provided you win, of course.'

'Putting conditions on sex is probably grounds for divorce, you know. Unreasonable behaviour or something.'

'No it's not. I'd cross-petition on insatiable sexual appetite. At eight-thirteen on a Friday morning the judge'd be right behind me. Leave the divorce law to me. You concentrate on making the commercials.'

Stephen sat down on the bed and put his socks on. They were tartàn and matched his underpants. Not that anyone would know, he thought morosely. A lock of dark curly hair fell across his face. It was getting long again but Tess liked it best like that. She said it made him look poetic. *Poetic*, for Christ's sake. Poncy, more like. It was the eyelashes that did it. He'd always had long vampy eyelashes, the kind women yearn for.

Not to mention the Head Boy of his public school who'd offered eight conkers and a recommendation for prefect if Stephen batted them in his direction. Stephen had wisely taken up boxing instead.

There wasn't much call for poetry, he reflected, if you were an ad man. He zapped the TV's remote control wondering if his washing machine commercial would come on and what its chances were of winning tonight. He'd never been in line for an award before, especially a Golden Apple for Best Art Direction. He sat through an ad for Sega Megadrive, another for Super Mario, one for Mortal Kombat and another featuring a ghastly little girl building a beauty parlour out of pink Lego. Children were never too young to be the adman's target. What was it the Jesuits had said? Give me the first seven years of a child's life and you can keep the rest. A smart bunch, the Jesuits. They'd have made a great agency. Iggy Loyola & Company. They'd have creamed off every award going.

He pulled on the trousers of his unstructured suit, trying to shake off his cynicism. Today of all days he ought to feel wholeheartedly excited. If he won the award tonight he would have really made it. But was advertising really a job for a grown man? There you go again, he told himself, shaking his head and trying to clear away the corrosive thoughts. For once, just let yourself believe the bullshit.

Downstairs in the hall, Tess picked her way between Luke's bicycle and his rollerblades, noticing the pile of unopened letters addressed to Stephen, a number of them bills. She unzipped the plastic suit bag she'd hung on the coat-stand with her clothes for tonight. The pink silk jacket inside glowed back at her dazzlingly. Briefly she remembered the look on the shop assistant's face when she'd selected it. *Pink?* the girl's

3

expression had said, with *your* colour hair? Tess had bought it anyway. Why should redheads be stuck with twenty-nine shades of green? Her best friend Phil was always advising her to go to a colour counsellor but Tess loathed the idea. She didn't want to go round dressed like an autumn leaf, expected to take colour swatches with her every time she nipped into Next.

The pink would be fine. After she'd zipped it up again Tess turned and tripped on a black bag of old clothes left in the hall. They were supposed to be taken to Oxfam, but, life being life, seemed to have taken up permanent residence in the hall. She dropped down onto the stairs, rubbing her ankle and swearing in a way that would have shocked the judges, who liked to think her a nice, wholesome girl, if a mite spirited.

What she needed, Tess thought angrily, wasn't a colour counsellor, but a crap counsellor. Someone who would zip through her life chucking out everything she didn't need, ignoring all pleas of sentimental value or that it might come in useful one day. Sometimes she fantasized about a burglar who would come and steal everything in the house, leaving it completely bare. But she knew the reality. They'd take the telly and the video and leave the old newspapers, empty cassette boxes, clothes not worn for five years which she couldn't bring herself to chuck out, not to mention those mysterious plastic game parts, useless until thrown away and then rendered somehow vital and irreplaceable. She stopped herself there – no point in getting carried away – remembering that she needed a grey silk top which she suspected her sixteen-year-old daughter had pinched. She ran upstairs and put her head round Ellie's door.

The room, just visible beneath a sea of clothes, was empty. In one corner a two-foot pile of old copies of *Company* magazine served as dressing table, crowned by Stephen's missing shaving mirror. Next to the bed a coffee cup was quietly making enough penicillin to save an entire African tribe. The window was wide open, and on the sill Ellie had thoughtfully placed the black clodhoppers she wore with everything, from swimsuit to party frock to air.

The bathroom door opened and Ellie emerged in a blare of Kiss FM, leaving it steamier than the Amazon jungle, a fact which amazed Tess since she herself never managed to get bathwater that was more than lukewarm.

'What have you done with my silk top, you wretched child?' she demanded.

'Really, Mum.' Ellie mustered all the disdain of a punk rocker accused of wearing her mother's twinset and pearls. 'What makes you think I'd borrow anything of yours?'

Tess felt her temper rising. 'Bitter experience.' She spotted the missing top underneath a white crocheted bolero so tiny it reminded her of two of the doilies her mother used to make tacked together. 'What's this then?'

'Oh, that old thing,' shrugged Ellie, looking at seventy pounds' worth of designer camisole, given to Tess by Phil last Christmas. 'Well, you wouldn't want me to go out with nothing underneath the crochet, would you?'

Tess grabbed her silk top. Not only was it crumpled beyond ironing but drenched in patchouli. Great. Now she would look like a bag lady and smell like a flower child.

By the time she got downstairs Stephen and Luke

were quietly eating cereal and watching a video. Tess turned it off.

'Hey,' protested Stephen, 'that was *Kindergarten Cop*. My favourite. If I can't have sex at least leave me violence.'

'You haven't got time,' Tess explained patiently. 'I've got to go in early so I can leave on time for your do. That means you've got to take the kids to school and Inge hasn't had her cup of tea yet.' She kissed the top of his curly head before he could protest.

Stephen followed her into the kitchen testily. 'Correct me if I'm wrong, but isn't the idea of an au pair that they make tea for you rather than vice versa?'

'Usually,' Tess conceded, 'but not in our case.'

'Just remind me why that is?'

'Because our life depends on her.' Tess knew she let Inge get away with murder but was damned if she was going to feel guilty about it. On the whole Inge was an asset, and like most busy working women Tess was prepared to overlook the rest. 'Because the last three bonked their way into the *Guinness Book of Records*. Because you and I don't have time to take Luke to computer club, chess club, and all his other clubs. Because she phones home after eight instead of at peak time. Because Luke adores her. Stephen,' she pointed out as he boiled the kettle, 'you're using PG Tips. You know she prefers Earl Grey.'

Ten minutes later Stephen packed Ellie and Luke into the car as Inge, finally up and dressed in a pastel tracksuit, stood decoratively on the pavement waving them all goodbye. As she did so she indulged in her favourite fantasy of herself as Stephen's wife. She would, she mused, be far better at it than Tess. Poor Stephen, so handsome and young-looking, with a wife who neglected him for a job.

6

With a sigh Inge went inside. And now she had to clear up the breakfast things. Life was hard for au pairs.

Back in the kitchen she ignored the washing up and made herself a cup of coffee with one of the individual filters Tess used for dinner parties. Amongst the post a copy of *Marie-Claire* addressed to Mrs Tess Gilfillan gazed up at her invitingly. On the cover a headline caught her eye: 'WHY EVEN DEVOTED HUSBANDS CHEAT'. Inge sat down and opened it carefully. She could always put it back in the plastic cover after she'd read it. Curled up on the sofa with her coffee she felt more cheerful already.

As Tess squeezed her way through the glamorous crowd packing the Great Room of the Grosvenor House Hotel in Park Lane, she was deeply conscious of the difference between Stephen's world and her own. In the law you were considered over the top if you wore colours. Yet here tonight there was enough glitter and sequins to warm the heart of the most outrageous drag queen. Here you were more remark-able if your neckline *didn't* plunge to your navel. Subtlety wasn't a quality much prized by advertising people. And yet, mixed in amongst the birds of para-dise were a few dull thrushes in polyester pastel, clearly the wives of The Client, up from the suburbs, their handbags clamped to their sides as though they might at any moment be wrenched from their grasp by some raffish account exec.

Tess, aware that in her pink silk jacket and patchouli-scented camisole she probably looked as though she belonged to neither group, craned her neck looking for Stephen.

Around the stage area, where a cut-price Courtney

7

Pine combo jammed away ignored by everyone, about a hundred tables were ranged. It was a point of honour among the hot agencies to be seen at the front, and if they couldn't get ringside seats they sulked and stayed away. Stephen's agency was not hot. To be truthful it wasn't even tepid. But Stephen liked it because it was small, and British-owned, and not, as so many agencies were, answerable to some absentee landlord in Madison Avenue eager to squeeze out the last drop of profit.

'Tess! Over here!' Tess swung round to find Stephen, looking ludicrously attractive in his father's aged dinner jacket, standing by one of the front tables with his boss, Ted. He picked up a bottle of champagne from an ice-bucket and deftly opened it, handing her a glass.

'Nice table,' she remarked.

Ted grinned from ear to ear, looking to Tess like a leprechaun in a Moss Bros outfit. 'Those bastards from CCDO' – CCDO was currently the most prestigious agency in town – 'offered us a grand to change tables because theirs is stuck out in no man's land. We told them to stick their heads up their orifices.' He fell about at his dazzling wit.

'You look gorgeous,' murmured Stephen as Ted turned to offer a glass of champagne to one of his biggest rivals. 'Pink suits you. It shows you aren't hidebound by conventional ideas of colour.'

'You mean it screams at my hair.'

Stephen grinned.

She put her head close to his dark one and whispered, 'This table must have cost you a bomb.'

'It did. But we've got a lot at stake tonight.'

Tess brushed away a lock of curly hair that had fallen over his eyes. 'Don't be too disappointed if you don't win.' She was aware of a streak of protectiveness, almost as though he were Ellie or Luke.

'Don't worry, I'm a big boy now. It'd be brilliant for the agency though. Lots of new business just when we need it.' Over her shoulder he noticed a couple walking towards them. 'Aye, aye,' he said softly. 'Here comes The Adulterer. With Trophy Wife in tow.'

Tess looked round to find Greg, Phil's recently ex-husband, coming towards them with a walking, talking Barbie doll on his arm. Even her name sounded like some invention by a toy manufacturer.

'Tess, Stephen,' Greg hailed them both, beaming. 'You know Linzi, don't you?'

Tess surveyed the girl who had broken up her best friend's marriage and deprived Dan and Hattie of their father. 'Yes, of course. Hello, Sindy.'

'Linzi,' she corrected, revealing a flash of steel beneath the plastic.

'You can be the first to hear our good news,' smiled Greg.

Tess's sense of devilment rose. 'Don't tell me you're splitting up already?'

Greg looked at her oddly, but Linzi was too pleased with herself to notice. She smiled beatifically. 'We're having a baby. Greg's so thrilled.'

Tess felt a stab of fury on Phil's account. Really, the girl didn't have to sound so smug. What on earth was she going to tell Phil? Her friend was still reeling from the pain of the divorce even though it had been more than a year ago.

'Really? I thought he had two already?'

Stephen shot her a warning look. 'I think it's time we sat down. Everyone's going back to their tables.'

Breezily Greg and Linzi air-kissed Stephen and Tess

9

goodbye and fought their way through the glittering crowds.

'You didn't have to be quite so rude,' chided Stephen gently.

'Why not?' snorted Tess. 'There's nothing wrong with a bit of good old-fashioned disapproval.'

'What happened to Tess Brien, the great liberal?'

Tess grinned. 'She gets a bit lost where people she loves are concerned.'

The popping of a champagne cork two inches from Tess's ear brought a welcome diversion and she turned her attention to watching a thousand of London's top ad people shriek and kiss their way back to their tables. Suddenly millions of kilowatts of blinding white light beamed on, music started and Richard Kaye, Britain's highest-paid chat-show host, climbed on to the platform in a welter of cheers and applause. Tess had forgotten the event was to be televised. She felt a moment's surprise that the public would be that interested, then remembered that people often said they preferred the ads to the programmes.

For the next hour, as tension brought sweat to the armpits of even the most expensive dinner suits, Tess watched the assembled might of the ad industry wait and hope. Winning a major award here tonight meant both prestige and moving a couple of rungs up the corporate ladder. In advertising image was all. Agencies were 'hot' one moment and out of favour the next, winning and losing contracts worth millions of pounds as a way of life.

Tess had to admit the clips were entertaining. Humour had always been the thing the UK did best, though one or two ads were so strange that she couldn't help wondering what the ad men were on when they'd dreamed them up.

Then, finally, it was Stephen's category.

'And now,' intoned Richard Kaye reverently. 'One of the most prestigious awards of the night, Best Art Direction. There are four entries in this section.' A clip flashed on to the giant screen above their heads. 'First: Capel, Kramm, Robinson for their celebrated campaign for Silvertip Filter Cigarettes.'

Tess found herself hoping, rather ignobly since she had only given up smoking herself a few years ago, that surely in these days of political correctness a cigarette manufacturer couldn't walk off with the top award. But then, she reminded herself, advertising was hardly the guardian of the nation's morality.

A hush had fallen on the huge room, denoting the almost sacramental nature of the occasion. Tess smiled.

'Next: Butcher, Collins, Beckstein for Envy Jeans.' The BCB contingent cheered loudly, knowing they had successfully managed – with the help of a top film director and a budget that would have funded a minor Hollywood feature – to change the image of their product, blue jeans once worn by cowboys, to the leading brand bought by yuppies who didn't know one end of a horse from another.

The clip showed a Bardot-like blonde slowly undoing the fly buttons of a young man in a hotel which closely resembled the Ritz. The ad stopped just, but only just, short of porn. It was clearly serious competition though. Even Richard Kaye looked flustered as he continued his announcement.

'The third entry is Maxwell-Decourcey for British Water.' There was a universal cheer of support for this witty animation for the newly privatized water industry, which set out to persuade people that something which had hitherto been free, or almost free, was now a commodity beyond price.

Tess shifted in her seat and caught Stephen's eye. He raised an eyebrow in return, glancing round at the tensed-up faces at every table. How much money and creativity had been poured into these thirty-second mini-epics? And yet did they make a gram of difference to anyone? Most consumers couldn't even remember the name of the product.

And then it was the turn of his own ad. Richard Kaye was announcing the final contender – the D Agency's commercial for the Ultron X washing machine, shot on a tenth of the budget of most of his rivals. The ad which flashed above the room on giant screens featured three seals discussing the pros and cons of the Ultron washer-drier. It relied on wit and razor-sharp editing and even though shooting it had been a nightmare and he'd seen it at least a thousand times, it still made him laugh.

In spite of his cynicism, Stephen felt the atmosphere start to take him over. For the agency to win over its giant rivals would be amazing. But also, given the stiffness of the competition, highly unlikely.

'And the winner is . . .' Richard Kaye paused as though he were announcing Miss World and smiled directly into the lens of the camera, making the most of his moment, 'Stephen Gilfillan of the D Agency for the Ultron X washer-drier!'

Everything around them erupted while Stephen went up to accept the award. As he fought his way back to his seat Ultron's MD, a mild-mannered man from Wolverhampton, kissed him on both cheeks with the enthusiasm of Dickie Attenborough. Ted pumped his hand; friends, clients and prospective clients all homed in to pat him on the back. Only at the Envy Jeans table did the executives of Butcher, Collins, Beckstein murmur dissent. They too knew how much

Stephen's commercial had cost to make compared with their own. The chairman leaned across to his deputy. 'Sickening, isn't it, when Stephen Gilfillan's always slagging off the biz?'

'Absolutely,' endorsed the other man. 'Awards should go to people who believe in advertising.' He smiled. 'Or at least keep their mouths shut.'

A few feet away Stephen's friend, Greg, grinned to himself. Stephen was certainly getting up a few noses tonight. Not that it would do any him any harm. Every industry liked to have its *enfants terribles*. Someone to have a conscience so they didn't need to.

'You did it!' Tess shouted delightedly. 'You really did it!'

'You mean even my loving wife wasn't entirely confident in me?'

Tess laughed as a photographer from *Campaign* clicked away and a reporter from *Marketing Week* asked what it felt like to win when you were the rank outsider.

And finally it was over. The toasts drunk, the champagne bottles emptied, and they poured themselves into a taxi and poured themselves out again as the cab turned into their street at the wrong end of the King's Road.

In the hall Tess tripped over the Oxfam bag again but, instead of swearing, this time she giggled. In the kitchen she pulled Stephen to her and kissed him, almost bursting with pride. 'How about a nightcap for the conquering hero? Brandy? A malt whisky?'

'Ovaltine,' he stated firmly.

She laughed. A low rich chuckle full of sexual promise.

'That's the nice thing about marriage.' Stephen

13

watched as she searched for a milk pan. 'You dare to admit the truth. Ovaltine instead of single malt.'

Tess poured milk into the pan and looked at him challengingly. 'So, superstar, how does it feel to be the hottest ad man in town?'

'Come over here, know-all, and find out.' Tess saw the glint of arousal in Stephen's half-closed eyes as lazily he started to undo the buttons of her pink silk jacket, and this time she didn't stop him. 'Let's forget the Ovaltine, shall we?'

Behind them, unnoticed, the milk boiled over.

In the next few months Tess would look back on that night time and time again, searching for clues of what was to come, some sign of what was about to happen to their marriage. But there were none. Not yet.

CHAPTER TWO

'Congratulations, Dad!' Ellie threw her arms round her father and gave him a resounding kiss the next morning at breakfast

'Congratulations, Stephen,' Inge endorsed admiringly. 'It is like the Oscars, yes?'

'A bit,' Stephen conceded modestly.

Luke looked up from his World Wrestling Federation magazine. 'I was wondering, Dad . . .'

'Yes?' Stephen smiled at the seriousness on his twelve-year-old son's face.

'. . . what's advertising *for* exactly?'

Stephen laughed. 'Search me. I only work in it.' Tess listened, surprised. There was a a slight edge of sarcasm and a defensiveness in his tone that surprised her on this day of all days.

She leaned over and ruffled his hair, then started to search for her briefcase. She was usually the first to leave, except when it was her days to take Ellie and Luke to school. Mostly Inge did it.

'Mum, can I ask Lil and Penny round tonight?' enquired Ellie, referring to her two terrifyingly cool best friends.

'Not unless I have a chaperone,' said Stephen. 'Those two are shameless.'

Ellie giggled. 'They just fancy you, that's all.'

'Well I don't fancy them. They frighten the life out of me. They're Amazons. I blame all that brown bread and sunflower margarine. Anyway, haven't they heard of Lolita?'

'Absolutely,' Ellie insisted, 'and they're both right

behind her. Anyway it's your own fault.'

'*My* fault?' Stephen glanced at Ellie, puzzled. 'How can it be my fault?'

'You just don't look like other dads.' She stretched up and patted him condescendingly. 'Don't worry, you'll be old and bald soon.'

'Thanks a lot.' Stephen pushed her off affectionately. 'I'm glad I've got something to look forward to.'

'Do you want a lift to the tube station?' Tess offered, deciding he needed rescuing. But before she got to the front door the phone in the hall went. Tess picked it up. It was her mother.

'Hello, Mum.' She looked at her watch and raised her eyes to heaven. Her mother had an unerring knack of ringing at the wrong moment and then sounding wounded if Tess put her off.

Stephen grinned disloyally and mouthed the words 'I'll walk' at her. Tess's mother Dymphna, once on the line, was very difficult to dislodge.

'So how's life in London?' asked Dymphna. 'It obviously keeps you busy since you never phone me.' Tess sighed. It was amazing how Dymphna managed to get her disapproval both of Tess abandoning Liverpool, and of her daughter's busy lifestyle, into the first sentence.

Her mother had never understood why Tess had to leave their home town when her four sisters had all stayed nearby, providing Dymphna with a constant soap opera of crisis and catastrophe in which she was the chief soothsayer and giver of advice, a role she thrived on. And Tess had to admit Dymphna played the part brilliantly, always there, able to soothe any fretful baby to sleep within seconds on her ample chest, the kitchen of her council house constantly full of neighbours dropping in and out, the kettle forever on as they exchanged gossip and old wives' tales that made Tess's hair stand on end.

But Tess had wanted to spread her wings. Their first quarrel was when she chose London University in preference to Liverpool. 'They'll look down on you with your accent,' was Dymphna's dire warning. 'They'll say you keep coal in the bath.'

Tess had indeed met the odd snob who sneered when she opened her mouth, so one day she went into the Ladies loo and willed herself to lose her accent. And lose it she had. Much to her mother's disgust.

Tess decided to change the subject. 'Did you see Stephen on the telly last night?' Her mother had always liked Stephen, despite his upper-class background, which Dymphna was prepared to overlook since he had no airs. 'He won an award for that advert of his with the seals.'

Dymphna chortled. She disapproved of advertising, holding that it made people want what they couldn't afford and didn't need, but she liked that advert. 'Breda saw it,' she said. 'She went off pleased as punch to tell everyone down at the clinic about her clever brother-in-law.'

It always amazed Tess that her mother, a staunch Catholic, didn't object at all to her eldest daughter Breda working in a Family Planning Clinic, doling out contraceptives by the gross. But then Dymphna seemed certain that she had a personal hotline to God that conveniently by-passed Pope John Paul II and all his dicta. 'He's only a man, after all,' Dymphna was fond of saying, 'and what do men know about getting pregnant?' The only question she and His Holiness were in complete agreement over was divorce. Another reason she disapproved of Tess's career choice.

'And what difference will this award make?' enquired her mother pragmatically.

'He might get more money.'

'And what do you need with more money?' Tess had never been able to explain convincingly to Dymphna that working as she did for a firm of reasonably radical lawyers, her own salary was much less than her mother imagined and that since Stephen's agency was small and struggling he was a long way from the cocaine-and-convertible lifestyle Dymphna imagined all advertising people enjoyed.

'You worry too much about money,' sniffed her mother. 'We managed all right, didn't we, with five children and your sainted father not always able to work?'

Tess smiled bitterly. The reason her sainted father hadn't been able to get work was because he used to stay up all night drinking Irish whiskey with his cronies, then spend a lot of his days in the betting shop. Yet theirs hadn't been poverty in the classic sense because when he worked he'd had quite good jobs. In a way it had been worse. It was the unpredictability of it Tess hadn't been able to stand. Never knowing whether she'd have her dinner money or not, or whether she could go on school trips or afford a party for her birthday to which she could ask her friends. Usually she'd just said no to things; that way she didn't have to explain when the money wasn't there. But she'd decided one thing: it was never going to happen to her kids.

'If you're short of money why doesn't that selfish old father of Stephen's give you any? He's rich as Croesus, that one.' Tess knew perfectly well Dymphna had a soft spot for Stephen's father Julius, ever since he'd charmed her with tales of his Bohemian youth and made her drink several too many glasses of Spanish sherry at their wedding reception.

'Stephen would never ask him. You know what it's like between those two.' She waved goodbye to Ellie and Luke, who were being chivvied reluctantly out of the house by Inge, and psyched herself up to interrupting her mother and getting off the phone without feeling guilty.

'Look, Mum, I really do have to go now. This call must be costing a fortune.'

'I know, I know and out of my pension too.' Dymphna seemed to be conveniently forgetting that Tess paid her phone rentals and all her bills. 'Give that son-in-law of mine a hug and tell him he's a clever boy.'

Finally Tess managed to put down the phone, noticing as she did the familiar peeling strip of terracotta wallpaper behind the hall stand. They'd been here eight years now and never seemed to have the money to get a decorator in. Of course they could do it themselves, but the one room they'd stripped had stayed like that for nearly a year because both of them were so busy.

Maybe her mother was right. Maybe she did worry about money too much. After all, Stephen might get a rise now, and Will Kingsmill, her own boss, had promised that when the next partnership came up at Kingsmill's, it would be hers. Feeling optimistic Tess leaned forward and pulled off a long section of the wallpaper. She'd wanted to do that for ages.

Humming, she grabbed her briefcase and set off for work.

Stephen whistled as he ran up the escalators at Tottenham Court Road tube station. It was good for you to walk up now and then.

At the north end of Soho Square he was greeted by the grinning tramp he saw every morning.

'Fine morning, sorr.' The man indicated the March sunshine. 'Good to be alive. Would you have a pound for a wee whisky at all, sorr?'

Stephen liked the man's candour. None of this nonsense about wanting a cup of tea, though he looked like Buckfast Tonic Wine might be more his tipple. Stephen delved into his pocket and handed him fifty pence. He could have the other fifty another time.

'Thank you, sorr. Have a nice day now, sorr.'

Stephen waved goodbye, still smiling, as he pushed open the swing doors of the D Agency thinking, as he often did, that it was a very nice location. Much more pleasant, in fact, than the offices of some of the bigger, more prestigious agencies.

'Congratulations, Mr Gilfillan,' offered the security man, rushing up to press the button and summon the lift before Stephen had to lift a finger. 'A real honour for the agency.'

'Thanks, George.'

The middle-aged receptionist, ignoring a long line of supplicants for her attention, patted her hair and called over the top of their heads: 'Really fantastic, Stephen. We all watched it.' As she punched out the queue's visitors' passes on her machine she reflected that if she had to choose one man, instead of one commercial, it would still be Stephen. She'd always liked men with curly hair and blue eyes. A real Irish charmer, even if he was only half-Irish and had grown up in London. It was in the blood. She liked a Celt. They had souls. Not like the bloody repressed English. And she found herself humming the tune of 'The Wild Rover' as she punched out the final pass.

On the third floor Stephen found Ted's secretary

camping outside his door. 'Well,' she said. 'His Royal Lowness is in a good mood this morning, thanks to your award.' Stephen smiled again as he unlocked his door. The whole building seemed to feel the same. 'He says can you come and see him as soon as you get here. He's got some good news.'

As Tess ran up the front steps of Kingsmill's, which was tucked away in a corner of Paddington between a fifties council block and a peeling Victorian terrace, she felt the usual lift to her heart. She loved her work. And now and then she even felt she might be making a difference to someone's life.

Despite the rather seedy exterior Kingsmill's was surprisingly smart inside, having just undergone a complete facelift. Until recently the offices, furnished with tatty olive-green rugs and peeling radical posters, had had the feel of the campaign HQ of a left-wing political party or one of the larger Third World charities. But now all that had been swept away in favour of a smart new image, in keeping with the more commercial spirit of the times. The entire office had been transformed by wall-to-wall carpeting in a daring shade of lilac, the ageing furniture thrown out and replaced by smart modular units, and copies of *Tatler* and *Elle* had taken over from the faded copies of *New Statesman & Society* or the *New Left Review*. Except outside Tess's office. Because she was a family lawyer, Tess had resisted this sweeping gentrification and had hung on to her stacking boxes full of toys in bright primary colours, half-chewn board books, and a rocking horse with one ear that had once belonged to Ellie and Luke. Consequently her corner looked more like an antenatal clinic than a solicitor's office – which was just how Tess liked it.

As soon as she arrived – fifteen minutes later than usual thanks to her mother's phone call – she was pounced on by Jacqui, her secretary, holding a cup of coffee in one hand and an armload of files in the other.

'Don't worry,' said Jacqui soothingly, 'this is just this morning's. There's an even bigger pile this afternoon.'

Tess smiled at the attractive black girl. She was super-efficient as usual and, Tess knew for a fact, at least as bright as half of the trainee solicitors.

'Jacqui?'

'Yup.'

'Why don't you give up being a secretary and go to law school? You're twice as sharp as most of the articled clerks.'

Jacqui laughed. It wasn't the first time they'd had this conversation.

'What, and become a divorce hotshot like you?' She gestured at the pile of documents Tess was going to have to work her way through today. 'No chance. I work to live, not live to work.' She opened Tess's appointments book with a snap. There were solid entries till six p.m. 'And then I like switching off and having fun.'

Tess shrugged. 'Point taken.'

'Shall I wheel the first one in?' asked Jacqui, handing her a file.

Janice Brown. A young mother from the council estate next door who wanted to divorce her husband on the grounds of unreasonable behaviour because he dressed up in women's clothing and walloped her. And when the police had been round to ask for Mr Ivor Brown a vision had opened the door in a black leather miniskirt and diamanté earrings who'd told them he *was* Mr Ivor Brown. Sounded unreasonable to Tess. The only way to survive the messes some of her clients got into was to laugh occasionally. Otherwise you'd cry.

'By the way,' said Jacqui as she opened the door to summon Tess's first client, 'Patricia Greene wants a word later.'

Tess made a face. Patricia Greene was Tess's polar opposite at Kingsmill's. She specialized in tax and corporate work and brought far more income into the firm than Tess did. Although she claimed to have nothing against the underprivileged, Tess suspected she hated them cluttering up the waiting room. It was bad for the new image.

'Stephen, Stevie, come in, come in.' Ted's small rotund body could hardly contain its energy. It bounced from place to place like a demented wallaby. 'Do you know who I got a call from first thing this morning?' Stephen marvelled at Ted's capacity to look gleeful and conspiratorial at the same time. 'Worldwide Motors! They want us to do a beauty contest!'

Stephen raised an eyebrow. Worldwide were one of the biggest US car manufacturers, a real catch. 'I thought Worldwide were happy with CKR.'

'They were until they came to the awards last night and saw that crummy – and very expensive – cigarette ad compared to your washing machine epic. They reckon if you can do that with a household appliance what could you do with their brand-new car launch?'

'And they want us to pitch for the car launch?'

Ted's grin was so wide Stephen thought his face might split. 'It'd be the biggest campaign we've landed for years. Four million spend. Two of it on TV airtime alone. All we have to do is show them we have more brilliant ideas where the seals came from.'

23

Stephen stood up. 'When for?'

Ted had the grace to look embarrassed. 'Next week?'

Stephen laughed. 'Then I'd better get cracking.'

Ted slammed his first into the palm of his other hand. 'That's my boy!' he commented admiringly to Stephen's departing back.

Tess glanced at her desk diary to find that her next client was one of her favourites, Terry Worth. After an hour of tales of transvestite husbands Terry's down-to-earth solidity would be a welcome breather. Terry Worth was a classic case of barrow-boy to millionaire whose rise and rise had only been halted by one mistake: meeting and marrying a middle-class girl who enjoyed outraging her parents. They'd had two months of fun before discovering just how different they were. Just long enough for Angela to get pregnant. Then, once the marriage was already beyond repair, they'd tried to mend it by having another baby.

Tess had handled the divorce and had been amazed at how generous Terry had been. And Angela had thanked him by being as difficult as possible. The amazing thing was how they had fallen for each other in the first place. Terry was a steak eater who liked nothing better than to take the children for a Big Mac and a spending spree at Toys 'R Us. Angela was a committed vegetarian who believed in saving and the benefits of delayed gratification. Tess knew which of them she preferred.

Jacqui showed Terry in. As usual Tess found herself smiling simply at the warmth of the man and his bearlike physical presence. Even the immaculately handsewn suits couldn't disguise Terry's origins, but they simply made him seem bigger and more alive.

'Tess, gel,' Terry wrung her hand enthusiastically. 'How're you keeping?'

'Fine, Terry. Fine.'

'I saw hubby on the telly last night. Doing well, the lad. Maybe I'll have a bit of business to put his way myself one of these days. What do you say to Truthful Tel presenting his own TV commercials?'

Tess laughed. He'd be brilliant, of course. 'So what's the problem this time, Terry?'

All the fun drained instantly from Terry's face. 'It's Angela, of course. I'm having trouble getting to see the kids.'

By the time the hour was up Tess was feeling wrung out like an old sponge. Love might make the world go round but there were so many ways it screwed people up.

The only thought that cheered her was that she was having lunch with Phil. Then she remembered Linzi and the baby. What was the matter with everyone? Couldn't anyone sustain a happy marriage any more? Look, she told herself sternly as she saw Terry out, if it's romance you want, you're in the wrong business. Briefly she picked up the photo of Stephen with his arms round Ellie and Luke, which she kept on her desk. Touching his face with her finger she allowed herself a smile. Thank God they were happy at least.

She grabbed her coat and strode out of her office to find Terry still there chatting to Jacqui. 'Are you going my way?' he asked. 'The Roller's just outside.' Tess decided it was too good an offer to refuse.

As they drew up outside Forbo in Covent Garden they were met by an arresting sight. A cab was blocking most of the frontage of Exeter Street. Yet none of the cars and taxis stacked up behind it were hooting or shouting abuse in the usual manner. Tess craned her neck and immediately saw why. Protruding from the back of the taxi was an almost indecent amount of leg encased in velvet hotpants. Tess recognized the owner at once. Phil had lost another contact lens.

As Tess said goodbye to Terry, Phil emerged victorious and blew a kiss at the crowd of onlookers.

'That's my friend Phil,' Tess explained, 'we're having lunch in Forbo.'

Terry winked. 'Well, well, what a coincidence. I was just wondering where to take my client for lunch today.' Tess looked at him disbelievingly as he studied Phil walking towards them. Only Phil would consider scarlet hot pants with thick tights and a pair of tartan Doctor Martens (which Ellie would have given her eyes for) as an appropriate outfit for a thirty-five-year-old working woman. But then, conceded Tess, she did work in PR.

Tess waved a final goodbye and joined Phil on the pavement. Together they walked down the steps to the basement restaurant. 'Hmmm,' commented Phil, glancing back at Terry, 'nice.'

'The man or the car?' enquired Tess grinning.

'Theresa Brien, what do you take me for?'

Tess decided not to answer that one. Instead she changed the subject as they waited in the queue to be seated. Forbo was one of London's most popular lunching spots. Like almost everyone else in the restaurant she was studying Phil's outfit. 'You look very sixties. I had a pair of shorts like that once.'

Phil shook her head. 'I do not look very sixties. A witty comment on the sixties perhaps; a homage to the sixties; a pastiche even; but I don't look simply sixties. And you didn't have a pair of these. They're too expensive.'

26

'Who're they by?'

'Gianni Versace.'

'Mine were C&A.'

'Precisely.'

Finally they reached the front of the queue and the greeter turned to Phil like a long-lost friend, kissing her extravagantly on both cheeks.

'You're well known here,' said Tess admiringly as she sat down and scanned the menu. It all looked delicious but she had a full afternoon. She selected a seafood pasta.

'Nah.' Phil shook her head. 'They don't know me from Adam. It's just part of the treatment.' And indeed behind Phil's head she saw the woman greeting someone else equally effusively. She looked again. It was Terry.

Two minutes later the waitress arrived to take their order. She carried a tray with two glasses of pink fizz. Tess looked at them, puzzled. 'There must be some mistake. We didn't order these.'

The girl gestured behind her somewhere in the middle distance. 'From the gentleman over there,' she said vaguely.

Phil sipped hers at once. 'How thoughtful. Kir Royale. Just the thing to pep up your lunch. Who is he?'

For some reason Tess looked evasive. 'A client of mine.'

'So what's he like?'

'Nice,' she conceded. 'Funny too. But trouble.'

'Sounds interesting.' Phil sipped her drink. 'Married?' Ever since her divorce was finalized a year ago Phil had been trying to get over the pain by searching diligently for Mr Right This Time.

'Divorced. With complications.'

27

'Mmm.' Phil sounded as though she were surveying the sweet trolley. 'Sounds even more interesting.'

Fortunately their food arrived and Tess was able to divert Phil's attention. They chatted away about work and children as women lunching do. 'Hey,' Tess demanded after they'd caught up with each other's gossip, 'did you hear about Stephen's award? He got best art direction.'

'Absolutely. How crass of me not to mention it. All the headhunters will be knocking at his door now. To win an award – *and* on a small budget. The client must think he's died and gone to heaven. So . . .' Phil paused for a moment. Tess guessed exactly what she was going to say next. Phil was about as difficult to read as the front page of the *Sun*. 'I suppose you saw my bastard ex with that floozy of his? Sorry, Vice-president of External Relations? I hope you poured your wine in her lap.'

Tess reached out and touched her friend's hand. She knew how much it still hurt. Should she tell her about the baby? Would it be better coming from her than some stranger? Tess took her courage in both hands. 'Phil, there's something I ought to tell you . . .'

But Phil wasn't watching her any longer. She was smiling broadly at someone behind Tess's left ear. Tess turned.

Terry Worth was standing immediately behind her chair carrying a bottle of champagne and three glasses. 'My client had to go, so I've been left all alone. Can I offer you ladies a drink?'

Tess looked at her watch. They'd chatted so long it was after two and she was expecting a client at two-thirty. 'Thanks, Terry, but I'm afraid I have to get back.' She looked at Phil purposefully. 'And I'm sure you do, too, don't you, Phil?'

'Me?' asked Phil innocently. 'As a matter of fact,' she lied, 'I've got a very light afternoon.'

'I thought you had a budgeting meeting on Fridays?' Meanly Tess couldn't resist asking.

'Oh, that.' Phil smiled, recalling the ten people who would be waiting for her to come and chair it. 'I'm sure it can wait.'

Tess stood up, bowing to the inevitable, 'Philomena Doyle, this is Terry Worth.'

'I knew my husband was having an affair. But the question was who with?'

Tess looked across at the woman opposite her, trying not to think about how Phil and Terry might be getting on in the restaurant. The woman wasn't that different to Tess herself. Late thirties, busy, holding down a job and family.

'I thought at first it had to be a colleague. They're always the worst. Having sex *and* being able to talk about business afterwards. Lethal. Then I worked it out. There was only person it could be. The nanny.' The woman certainly had her full attention now. 'I mean, the *nanny* of all people. It's the ultimate middle-class betrayal, isn't it? Of course, he denied everything. So do you know what I did?'

Tess shook her head, imagining the well-dressed woman in front of her lurking in the wardrobe ready to jump out with her Polaroid at the ready.

'I taped them!' She removed a small cassette player from her bag and switched it on.

A series of groans and grunts, building dangerously towards a crescendo, emanated from the machine. Tess cringed, twisting in her seat, appalled yet riveted. It certainly made Serge Gainsbourg and Jane Birkin sound tame.

29

Opposite her the wife of the protagonist in this dirty-mac masterpiece seemed to have lost all sense of pain and rejection. In fact her face gleamed with triumph at having actually caught them at it.

Seconds from the orgasm Tess decided enough was enough. Firmly she turned the machine off, noting a look almost of disappointment flit across her client's face. What people were prepared to do to one another once love had died perpetually amazed Tess.

'So.' She handed the woman back her cassette machine, fascinated despite her attempt to be neutral and professional. 'What did he say when you played it to him?'

The woman leaned forward, as smug as a cat. 'Oh, I haven't played it to him yet.' She put the tape safely away in her handbag. 'I thought I'd save that up for the divorce.'

After her soft porn session Tess decided she needed a reviving cup of tea before braving the next chapter of marital betrayal. There were times when she wished she'd stuck to Landlord & Tenant.

Outside her office, Jacqui was nowhere to be seen so Tess switched on the kettle and opened the cupboard where Jacqui kept the tea and coffee. Staring her in the face was a photo of Lyall Gibson, the firm's whiz kid, cut out of the *Law Society Gazette*. Tess grinned. So that was the way the land lay.

Suddenly she was aware of Jacqui standing behind her, a blush firing up her caramel skin.

'So. Lyall Gibson, eh?' Tess teased. 'I didn't know you had the hots for Mr LA Law.'

Jacqui took the tea out of Tess's hands with brusque efficiency. 'Don't be so ridiculous,' she snapped, slamming the cupboard shut.

Tess tried hard to wipe the smile from her face and failed. 'I don't suppose there's any chance of a spoon?'

Jacqui opened the cupboard and handed one to Tess. As she closed it again the picture caught her eye.

'I see what you mean.' Her face softened. 'He does look a bit like Harry Hamlin, doesn't he? Only much better looking.'

Half an hour later Tess was quietly enjoying a brief respite between clients when there was a knock on her door and Jacqui put her head round. 'Patricia Greene's here. Can you see her now?'

Tess made a face. Patricia coming to see her was bound to be bad news. She knew that Patricia, with her degree in business studies on top of her LLB, saw herself as the prefect and Tess as the naughty girl giggling at the back of the classroom. The socially responsible thing to do, in Patricia's view, was not to take on endless clients who might not be able to pay their way, and then undercharge them, as Tess sometimes did if she felt sorry for them. The responsible thing to do was to take on customers who could make the firm more profitable, and bill them promptly and fully. Tess sighed.

'Show her in.'

Before Tess saw Patricia, she heard her. Patricia was going through a heavy accessories phase. Earrings, bracelets, necklaces, even chains on her shoes and hairband. Patricia had more gilt than Selfridges jewellery counter. Tess felt tempted to point out if she had her nose pierced she could fit a few more links in.

'Good of you to make time for me.' Patricia sat down, smiling patricianly. 'By the way, one of your client's children's just been sick on the carpet.'

'Oh, God,' groaned Tess, jumping up.

'Don't worry,' Jacqui reassured her, 'I'll handle it.'

Tess thanked her gratefully, then decided she'd get straight to the point in the hope Patricia's visit would be a short one. She wanted to leave on time and see how Stephen had got on at work today. 'So what can I do for you?'

'I just wondered if you'd heard the rumour?'

'What rumour's that?'

'That they're thinking of making a new partner?'

Tess kept her face dead-pan. She certainly hadn't heard such a rumour, even though the senior partner had promised her faithfully that the next partnership would definitely be hers. Had they decided to do it and just not told her yet? Tess began to feel a flood of excitement. How terrific that would be. Just after Stephen's triumph too.

But Patricia was still speaking.

'If you haven't heard anything then maybe I'd better tell you what people are saying. The word is that they're definitely going to make a new partner.' She smiled at Tess with the certainty of one who can afford to be generous. 'But they can't make up their minds whether it should be you or me.'

CHAPTER THREE

Stephen chewed the end of his drawing Pentel and looked down at the pad in front of him. He'd been sitting here for half an hour trying to dream up ideas that would hit the bosses of Worldwide Motors right between the eyes and convince them they should abandon the hottest agency in London and hand their business over to him. But nothing was coming. He knew what the trouble was. The brief. Worldwide was launching a new range of gas-guzzling, top-of-the-range cars, and Stephen couldn't help asking himself if this was what people actually needed right in the middle of the worst recession (unless you believed the Government who were trying to convince everyone it was over) since the thirties.

He got up and wandered over to the window, noting that his tramp friend now seemed to be having a party down in the gardens. As he turned back to his desk the award from last night caught his eye and he picked it up. A ghastly piece of metal, but worth its weight in kudos. Already he'd had several lunch invitations from directors of other agencies, no doubt to put feelers out to see if he was poachable on the right terms.

Stephen put the award back on the window sill. What was the matter with him, for Christ's sake? This ought to be the high point of his working life. Instead he kept feeling a creeping sense of dissatisfaction he couldn't shake off. And then there'd been Luke's question this morning. *What's advertising for, Dad?* He'd laughed it off but he didn't have an answer he believed himself. Maybe it was just anti-climax after the build-up of the awards.

He turned to find Bill Barclay, the young account exec who'd also worked on Ultron, with his head round the door grinning away like Popeye on double spinach.

'Guess what?' His eyes twinkled above his Turnbull & Asser shirt and sporty red braces. Account executives were always snappy dressers.

'What?' repeated Stephen, smiling back. There was something irresistible about Bill's enthusiasm. He was the kind of person who, when asked a simple question like 'How are you?', would beam and say 'Sparkling!' thereby ruining the other person's day.

'I'm going to work with you on the Worldwide account.'

'If we get it.'

'Of course we'll get it. With your talent and my charm? Bound to. Is that it?' He indicated the award reverently, as though he were in the presence of a relic.

'That's it. Hideous, isn't it?'

Bill ignored him. 'I know people who'd kill for that. It must be worth a few grand on salary. Plus a move up from a three series to a five series at least.'

Stephen laughed. Bill had made it his life's work to calculate the finest gradations of status in the world of advertising. The difference in prestige between a three series and a five series BMW was something Bill could write a thesis on.

'Anyway, come on,' Bill said. 'The boozer's been open a good half-hour. Let me buy you a celebration drink.'

Stephen relaxed. What he was feeling probably wouldn't last.

'Great idea. Moët, did you say?'

Bill laughed. Stephen was his idol, but just for a minute there he'd been a bit worried about him.

Tess had just put on her coat and was heading for the door when she spotted Will Kingsmill coming out of his office and realized it was too good an opportunity to miss.

'Will!' she called. 'Do you think I could have a word?'

Will turned, looking like a rather pink salmon who had just been landed unexpectedly and was wondering if there was any way he could wriggle off the hook. He'd put on weight recently and no longer ressembled the lean and hungry radical who had founded the firm twenty years ago at the height of his reforming fervour. Now he seemed more like a representative of the Tory shires, eager to enjoy the good life and all it offered.

'Certainly, Tess. Have you time for a drink?' His tone was conciliatory. Tess knew her one advantage was that he was a tiny bit nervous of her. He'd hired her because she was passionate and committed and spoke her mind, but that had been five years ago. Now, she suspected, those qualities made him feel uncomfortable. He stood aside to let her into his office.

'Thanks. A glass of white wine would be lovely.'

'So. What can I do for you?'

'It's about this rumour.'

'What rumour is that?' Will poured himself a generous whisky. He would miss his usual train and be home late. He felt he deserved a little compensation.

'That you're creating a new partnership.' She almost added, And you can't decide who to give it to, me or Patricia, but decided it'd be safer not to put ideas into

35

his head. After all, the whole thing might just be Patricia being devious.

'Tess, Tess.' Will sat down opposite her clucking in a fatherly manner. Tess sometimes thought he'd decided to by-pass middle age altogether and go straight to the octogenarian judge phase. 'I told you that you would be the first to know, and you will. Please don't listen to gossip.'

Tess drank up her wine. She didn't know whether to believe him or not, but there wasn't much she could do. She stood up. 'Fine, because I'd be very unhappy now that you've promised me the next partnership, if you were to change your mind and give it to someone else.'

'My dear girl.' Tess marvelled at how well he pulled this likeable old buffer act off; after all he couldn't be more than ten years older than her. 'Do you think I'd go back on my word?'

Tess closed the front door behind her and listened. The house seemed strangely quiet. She went into the kitchen and slung her briefcase on a chair. An ominous crunching underfoot reassured her that Luke must be back because there were cornflakes all over the floor. For nearly a year now Luke had being going through his Cereal Period. The only thing he would eat came out of a cardboard box, and Tess had had to give him vitamin supplements in case it was true that there was more nourishment in the packet than the cornflakes themselves. Lately he'd moved on to eating anything that was covered in breadcrumbs and went in the oven. It had to be a step in the right direction, Tess told herself.

Upstairs she heard a sudden shout from the room where he kept his Scalextric. He'd probably got his two friends, Tom and Ben, round. She took off her jacket and followed the noise.

But it wasn't Tom or Ben engaged in the life-or-death battle. It was Stephen and Luke, with Inge watching from the sidelines with all the proud concern of a Mrs Niki Lauda. Loud music blaring from Ellie's bedroom denoted her usual disapproval of such noisy male pursuits.

'Ellie,' shouted Tess, 'can you turn that down please?' Then she put her head round Ellie's door. 'Haven't you got any homework to do?'

Ellie reluctantly lowered her copy of *Company*. 'How can I work with that noise going on? Why are men so *stupid*, Mum? Even the nice ones like Dad?'

Tess smiled. This was one of Ellie's favourite themes at the moment.

'Pen and Lil and I,' Ellie added nonchalantly, 'are thinking of being gay.'

'Ah,' nodded Tess, deciding to play this one by ear.

'Only theoretically,' Ellie reassured her. 'It's very cool, you know.'

'I see.' Tess sat down on the bed for a moment. 'Why don't I get those boys to shut up. Stephen!' she shouted. 'Ellie can't do her homework with all that racket.'

Stephen emerged from the Scalextric Grand Prix, grinning. 'We can't have that, can we?'

Ellie looked back at her parents resentfully, correctly detecting their mirth. 'It's all right for you,' she said looking accusingly at Tess, 'you had a deprived childhood. Luke and I have had everything handed to us on a plate. It really isn't fair.'

Tess, remembering the joys of her deprived childhood, caught Stephen's eye and they both burst out laughing.

'Right,' said Stephen decisively, 'no more allowance for you and let's see how it benefits your schoolwork.'

As they closed Ellie's door he noticed that under the laughter Tess was looking tired.

'Rough day at the office?' he asked.

'Oh, you know, the usual. Patricia stirring. Clients weeping. Husbands fighting wives for the children. Fairly average . . . Actually' – she brightened at the memory – 'I did catch Will just as he was leaving and give him what for just in case he was thinking of changing his mind about my partnership.'

Stephen smiled, imagining the scene. 'Poor Will, a redheaded firebrand pouncing on him just when he was off to catch the six-ten to Newbury.'

'As a matter of fact, I kept my cool quite beautifully.'

Stephen ran his hands through her luxuriant hair and looked down at her. 'Trust me to marry a redhead! Do you remember when Miles, the Old Etonian, called you my bit of radical rough back at college? You went for him hammer and tongs! Told him he and his family were parasites living off the back of the working class!'

Tess was embarrassed. 'I didn't really say that, did I? How crass.'

'You've mellowed a bit since then, but I won't let on to Will Kingsmill.' He touched the dark shadows under her eyes. 'Why don't you go and sit down? I'll cook supper.'

Tess looked at him gratefully. She was feeling worn out. How on earth had she managed to find him?

'I know.' He shrugged expansively, correctly reading her thoughts. 'Good looks *and* he makes a mean spag bol. Aren't you a lucky girl?'

'I would be,' she shouted after him in case he got

above himself, 'if you didn't use every pan in the kitchen!'

Ten minutes later she went downstairs to the kitchen to find Stephen making garlic bread and salad to go with his spaghetti. 'I should really be doing this for you, the conquering hero.'

'I know,' Stephen agreed mournfully, 'I'm just a henpecked husband.'

Tess put her arms round him as he stirred the sauce. 'I do love you, you know. How was it today? Did they strew your path with rose petals and offer you increased pension plans?'

He laughed, kissing the top of her head as she leaned on his shoulder. 'Not quite. But we did get asked to pitch for a huge new account. Worldwide Motors. They're with one of the biggies, but unhappy apparently.'

'Stephen, that's great!' Tess kissed him full on the lips and encountered an unexpected taste of tomato purée.

'Well . . .' Stephen thought about voicing his doubts but didn't get the chance.

'God,' said Ellie, following her nose into the kitchen and finding her parents locked in an embrace, 'can't you two ever leave each other alone?'

Tess thumbed her nose in a thoroughly unmaternal gesture, then put her arm round her daughter who was grinning unrepentantly. 'Come on, you. Go and get your brother. A feast like this deserves a climax. Let's go and get some Häagen Dazs.'

'Thank God for that.' Ellie skipped out of the kitchen before her mother could reach her. 'I thought for a ghastly moment you might be going to cook something yourself.'

CHAPTER FOUR

'Ready for the big meeting then?' Bill Barclay was taking no chances with Stephen over the presentation to Worldwide and had decided to come and get him personally. 'They've sent the top brass. Raf Walensky himself, no less.'

Stephen looked up from his folder, surprised. Raf Walensky was the UK Group Head, a notorious toughie. Stephen had never met the man but had heard plenty of stories about him. Worldwide must be serious.

In the agency's meeting room, probably no more than a cupboard compared to the Worldwide board-room, Ted was already waiting with Walensky and his entourage.

Ted made the introductions and then sat back, trying not to look hurt, as Walensky ignored him and took control of the meeting himself. When Bill Barclay cracked a harmless joke to try and lighten the tension Walensky squashed him like a snail under his boot. Clearly no one had told Raf Walensky about corporate democracy. Instead he addressed himself to Stephen as though they were the only two people in the room.

'Now, Stephen, you may be wondering why we're launching a range of prestige cars in an era of recession.' Walensky fixed him with an evangelical eye. 'The answer is that we're making a statement, taking the lead. What we've seen over the last few years is no less than an abandonment of consumerism.' Walensky leaned back in his chair, warming to his theme. 'The eighties has become a discredited decade. Spending is a dirty word. All we're left with is a world of lefties and veggies and people who probably recycle their own shit. And they're all saying we should spend less, consume less. And it's catching on! Stephen, we've got to make people proud of spending again, proud to consume, to have a bigger, better car than their neighbour's and we want you to come up with the image that says it all.'

He stood up so fired by his own eloquence that he began to pace the room. 'Now we've got to think big, dramatic. What I had in mind was the dawn of the world.' Stephen bit his lip. The man was serious! 'You know, like in *2001*. That incredible music. "Thus spake . . ." What was it . . . "Zorba"?'

Stephen's mouth twitched. ' "Zarathustra?" '

'That's it!' Walensky's eyes were alight with his vision. 'And all those goddam monkeys crowding round looking at the first creation of the world . . . our new baby!' And his eyes closed in reverence.

'Yes,' agreed Stephen. 'There's a lot of potential for humour there.'

The Worldwide contingent looked at Stephen as though he'd just farted in church. 'Humour?' snapped Walensky. 'This is the most serious project you'll ever work on. It'd better be, with twenty million dollars riding on it.'

For a moment Stephen imagined putting together a subtly witty campaign and trying to explain it to Walensky. He found himself sympathizing with the veggies and lefties. Luke's question flashed into his mind again. What was advertising *for*? Of course he knew all the textbook answers about market forces and mixed economies. But as he sat there looking at Walensky's overfed face, a sense of the utter absurdity of his job washed over him.

'Fine,' he said, resisting the desire to laugh out loud, 'monkeys it is.'

He caught Ted looking at him suspiciously.

Finally wresting control of the meeting back from Walensky before Stephen said anything more, Ted closed the discussion as quickly as possible.

Immediately Stephen got up and headed for the door. He'd had as much as he could take for one day.

'What's the matter with *him*?' asked Bill quietly as the Worldwide contingent gathered up their things.

'I don't know.' Ted narrowed his eyes. 'But I intend to bloody well find out. By the way, Bill, do you think you could spare me five minutes? I want a quiet word with you.'

Back in his office, Stephen threw down his papers. Walensky's face stared up at him from his pad and he realized that in his anger he must have done a doodle of the creep. It was only a few dashed-off lines and yet it somehow caught the man in all his domineering unpleasantness.

What the hell was he doing with his life? Training gorillas and seals to sell cars and washing machines for shits like Walensky to reap the profits? He'd be forty soon. Maybe it was time for a rethink. He wondered what Tess really thought of his job. She did something useful, after all. When she got home tonight he'd talk to her about it. Then he remembered it was her late night, and felt a sharp stab of disappointment. Every two weeks she did a stint as duty solicitor at the local police station so that anyone suddenly needing a lawyer could get one. The law's equivalent of Casualty. Inge would be babysitting. He was free just when he didn't want to be.

He was about to leave when Bill Barclay appeared at

his door, looking deflated, like those expensive helium balloons do by the time you get them home. 'What's up?'

Bill sat down heavily, still holding on to his briefcase. 'Oh, nothing. Just had a gruesome session with Ted.'

Stephen wondered whether he should ask him what about, but before he could Bill caught sight of the sketch of Walensky.

'Hey, that's brilliant! You've caught that mean and hungry look to the life! I didn't know you could draw.'

Stephen thanked him, surprised. He'd thought Bill would admire Walensky on principle. 'It's just a knack. No real talent involved.'

'Could you do me?' Bill asked taking off his coat. 'A sort of memento of working here.'

'Why? You're not thinking of leaving, are you?'

Bill avoided his glance and sat, jaw jutting in a heroic manner, for Stephen to sketch.

Five minutes later it was done. Bill sat staring at it intently until Stephen, sensing that something really might be wrong, suggested they go for a drink. He didn't particularly feel like it but Bill obviously needed cheering up. Three Budweisers later Bill had spilled it all out. His wife, a go-getting sales rep with her own Vauxhall Calibra, wanted him to move out of the house they'd bought together on a giant housing boom mortgage. She'd met someone else. Bill had nowhere to go and had sunk everything into the house. And it sounded as though he still loved the woman. Jesus. It was the kind of story Tess had to listen to every day of the week and Stephen marvelled at her stamina. The thought of Tess made him eager to leave but he sat through several more rounds, realizing Bill needed the sympathy.

Finally he asked, 'So, what did Ted have to say to you earlier?'

'Oh,' Bill stiffened, 'nothing much. Must try harder. You know Ted. He expects body and soul.'

As they stood on the pavement outside the bar Stephen felt his colleague droop. There was something beaten and defeated about him that worried Stephen in someone as naturally ebullient as Bill. Stephen almost invited him to come home then remembered he wanted to talk to Tess. Instead he flagged down a taxi and helped Bill into it, giving the driver Bill's address in the suburbs and pressing a tenner into the man's palm in case Bill passed out. Then he waved goodbye and waited for another cab.

The house was quiet for once and there was still no sign of Tess. He looked in on Luke, asleep cuddling his Game Boy which Stephen gently removed and switched off. In his day it had been tattered copies of *Just William* or *Billy Bunter*.

Ellie's door was shut and he decided not to risk waking her by knocking. Five minutes later he was in bed. But the moment his head hit the pillow he felt a switch click and he knew with absolute certainty that he wasn't going to sleep. As he lay there a nameless fear swept over him and he felt a knot of stress forming in his stomach. If these genuine doubts about his future kept coming back, what the hell should he do about them? He was a success, a big noise, surely he'd be mad even to think of turning his back on all that? And if he gave up advertising what would he do instead?

Finally, after what seemed like hours, he heard Tess coming back and his heart lifted. Just the thought of her lying next to him made him feel better.

Tess, bone tired after spending the last two hours in

the cells trying to make a young Pakistani mother, just arrested for drug smuggling, understand the seriousness of her position, trudged wearily up the stairs to find Stephen sitting up in bed waiting for her.

'Still awake?' she asked, surprised. She started to get undressed, glancing as she did at the clock radio by the bed. It was after one a.m.

'I couldn't sleep.' He knew it would be selfish to burden her at this hour, but couldn't help himself. 'Look, Tess. I know it's late but I've been thinking for hours. I'm not sure I want to go on working in advertising.'

Tess looked at him blankly, her brain working slowly. What on earth was he on about? She leaned forwards to kiss him and caught the smell of Budweiser on his breath. She felt a faint stirring of resentment. All right for some. 'Let's talk about it in the morning, shall we?' Her eyes felt as though they'd been super-glued shut. 'It'll keep, won't it?' And falling into bed next to him she snapped out the light.

The next morning they were both so tired they overslept and it was only the sound of a neighbour's car alarm going off that woke them. Tess jumped out of bed and dressed hurriedly, stooping to give Stephen a brief kiss. He put his head under the pillow. The Budweisers had caught up with him.

'Tsk, tsk. Breath like a badger's bum,' Tess pointed out unsympathetically, reaching for her shoes.

Downstairs Luke and Ellie were bickering as usual. 'Mum,' shouted Ellie, getting in first, 'Luke hijacked the telly last night for his stupid Sega when Penny and Lil had come round specially to watch *Top of the Pops*.'

'I've already told Ellie,' Luke pointed out patiently,

45

'that *Top of the Pops* is old hat. All the cool people watch *The Word*.'

Tess shook her head. They were exactly the same as they'd been aged three and seven when they'd fought continually over wanting Tess to read them *Swallows and Amazons* or *Topsy and Tim*. A panic then ensued because Luke had lost his trainers.

'Wear your old ones,' advised Tess.

'*Mum!*' Luke shook his head in disbelief. 'I can't. They're Hi-tops. No one wears Hi-tops any more.'

'Too bad.' Tess went back to her paper remembering the outrageous cost of the trainers and Luke's insistence six months ago that he would be a social leper if he didn't possess them. 'A bit of peer group disapproval won't do you any harm.'

As she got up to gather her own things to go to work, she felt a faint pang of guilt about Stephen's attempt to talk. Perhaps she'd been too unsympathetic.

But Stephen appeared to think he was the one who needed to apologize. He followed her into the hall. 'Look, I'm sorry about last night. It was a ludicrous time to start a serious conversation.'

Tess put down her briefcase. 'Was it a serious conversation?'

'I don't know.' He reached for her and suddenly kissed her on the lips with surprising passion.

Tess touched his face and smiled. 'What's Inge been putting in *your* porridge?'

'Tess . . .' He paused, still holding her, his tone suddenly serious. 'You don't just love me because I'm successful, do you?'

Tess stroked his hair, wondering what was behind all this. 'Of course not. I'm proud of you because you're successful. But I love you because you're you.'

'Thank God, because . . .' began Stephen, when the post thudded on the mat next to them. On top of the pile was an expensive-looking envelope written in a bold italic hand. Tess and Stephen looked at each other. There was no mistaking that handwriting. It was as flamboyant as its creator.

Stephen bent down and picked it up. Tess watched his face as he opened the letter and thought how Julius, Stephen's famous father, had done it again. Even from three hundred miles away over the water in Ireland he still had the power to affect Stephen just as he always had done.

'Isn't that touching?' Stephen said with more than a shade of bitterness. 'An invitation to their Golden Wedding. They're having a party to celebrate fifty years of tearing each other's hearts out.'

Tess took his hand, wishing as she often did that his relationship with his father were easier. But then Julius Gilfillan wasn't an easy man. A genius perhaps. And certainly a genius at self-promotion. He was the *bête noire* of the art world, the portrait painter everyone famous had to be painted by, even if they loathed the end result. Which they often did. The richer and more famous the subject, the more Julius brought out their worst features.

Tess remembered the first time she had met Stephen's parents. She, the working-class girl from Liverpool, being taken to lunch to meet his mother: superior, icy Stella who reminded her faintly of a headmistress crossed with Edith Sitwell. And wicked, provocative Julius who'd insulted Stella constantly as she listened, unmoved. And the conversation. Their own child was expected to be witty and clever and knowledgeable or he was expected to keep his mouth shut. It had struck Tess that her own family might be humble, but at least you didn't have to prove yourself to be loved in it.

And yet she had a soft spot for Julius. Despite his selfishness he'd taken to Tess instantly and always made a fuss of her. He'd said he liked her spirit, but she suspected it was just as much to annoy Stella.

'Do you want to go?' Tess's mind flashed to the beauty of West Cork in the spring, and the faded Georgian splendour of Killamalooe House. And she found herself hoping he would say yes.

'Knowing Father, he'll hardly notice if we go or not, just as long as the gentlemen of the press are there in droves. That's probably the only reason he's having it. He loathes sentiment, but he certainly knows an opportunity to wring out more column inches.'

'Luke and Ellie would love it,' pointed out Tess.

'Maybe we should talk about it then.'

'And the work thing,' Tess added. After all he had listened to her professional problems often enough.

'Yes,' agreed Stephen, 'maybe we should talk about that too.'

And then the hall filled up with Ellie and Luke and their school gear.

'Can you drop us off today, Dad?' pleaded Luke. 'Inge's done it for *weeks*.'

Stephen agreed and they all poured out on to the pavement and into his company BMW.

'Can we have the roof down? Lil and Penny will be *sick* with envy.'

'In March?'

'Absolutely . . .'

Tess smiled as she opened her own rusting old Vauxhall – Kingsmill's didn't run to company cars – feeling much more cheerful.

*

48

As soon as she arrived Tess was greeted by the usual avalanche of clients and crises. But through the morning she found it hard to summon her usual concentration. Her mind kept drifting back to Stephen. There was clearly something worrying him, and she hadn't been particularly sensitive about it.

At lunchtime she phoned him to see if he was free for a quick bite but he was with a client. She was probably making too much of all this. If he wanted to talk to her he'd find time – and whatever it was he'd probably forgotten about it already. Since she had five minutes to spare she decided to phone Phil and see what she thought.

What Phil thought was that she should come straight over and share a sandwich.

Tess always enjoyed visiting Outrageous PR. With its terracotta walls, leopardskin couches, and staff who all looked like they were auditioning for the revival of *Hair*, it was a world away from life at Kingsmill's. And Phil was Queen Bee there. Her office was a hymn to status, minimalist and bare, its only decoration a large cactus with man-eating spikes, both daunting and phallic. Phil's huge desk was, as usual, empty. Remembering her own office, packed with filing cabinets and box files piled up the walls, Tess couldn't help feeling impressed.

'Where on earth do you keep everything?' she marvelled as Phil got up and kissed her.

'It's management policy. We operate a paperless office. And a clear-desk philosophy. It's supposed to impress the clients with our uncluttered thought.' She opened her drawer. 'So I keep all the crap in here. And in my secretary's office.' She leaned back and pushed open a door. The adjoining room was full of filing cabinets.

The only object on her desk, apart from the constantly buzzing telephone, was her customized black computer. The press release she'd been working on stared out at them. 'Did you know that nine out of ten men would like to see their women in sexier underwear? I tell you, since working on this survey I've thrown out my cotton M&S and gone for the hooker look.'

'Phil, you're daft. You're not even in a relationship.'

'Not yet. But when Mr Right comes along I don't want to screw up my chances by wearing the wrong bra, do I?' She switched off her computer and the press release disappeared. 'So how's the golden boy of the ad world?'

'That's what I wanted to talk about. He was lying in wait for me last night. He started saying he thought he might want to give it all up and do something else.'

'Just when he's won the biggest award the industry offers?' Phil asked suspiciously. 'He's not having an affair is he? That makes them do weird things in my experience.'

Tess shook her head, laughing. 'Not as far as I know. You've got sex on the brain! Affairs aren't the only thing that make people behave oddly, you know.'

'Oh really. Tell Greg that. How do you know you'd know, so to speak? I had no idea Greg was getting his end away. He was much nicer to me than usual, the duplicitous shitbag.'

'I bloody well ought to know,' retorted Tess, 'I spend half my life listening to tales of infidelity.' Suddenly she giggled. 'Did I ever tell you about the client I had who was convinced his wife was being unfaithful but she kept denying it?'

'No,' Phil leaned across her vast desk, riveted. 'What did he do?'

'He waited till she got back late one night, then took her knickers out of the dirty clothes basket and sent them off for DNA analysis!'

'My God,' Phil whispered, 'and was she?'

'Yes.'

'Dear me.' Tess realized she'd finally shocked Phil. 'Whatever happened to good old-fashioned trust? It shakes your faith in human nature, doesn't it? So, if it isn't the one-eyed trouser snake, what is Stephen's problem?'

'I think he may be losing his faith in advertising.'

'That sounds perfectly sensible to me.'

'Not if you work in it.'

'I suppose not. Mind you, there's nothing wrong with a bit of healthy cynicism.'

'Stephen's not the cynical type.'

'No,' conceded Phil, 'he runs more on passion and enthusiasm, doesn't he? So. A mid-life crisis, eh? Don't worry. He'll probably just get religion or go and work for Christian Aid for a couple of months till he realizes what it's like not having an American Express card.'

'Oh, Phil, be serious. And do you know, all I wanted to do was snap at him and tell him to stop behaving like a teenager.'

Phil laughed. 'You never did know when to shut up. Do you remember that Retreat at school when the priest asked if there was anyone in the room who didn't believe in God? And you went and put your hand up? Humour Stephen a bit. Be understanding. Persuade him to think things through. That should take a few months and by then he'll probably have got over it. By the way –' Tess realized from the sudden enthusiasm in Phil's tone that she was about to shift the conversation back to herself. 'Has that Terry Worth asked all about me yet?'

'No. He has not,' Tess replied briskly.

'Tsk, tsk,' Phil tutted, shocked. 'I must be losing my touch.'

Taking Phil's advice, Tess dashed home promptly after work, glad that it was Friday, determined to be more understanding. There was no sign of Stephen yet, only Ellie and Luke, making a mess of the kitchen as they fixed yet another snack. Their eating habits were a running battle between them and their parents, who wanted them to sit down and have a meal together every now and then. 'But, Mum,' Ellie usually protested, munching her way through a triple-decker sandwich containing most of the contents of the fridge, 'eating a meal's a waste of time. I've got more interesting things to do.'

Both looked at her in amazement when Tess announced the intention of cooking a romantic dinner for Stephen. Ellie in particular had a rock-bottom opinion of her mother's culinary talents. 'Tell you what, Mum,' she counselled from the collected wisdom of her sixteen years, 'wouldn't it be safer just to send out for a pizza?'

Stephen came out of Sloane Square tube station and watched his bus departing seconds before he made it to the bus stop. Instead of waiting for another one he decided to start walking down the King's Road. The evenings were just beginning to get a bit lighter and London was looking spruce and inviting, daffodils standing to attention in every window box. The city always looked its best in spring and autumn. By summer it had a grubby air which even flowerbeds full of roses couldn't quite dispel.

The street that had once been the epicentre of

Swinging London still had its own charm, with risqué leather shops cheek by jowl with antique markets and interior design emporia, all presided over by that rather auntlike presence, Peter Jones department store. Stephen strode down the right-hand side, window shopping and watching the gays and Goths and braying bankers who made up its permanent population.

Halfway down he stopped outside Chelsea College of Art where a large sign informed passers-by that its evening classes in life drawing were undersubscribed and in danger of having to close.

Stephen put down his briefcase and stared at it. He'd always wanted to learn life drawing, recognizing that like scales were to the piano, life drawing was the universally acknowledged basis for every area of art.

Stephen picked up his briefcase and walked on. What was he thinking of? Painting was his father's domain and all his life he'd tried to scramble out from his father's vast shadow. And yet he knew he'd had some talent once. His art teacher at school had been furious when he'd opted to go to university instead of art college. A mild-mannered man, he'd suddenly turned evangelical and had a go at Stephen. Talent is like an itch, he'd shouted, not scratching it might be sensible, but in the end it would drive you mad.

Maybe this dissatisfaction he'd been feeling wasn't as fundamental as he'd feared. He'd had the sense lately not that he didn't possess creativity, but that he might be wasting the creativity he did have. It could be that all it needed was a real outlet. Anyway, what had he got to lose? Evening classes cost virtually nothing and he could always give up if it was a mistake. Besides, he'd be doing them a favour. If they didn't get more students they'd have to shut up shop.

He turned back, went in and registered, paying a ten-pound deposit. As he came out again he felt a lifting of his spirits as though some pressure had been surgically removed from his brain. He'd done something; taken some action. After all, he didn't need even to mention it to his father.

As he opened the front door he smelt the instantly recognizable aroma of his favourite American Hot pizza from the place round the corner. In the dining room, which, being kitchen people, they hardly ever used, Tess had put a green linen cloth on the table and lit candles, as though it were a banquet.

As he put down his bag he caught the look of anxiety in her eyes and realized all this was because she'd been concerned about him. He held open his arms. 'Don't worry, I'll be fine. And you'll never guess what I've just done. Enrolled in evening classes for life drawing!'

Tess looked at him in amazement. 'I thought painting was your father's thing?'

'It is. But I used to have a little talent too. I want to know how much.'

He sat down and Tess handed him a slice of pizza. Thank heavens he seemed quite different from the way he had this morning. The gloom had cleared. Maybe, as he said, all he needed was an outlet. Unexpectedly the evening she'd been dreading turned into a merry lark. Two glasses of wine later, Tess realized what she was feeling was relief.

Next morning Tess woke and stretched in the luxurious knowledge that it was Saturday. Stephen was still asleep, his eyes hidden by a lock of unruly hair.

Quietly, so as not to wake him, she went down and brought them a cup of tea.

At the rattle of the teacups, magically he woke up. 'Have I died and gone to heaven?'

'I'm just softening you up.'

'What for?' he asked, hopefully slipping a hand up her nightdress.

Tess put down her cup, mustering the most enticing expression she could. 'For the supermarket run,' she purred. 'I'm afraid it's your turn.'

'Oh God.' Stephen collapsed and put his head back under the pillow. 'Is it really?'.

'Don't worry, Luke'll help you. He loves super-markets.'

So after breakfast Stephen and Luke set off in one direction while Tess went off in another to drop Ellie at her friend Lily's where she would no doubt spend the day watching educationally stretching videos such as *Don't Tell Mom, the Babysitter's a Zombie*.

As Luke cruised the aisles of the superstore in search of food that showed as little relation as possible to its origins, Stephen marvelled at the wonders of marketing, from dinosaur-shaped pasta to cook-chill Yorkshire puddings. Fortunately Tess had given them a compre-hensive list and Stephen decided to insist on No Devia-tion or they'd be there all day. The only pitched battle arose, surprisingly, at the washing powder section.

Stephen selected Safeway's own brand, but Luke returned it firmly to the shelf. 'Mum prefers Colorbrite because it keeps brights bright,' he explained to his father, kindly quoting the TV jingle.

'But that's nonsense.' Stephen tried to swap the brands.

'No it isn't,' insisted Luke smugly. 'Mum says so.'

'But I worked on that ad. It's complete crap; we just couldn't think of anything else to say about it. And it's more expensive.'

'Mum still prefers it.'

Stephen gave up. As an object lesson in how advertising worked it was pretty convincing. He'd even managed to fool his own wife.

To Stephen's great relief they had the evening to themselves. Luke was staying with his friend Ben and Ellie was off to a party. Even Inge passed them in a swathe of minidress and Calvin Klein perfume.

'Where's she off to looking so glam?' asked Stephen.

'An EFL disco.'

'Who're EFL? I stopped at Emerson, Lake and Palmer.'

Tess giggled. 'English as a Foreign Language, you twit.'

Stephen sipped his wine. 'Thank God I'm not young any more.'

He and Tess had just demolished a delicious Penne Amatriciana and were settling down to Chianti and pecorino cheese when Ellie made her appearance. Stephen nearly dropped his wine glass. She had paired a skimpy black swimsuit with tiny cut-off shorts, enormous clumpy boots and completed the ensemble with a large tattoo on her shoulder of a grinning skull with a rose in its teeth.

Stephen closed his eyes. 'Tess,' he whispered in disbelief, 'have you seen her shoulder? How the hell could you've let her do it?'

'Oh, Dad.' Ellie stuck her finger in her mouth, then she rubbed her skin gently. The tattoo smudged slightly. 'Haven't you ever heard of transfers? They must have had them in bubble gum even when *you* were young!'

Stephen gulped his wine looking marginally relieved. But he hadn't given up yet. 'I see subtlety is out of vogue. So where are you going all got up like a call girl in the Bois de Boulogne?'

'To a party. I told you. And no, I'm not going out on the street dressed like this. Lil's dad's dropping us off and Mum's given me the money for a taxi home.'

'That's something, I suppose.' Suddenly another thought hit him. He grabbed her hand and pulled her on to a chair. 'Ellie, you do know the facts of life, don't you?'

Ellie groaned. 'Yes, Dad. You told me them when I was four.'

Stephen looked stunned. 'Did I?'

'In glowing detail, except the fact that it was fun doing it. For some reason you left that bit out.'

'And how do you know about the fun bit?' Stephen demanded suspiciously.

'From your and Mum's expressions on Saturday mornings when you had a lie-in and we watched *Multi-Coloured Swap Shop*.'

Tess smirked, but Stephen was determined to be serious.

'Ellie, do you carry condoms?'

'*Dad*,' protested Ellie, making a face.

'Well, do you?'

'Do *you*?' Ellie demanded. 'Give me some credit for knowing my own mind. I don't carry them because I don't intend to sleep with anyone. Look, Dad, I probably know more about safe sex than you do. I bet you've never put a condom on a banana in the dark.'

'Certainly not.'

'Well we have. At school. It's fine actually. As long as you don't try and eat the banana afterwards.' She scooted out before Stephen could react. 'Don't wait up. I'll be very responsible. Honestly.'

And then the house was empty.

'It wasn't like that in our day, was it?'

'No,' agreed Tess, 'but then it wasn't *that* great in

our day. Everyone frightened of getting pregnant. And if they didn't get pregnant, even worse, they got *talked about*.'

'I suppose you're right,' said Stephen. 'I just didn't ever expect to be a parent. Tell you what. Let's be daring and leave the washing-up.' He led Tess over to the sofa and they sat down.

'You ought to trust her, you know,' Tess chided him. 'She's very sensible.'

'I know, I'm sorry, it's just my paranoia. It's the boys I don't trust. I used to be one, remember.' He cuddled up closer to her. 'I don't suppose,' he asked, pushing her back against the cushions, 'you fancy putting a condom on my banana?'

Tess laughed as Stephen began to kiss her and stroke her body, one hand slipping down between her thighs until she closed her eyes and arched her body towards him. And then, out of nowhere, there was a deafening explosion of electronic sound, like the screeching of ten car alarms or the jackpot being hit in a video arcade. It was Luke's newest computer game.

'Oh God,' muttered Stephen, sitting bolt upright as Tess struggled to turn the monstrous thing off, 'I think I've put my back out.'

Tess, knowing she should be sympathetic and wifely, collapsed instead in a peal of helpless laughter.

She had just managed to straighten him up with the help of every cushion in the sitting room when the phone went.

To her surprise it was Terry Worth, and he sounded anxious.

'Look, Tess, I'm really sorry to ring you like this on Saturday night but it's the kids. I've been stuck here at this bloody service station waiting for Angela to bring them for three hours. Is there anything I can do?'

'Have you tried ringing her?'

'The answering machine's on.'

'And what about the police, just in case there's been an accident?'

'I've tried that.'

'Maybe Angela's made a mistake about the arrangements.' Even as she said it Tess admitted to herself that Angela was one of the most chillingly efficient women she'd ever met.

'I suppose that's a possibility.' This was clearly the option Terry wanted to believe.

'Then I think if I were you I'd go home.'

'OK, Tess, thanks a lot.'

She put the phone down. What a bitch Angela was. The first thing she'd done after she got the settlement was move the children to somewhere Terry couldn't visit easily. Now it sounded as though she was making life even harder for him.

'Who was that?' asked Stephen.

'Terry Worth. You know, the Cockney millionaire. His ex-wife's playing him up over access to the kids. It's so shitty of her because he's a lovely man and he adores his kids.'

Stephen took her hand. 'Just promise me one thing.'

'What's that?'

'That we won't ever do that to each other. Or to the kids.'

'I promise,' smiled Tess, loving him for thinking the same thing she was.

'Now,' said Stephen, who was looking remarkably recovered, 'where were we?'

CHAPTER FIVE

'Tessie, Stephen, hello!' Their oldest friends, Josh and Catherine, stood in the drive outside their lovely flint-faced house high on the South Downs waving and holding the dog so that it wouldn't jump up and scratch the paintwork on Stephen's shiny BMW.

'So you didn't bring the children,' said Catherine, opening Tess's door. Their own four, ranging from six to fifteen, were dotted round the house and garden. 'Giving yourselves a day off?'

'Luke's with a friend and Ellie had a late night,' explained Tess. 'Isn't it great?'

Tess hugged Catherine, thrilled to be seeing her after months of being too busy. Josh and Catherine were Tess's Ideal Couple, the perfect antidote to her job. They had been married for eighteen years and were blissfully happy.

Josh taught at Sussex University and Catherine helped out part time at a local health centre. Money was tight and their house had become increasingly scruffy over the years, but neither Josh nor Catherine seemed to notice. Tess often wondered what it was that made their marriage work so well. They just seemed to fit together like a pair of old gardening gloves.

'Stephen!' Josh greeted him as though he hadn't seen him for years. 'Just the man! You can come and help me with some wood chopping. We're right down to the last few logs and it'll get cold later. Emma! Get that tricycle out of the woodshed!' His six-year-old daughter scuttled off. Clearly he liked playing the paterfamilias and was good at it.

Stephen followed Josh to the bottom of the garden while Tess and Catherine headed for the warmth of the kitchen to finish preparing lunch. Even though it was April the sun had no real warmth yet.

'You hold on to that,' commanded Josh, pointing to a narrow treetrunk. Stephen did as he was told, noticing as he looked around that there were wild daffodils in the nearby copse and wood pigeons cooing reassuringly in the branches. Probably too early for a cuckoo. And at that moment he heard one and both he and Josh grinned.

'Horrible bird. Pushes all the host's fledglings out of their own nest to get all the food. God knows how it got to be the symbol of rural peace.'

Stephen laughed. He'd never liked Josh quite as much as Tess did Catherine. Always found him a bit too Real Ale, maybe even a touch smug about his provincial cosiness. But today Stephen found himself envying him. Josh really liked what he did.

'Josh?' Stephen caught the logs as Josh chopped them and chucked them into the basket. It was oddly rewarding watching the basket fill up.

Something in Stephen's tone made Josh stop chopping for a moment. 'Mmmm?'

'What would you do if you got fed up with teaching? After all, you've got four kids to support.'

'Work out if there's anything else I could do, I suppose. Which I doubt.'

Stephen picked a wood louse off the log he was holding and dropped it gently to the ground. 'Maybe I should think about teaching.'

Josh laughed out loud. 'Oh, come on, Stephen, you couldn't survive on an academic's salary. It wouldn't keep you in Paul Smith ties let alone BMWs.' He picked up the basket of logs and headed towards the garden. They passed Stephen's car. 'Fortunately I've never fancied a penis extension like yours.' He tilted his head towards the gleaming BMW parked next to his own ancient Saab.

'Laugh while you can,' Stephen replied. 'I may not have it much longer.'

In the kitchen Tess and Catherine were peeling sprouts and sipping wine with Emma, Catherine's youngest daughter, sitting next to them massacring any they handed her with a blunt knife.

'Go on,' Tess encouraged her, 'tell me. What's your secret? Why does your marriage work so well?'

'Does it? I always think we're too caught up with family. That we ought to talk about Freud at breakfast and the threat to the ozone layer. Not just whether Tim's behind with his homework or whose turn it is to take the rubbish out.'

Tess laughed. 'I once used a shrink as an expert witness and he told me couples who talk about Freud at breakfast usually have relationships that are in deep shit.'

Emma looked at her with delighted amazement. 'You mean pooh,' she corrected amiably.

'So I do,' conceded Tess. Fortunately Emma decided that with this nugget she'd had the best of the conversation and went off to tease the dog.

'Anyway,' Tess prodded, 'you haven't answered my question. What makes your marriage work?'

Catherine laughed. 'It didn't always. We had some very rocky years. Josh was my first boyfriend and I married him for security. I didn't want to face the world. But though I got away from the world, he didn't. He was out there with all those adoring young students; all those pretty young girls putting him on a pedestal. He'd been just an ordinary working-class bloke from an ordinary background; now they all thought he was God. And for a while he started thinking he was too. It was nearly the end of us.' Catherine's face took on a look of pain, remembering. 'But I decided to trust him, see how he turned out. Frankly with three children under five I didn't have a lot of choice. I couldn't stop him changing. We were married at twenty; he was bound to. I just had to see if I liked what he changed into. Fortunately I did.' She picked up the sharp knife again. 'I never found out what did it, a girl or what, but he stopped believing he was God and went back to being Josh.'

Tess smiled in sympathy. Maybe she needed to just trust Stephen. Maybe he was changing too and she should wait and see what happened. And then the door opened and Josh and Stephen came in with the basket of logs, followed by Rocky the dog looking very pleased with himself carrying a leg of lamb in his mouth.

'Oh my God,' shrieked Catherine, 'he's got Mrs D.'s Sunday joint!' Josh threw down the basket of logs and wrestled the meat from Rocky's teeth.

Catherine rinsed it under the tap and inspected it for teethmarks. 'He's your dog,' she accused Josh, laughing, 'you take it back.'

'Bad dog!' said Josh, wrapping the meat in kitchen paper and disappearing out of the front door. 'You didn't even remember the mint sauce.'

It was dark by the time Tess and Stephen tore themselves away from the warmth and merriment of Hope Lodge's kitchen and set off back for London. Josh, Catherine and the children all came out to wave them goodbye.

'Well, well,' said Josh, picking up Emma's tricycle

and putting it in the front porch. 'There's someone who, if I'm not much mistaken, is about to huff and puff and blow his house down.'

'Oh God,' Catherine turned, kicking some loose plaster off the porch wall and wondering if that explained Tess's curious question. 'Poor Tess. I do hope you're wrong.'

'So, are we going to your parents' anniversary party or not?' Tess asked Stephen. Stella, her mother-in-law, had phoned late the previous night asking if they'd made up their minds yet.

'Please, Dad, do let's,' chorused Luke and Ellie. They both loved it at Killamalooe because Julius treated them like grownups and let them join in the conversations and drink wine all night.

'Your mother says you and I can have the cottage while Ellie and Luke stay in the big house so we can have some privacy.' They both knew his mother was being tactful, because that way Stephen could get away from too much exposure to Julius.

He looked at the three eager faces, even Tess, all wanting him to agree.

'All right,' he gave in reluctantly, 'as long as we're staying in the cottage.'

'Yippee!' whooped Ellie. 'Back to the auld sod!'

'In more ways than one,' grinned Stephen.

From the hall Inge called that it was time to leave for school and Ellie and Luke reluctantly kissed their parents goodbye. Tess got up too.

'One thing,' Stephen added, looking faintly embarrassed. 'You won't mention the art classes, will you?'

Sad that he should feel like that, Tess agreed. 'Of course not. I wouldn't dream of it.'

★

Stephen watched the woman arrange herself on the platform in the middle of the floor with fascination. It was difficult to put an age on her. Her face looked sixtyish but her naked body far older. It was clearly a body that had lived, a body with a history. The breasts drooped, stretch marks were still visible on her hips and thighs, and the uneven scar of a Caesarean formed a faint line above her pubic hair. Yet her face had about it a challenging aliveness, a sense of still being ready for anything that chance might bowl in her direction. She wasn't a ground-down victim too frightened to cross her own threshold. Stephen sensed that this was a woman who still left life's door wide open.

As the other students worked steadily Stephen still watched. He'd never attempted life drawing and he was conscious he might fail. And then, for a fraction of a second the model looked him in the eye and almost imperceptibly winked.

Stephen laughed and glanced at the clock on the studio wall. Half an hour had passed. What did it matter if he screwed up? It was time he got down to it.

The lecturer looked at her watch too and wished she didn't have to supplement her painting by teaching evening classes. She felt a flash of guilt that her leftie principles were slipping. Not that evening classes weren't a wonderful institution, the only way most ordinary people had a chance to get away from their dull daytime jobs and exercise their artistic fantasies. It was just that most students were so pedestrian. Through most of the course they would struggle with their charcoal, drawing tiny, terrified lines, rubbing out continually, never daring to try the broad sweeps that would pin down the reality of the woman in front of them. Ah, well. At least she had, thanks to the sign she'd put up, three new pupils and the course would –

for the moment – be saved. Until another couple of women from the estate over the road decided they'd rather go back to watching *Taggart* and the local authority threatened the course with closure again.

The lecturer sighed. Maybe she ought to be more encouraging. She started to do the rounds, willing herself to see the positive in the uninspiring efforts that met her gaze.

She had almost worked her way round the class when she realized it was time to pack up. The caretaker was very fussy about easels being put away before nine-forty-five and grouched endlessly if the last person wasn't out of the building by ten. She'd just have to assess the remaining students at the beginning of next week.

'Sorry, everyone, time to go home. Could you take your drawings home with you and bring them back for the next class?'

Quite a lot of the class, she noticed, put away their things with great enthusiasm. Probably eager to get to the pub round the corner where a lot of people went for a drink afterwards. It was a well-known fact, suggested in every woman's magazine article, that evening classes were a good way to meet the opposite sex.

She supervised the stacking of the easels and collected up the charcoal as the model, entirely careless of her naked state, disappeared behind the screen to get dressed. To the teacher's annoyance one of the new students at the back seemed to have made no effort to pack up his things and was still sketching.

She strode over and enquired in an irritable tone if he would kindly stop, realizing it was one of the students she hadn't got round to tonight.

The man, tall and attractive, in his mid-thirties, was bending over his drawing as she approached, shading in the tender area of the inner thigh. He ignored her and went on drawing.

'I did ask you to pack up ten minutes ago, you know,' she pointed out, her irritation spilling over into rudeness.

'Sorry.' Stephen stood back, fixing her with one of his most engaging smiles. 'I didn't know whether we'd be having the same model next time, so I wanted to finish tonight.'

The lecturer glanced from his face to the drawing and stared, feeling as though a complete stranger had just come up and handed her a thousand pounds. The drawing had captured the woman in living, breathing reality. Every line and crevice of her raddled body was there. But more, far more than that, he had captured her spirit, the unbowed, two-fingered rebelliousness of the young woman that lived on in an old woman's body.

It was the best thing she'd seen in twenty years of teaching.

The excitement Stephen felt at the lecturer's reaction lasted all the way down the King's Road and the New King's Road to his own front door. He almost bounced up the front steps and into the kitchen to find Tess sitting at the pine table, surrounded by bills. He felt a prick of guilt. Doing the bills was his job, in the division of labour they'd worked out.

Tess looked up but didn't smile. She was annoyed with him. The phone company had rung today and told Inge they were three months behind with the bill and they were going to cut off the phone unless it was settled in three days. So instead of putting her feet up and watching TV after a knackering day at work she'd spent the evening writing cheques. She'd found a surprising number of bills unpaid. And Luke and Ellie's school fees would be due in two weeks. It had all brought a shiver of recognition. Sometimes when she'd been a child her mother had suddenly turned out all the lights and told them not to speak because the rent-collector was knocking on the door. Tess had never forgotten that feeling of panic.

'Sorry, Tess love. I should have done all that.'

Tess's resentment bubbled a little lower. There was a kind of white-hot energy about him tonight that made it hard to go on being angry with him.

Stephen moved closer, knowing that this probably wasn't the right moment but, unable to contain his excitement, he went on anyway. 'Tess, something really amazing happened tonight. My art teacher thought my drawing was brilliant.'

Tess smiled in acknowledgement, trying to share his obvious pleasure and suppress a creeping wariness about what was coming next.

'Tessie, you know how restless I've been at work lately. Well, I think I'm beginning to understand why. I thought at first it might simply go away, that it was just disillusion with advertising and I could shake it off. But, Tess, it's more than that. It's deeper than merely a reaction against something. I need something more positive in my life, something I actually *want* to do.' He raked her face with his eyes, hoping for some kind of understanding there, but Tess's look was fixed. 'I think I want be a painter.'

Listening to him, Tess felt panic spread through her. Then she took told of herself. Maybe he meant one day.

'When?' she asked, willing herself to stay calm and dismiss the ingrained fear of poverty and insecurity which made her so terrified of change.

He looked her in the eye, confirming the worst. 'As soon as possible.'

Remembering the piles of bills and red reminders Tess felt a surge of fury ran through her. How could he just jump this on her out of the blue?

'Look, Stephen.' She was trying to sound reasonable but sensed her tone was coming out patronizing. 'Thousands of people probably want to be painters. Shrinks. Plumbers. Accountants. But you can't just do it overnight.' She pointed to the sheafs of bills, enough it seemed to her, to run a small business. 'We already spend everything we earn and more. If you want to change your life we'll have to work up to it. Save. Economize. Work out how to pay the mortgage and the school fees. We can't do it all on my salary.'

Stephen looked at her almost pleadingly. 'I don't know how long I can wait. I'm beginning to hate what I do.'

Tess felt her temper crack. Stephen sounded like a restless teenager, not a man with a house and two kids. 'Oh for God's sake, Stephen. Of course you can wait. Be a Sunday painter for a bit.'

'My father didn't.'

How dared he quote his father as any kind of model? 'Yes. And for ten years you went barefoot and lived like a gypsy all over Europe till he made any money. Stephen, we've got a house, commitments, a way of life.'

'Yes,' sighed Stephen, acknowledging the truth of what she was saying but wishing she wouldn't say it all the same. He stood up and turned away. 'Of course you're absolutely right.'

Tess watched him leave the room, the energy that had lit him up snuffed like a candle. Had her childhood memories made her too terrified of taking risks, or was she behaving perfectly reasonably?

CHAPTER SIX

Tess woke up and instantly remembered the quarrel she and Stephen had had last night. They had gone to bed without making it up, and did not even roll together across the cold, wide space by accident. It was as though their unconscious as well as their conscious minds felt the hostility.

She looked across at him. He was still asleep. Instead of waking him she closed her eyes and pictured the wide sweep of beach at Killamalooe, with the abandoned tower at one end that she sometimes liked to climb and sit in staring out to sea like the Lady of Shalott. At the other end of the bay was the lighthouse, and in between the shell-strewn beach where she and Ellie had spent hours looking for mother-of-pearl. Even the thought of it was balm to the spirit.

The prospect of Killamalooe made her wonder briefly what Julius would make of Stephen's sudden interest in art. Julius was so exasperating. Part of her warmed to him, to his outrageous sense of humour, and to the unexpected kindness he'd always shown her. Unlike Stella. There was nothing like approval from someone to predispose you to like them. So she'd tried to make allowances for his selfishness and his utter belief that nothing existed beyond the needs of Julius Gilfillan, genius. But when it came to Stephen she couldn't forgive him. It was clear to her that despite Stephen's rejection of his father's lifestyle, he desperately wanted his approval. Yet Julius, almost cruelly, withheld it.

Families, thought Tess, leaning down to Stephen

and kissing him. He didn't stir. Were they more of a blessing than a curse? Sometimes it was a close-run thing.

Stephen decided to get the bus to work. Somehow he couldn't face going underground; his mood was already too bleak. Most of the time he didn't begrudge Inge the car to do the ferrying to and from school and the countless other activities London children engaged in, but just for today he would have welcomed his own little private bubble. Tess had seemed less angry, admittedly, this morning. But he still sensed an under-lying resentment in her. In a way it had frightened him because he half understood it, but it was also the first gulf that had opened between them and he didn't know how to bridge it.

He got off at the corner of Shaftesbury Avenue and Greek Street and walked up towards Soho Square, hoping the spring sunshine would lighten his mood. Taking his usual short-cut through the square gardens he saw their friendly neighbourhood drunk peel away from a group of others breakfasting on Tennants Super.

'Good morning, sorr. Could I trouble you for a quid now, sorr?'

Stephen gave him the fifty pence he'd held back last time and the man went off chortling to himself. They seemed a carefree bunch. Jesus, Stephen muttered to himself, get a grip on yourself. You're not starting to envy the winos?

As he pushed open the swing door of the agency he tried to focus his mind on the meeting scheduled this morning with Worldwide Motors. The prospect did nothing to raise his spirits.

He'd only just opened the door of his office when

Ted's secretary was on the phone asking him to come up. Assuming it was a pre-meeting briefing, Stephen grabbed his folder and summoned the lift.

Unusually the door of Ted's office was open and Ted sat, pale and sweating, behind his desk despite the cool weather. Stephen noticed dark patches under the arms of his shirtsleeves and that his hands were shaking. He wondered if Ted had had a rough night taking clients out. The provincial ones, suddenly away from their wives, often wanted to be shown the *A–Z* of sleaze, which could be deeply wearing on their hosts.

'I want you to know,' said Ted before Stephen had a chance to make any comment, 'that I don't consider any of this my responsibility. I had no idea about Bill's home situation. I simply acted because he'd lost his sense of proportion. Wouldn't you agree with that, Stephen?'

Stephen had no idea what Ted was talking about. 'Bill Barclay, do you mean?' Stephen thought about Bill's revelations of the other night. He clearly had personal problems, but it hadn't seemed to affect his work. He was like a puppy on its first outing where the Worldwide account was concerned. 'He's a bit of a workaholic, if that's what you mean. Spends every waking hour in this building, but I always thought you approved of that, Ted. I thought that was considered being a good boy. What's the matter with Bill?'

Ted's hands started shaking again. His secretary gave him a black coffee. 'Look, Stephen, I took him off the account. He was too inexperienced.'

'Oh, come on, Ted,' Stephen felt a spurt of anger on Bill's behalf, 'He's been here five years at least.'

'Walensky didn't like him.'

'Ah, now we have the truth. Walensky didn't like him so you chucked him out. How's he taken it?'

'Jesus.' Ted's hands rattled his coffee cup as though he were sitting on a high-speed train. 'He didn't take it. The stupid young sod locked himself in the garage and sat in his bloody company car with the engine running.'

'He isn't . . .?' Stephen couldn't bring himself to say it. He pictured Bill in his office the other day envying the award and explaining the exact status of each class of BMW.

'Dead. Yes he is bloody dead. And you know what people will say, don't you? That he did it because I took him off the effing account. Shit.'

Stephen turned away. Images of Bill slumped in his car feeling betrayed by the agency he'd given his more-than-all to rushed through his mind.

'Stephen, what am I going to do? I had no idea about all this stuff with his wife.'

'His wife sounded like a cow from what he told me. But what about his kids? You could set up a trust for them, at least. Make sure they don't suffer financially.'

Ted looked appalled, his sense of self-preservation beginning to win over his panic. 'I can't do that. It'll look as though I'm accepting responsibility.' He turned to his secretary. 'Janine. Get on the blower, love. Find out when the funeral is. Send the biggest bloody bouquet of flowers you can find. And sign it from the company. Not me personally. Got that?'

'How touching. Bill would have appreciated that.' Stephen turned away and walked as fast as he could out of the room, ignoring Ted's appeals for him to stay. He slammed the door of his office, feeling sick. To throw your life away for advertising? Jesus. He opened the folder he'd been carrying and looked down at the obscene gas-guzzling cars. And yet wasn't that exactly what he was doing too? Wasting his life?

73

The thought of Bill looking punctured and pathetic outside the bar the other night kept coming back to haunt him. If only he could have persuaded Bill what he believed himself, how little advertising mattered. Stephen didn't know how long he sat looking at the same illustration but it was only moments later that the phone cut through his thoughts. It was Ted's secretary again, to say that Mr Walensky was here and the meeting would go ahead as planned. Stephen couldn't believe what he was hearing.

'Surely Ted must have put him off, today of all days?'

'Well, he's here, and in none too good a mood, I gather.' The girl sounded both upset and embarrassed. 'Something to do with having to hang around in reception while you and Ted were talking.'

Stephen flipped the folder shut and picked it up angrily, his dislike for Walensky growing.

In the meeting room he found Ted already there, placating Walensky. But the man wasn't having any. 'I've been kicking my heels downstairs for half an hour.' He repeated it as though he couldn't quite believe the magnitude of the sin. 'Half an hour. What are you running here anyway? An advertising shop or a fucking *tea*shop?'

That was it. Stephen tossed his folder down on to the table. 'As a matter of fact,' he said nastily, 'some of this is your responsibility. You didn't like the account executive we'd allocated so Ted took him off the account.'

'Well?' Walensky clearly thought this was only to be expected.

'Unfortunately the man had personal problems as well and last night he committed suicide.'

Walensky seemed supremely unmoved. 'Maybe you

should be more careful whom you hire. If they can't stand the heat . . .'

Stephen looked at the man in disbelief. 'Has it ever occurred to you, Mr Walensky' – he made his voice as even and pleasant as possible – 'that you are an unpleasant shit with third-class ideas?'

The room was suddenly filled with waxworks, their eyes fixed straight ahead. Stephen waited to see whose part Ted was going to take. Ted said nothing but moved perhaps half an inch closer to Walensky. Maybe he already felt he'd said too much to Stephen, thus rendering him an embarrassment.

Without saying a word Walensky turned, picked up his papers and walked out, followed by his scuttling yes-men.

Stephen watched Ted's face. He looked more composed now, his conscience firmly shrink-wrapped and out of sight. 'Come on, Stephen,' he said, with almost a teasing tone to his voice that made Stephen want to gag, 'you know you can't talk to a major client like that. You'll have to apologize.'

'I'm sorry, Ted, but that's not possible. Bill's dead and that lump of lard didn't give a toss.'

'Stephen, don't be ludicrous. This is business. You don't have to like the man to work with him. Go on, run after him. I can't stand by while he takes the campaign to another agency just because of your scruples. This isn't fucking Christian Aid, you know.'

'Sorry, Ted.' Stephen stayed where he was.

'Then you can bloody well consider yourself fired.'

Stephen shrugged. 'It'll be a pleasure.' He walked slowly towards the door, then turned. 'And don't worry about me, Ted.' His voice was all honeyed sarcasm. 'I'm not the type to sit in my car with the exhaust on.'

*

75

Tess's meeting finished early and she walked past the British Museum wondering if she had time to go in and look at the Egyptian Room, a place she loved. But then she remembered the more pressing task of finding a present for Julius and Stella. What on earth did you give one of the most highly paid painters in the world? Their house was already stuffed with antiques and exquisite objects gathered from abroad when Julius went on lecture-tours. Something gold, presumably, as it was their golden wedding. On the corner of Museum Street she spotted an intriguing sign advertising Rameses Egyptian Bazaar. She ducked down into the basement and was amazed. It was just like stepping into Cairo or Luxor. At the bottom of the steps two enormous statues guarded the entrance as though it were a tomb. Above the door was a gold eye, designed to shame and discourage tomb robbers and remind them of their fate if they crossed the sacred threshold.

Inside there were statues of every shape and size, papyri of the whole panoply of Egyptian gods and goddesses, shabti figures in metal and ceramic, brass temple bells, tiny perfume bottles encased in silver.

And a whole shelf of cats. Tess had an inspiration. Stella liked cats. Most of the statues were green, carved in jade or malachite, but there were a few in black.

'Do you have anything in gold?' Tess asked, picking up a particularly attractive malachite one about the size of a thimble with green chips for eyes. 'It's a golden wedding anniversary present, you see.'

'We don't stock real gold,' the assistant answered. 'Too expensive. But I'll have a look.'

He disappeared, leaving her once more with the illusion that she was in Egypt. Then, a minute or two later, he came back with a black cat, about nine or ten inches high, with a fabulous necklace in solid gold.

It was perfect. As the shopkeeper boxed it up she saw him pick up the tiny malachite cat she'd admired and put it in too.

'There must be some mistake,' she protested.

He smiled, reminding her of the gentle, tolerant expression on the mask of the boy-king. 'For luck. No extra charge. Perhaps you may need it one day.'

As she came out, blinking, into the daylight, she decided to take it as an omen. If Stephen wanted to change his life, why shouldn't he? If he was serious about painting they had better start thinking ahead, making economies, saving up what the Americans called 'Fuck You' money. In a couple of years it should be possible. She decided not to go back to the office after all. She had no more meetings today anyway. Instead she'd go home and she and Stephen could sit down and plan the future. At the bottom of her bag the tiny good luck cat winked its eyes unseen in the darkness of its cardboard box.

'Look, Mum, Dad's home!' Luke shouted to her excitedly as she opened the front door. 'He was here when we got back from school.' He dragged her into the kitchen where she found Stephen making a cup of tea with Ellie.

'Hello, love. I've just found the most fabulous present for Julius and Stella. I'll show you in a moment. What brings you home so early?'

'Well, actually . . .' Stephen decided there wasn't much point being indirect. 'The truth is, I've been fired.'

CHAPTER SEVEN

'Gosh, Dad,' teased Luke, not realizing the seriousness of the situation. 'Does that mean I can't have that new computer you promised me?'

Ellie, sensing with rare discretion that this was one discussion they should keep out of, grabbed him and dragged him upstairs protesting loudly. Inge followed and disappeared into her room to turn up the volume on her TV tactfully.

Tess, halfway through unpacking her briefcase, stared at Stephen in disbelief. He couldn't really have been fired, not out of the blue, especially after the award. It had to be his fault. He'd been working up to this, she knew it. The truth was, while she'd been sensibly planning his escape he had simply thrown everything away with no thought for the rest of them. Suddenly she felt overwhelmingly angry. 'So you're happy now, are you? Now that you've managed to get what you want? And how exactly are we going to pay the mortgage?'

'There may be some kind of pay-off from the agency,' Stephen said quietly. How stupid of him to expect Tess to be sympathetic, to want to know why.

'Do you mean you don't even *know*?' Tess heard her voice rising in fury. 'You didn't even bother to find out? No, I don't suppose you even thought about your family, did you? You just did the macho thing and stood on your dignity.' Carried away by the intensity of her anger Tess didn't realize quite how sarcastic she sounded. 'So, what vital principle were you fighting for? Artistic integrity in Levi commercials or just bigger company cars?'

Stephen didn't even answer. He simply got up and walked towards the front door. Seconds later Tess heard it bang.

She sat down at the kitchen table utterly drained. If he was going to behave like a sulky adolescent and not even bother to give her an explanation, then fine. She closed her eyes and breathed deeply, trying to calm down.

Gradually she felt her anger subside and a slight misgiving set in. OK, she'd lost her temper; it was a fault of hers. But surely she'd had plenty of provocation? She got up, went to the fridge and poured herself a soothing glass of wine. And as she sat down again the thought struck her that she'd been too furious to ask Stephen exactly why he *had* been fired.

Stephen walked fast along the New King's Road towards Parsons Green. Litter was blowing everywhere in the sharp April wind and he hadn't even brought his coat. Viciously, he kicked a Coke can banging along on the pavement. He couldn't *believe* Tess. The famed caring, compassionate Tess Brien, champion of the underdog, hadn't even listened to his side of the story, hadn't even wanted to hear him out. Jesus, Bill had killed himself in some pathetic suburban garage over some ludicrous ad campaign and all Tess was worried about was the sodding mortgage.

He arrived at Parsons Green, filled to overflowing with noisy laughing yuppies spilling out of the wine bars, sitting out at the pavement tables outside the pasta restaurants despite the chill spring weather. Watching them, he felt jealous of their freedom, of their capacity to do what they wanted, to drop everything and bum round the world, unsaddled by family commitments and endless bills and pension schemes.

A dark-haired girl in a linen suit sat at one of the outside tables, alone. He realized that she was watching him. As he walked towards her she smiled a broad, straightforward smile of invitation. For a split second he was tempted to sit down with her. Why the hell not? That smile vaguely reminded him of someone. And then he remembered who. When he was a student he'd taken out a girl with the same bold inviting smile. At the end of the evening, as was the way in those times, they'd ended up in her flat. And just before they'd gone to bed together he'd held her for a moment. *This isn't just going to be a one-night stand, is it?* he'd asked her. *Because if so I'm not really interested.* A look of shock had flitted across her eyes. *Isn't that supposed to be my line*, she'd asked, her tone hard and sarcastic as though he'd broken the rules. Men weren't supposed to feel emotion, only to want sex. And he'd got up politely from her bed and taken himself home, never sure whether he was a fool or not.

Stephen returned the girl's smile and walked on. She wouldn't solve anything. The truth was he loved Tess and his family. It was just that she could be such a bitch when she lost her temper. Usually she regretted it the next day. But by then the words had already been spoken.

Tess, wearing jeans and a T-shirt, her long red hair tied back in a red bandanna, manically mopped the kitchen floor, trying to atone for her outburst through housework. The only time she remembered such old-fashioned virtues as spring-cleaning was when she felt guilty. Then, even if it was two o'clock in the morning, she'd scrub and polish until she dropped from physical exhaustion.

Ellie and Luke, hearing the front door bang, closely followed by the sound of ferocious hoovering, had sensibly decided to stay upstairs until things blew over. This wasn't the first time their parents had fallen out, though on the Relate scale of marital disharmony, this was clearly somewhere between gale force 8 and a hurricane.

When the phone rang around ten, Tess was so absorbed in scouring the oven, aided and abetted by a Marvin Gaye tape turned to full volume, that she didn't even hear it. Luke had to run downstairs and tell her that Ted was on the line.

Tess put down her Brillo pad and rinsed her hands. Maybe Ted was offering Stephen another chance. Eagerly she picked up the phone from the kitchen wall.

'Tess, hello. How's Stephen? Has he calmed down yet?' Ted's voice sounded oddly shifty. 'Look, if you could persuade him to apologize to Walensky I'm sure the whole thing'll blow over. After all the man's a human being. He'll understand how cut up Stephen was about Bill. As we all are,' he added sanctimoniously.

Tess had no idea what he was talking about. Wasn't Walensky the big noise from Worldwide Motors? So Stephen had fallen out with him. 'Of course I'll try and talk him round. But, Ted, I don't really understand. What about Bill? Why should he be so upset about Bill Barclay?'

There was a long pause. 'Jesus, Tess.' Ted sounded incredulous. 'Didn't Stephen tell you? Bill Barclay went and topped himself, the stupid young shit. And all over a sodding car campaign. Then Walensky makes some tactless remark and Stephen jumps down his throat.' There was a slightly apologetic pause. 'I gave him the chance to climb down, Tess, but he just wouldn't do it. And I can't afford to lose Walensky's business. So you see my position. Of course I want to keep Stephen, too. He's a very talented man. As you know.'

But Tess wasn't listening. She stood in the middle of her shiny clean kitchen floor, a strand of damp hair falling down over her eyes and a sick feeling spreading from the pit of her stomach. Bill Barclay had killed himself. And Stephen had clearly been fired for blaming Ted.

'Tess?' said the voice on the phone. 'Tess, are you still there?'

Stephen drained his glass and looked round the wine bar. It was nearly one a.m. and he was almost the last person in the place. Even the noisy group of estate agents in the far corner, who had been celebrating all evening either because the housing market was picking up or because they'd decided it couldn't get any worse, were picking up their coats and paying the bill. Judging by the number of empty bottles on the table they were probably about to make some policeman's evening as he flagged down their Golf GTIs and breathalysed them on the way home.

The trouble was that Stephen didn't feel drunk. He felt entirely sober. And still furious. He'd walked until he was physically exhausted but his brain hadn't done him the favour of feeling the same. He said goodnight to the waitress, noting with a wry smile quite how quickly she put his chair on top of the table when he got out of it, and climbed back upstairs to the Green and headed slowly for home.

But as he walked down their street, half shabby, half gentrified, he knew he didn't want to go in. The thought of Tess already in bed asleep, her rigid and unforgiving back towards him, just made him feel more depressed.

Maybe he should go and find a hotel and brave the curious looks he'd get from the night desk arriving so late and without luggage. Then he noticed his car parked opposite their house. The car that would have to be returned to the agency any day. It might as well come in useful one last time.

He climbed into the back and stretched his long body as much as he could along the seat. Fortunately he hadn't parked it under a streetlamp. Within five minutes he'd fallen into the dreamless sleep of total exhaustion.

Upstairs in their bedroom Tess wasn't lying rigid and unforgiving in their bed. She was pacing about, riven with guilt at how badly she'd behaved, at the unfair conclusion she'd jumped to. Every few moments she looked out into the street to see if there was any sign of him, but there wasn't. Finally she went back downstairs and lay on the sofa trying to read a book and drinking strong coffee, wondering where Stephen could have gone. To a friend's maybe, or to someone from the agency. Or maybe he'd still come back. She decided to wait up a little longer. She switched on the TV. Phil Donahue was debating whether or not fidelity was an impossible ideal in the late twentieth century. For the first ten minutes she watched, riveted. Then she fell deeply asleep with the future of fidelity still hanging nervously in the balance.

Bright sunlight was streaming in when she woke up, and she could hear the milkman rattling the bottles out on the front steps. She was stiff all over, and absolutely freezing. She sat for a moment taking in the fact that Stephen hadn't returned, then stumbled into the hall and opened the front door. The milkman was still standing there, the same one they've had ever since they'd moved in when Luke was little, begging for rides on his milkfloat. By now he was an old family friend.

'Oh dearie, dearie me,' he tutted, taking in Tess's dishevelled appearance. 'Fallen out with the old man, have we?' Tess looked at him too astonished to be insulted. Was the man a mindreader?

The milkman grinned. 'He's over there. Kipping in the back of the motor. Maybe a nice cuppa might help sort things out? Always pour tea on troubled waters, my wife says.' He handed over her milk and departed, whistling and grinning. He liked Tess. She always had a smile and a word for him even when she was in a hurry, not like some down this street. He kicked a double-parked Volvo as he passed. And they call *us* yobbos, he muttered.

Tess, feeling nervous and clumsy, decided to take his advice and made a pot of tea. Usually they had this in bed every morning as part of their waking-up ritual. Maybe the oddness of having it in the car would cut the ice. Carefully she poured two mugs, tucked a packet of biscuits under her arm and crossed the road. This would give the neighbours something to talk about.

In spite of the sunshine Stephen was still asleep. Tess put down one mug of tea on the pavement and knocked on the window, watching him wake with a start, uncertain for a moment where he was. Then he saw Tess and opened the door.

'I thought you might like a cup of tea,' she said tentatively, not sure of her reception. 'I'm so sorry, love,' she rushed on before he could say anything. 'Ted rang last night and told me about Bill. You must have thought I was a heartless cow.'

84

'A heartless bitch,' he amended with the ghost of a smile.

'A heartless bitch then.'

He took the mug of tea and beckoned her in next to him. 'Maybe I should blame this.' He ruffled her red hair with his free hand. 'Why the hell did I marry a redhead?' He sipped his tea, taking in her creased clothes, smudged eye make-up and a crest of hair which was standing up like an aggressive cockerel's. 'God, you look a mess,' he pointed out with a smile of satisfaction.

Tess laughed and sipped her tea. 'I've been awake all night worrying where you'd got to.'

Tenderly he reached for her and removed the mug from her hand and put it on the floor next to him. She might lose her temper and behave like a demented banshee but at least she was genuinely sorry. He leaned towards her and kissed her just as Luke opened the front door to see what had happened to the newsboy with his computer magazine.

He turned to Ellie who was coming down the stairs behind him. 'Why on earth are Mum and Dad snogging in the back of the car at seven-thirty in the morning?' he demanded.

Ellie glanced over his shoulder, relieved that though this certainly counted as unpredictable behaviour it was a lot better than last night. 'Search me,' she said in tones of world-weary tolerance, 'maybe Mum's been reading too many articles on keeping the magic alive in your marriage.'

As she showered and dressed, Tess remembered that in all the worry over Stephen's job she'd forgotten this Saturday was the weekend of Julius and Stella's anniversary. They could sit down and be practical when

85

they got back. At first, she'd wondered if the whole thing might blow over at the agency. Walensky himself might climb down or some way be found for egos to be soothed. But she'd come to see that with Stephen it went deeper. Bill's tragedy hadn't been the cause of his departure, it had simply lit the touchpaper. Anyway, she told herself, look on the bright side. Maybe she'd get the partnership after all. God knew, they needed the extra money now. But what they needed even more was some time together to heal the wounds of the last few days, and to try and remind themselves why it was they'd married each other in the first place. She hoped that despite Julius Killamalooe would be just the place.

By Friday, despite the workload that always piled up if she went away, Tess couldn't resist the creeping sense of excitement. At best Ireland would give them the chance to think things through, at worst it meant they could put off reality for a few days more.

Tess went in early and worked her way steadily through the pile of documents, telling Jacqui to put only the most urgent calls through. By lunchtime she'd finished and was about to make a mad dash for home when the phone went.

'I don't know whether you count this as urgent' – Jacqui was used to calls from Dymphna – 'but it's your mother.'

Tess ignobly considered getting Jacqui to say she'd already left but decided against it. At least she had a real excuse to cut her mother short today.

'Hello, Ma.' Tess cradled the phone under her chin while packing her briefcase at the same time.

'You sound strange,' Dymphna accused her. 'You haven't got laryngitis again?'

'No, I haven't. I've got the phone wrapped round my neck so that I can pack a little bit of work to take to Ireland. I'm off in a minute.'

'I know. That's why I'm ringing. I want you to say happy anniversary to the old devil for me. And to Stella, of course,' she added dutifully. 'And forget the work. You're only going for four days, for pity's sake! How long's Stephen got off?'

Tess hesitated, uncertain whether to tell her mother the truth and decided now wasn't a bad time. At least she'd have to keep her opinions brief. Even Dymphna couldn't delay Aer Lingus's schedules.

'Well, as a matter of fact I was going to phone you. He's been fired.'

'Fired? But he's just won that award thingummy.'

'I know. It's a long story. Someone at his firm killed themselves and Stephen felt it was because they'd been badly treated.'

'I knew London was a terrible place.' Dymphna spoke as though Tess had confirmed that suicides were an hourly occurence in the capital's business world. 'How's Stephen taking it? He'll get another job easily enough, surely?'

'Mum, I think he wants to give it up and be a painter.'

'Well, now. There's a thing. I never thought advertising was much of a job for a grown man.'

'It pays well, though. I don't know how we'll get by on my salary.'

'Go on with you! You'll be fine. Get rid of those fancy cars and that idle Swede. You were always too worried about money. When your sainted father was alive we never knew when we'd have a few bob from one day to the next but we were quite happy, weren't we?'

Tess gritted her teeth at the familiar refrain. She was on the point of reminding her mother that her sainted father's gambling had caused them far more misery than happiness and that if she had a hang-up about money it was precisely *because* they'd never known whether they'd have any from one day to the next, but she didn't. Her father's memory was sacred. Only one rung below God the Father and certainly above John Paul II.

'Go on, now, the future'll take care of itself. I'll light a candle for you.'

Oh well, Tess almost said, that'll be all right then. 'Thanks, Mum. I'll send your love to the happy couple.'

'Enjoy yourself. And leave that briefcase behind –' Her mother was still talking when Tess put down the phone and rushed out.

At home there were so many suitcases in the hall that Tess could hardly get by them. At the bottom of the stairs Stephen was arguing with Luke over whether he could bring his Sonic the Hedgehog computer game. 'You're going to an outdoor paradise. Sea, fresh air, wild empty beaches, no one as far as the eye can see!'

'God, Dad,' Luke protested gloomily, 'surely it can't be as bad as all that?'

Finally Inge brought the car round and they packed what looked like enough luggage for four weeks instead of four days. At the last minute Tess brought her briefcase back in and left it in the hall. Her mother was probably right. Without it she felt far more cheerful and did a little dance as she made her way back to the car. Three faces looked out at her in embarrassment.

As it was Friday afternoon the airport was packed.

Stephen thought of the ludicrous advert the agency had just made of passengers doing the Birdie Dance all round the concourse to demonstrate what good fun airports can be. As he'd tried to point out in the planning meeting, how would that get over the fact that most people knew airports to be overcrowded, full of litter, with inadequate seating and staff trained in good manners by the Spanish Inquisition?

Today was no exception. They seemed to be sharing the seating area with the entire London Irish rugby club. The fans had clearly decided to get into the mood early and Stephen doubted whether some of them would still be conscious by the time the game started. The man on Stephen's left, as delicately built as a prop forward, offered Stephen his can of Guinness. An overwhelming feeling of being demob-happy descended on Stephen and he took a healthy swig. The man clapped him on the back. Stephen caught Tess's eye and smiled just as their flight was called.

They boarded the plane, mercifully without the rugger buggers. 'Pity,' said Ellie, 'I could have taken one home for Inge. It might have taken her mind off someone else.'

When they landed at Cork it was a gloriously sunny afternoon. A jazz band was playing in the terminal building. They smiled, the irresistible welcome of Ireland getting to all of them.

Stephen retrieved their cases and walked towards the exit. He knew with absolute certainty that his father wouldn't be there to meet them. And yet as he pushed the trolley, dangerously piled with bags, he felt, as he always did when coming home – even when his visit was unexpected – an absurd irrational hope that this time he might.

Suddenly Tess elbowed him, amazed. 'Isn't that Julius over there?'

A white-haired old man, his skin tanned but blotched with dark patches, wearing a battered Panama hat, an ancient pair of cricketing trousers and a baggy white jacket, with a red bargee's scarf tied round his neck, appeared at the other end of the hall.

Stephen felt his stomach twist. In thirty-eight years his father had never met him. Not once. Not from boarding school at the end of term, though Stephen would have given anything to have seen his face there at the station; nor from any of the holidays Stephen went on with his mother while Julius stayed to paint; not even when he came home after spending two weeks in hospital.

And here he was today, walking towards them with his hand outstretched in loving greeting. His heart somersaulting, Stephen almost ran towards him.

And then, from the other side of the airport book-stall, a soundman's boom appeared followed by a soundman and a whole TV crew.

His father was coming to meet him simply for the benefit of the television cameras.

CHAPTER EIGHT

'Stephen, love, welcome to Cork!' Julius threw open his arms in a theatrical gesture of such shamelessness that it took his son's breath away.

The intense delight of a moment ago transformed itself into a familiar stab of anger and Stephen felt the temptation simply to turn away. That would be one for the cameras.

And then he caught sight of Tess's face as she stood next to him. She was shaking her head and laughing. Without looking in his direction she reached over and squeezed his hand, and he realized that she understood. Stephen felt his anger begin to dissolve. He ought to know his father by now.

'Hello, Fa. How nice of you to come and meet us.' The irony was lost on Julius.

'A pleasure, love, a pleasure.' Julius embraced Tess as though coming to meet them at the airport was entirely second nature to him. 'And how are my two precocious grandchildren? Loaded down as usual with hi-tech gadgetry?'

Ellie and Luke responded by throwing themselves into his arms with genuine affection. 'Luke's brought his Sonic the Hedgehog,' accused Ellie disloyally.

'My dear chap,' tutted Julius, 'you can stay up late with me and we'll drink some brandy and go and find a real hedgehog, a whole bloody family of hedgehogs.' He made it sound far more alluring than sitting in front of a computer screen.

For once Luke showed interest in the Great Outdoors. 'That'd be great, Grampa!'

'And you, Lady Eleanor' – he always used this pet name for her – 'have been invited to listen to some group or other at Slane Castle. U3, I believe they're called.'

Ellie almost fainted on the spot. 'Grampa! You don't mean U2? They're only the world's number one rock band!'

'Ah, possibly.' Tess had the distinct impression that Julius knew exactly whom he was talking about. 'Your grandmother has the details.'

And then, with perfect timing, at the precise moment the videotape ran out in the camera. Julius turned to the crew. 'Was that OK, boys?'

'Gosh,' said Luke, every overtone of the situation lost on him, 'are we going to be on TV?'

There was a brief moment of silence. Then Tess remembered that, since they hadn't been expecting to be met, they'd reserved a car from Avis. She turned to Stephen. 'What shall do I about the hire car? Do you want me to drive it while you go with Julius?'

'Well, actually . . .' For once even Julius had the grace to look embarrassed. 'We've got to go on and do some more filming, haven't we, Sebastian?'

'I just don't believe the gall of him.' Stephen drove the hire car out of the airport compound and turned west towards Killamalooe. 'He wasn't coming to meet us at all! The whole thing was a set-up for the TV people!'

'I know. I know,' soothed Tess, wishing they'd got off to a better start. 'But you ought to be used to him by now.'

Ellie leaned over Tess's shoulder from the back. 'Isn't it amazing about U2? Lil and Pen will die with envy!'

'I bloody well hope,' muttered Stephen grimly, 'that

he wasn't making *that* up for the benefit of the cameras.'

Tess looked at him. Even Julius wouldn't be that crass. 'Come on, Stephen. He wouldn't do that.' She thought for a moment. 'Would he?'

The sun was lowering in the sky as they neared Killamalooe, dropping down over the bay, creating a golden path of light, and with every mile Tess felt herself surrendering to the irresistible pull of West Cork.

And suddenly, there it was. Killamalooe House. A white Georgian mansion with lawns stretching down to the shore. Georgian mansions were two-a-penny in Ireland, often dilapidated and sold for knock-down prices to anyone with the cash and the nerve to shoo out the cattle who'd taken up residence and the patience to renovate them. Killamalooe had been no different until Stella fell in love with it thirty years ago and finally demanded Julius put down some roots.

For years, before Julius's paintings really started to sell, they had lived in one wing with no heating and stone-flagged floors with draughts from the sea winds that made it more like hell than heaven. Stephen could still remember the biting cold of that stone, even in high summer, as he ran, barefoot and Bohemian, from the kitchen to the garden. Stella, he remembered, had just read a book about the painter Vanessa Bell and the artistic commune she'd created at Charleston Farmhouse in Sussex, letting her children grow up wild as gypsies. Killamalooe, Stella had decided, could be a kind of Irish Charleston.

Thank God all that was in the past. Over the last couple of decades every comfort had been installed at Killamalooe. But thanks to Stella's taste they'd avoided suffocating it in the chintzy cosiness of a country hotel, and Killamalooe had kept its Georgian charm.

After the episode at the airport Tess half expected to find no one there to greet them but, as they swept up the drive, there was Stella, dignified in lavender-grey, standing on the steps between the two urns, waving.

'Where on earth's Julius?' she asked, holding out her arms to Ellie and Luke. 'I thought he'd gone to meet you.'

'He had to go and do more shooting,' said Stephen wryly, kissing his mother on her smooth powdered cheek.

'It really is too trying of him,' said Stella, embracing Tess with a warmth that surprised her. 'You know he's allowing them to film the dinner.'

'So much for an intimate family party,' said Stephen, raising an eyebrow.

'For three hundred?' Ellie reminded him.

Stella looked at her granddaughter. Clearly grunge hadn't hit West Cork yet. She surveyed Ellie's short hair, the torn tea dress under a baggy man's jacket and the Doctor Marten boots and shuddered. 'Darling, you look like a tinker girl.'

Tess was grateful that at least Ellie had left off the tattoo.

'Don't worry, Stella,' Tess reassured her, 'they all look like that in London.'

'Then I'm glad I'm buried over here.' Stella rang for tea as she shepherded them all into the drawing room.

Ellie's eyes lit up with devilment as she plonked herself down on the arm of a delicate antique sofa. 'Did I ever tell you, Gramma, that I was thinking of becoming a New Age Traveller?'

'Don't believe a word of it, Stella.' Tess gave Ellie a quelling look. 'She's working very hard for her A levels so that she can go to college and study art.'

'Gramma,' Ellie jumped off the sofa and put her arms round Stella's neck, 'Gramps said something about me going to see U2.'

Stella smiled. 'Yes. My friend Elizabeth's boy organizes concerts at Slane Castle. They're having one on Sunday.'

Stephen and Tess exchanged a look of relief. At least Julius hadn't made that one up.

The tea arrived and Luke and Ellie fell on it like refugees in a transit camp.

'You wouldn't believe,' pointed out Tess, 'that they've just had a full cream tea, complete with cucumber sandwiches, on the flight over, would you?'

As they had tea, Tess looked around her. Killamalooe was an amazing place. Not just because of its perfect proportions and magnificent views down to the sea, but because of the paintings. From Augustus John, Jack Yeats and Whistler to Lucian Freud and Francis Bacon. As well as endless sketches by other modern painters. She picked up her cup and wandered over to them. The most arresting was a bare landscape by an artist whose name she didn't recognize. Underneath there was an inscription: *To Julius. With thanks for all your help and patience.* Clearly art brought out the best in Julius.

'Now,' Stella stood up briskly, 'why don't you take your things over to the cottage? Luke can go and look at the horses while Eleanor helps me make table decorations for tomorrow.'

Five minutes later Tess and Stephen dumped their bags on the inviting-looking double bed and looked out of the window. The cottage was only yards from the beach.

'If we hurry we should just catch the sunset,' said Stephen, opening the door. They ran down towards the sea, breathing in the sharp salt air and feeling the wind whip their hair into salty tangles. In minutes they were on the wide arc of empty beach, their feet crunching on the dry shingle, listening to the sea whirling thousands of tiny pebbles as each wave withdrew and pounded in again.

Then, just as the sun started to disappear over the horizon, they reached their favourite place, a tiny cove known as Cowrie Beach. Tess loved it because everywhere you put your foot it sank ankle-deep in shells. Pink pyramids of painted topshells, pearlized dog whelks, the shiny russet of the Smooth Venus and, best of all, minute folded-over cowries, which always reminded her of miniature Cornish pasties. Everyone round here said they brought good luck. Good luck again, thought Tess.

She looked into Stephen's eyes, and saw the red glow of the sunset there, and something more besides. A hungry, shameless desire that made her muscles tighten in anticipation.

He reached for her hand. 'Let's go back to the cottage'.

Tess laughed recklessly, her long red hair billowing out behind her, not knowing what was coming over her. 'I don't think I can wait that long.'

His eyes holding hers, he stripped off his raincoat and threw it down over the carpet of shells. And as the sky darkened around them they lay down together and made love with the sea drowning out any doubts that this might not be proper behaviour for respectable married people.

The day of the party was chaos, even under Stella's

able supervision. By mid-afternoon thirty round tables were being set up in the ballroom, which Julius normally used as a studio because of the floor-to-ceiling windows with their perfect north light. Each table, designed to seat ten, was first covered with a thick blanket, a tip Ellie, of all people, had read in a magazine, and which turned out to be a huge success, giving, as the article had promised, added sumptuousness. Then a huge white Irish linen tablecloth was added, topped with a smaller round pink cloth. Finally they were set with hired white bone china, crystal glasses and crisp white napkins.

In the centre of each a flower arrangement was to be placed, which Stella and Ellie were finishing now. Stella had no patience with professional florists, claiming they made every occasion look like a Rotary Club dinner.

Finally the tables were finished and Stella cast a demanding eye over them. 'Hmmm,' she pronounced. 'Very nice but a bit predictable. They need something else and I don't know what it is.'

'I do,' Ellie announced mysteriously and disappeared into the gardens with a pair of secateurs. She returned triumphantly with a huge armful of ivy.

'What are you going to do with that?' asked Stella nervously.

'You wait and see,' commanded Ellie as she pushed Stella out of the ballroom. 'Go and check on how the food's getting on, Gramma.'

When she returned twenty minutes later, Stella was amazed. Ellie had draped the ivy in intricate patterns on each table. It gave just the touch of individuality that had been lacking.

Stella clapped her hands. 'She may look like a banshee but she really does have a touch, that girl,' she told Tess who had come to see if she could make herself useful. Tess glowed with maternal pride, though Ellie certainly hadn't got it from her.

In the huge hall with its Georgian fanlight window, streams of caterers, a string quartet and an Irish folk-rock band were all arriving at the same time, just as the TV crew were trying to set up their huge HMI stage lights. Julius was standing on the wide sweep of stairs, holding a bottle of claret and loving it all.

'So,' said Stephen, joining him and leaning over the banisters surveying the mêlée beneath, 'who's speaking tonight?'

'No one.' Julius took a sip of his claret. 'I can't stand all that self-important toasting claptrap.'

'Aren't you going to do anything to mark the occasion?' Stephen was surprised.

Julius grinned. 'Well, I thought I might just say a few words myself, as a matter of fact.'

'Why not?' congratulated Stephen drily. 'After all, no one else appreciates you quite as much as you do yourself.'

But Julius wasn't listening. He was trying to attract the attention of Sebastian, the director.

Ellie was the first to arrive downstairs dressed for the party. She stood in front of the fire in the drawing room wearing a 1950s garish turquoise cocktail frock, with hideous matching hat, delicately completing the ensemble with her usual Doc Marten boots.

Stella, who was next to arrive, stood transfixed with horror. 'Eleanor,' she yelped, 'surely you're not wearing those boots to the party?'

'But the boots are essential,' Ellie protested. 'They're an anti-fashion statement.' She looked at her grandmother patiently. 'Otherwise people might think I was taking the outfit seriously.'

Stella looked on, unable to follow the subtleties of retro fashion distinctions. 'Look,' she insisted, 'if you like old clothes come upstairs a minute.'

She led Ellie to a small room at the top of the house and threw open a trunk full of beaded flapper dresses from the 1920s, which had belonged to her own mother.

Ellie whooped with delight and threw the hideous cocktail frock to the floor. She tried on two or three before deciding on a slinky beaded confection in dusty pink.

'At least the twenties was an elegant era.' Stella surveyed her granddaughter, replacing the frightful hat with a dark pink feathered hairclip. Finally she stood back and smiled. 'I thought they'd suit you. But please, Eleanor,' wrinkling her aristocratic nose in disgust, 'take off those horrible boots.'

Tess had just put on her new ivory silk bra, more than a little hampered by Stephen's attempts to slide down the straps and kiss her rosy nipples, when Ellie twirled in in her flapper finery singing 'I Feel Pretty'.

Noticing Tess guiltily straightening her bra strap she rolled her eyes to heaven. 'Not at it again?' I don't know what's got into you two lately. I hope you're taking precautions. I'd die of embarrassment if Mum got up the spout at her age.'

'Thank you, Ellie, that's quite enough.' Tess shooed her out of the room. 'And I'll thank you to remember that plenty of women have their *first* baby at my age.'

'How's my favourite daughter-in-law? You look glorious.' Julius, distinctive in immaculate tails with a resplendent tartan waistcoat, greeted Tess approvingly when she finally walked down the sweeping staircase to the party. She did look good, she knew it, in her emerald-green taffeta ball-dress with the green glass dangly earrings Ellie had bought her.

Much to her amusement, Julius took her hand and helped her down the last step as though she were made of porcelain. 'You seem to belong here,' he said, gesturing at the grand surroundings, 'the milk of your skin and that outrageous hair. You were made for Ireland. I expect it's your ancestry.'

Tess smiled, thinking that it was something else altogether making her skin glow and her eyes shine. 'Except that I'm bog Irish,' she pointed out, taking a glass of champagne from a passing tray, 'and if I'd ever been allowed in a house like this it would probably have been to clean it.'

'Only until the Master spotted you and whisked you off to be his bride.'

'Whisked me into the linen cupboard and relieved me of my virtue among the damask tablecloths more like,' Tess corrected him. 'Vowing undying love until the day I told him I had a bun in the oven, my family had rejected me and the priest said I was a trollop. Upon which he'd have decided it was all my fault and sent me off to the workhouse or back home on the next boat to Liverpool.'

'What a depressing analysis. There speaks the hard-headed divorce lawyer.'

Across the room she saw Stephen accepting a Black Velvet and start drinking it too quickly. That wasn't like Stephen. Still, they were supposed to be relaxing. She sipped her champagne as he walked over to them.

'Stephen, I was just telling Tess how much at home she looks in Ireland.'

'So do you, Julius.' Tess considered him. 'Ireland suits you. Have you always wanted to come home?'

Before he could answer Stephen jumped in first. 'Don't accuse Father of sentiment, for God's sake. He lives here because cultural earnings are tax-free. It'd be the Cayman Islands if it weren't for his prickly heat.'

Tess winced at the unending bitterness between them, and tried to change the subject. 'Did Stephen tell you about his award? For best art direction.' Somehow it seemed a lifetime ago when it had only been a matter of weeks.

'Art?' Julius played deliberately naïve. 'What, pray, has art got to do with advertising?'

Even though he agreed Stephen felt the familiar anger rising. 'Why do you always have to belittle everything I do?'

'Oh come on,' Julius shrugged, 'awards like that are meaningless. They only exist to justify your salaries. You're not going to stand there and defend the artistic value of a Pepsi commercial.'

No, thought Stephen, but it'd be nice if for once you congratulated me, no matter how meaningless the award.

Before Tess could jump in and steer the conversation to calmer waters Julius was dragged off by the TV people, and dinner announced.

As they lined up to look at the seating plan, Tess was struck for the first time by what a glittering occasion it was. Even she, who knew herself to be painfully ignorant of the art world, recognized a mix of famous painters, TV arts personalities, and important critics. Once seated, she found the food was superb and the people on their table good company. The only worrying thing was that Stephen was still drinking steadily. By the time Julius, satisfied that the TV cameras all had their red lights on, stood up to speak, Stephen was more than half cut. Tess kept trying to move his wine glass subtly out of his reach and pour him mineral water, but he just drank from his neighbour's glass instead.

Recognizing a commanding presence when they saw one, the waiters and waitresses stopped shuffling and rattling and retired to the back of the room as soon as Julius stood up, ignoring even the most desperate signals from one or two guests with temporarily empty glasses.

The atmosphere in the ballroom was relaxed. Everyone knew that Julius was a good speaker and that given the circumstances they were in for some touching sentimentality, perhaps even a hymn to long and committed marriages which would make them all – even the much-divorced ones – rejoice in the permanence and security of matrimony. On an occasion like this they were even prepared to forget, as Julius no doubt would, his many falls from grace. That being over, they could drink the happy couple's health and proceed to the real business of the evening: drinking as much champagne as they could and having a bloody good time.

'In my life,' Julius began expansively, 'there has been one overriding passion . . .' He paused dramatically and every woman in the room looked enviously at Stella, who in turn smiled expectantly at Julius. 'Art.' Stella looked down at her plate. 'Perhaps passion isn't the right word. Maybe obsession would be more accurate. The kind of impulse that made artists starve in garrets, drink absinthe to keep going when no one bought their work, that drove Vincent to cut off his ear when he couldn't paint it, and Pablo to take essence of pregnant mare's urine in order to keep young and to keep painting. Obsession, of course, makes you selfish and I am the first to admit that I have been selfish over the years.'

'You can say that again,' murmured Stephen, as Tess gave him a quelling look.

'But in the end it's my belief that the true artist has no choice. He *has* to be selfish. When the spirit moves you you can't ask it to come back next week when it's more convenient.'

One or two polite laughs rippled through the guests. Tess, sensing a slight embarrassment, hoped he would get round to Stella soon and the life they'd had together.

'But in the end painting is its own reward. For me it has been both passion and obsession. But more than that. For more than fifty years it has been a lavish and generous mistress. Ladies and gentlemen, I would like to propose a toast.' There was an almost palpable sigh of relief round the room. It was coming at last. Julius filled his glass and looked directly into the lens of the camera. 'Ladies and gentlemen, painters, friends, critics . . . please raise your glasses to the greatest of all the muses, art!'

Stephen sat frozen with fury. Julius had spoken for ten minutes on the occasion of his golden wedding anniversary without once mentioning his wife. All around him he could see embarrassment written on the faces of half their guests as they joined in the toasts. Was it simply thoughtless, the product of an oversized ego, or was it deliberate? Was this the latest skirmish in his parents' fifty-year war of attrition?

He realized he didn't care. It was still offensive, whatever its motive. Flushed with anger and drink, Stephen started to push his way towards the front.

Instinctively Tess got half out of her chair to try and stop him, then sank back. There was nothing she could do. She filled her glass and waited for the worst to happen.

Julius didn't notice him until he was a few feet from the platform. For a second his face reflected uncertainty. Then his instincts to take control asserted themselves.

'Ladies and gentlemen, I think there is something my son would like to add.' He banged the microphone just as Stephen approached the top table and smiled suavely. 'My son Stephen is a big noise in advertising, not, I fear, a calling where passion is very familiar.' Stella looked on anxiously as Julius stepped back and announced: 'Ladies and gentlemen, Stephen Gilfillan.'

As Stephen stepped up to the microphone he realized he had no idea what he was going to say. His first impulse had been simply to agree. To say that Julius was indeed selfish. That he had been a terrible husband and a lousy father, and that he still was. That if art had been his mistress, not forgetting the dozens of others, there had been a price to pay and that it had been been he and his mother who had paid it.

Now, standing here with the TV cameras trained on him, he noticed Sebastian, the director, murmur to go for a close-up. Clearly they thought this was going to be their scoop.

Stephen felt himself calm down. He drank a sip of water, paced himself, and began. To everyone's surprise, his tone was light and humorous.

'Ladies and gentlemen. Artists, like absent-minded professors, are not noted for their social graces. Stanley Spencer was not thought to be the ideal dinner guest. Soutine would have painted the meat instead of eating it. Picasso would have tried to seduce the hostess.

Duncan Grant, the host.' There was a ripple of appreciative amusement. 'So we have to make excuses for my father when he leaves out that most vital part of his life – my mother.'

Tess could almost hear the sighs of relief that Stephen was not sabotaging but rescuing the occasion. 'There are some people whose names are inseparable because the success of the one depends upon the other – even if one may be in the foreground and the other in the shadow. Elizabeth and Philip, Winston and Clementine, maybe even Margaret and Denis.' The guests laughed again. 'And to that I would add another couple whose success is more intertwined than perhaps either knows. Ladies and gentlemen, I give you Stella and Julius.'

Tess almost cried with relief and with emotion to see her mother-in-law accept the tribute.

The guests sat down and began to talk amongst themselves as Stephen turned to leave the table. And then he clearly thought better of it and walked back to the microphone. He turned towards his father.

'One last thing you got wrong, Julius. I'm not a big noise in advertising any more. As a matter of fact I was fired last week.'

CHAPTER NINE

'Why on earth didn't you tell us?' Julius asked in irritation. 'You made me look a complete prat.'

'I thought you did a pretty good job of that without my help,' Stephen retorted.

'Come on now, you two.' Stella linked arms with both of them. 'This is supposed to be a happy occasion. It's time to start the dancing.'

A crowd of painters, deep in discussion about the merits of some technique, grabbed Julius and pulled him into the argument. Stella and Stephen made for the dance floor.

'Want to dance?' Stephen tapped his feet to the folk-rock group as it played a jazzed-up Irish air.

'I'd love to.' Stella smiled at him, so tall that she was looking directly into his eyes. 'And thank you, darling. That was a marvellous speech. You rescued the whole evening.'

Stephen looked embarrassed. 'I'm sorry I had to. I didn't mean to show Fa up.'

'Thank goodness you did. He thinks so too. He'll never admit it but I know him. He's probably very grateful.'

'He has a funny way of showing it then. Ma?' He looked at the elegant face as it greeted her guests over his shoulder. 'You protect him too much. He's a selfish old sod.'

Stella waved to one of their neighbours. 'I know.'

'Then why do you stay with him? He's not even faithful to you.'

Stella winced slightly. 'I sometimes ask myself that.

Habit, perhaps. Fear of being alone?' She glanced at Stephen half-apologetically. 'And he can be terrific fun, you know. Life's an adventure with Julius. Still. And I do believe in marriage, you know, the ups and the downs. You build something with a person over fifty years that can survive an awful lot.'

Stephen thought of Tess. He knew his desire for change could push their marriage to its limits. Did she see life with him as a great adventure? Sometimes he suspected she found security more attractive.

And then there she was, smiling at him, coming across the dance floor with Julius. She looked so stunning in her green taffeta with her glorious red hair that people were standing back for them, as though it were no less than their due.

Julius swept Tess into a spirited polka to the band's up-tempo version of 'The Leaving of Liverpool'. Gradually Stephen and the other dancers stopped and stood back, clapping. Julius always had to be in the spotlight.

When the music stopped they staggered, breathless, towards Stephen and Stella.

'Jaysus,' gasped Julius, 'I'm finished. How did they keep that up all evening, for God's sake?'

Stella subtly took Tess's arm and led her off to look for Luke and Ellie, leaving Julius and Stephen alone together.

'So.' Julius flopped on to a spindly gold chair at a nearby table and helped himself to another glass of claret. 'What will you do now, get another job in advertising?'

Stephen sat down next to him, suddenly feeling very sober. For a moment he toyed with the idea of telling his father the truth. That he wanted to be a painter. But he couldn't bear the idea of the dismissive reaction he might get, derision even.

'I don't know yet. I'll find something.'

There was a moment's silence, as though Julius wasn't sure how to go on. 'Well, if you're ever short of cash . . .' He trailed off.

'Don't worry, Fa,' Stephen said quickly, appalled at the thought of borrowing from his father. And yet he knew that coming from Julius this amounted to a gesture of apology. He glanced at his father, eager to say more. But talking had never been easy between them. Julius too looked as though he wanted to add something. Instead Luke bounced up to recite the disgraceful amount of food he'd eaten, closely followed by Tess who, too late, tried to stop him interrupting them.

'Thanks anyway, Fa.' Stephen stood up. 'But we'll survive.' He reached out for Tess's hand. 'After all, we've still got each other.'

The rest of their stay seemed to disappear in a whirl of activity. At first Stephen thought he was going to have to drive Ellie all the way to Slane Castle for her concert, but Stella's friend offered to meet her at the station, which Ellie much preferred. She didn't want her dad hanging round when she was going on an adventure like this.

On Sunday evening Luke and Julius went on the promised hedgehog hunt, taking a flask and sandwiches. No one had much faith in the expedition except Julius and were stunned when they came back with a baby hedgehog that had lost its mother. Luke was trying to persuade Julius to hand-rear it.

The only chance Tess and Stephen got for a long walk was in the morning before anyone else was up. They headed out along the shore, smiling at each other as they passed Cowrie Beach, but not brave enough for a repeat performance in broad daylight. Instead they worked off their energy climbing over the slippery rocks out towards the ruined tower at the end of the bay. Just beyond it they came upon an abandoned chapel with a tiny cemetery jutting out into the sea, which they'd forgotten existed. In the farthest corner a Celtic cross was built into the stone wall of the cemetery, on to which six or seven rosaries had been draped, each to mark a favour asked of God.

Stephen sighed and caught Tess in his arms, looking out to sea. It was rougher today, and steel-grey, with great billowing clouds. 'Not bad, as final resting places go.'

Tess laughed contentedly. 'Speaking of which, Stella's asked us here in the summer.'

'Do you want to come?'

Tess turned round. 'I'd love to. If you can stand Julius.'

'I can, if you can.' Together they stood, holding each other absolutely still as though they were as much a part of the landscape as the stone cross or the ruined chapel. Suddenly the sun came out from behind the clouds and lit up the scene for them. Tess felt a sense of perfect peace flood through her. Everything was going to be all right. She knew it was.

But on the flight home, as everyday reality beckoned, Tess could already sense a drooping of all their spirits.

Stephen was wondering if Julius wasn't the only selfish one who never thought about his family. For the first time it struck him that maybe he was repeating the pattern.

Ellie had disappeared into a dream world reliving the moment when U2's lead singer had actually talked to her, and not just 'Hello' either. 'Hi, you're Ellie, aren't you? Did you enjoy the set?' She repeated the words he'd spoken like a mantra, dying to impart them to Penny and Lily. Ten words just for her! And she was sure he'd put special warmth into them.

Luke looked at his watch anxiously and asked Tess if she thought Julius would have remembered Vincent the hedgehog's midday feed. Julius had selected the name on the grounds that its original owner had been equally prickly. Tess was sure he would have. Or rather Stella would have.

As they circled above Heathrow Airport Tess tried not to think about the bills that would already be piling up and how exactly they were going to pay them and glanced across at Stephen. He seemed preoccupied too.

She reached over and squeezed his hand. 'Don't worry. We'll be all right.'

'Look on the bright side, Dad.' Luke leaned across Tess encouragingly. 'Now you'll have to do that mural you promised me.'

Stephen felt an odd sensation as he drove his company car into Soho Square for the very last time. Not loss exactly. In spite of Josh's cracks about it being his penis extension, he'd never been particularly fond of it. Inge had driven it far more than him anyway. He thought briefly of Bill Barclay and his obsession with status. Poor sod. Status had never been one of Stephen's motivations. It only existed to prove to other people you were better than them and he couldn't be bothered with it. Maybe it was the finality of the gesture that was getting to him.

Inside the building he handed over the keys to the receptionist. He didn't want to see Ted and have to argue the whole thing through again. He'd made up his mind and it hadn't, whatever Ted thought, been really to do with Worldwide Motors.

As he turned to leave he noticed that the woman behind the desk, who usually seemed as sweet and sympathetic as the Iron Maiden of Nuremberg, was sniffling quietly. 'It won't be the same without you, Mr Gilfillan.'

'Thank you, Maureen,' he lied gently, 'I'll miss you too.'

Outside on the pavement Raf Walensky was just arriving in his ludicrous limo. Stephen skipped down the steps before Walensky saw him and disappeared into the crowd of office workers eating their sandwiches in the square gardens. He sat down on one of the benches feeling an overwhelming relief that he could now avoid the Walenskys of this world. His friend the wino spotted him and came to sit down next to him.

Before he had time to ask for the usual handout Stephen gave him a pound. A suitably grand farewell gesture. The drunk pocketed it delightedly and ambled off. 'Good luck now, sorr,' he shouted.

'Thanks. I'll need it.' Stephen got up and walked in the opposite direction, towards Leicester Square tube station. He had no idea what he was going to do next. Yet he was conscious of walking with a step lighter than he had for months.

Back at work, where Stephen couldn't see her, Tess was spending every spare moment doing sums on the back of envelopes. One thing was clear, without his salary their outgoings were nowhere near met by her earnings. She thought of the money she'd carefully saved for a rainy day. That would see them through this month at least. But after that, God alone knew. The trouble was, working her way through their spending, they didn't even seem that extravagant. No doubt,

Tess speculated, when she flicked through her household expenses, the Queen felt the same way.

She realized she had no idea what Stephen's plans were. To go to art school or to get another job? But for the moment there was one thing that was going to have to go. Inge.

'Inge, do you have a moment please?' Tess asked her that night. Inge followed dutifully and they sat, as they never did, either side of the kitchen table.

Tess had been thinking through what to say all afternoon. She hated firing people and Inge, despite some irritating habits, had been brilliant with Luke, ferrying him around from chess club to computer club to judo and he'd grown very attached to her. What's more she wasn't sure quite how they were going to survive without her. Working mothers couldn't trade favours in the way that stay-at-home ones could. Still, they had to economize and no doubt she'd cobble something together.

'Inge, as you know . . .'

'It's all right, Tess,' Inge interrupted. 'I know that you are going to give me the – how do you say it? – chop.' She beamed unnervingly. 'It's because Stephen has been fired from his job and you think that one way to economize would be to do without Inge. I understand that. So I have a plan.'

Tess laughed nervously, taken aback by Inge's sudden burst of Scandinavian efficiency.

'You see, I like my job here very much, and I love Luke extremely. Also, I think you do not know how complicated is his life. Without me he will have to give up a lot of things.'

'Well,' protested Tess, 'there is public transport. Plenty of children use that.'

'Not to get to Luke's chess club. It is very hard to

get to his chess club on public transport.' She had clearly given this her full attention. 'And Tess,' Inge went on, leaning forward as though being Swedish she was One Who Knew About Such Things, 'think of all the pervies on the tube!'

'Inge,' countered Tess trying not to think about the pervies, 'we have to economize. We'll be living on one salary.'

'That's good,' concluded Inge as though something had been settled. 'You don't pay me. Or maybe you give me pocket money to salve your liberal conscience. You will still give me a room and board. My father is rich. My allowance is much bigger than the small sum you pay me anyway. I don't need more money.'

Tess was stunned by Inge's logic. 'But I can't do that.'

'Yes, you can. Think of Luke. Think of the pervies. Think . . .' She paused. Clearly this was to be the masterstroke. 'Think of Stephen. How can he work if he has to think all day of where the children should be?'

Reluctantly, Tess caved in. 'OK. We'll give it a try. Just for a couple of weeks, to see how it works out.'

'Thank you, Tess. And don't worry. If I don't think it's fair I can always leave.'

Watching her go, Tess was surprised to find herself hoping this wouldn't happen.

After Tess had left for work the next morning and the house was quiet, Stephen sat down in the sitting room with a pad and pencil. He knew that he had to work out the next step before depression or apathy set in and he lost his confidence. The most sensible step, if he wanted to paint, was to go to art school. But would he get a grant? It was one thing to be temporarily unable to contribute much to the household kitty, but quite another to be dependent.

He rang the Royal College of Art and discovered it was just as he thought. Since he'd already been to university he'd be eligible for only the most limited grant. If he was serious about art school he'd have to get some kind of job and pay his way. But for the moment he was determined to enjoy the pleasures of family life. After all, this might be his only chance.

When Tess got home from work and opened the front door she sensed instantly that the house felt different. For once the TV wasn't blaring. She put her briefcase down and stopped to listen. There was an unfamiliar but welcoming smell drifting through the house and squeals of laughter coming from the kitchen.

Inside, Stephen and Luke, both in stripy butchers' aprons, were standing by the cooker making popcorn. An American cookbook was propped up on the dresser. Corn was popping everywhere with Stephen and Luke both chasing it. Stephen caught some and gave it to Tess, tears of laughter pouring from his eyes.

'I don't suppose,' asked Tess looking over Stephen's shoulder at the recipe, 'you've got the temperature wrong, have you?'

'O ye of little faith,' tutted Stephen, glancing pompously at the recipe book before leaping into the air to catch a high-jumping popcorn. 'Do you know, Luke,' he said, popping it into Luke's mouth, 'I'm afraid we've got the temperature wrong.' Both fell about, as though this piece of information made the whole experience even more perfect.

'Tell you what, Mum.' Luke wiped the tears from his eyes and sat down. 'It isn't half fun having Dad home.'

'Yes,' agreed Tess weakly, looking at the corn all over the kitchen floor and then starting to laugh herself, 'I suppose it must be.'

However, over the next few weeks Tess found her patience being pushed to the limit. In an attempt to economize Stephen decided to do all the odd jobs that had been hanging round the house for years himself. As far as Tess could see, this involved going out and buying expensive materials, in too great quantities, and then bodging the job.

Her patience finally ran out when she got back to find Inge surveying a large hole in the wall, where Stephen had been attempting to put up new shelving. Stephen was nowhere to be found. Eventually she tracked him down to their bedroom, where he had retreated. He was fast asleep, completely hidden under the duvet.

'Perhaps,' suggested Inge when Tess went back downstairs, 'he should take some more evening classes. Maybe in woodwork this time.'

Tess sat at her desk glaring at the estimate the builders had faxed for repairing Stephen's hole in the wall. Really it was too much. Not only was he not earning but his efforts to save money were costing them a fortune. She knew he meant well, but she wanted to kill him all the same. Only the thought of seeing Phil and being as rude about him as she liked kept her from ringing him up and being extremely unpleasant.

Just as she was putting on her coat, Patricia ran in, looking as close to excited as Patricia ever looked, closely followed by Jacqui. 'Quick! Quick!' She grabbed Tess's remote control, 'Lyall's on the lunchtime news! He's won his medical negligence case. The kid's parents have been awarded a million pounds!'

The TV jumped into life and Lyall's face appeared in twenty-one inches of glorious colour. 'There,' said Jacqui, her face only millimetres from the screen, 'I told you he looked like Harry Hamlin. You can see it when he's on the box. Isn't he wonderful?'

'This won't do him any harm,' Patricia pronounced. 'Have you heard, now solicitors can sit on the bench they're considering him as a part-time judge? He'd be the youngest ever.'

'No, I hadn't,' said Tess thoughtfully.

Patricia snapped off the TV. 'What's this I hear about Stephen giving up his job to be a househusband? That's brave of him.'

Tess felt a wave of fury. She knew it was irrational and that if Stephen *had* decided to stay at home and look after the kids, it should be perfectly acceptable. She also knew that Patricia didn't think so. It was ridiculous, she told herself, Stephen's status shouldn't matter to her. But somehow it did – especially when talking to Patricia. 'He's decided on a change of direction, that's all.'

'So, how's it going, having Stephen at home all day?' Phil asked as they sat down at their table.

'Well . . . it's wonderful for Luke and Ellie.'

'And . . .?'

'To tell you the truth it's driving me spare. He keeps spending a fortune in B&Q then bodging everything he touches. Yesterday he came back from the library with a book on how to insulate your loft and I understood a dreadful fact about myself. I don't want to be married to a man who knows about loft insulation.' Phil burst out laughing. 'And then, as I was leaving work just now there was Lyall Gibson, one of my colleagues, being interviewed on the lunchtime

116

news and poxy Patricia tells me he's going to be the youngest ever judge and, oh Phil, we're so *broke* and do you know what I thought?'

'You wished Stephen could be more like this paragon Lyall.'

Tess nodded her head miserably.

'But the truth is, Tessie, Lyall's probably not a patch on Stephen.' Phil had always had time for Stephen ever since he'd been the only man she knew prepared to fish down the toilet bowl for her lost contact lens. And find it. 'Stephen's fun. This Lyall sounds like the type who knows where he'll be standing in five years' time.'

Tess realized that this was true. Lyall was a mite predictable. Though just at this very moment the thought of that was rather comforting.

'With someone like him you'd die of boredom. Anyway, maybe Stephen'll get another job.'

'I don't know whether he wants one. Or certainly only one that'll let him paint. And who are you to lecture on suitable men? You like vagabonds like Terry Worth.'

'Speaking of whom' – Phil looked a tiny bit piqued – 'still no enquiries?'

'As a matter of fact, he did ask for your number,' Tess lied, 'but I refused to give it to him.'

Tess smiled to herself when she got back from the lunch, her spleen against the male sex and Stephen in particular well vented. Phil was genuinely piqued that Terry hadn't made contact. But really it was probably all for the best. Terry was charming but someone with his family troubles you wouldn't wish on your worst enemy. On the other hand she was surprised at Terry. He'd seemed genuinely taken with Phil, and Tess had him down as a man of action. She didn't have long to wait. Later that afternoon, there he was, on the phone.

'Tess, hello. I've rung for some advice. I'm due to have the kids this weekend and I wondered how I can make sure there aren't any more misunderstandings this time.'

Tess thought for a moment. 'Why don't you send Angela a letter with all the details in and keep a copy. That way it'll be harder for her to say she got it wrong.'

'Great idea. I'll write to her now.'

Tess held on since she had the distinct impression this wasn't the only thing Terry was ringing about.

'By the way,' he asked casually, 'how's that friend of yours, the one who dresses like a King's Cross brass?'

Tess tried to suppress a giggle. So much for Gianni Versace. This was one remark she didn't think she'd repeat to Phil. 'She's very well.' And then in a moment of devilment she added, 'As a matter of fact, she often asks after you.'

'Does she now?' Terry sounded as though Tess had just made his day. 'Well, well, well.'

When Tess got home she found, to her surprise, the house, usually bustling at this time, was empty. She changed out of her suit into jeans and a sweatshirt just as she heard familiar voices shouting in the street. Stephen, looking like something from *Those Magnificent Men In Their Flying Machines* in helmet and goggles and an ancient pair of skates, was leading a chain consisting of Ellie and Luke on rollerblades, with Inge pushing at the back.

Tess watched them as Stephen stopped to wave and they careered into each other falling into a giggling heap outside the house. Phil was right. She couldn't imagine Lyall Gibson on roller skates. Stephen might not aspire to being a part-time judge and appearing on the lunchtime news but he was a brilliant father. She just wished he'd hurry up and decide what he wanted to do with the rest of his life.

Still at her office long after everyone else had left, Phil was catching up on the work she hadn't got through during the day. Although she liked to create the impression of being a scatty airhead who never gave work a second thought, her friends knew she was a dedicated – if occasionally irresponsible – pro. Her bosses astutely recognized that Outrageous PR *was* Phil Doyle and allowed her a little latitude denied less crucial members of staff.

Phil was packing up to leave when her red phone, the one she kept for close friends and high-powered clients, beeped discreetly from the corner of her desk. If it had been the other phone she would have ignored it; instead she sat down again and answered it.

To her surprise it was Josephine Quinn, the driving force behind Richmond & Quinn, one of her most important clients. Richmond & Quinn had been one of the big success stories of the eighties with their pretty and nostalgic range of toiletries. Now, rumour had it, they were considering launching in America.

'Josephine, great to hear from you.' Phil looked at her watch. Jesus, it was after nine p.m. The woman must be a serious workaholic. 'Why aren't you at some private view?' Josephine was a well-known patron of the arts. 'What can I do for you?'

'I wondered if you might feel like a little headhunting. We're trying to find a consultant to help us launch a perfume in the States. Both Hugo and I are too busy to give it all our energy.'

'Business must be good this side of the pond then.'

'Yes. We're still opening quite a lot of new shops.'

'Lucky you.' Phil thought of some of her clients who far from expanding were hanging on by their well-manicured fingernails.

'Come on, Phil, you know luck has nothing to do with it.'

There were times when Phil found Josephine Quinn a little *too* confident. Maybe being rich *and* stunning made it hard for a girl to be nice too. Some problem.

'So, what kind of person are you looking for?'

'Someone with a good design eye, who understands marketing. Preferably with contacts in the US. We won't need them permanently, Hugo or I will take over, but for six months anyway. And, Phil?'

'Yup?' Bloody hell, Phil was thinking, she's not asking much.

'They have to be good. Look what happened to Undercover.'

They both devoted a minute's silence to the terrifying example of the posh underwear chain which had expanded into the US, made some classic mistakes, and promptly gone bust.

'Of course they have to be good, Josephine,' Phil said sweetly, 'or you wouldn't be prepared to work with them.'

'Exactly. Any thoughts?'

'Not off the top of my head. But my database is at your command. I'll look through it tomorrow.'

'Thanks, Phil. As Hugo said to me, "Call Phil Doyle. She knows everyone."'

Phil allowed herself to feel flattered. 'OK, I'll call back soon as I have any ideas. Sleep tight.' She put down the phone and thought for a moment. No one who would fit Josephine's demanding bill sprang to mind.

And then it hit her. The perfect person. He could take the job, so they could stop worrying about money, and still keep his options open for what he wanted to do later. Stephen Gilfillan.

Phil reached for the phone to call Tess, then stopped for a moment. Josephine was both sensational-looking and a real toughie. In fact she was one of the few clients Phil was just a tad nervous of – not that she'd ever dream of showing it. Was Josephine Quinn what Tess needed in her life at the moment?

Don't be so ridiculous, Phil told herself. Stephen can stand up for himself and so can Tess. She dialled Tess's home number.

CHAPTER TEN

'So tell me more about this client of Phil's.' Stephen helped himself to a third piece of toast the next morning. Unemployment seemed to have done wonders for his appetite.

'You must have heard of her. Josephine Quinn, the whiz behind Richmond & Quinn, those maroon shops you see everywhere with the Victorian knick-knacks in the window. There are almost as many of them as Laura Ashley or the Body Shop.'

'And what does she want this consultant to do?'

'To help launch some new perfume in the States. They need someone who knows about design and marketing to mastermind it all.'

'And Phil thought of me.'

'It's a brilliant opportunity. They reckon they only need someone for six months or so. We could try and live mostly on my income and you could save yours for art school or whatever.'

'There is one little problem,' Stephen said as he got up to wave her goodbye like a good househusband, 'I know sod all about perfume.'

Tess kissed him. 'Ah, but you're a fast learner, aren't you?'

Stephen picked up the post and opened the front door for her. On top of the pile was a red reminder from the gas board. 'OK, fair enough,' he conceded, 'the gasman's just convinced me. I'll phone Phil later.'

Tess ran down the steps and blew him a kiss. 'So this is why I gave up my brilliant career,' he shouted after her, 'to launch a scent!'

★

All day Tess found herself having to resist ringing him to find out if there was any news. She knew she mustn't hassle him or he might turn against the whole venture. She'd just have to wait till she was home.

But to her extreme annoyance by the time she got back, he'd already left for his art class. There was silence apart from the murmur of Inge's television. Luke must be doing his homework.

Quietly she crept upstairs to watch him. She loved the look of total absorption he wore when he was doing maths or science, his favourite subjects.

Luke's door was almost closed, with only a crack of light confirming that he was inside. Gently she pushed it open. He wasn't sitting at his desk as she'd expected, but was lying on the bed with just the look of concentration she'd pictured. She smiled and came into the room to give him a kiss and ask how his day had been.

Luke jumped as though a wasp had stung him and stuffed whatever he was reading under the pillow.

'What on earth was that?' Tess indicated the pillow.

'Oh nothing. Just something someone at school lent me.' Luke had never been much of a liar and guilt oozed out of his every pore.

'Come on, hand it over.'

'Mum, it's nothing to do with you.'

'I said hand it over.'

Reluctantly Luke delved under the pillow and pulled out what he'd been reading. To her horror it was a girly mag.

'Luke,' she gasped, appalled, 'where did you get this from?'

'I bought it with my pocket money. You said I could buy whatever I wanted with it.' He pointed to the large-breasted girl who was posing with one hand

123

in her very brief briefs. 'I bought it because she reminded me of Inge.' He threw the offending magazine
on the floor. 'And please, Mum, don't tell me sex
should be part of a relationship. I just liked the
pictures.'

Tess realized she had no idea what to say. He was
growing up and she hadn't even noticed. Until now all
he'd been really interested in was computers and
WWF Wrestling. He'd never even noticed girls.

She ruffled his dark head. 'Well, don't buy it again.'

'I won't.'

'And certainly not from the newsagent where we
have our account. He might think it's for your father.'

'So, did you phone Phil?' Tess made herself wait a
whole minute before she dived in.

'Yes, I phoned Phil,' Stephen answered with infuriating calm as he took his coat off.

'And what did you think of her proposal?'

'I said I'd think about it.'

'Is that all?' Tess tried not to sound disappointed.
He wouldn't get a chance like this again, something interesting and short-term offered to him on a plate without going through a humiliating round of rejections.

'No that's not all.' He went into the sitting room
and sat down, enjoying keeping her in suspense.
'As a matter of fact I'm meeting Josephine Quinn
next week. There's only one drawback Phil forgot to
mention.'

'What's that?' She thought for a moment he was
going to say the job was based in New York.

'Richmond & Quinn's offices are in Winchester.'

Tess laughed with relief. 'That's only an hour down
the M3. You'd just be commuting in reverse. I can see
you now,' she teased, 'same seat on the train every

day, glaring at anyone who dares try and take your place. G & T on the way home, doing the crossword in the *Evening Standard*.'

'What a nightmarish picture. What if it was working late every evening, last train back and you meeting me at the station?'

'I could live with that for a month or two.'

Stephen shook his head. Tess was so transparent. 'Am I to deduce that you're just a little keen for me to get this job, my love?'

Tess sat down on his knee. 'Frankly, my dear, I don't give a damn. But the mortgage company might appreciate it.'

Jacqui giggled loudly as she read the article in *GQ* out to her friend Suzanne from accounts. Tess could hear the oohing and aahing halfway down the corridor.

'So what's in this magazine that's making you two behave like a couple of ten-year-olds?' Tess tried to peek over Jacqui's shoulder and see the cause of all the mirth. Jacqui hid it from her. So Tess chased her round the office, but Jacqui, a schoolgirl sprinter, got away from her easily. She flopped down into Tess's chair. 'OK, since you're so fascinated, it's about London's top ten bachelors. And look who's number eight.'

Tess wrested the magazine from Jacqui's grasp and read it out loud in pompous tones. '"Lyall Gibson, thirty-seven, leading London lawyer, specializing in negligence cases. Tall, dark-haired, brown eyes, shy ..." aah! ... "Not known to frequent pubs and night-clubs, so hard to track down ... intrepid girls might have to join the Wig & Pen Club. Likes Turkish baths and massages ..." Jacq, your luck's in. Didn't you do a course in aromatherapy? "So far,"' continued Tess, '"the elusive Mr Gibson has kept his briefs to himself . . ."'

'Oh God, terrible joke.' Jacqui shook her head.

'"So any eligible girl who wants to meet him may have to get herself run over (nothing disfiguring, a broken ankle perhaps) and preferably blame a multinational company. Prefers blondes." Well, that rules out us three.'

'Especially me,' giggled Jacqui and they all dissolved in helpless laughter until Suzanne spotted the object of the article walking into reception.

'Oh God. Sssh!'

Seconds later Lyall put his head through the door. 'Sounds like fun in here. What's going on?'

Jacqui and Suzanne descended into near-hysteria, leaving Tess to deal with the situation.

'We were just . . . er . . .' – Tess thought desperately – '. . . planning the office Christmas party. We thought we might hire a karaoke machine. What do you think?'

'Good idea. I do a mean "Heartbreak Hotel".' Lyall transformed himself briefly into Elvis while Jacqui slumped, clutching her ribs because they hurt so much from laughing. He shook his head at these girlish antics, and started for the door. 'Hang on a minute,' he pointed out, puzzled, 'it's another seven months till Christmas.'

At this, Jacqui started actually to choke.

'We know,' Tess replied, finding it almost impossible to keep a straight face, 'we just like to start our plans early.'

After Lyall had disappeared and Suzanne remembered she had some figures to check, a semblance of normality returned.

'By the way,' said Jacqui, wiping away the last of

the tears from her eyes, 'Suzanne mentioned something I thought you ought to know.'

'What's that?' Tess was inspecting her face for black smudges in the mirror.

'It's about Patricia Greene. She's been asking the accounts department for information about you.'

Tess stopped cleaning her face. 'What kind of information?'

'How much you've been charging your clients over the last couple of years, for a start. Suzanne reckons she must be doing some kind of calculation on exactly how much you bring into the firm.'

Tess felt a great splash of anger. She knew Patricia felt Tess brought in too many low-paying clients, but her reputation attracted plenty of high-paying ones too. Overall it evened out. Anyway, how dare Patricia check up on her? For a moment she was tempted to storm into Patricia's office and demand to know what she was up to. But some instinct told her not to. What would be far more useful would be to find out what Patricia intended to do with the information.

'Thanks for telling me.' Tess snapped her mirror shut and put it back in her bag, 'And Jacq, do you think you could make sure this doesn't go any further?'

Jacqui nodded. 'Gotcha. I already told Suzanne to swallow the evidence.'

'Has Stephen made contact with Josephine Quinn yet?' Phil knew she could have rung Stephen herself, but for once she was having the good sense to tread carefully. She and Tess were having a quick drink after work in the wine bar round the corner from Tess's office. It was soulless but convenient.

'He must have. He's seeing her next Thursday.'

'Tell him to take it seriously, won't you? Bone up on their background and everything. And if he doesn't know about fragrances, make sure he finds out.' Phil leaned forward so that her outrageous earrings clattered against the gold buttons of her mauve, lilac and fuchsia tweed suit. 'Josephine Quinn is one of the smartest businesswomen around. He's not dealing with some old biddy launching English Lavender Water. I hope he realizes that.'

'Philomena,' Tess folded her arms a shade huffily, while hoping that Stephen would indeed follow this advice. 'Stephen isn't a complete innocent, you know. The agency would have him back tomorrow if he really wanted to go.'

Phil grinned. 'I know. It's just that jobs like this don't come knocking every day. And it's so perfect for him. Who knows, he might really like it and forget all about this painting thing.'

'I doubt that. Anyway, here's the waitress. An Australian Chardonnay for me, please.'

'No, you don't,' corrected Phil, 'I'm buying. A jug of Margaritas please. And some Taco chips.'

'So what are we celebrating?' Tess knew her friend very well.

'What do you think I've got on my desk?' Phil closed her eyes to summon up the delicious memory.

'A telephone?' asked Tess meanly. 'A word processor? Some paperclips? A desk tidy? Don't say I'm not perceptive.'

Phil ignored her. 'Two dozen red roses,' she purred, 'and who do you think they're from?'

'Well it can't be Terry Worth because I made that up about him asking for your phone number.'

'You underestimate a man in love.' Phil sighed

luxuriously. 'He wrote down my car number and got a friend to check it out via the police computer.'

'But that's illegal!'

'I know.' Phil nodded delightedly. 'Isn't it romantic?'

Phil clearly relished the idea of Terry's illicit connections. Knowing her, she was probably hoping he'd turn out to be one of the Great Train Robbers.

'Phil, are you sure you know what you're getting into? Terry's a lovely man but he's really screwed up over losing his kids. And his ex-wife's appalling.' Tess knew it would be unpopular but felt it had to be said.

But Phil was too far gone to listen. 'I know,' she said, sipping her Margarita dreamily. 'Poor lamb. He's had a really rough time. What he needs is the love of a good woman.'

Stephen got up earlier than usual and ironed his favourite jade-green shirt listening to *Farming Today*. There was something extraordinarily soothing about hearing farmers discussing crop rotation and set-aside and the price of dairy cows when you were safe in the middle of Chelsea. You felt grateful you weren't required to farm the land yourself but were glad somebody was. The same was true of the shipping forecast. It bore not an atom of relevance to an urban existence, but it was comforting to think of fishermen tuning in their radios in Fisher and Dogger and German Bight and sailing safely to shore. No doubt it was irrational nonsense like this that explained the phenomenal success of Richmond & Quinn, who packaged manufactured memories of a bygone age with every bottle of perfume and bar of scented soap. It had certainly worked for them.

He held a medium-to-loud tie up against his shirt

and considered it. He had no idea what would be the right impression to make on Josephine Quinn and her partner Hugo Richmond, so he might as well just be himself. After all, he didn't even know yet if he wanted this job.

Tess appeared behind him in her towelling dressing-gown. She was barefoot and he hadn't heard her coming.

'You're up early.'

'I said I'd be there by nine-thirty.'

She straightened his tie, a little wifely gesture that was quite unnecessary, and thought how incredibly handsome he looked. 'Did you get time to prepare at all?' She was remembering Phil's advice about not underestimating Josephine Quinn.

'I didn't think I'd bother. I mean if they ask me about perfume I'll say I'm just an ad man and we leave that sort of thing to the research boys.' He grinned at the horror on her face. 'I suppose you think I spend my days watching Oprah Winfrey with Inge.' He picked up a folder and flipped it open. It was full of press cuttings, marketing supplements and sheafs of statistics. 'I've picked up quite a lot in the last few days. Perfume's always fascinated me. There's something about taking billions of rosepetals and the content of a deer's bollocks and turning it into Midnight in Paris that's always struck me as magical.'

Tess ruffled his hair. She might have known she wouldn't have to worry about Stephen.

The train journey, going in the opposite direction from the flood of commuters, was remarkably painless and within two hours Stephen was being driven in a taxi from Winchester Station to Richmond & Quinn's offices on the outskirts of the city. As they drove past sprawling Victorian houses into the clipped and manicured countryside Stephen reflected how pleasant it was to be out of London. This wasn't his kind of landscape – it was the wild sweeps of Ireland that pulled his heartstrings – but it was pleasant enough.

As they turned off the main road he saw a sign for Richmond & Quinn down a small country lane. It was amazing what a success they'd been yet had still managed to stay out of London. But it was all part of the myth, so Phil had insisted, and Josephine had always refused to consider a move.

As they turned up the drive he could see why. The grounds were actually much closer to the city centre than he'd realized, with lawns running down to the banks of the river Itchen, the spires of the cathedral in the background and sheep grazing in the water-meadows on the opposite bank.

'Which do you want, the offices or the Lodge?' The driver, who was clearly on familiar ground, indicated a brick and glass block half hidden by a clump of trees or the large Gothic house at one side of the wide sweep of green.

Stephen had been told to ask for the Lodge and the driver dropped him off. The Lodge was clearly lived in. But by Richmond or Quinn? Or maybe both. He wished he'd asked Phil the exact nature of their relationship. Were they husband and wife, lovers, or simply partners in the business sense?

As he got out of the car and walked towards the house, his feet crunching noisily on the gravel in the extraordinary tranquillity of the setting, he was surprised to feel a touch of excitement. And not about the job. It was at the prospect of meeting the famous Josephine Quinn.

CHAPTER ELEVEN

Stephen rang the heavy doorbell, expecting some kind of servant or perhaps a Filipino housekeeper to come and open it. It turned out to be a young boy in a maroon sweatshirt with the R&Q logo emblazoned on the front. He showed Stephen into a huge sitting room.

'I'll go and get Josephine. She's in the office.'

While he waited Stephen couldn't resist looking round the room. Along one wall was a vast inglenook fireplace, so big that there were wooden seats actually within the chimneypiece. A pair of medieval fire-dogs stood in the grate, side by side with an enormous wooden box of logs. Antique wall-hangings in the style of or, God knew, given the woman's reputation, maybe actually by Burne-Jones decorated every wall. The sofas were huge and deep, covered in faded tapestries. A row of velvet cushions in ruby and midnight-blue and jade-green picked out the beauty of their colours. With the morning sun filtering in through the high arched windows it seemed to Stephen that whoever decorated it had achieved the impossible. Grandeur *and* cosiness.

Behind him he heard the swish of silk and turned to find a tall, slim woman walking towards him wearing a mole-brown mannish suit that exactly matched the shade of her sleek bobbed hair. The face that smiled at him wasn't beautiful, but had a subtle intelligence about it which was somehow more arresting. In Stephen's experience most women disliked their bodies, or at least some part of them. But not this woman. She exuded an intense self-confidence about herself and the way she looked. Here was a woman who was used to being looked at and enjoyed it.

'Hello, I'm Josephine Quinn.' The handshake was assertive, almost masculine, and there was absolutely no sense of flirtation in her manner. 'Thanks for coming. Why don't I show you round? Then we can talk over lunch.'

Stephen put down his portfolio and nodded, admitting to himself how intrigued he was to see Josephine Quinn's domain. There was still no mention of Richmond. It was obvious who made the running in this partnership.

Josephine led him across the lawns to the tasteful brick and glass building he'd glimpsed earlier. The entrance led into a central glass atrium, rising into a dome, from which all the offices radiated in wings. She pushed open the door of the first wing and stood aside to let him pass.

'You're probably wondering why on earth we stay in Winchester. Isn't it commercial suicide to be out of London?'

Stephen smiled. This was indeed what he'd been asking himself.

'I realized what I wanted for myself was to live and work in the same place, to be part of a small community which shared a sense of purpose. And that's what we've got here. We draw our workforce from the immediate area and give them good working conditions. So they stay. Most of the people you'll meet today have been here since the beginning.' They entered a small lab where white-coated technicians, mostly women, were busy testing out different kinds of sprays and aerosols. 'Hello, Mary, how's it going?'

'Terrific, Josephine. We're nearly there on the spray for the new perfume.'

Josephine ushered him out. 'As you see, it's Christian names only here. There may be some other surprises for you. We don't have a traditional management structure, no titles, no clocking on or off. We believe in treating people like adults, not naughty children who'll only work if you threaten them. Each section is more or less autonomous. They manage their own budgets. We have no finance department.' She smiled at the astonishment on his face. 'We're even moving towards letting everyone fix their own pay. Providing their section is in profit, of course.'

'It sounds like the nineteenth-century industrialists with their model towns.'

Josephine led him into the next wing. 'A bit. But we don't make our workers do evening classes and spend their Sundays in church. They're allowed to spend the sabbath in B&Q or Homebase like everyone else.' Stephen laughed. 'It works, you know. Our profits have soared since we kicked out the structure.'

Stephen listened, amazed, as she showed him round section after section. It was like no business he'd ever seen or heard of. He could hardly believe what Josephine was telling him. Yet he had the evidence in his briefcase. Richmond & Quinn was a highly successful multinational company.

She finished the tour and led him back outside. Stephen was beginning to feel the stirrings of excitement about the venture. He'd tried working in an industry full of autocrats who thought they could kick the shit out of people because they were the paymasters; why not try something that seemed to be rejecting those values?

As they walked back slowly through the bright May

sunshine Stephen noticed a young girl leaning against the warmth of a red-brick wall eating a sandwich. He smiled at the peacefulness of the scene and waved a greeting to her. But the instant she saw them coming towards her her attitude transformed. She hid the sandwich behind her back, a look almost of panic on her face. Stephen glanced covertly at Josephine. So Richmond & Quinn wasn't quite the democratic paradise she'd led him to believe. It was clear from the girl's demeanour that Josephine could inspire fear as well as loyalty in her well-ordered world.

Back inside the house Stephen found himself looking for more clues about the woman and her personal life. But there was nothing to enlighten him. Only good taste as far as the eye could see. There were certainly no signs of family life. Stephen thought for a moment of his own home, scruffy and lived-in, with its half-finished décor because they'd never had enough money or time to get it done properly. Ellie's greatcoat permanently hanging on the bottom of the banisters, even in summer, like a relic from the Russian retreat. Luke's swimming things drying on the radiator in the hall. The Scalextric track in the spare bedroom. He tried to imagine living in the calm order of a house like this and supposed that, if you tried hard enough, you could get used to it.

'Ready for lunch yet?'

Stephen nodded and Josephine led him into a sunny dining room, decorated in pale yellow, with a round table set for three. It looked as though he was finally about to meet the elusive Hugo Richmond. A cold lunch of seafood salad with a a wonderful assortment of breads waited for them. Stephen couldn't resist touching them. They were still warm. Assuming that Hugo hadn't been in the kitchen all morning up to his elbows in flour, she had an amazing line in invisible servants.

To his surprise, Josephine poured them both a glass of wine. He'd had her down for the iron-disciplined mineral-water-only kind of luncher. She was about to put the bottle down when a man in his forties dressed in a blue suit with a collarless shirt joined them, talking into a portable phone.

'God, Hugo, put that bloody thing away, will you? At least over lunch.' Josephine poured a third glass of wine and handed it to him. In spite of the sunny day Stephen sensed a dip in the atmosphere, as though a strict father had just opened the front door.

'Stephen, this is my partner, Hugo Richmond.'

Hugo put the phone down on the yellow-painted dresser and shook hands. His were cool and smooth and oddly lifeless.

'So, Mr Gilfillan, I expect Josephine's told you about the company and our ideals. Now we're planning to put a toe in the shark-infested waters of the US, and we need someone to make sure we don't get it bitten off.' He helped himself to the food and Stephen noticed that he kept each thing in a little pile, separated from the rest. 'Perhaps you could explain exactly what you think you could bring to the venture?' Clearly Hugo wasn't a man for small-talk. And the formal greeting sat oddly in this allegedly democratic set-up. Maybe Hugo was reminding him he wasn't part of it yet.

Stephen felt the adrenalin flow. A combative attitude had always stirred him into action. He just didn't like to be treated as the kind of lackey the Walenskys of the world expected. Calmly he laid out his ideas. He'd already made a few calls to friends and contacts in New York and had a reasonable idea of the state of the fragrance market and its receptiveness to a new entrant.

'So, your opinion's that this is a reasonable time for us to be making our move?'

'Absolutely. Your name's already well known to discerning tourists who come to London. They buy Richmond & Quinn along with Penhaligon's and Crabtree & Evelyn. The trick's to stop you being just a well-kept secret and make you a big noise.'

Stephen knew perfectly well that operators as smart as Hugo and Josephine would hardly have got this far without doing basic research. So what Hugo must be looking for was something more impressionistic, the reactions of the style-setters. So that's what he'd give him.

By the end of lunch Hugo, though still formal, had at least unbent a little. At two-twenty-five precisely he put his knife and fork together and stood up. 'I must get back, as I assume you must too, Josephine.' He raised an eyebrow as though offering her a way of politely drawing the lunch to a close. Josephine ignored him.

'Would you like some coffee?' she asked Stephen instead, taking a cafetière from the dresser.

Stephen wondered if this was some kind of test, but it smelled so good he immediately agreed. Hugo picked up his phone and left them. Without him the atmosphere lightened again. Stephen helped himself to a peach from the fruit bowl and wondered if it would be ripe. He and Tess usually shopped in supermarkets to save time, consequently the peaches and nectarines they bought were always hard, almost like apples. Somehow he knew this peach would be different. And it was. The sweetness exploded on his palate, and the delicious juice ran down his chin. If he closed his eyes he could almost imagine himself in the Mediterranean sun. He'd have to watch himself. He could get used to all this.

He was amazed, when he finally looked at his watch, to find that it was mid-afternoon. 'I really ought to be going. The lunch was delicious.'

Josephine stood up. Together they walked through the oak-panelled rooms towards the front door.

'Did you have a coat?'

'No. Only this.' Stephen reached for the portfolio he'd left in the hall.

'Can I look before you go?' She reached out a slender hand. She wore only modern jewellery, he noticed, and her nails were neat and regular and looked consciously unpainted.

Almost reluctantly, but with a sense of excitement too, he handed it over. At the top were some rough designs for their new packaging. She held them up one by one saying nothing until she'd considered them all. 'They're lovely. You have a real feel for our mood. That's harder than you'd think.'

Then she came to the life drawings Stephen had forgotten to take out in his hurry to start early this morning.

She looked at each one in turn, but it was the drawing of the old woman that really caught her attention. She took it carefully out of the folder and propped it up on the hall table. Then she stood six feet away and stared at it.

Stephen felt as foolish as a sixth-former. Josephine Quinn wasn't an evening-class teacher struggling to see the best in a bunch of mediocre students, she was a genuine collector.

She took down the drawing and put it carefully back in his folder, then turned to him, her face serious.

'You shouldn't waste talent like that. It's spitting in the eye of the Almighty.'

Stephen smiled nervously, slightly shamefaced. 'Is it?'

'Do you want to see what really excites me?' she asked, completely taking him by surprise as she closed the portfolio.

It didn't sound like the kind of offer you could refuse, so, feeling slightly apprehensive, Stephen followed her through the kitchen right at the back of the house, where a young woman, clearly the source of the wonderful lunch, was loading a dishwasher, towards the gardens. Finally Josephine flung open the door to a vast extension with panoramic windows looking straight down to the river.

Canvases lay around everywhere and two easels were set up in the middle of the room with half-finished paintings on them, one of them a nude closely resembling the girl in the kitchen.

'What an incredible studio!' Stephen congratulated her.

'I designed it with glass everywhere so it'd get every last shred of light,' Josephine announced with a hint of pride, her voice suddenly sounding young and enthusiastic, with no sign of the hard edge of professionalism about it.

Stephen looked around the room, completely unprepared for what he was about to experience. Something was grabbing him and pulling him back to his childhood. He closed his eyes and breathed in, realizing what it was. The smell of oil paint laced with turpentine, of linseed oil and oil of spike lavender, headier and more evocative than any perfume. It was the smell of his childhood.

In a fraction of a second he was back in his father's

139

studio in Northumberland Wharf, on the bank of the Thames between Hammersmith Bridge and Chiswick, long before they moved to Ireland. He could hear the river lap against the bank when a boat passed. There was the smell of paraffin too, from the heater. He was sitting on the floor playing, forgotten. Above him adults wandered in to talk to his father carrying tumblers overflowing with Dubonnet, which Julius said was cheaper than Martini, with twists of tangerine peel because the lemons had run out. If he kept quiet no one would notice him.

As he stood there in the afternoon sunshine Stephen felt overwhelmed by one of the most powerful emotions he'd ever felt.

He had to try and be a painter.

And he knew that all his life he'd run away from this admission because of his father, because Julius's personality and achievement were so overpowering.

He opened his eyes. The experience had been so intense that he'd almost forgotten where he was. A few feet away Josephine stood watching him, a faint smile on her face, as if – impossible though it was – she understood exactly what he'd been thinking.

'You're his son, aren't you?' she asked quietly. 'And don't say whose son.'

'Yes,' said Stephen levelly. 'Yes, I am.'

'That must be hard for you.'

'You could say that.' And he saw that she did understand. She didn't try, like other people, even Tess, to tell him to grow up, to stop letting his father affect his life. Swiftly Stephen changed the subject. 'So why have you got this fine studio? Are you a painter when you're not being a tycoon?'

'Not any more. I gave up painting a long time ago when I realized if I worked very hard I might be good, but no more. I'm afraid I'm too much of a perfectionist to settle for that. So now I just lend the studio to people who have nowhere to paint. Talent by association, you might say.' She looked directly at him for a moment. 'Now that you've given up advertising why don't you just become a painter instead?'

It was an odd question from a potential employer but Stephen suspected she was genuinely interested rather than thinking of holding it against him. Did some instinct tell her that was what he really longed to do? She made it sound so simple but reality rushed back, puncturing the moment. 'Because I'd be penniless. I've got a wife and children. A mortgage. School fees. I need to earn. I can't go rushing off to art school like some kid. At least not yet.'

She straightened one of the canvases unnecessarily. 'Look, it's almost June now. Why don't you at least try the Bryant Summer School? It's only for four weeks. You could do that before starting here. I could probably swing it for you. One of my friends is a tutor.' She broke off, conscious that she was being too enthusiastic, offering too much. Her voice became stiffer, more formal. 'That is if we do decide to offer you the job.'

Behind her a door opened and Hugo appeared a few feet away. 'Quite. Don't let's jump the gun. After all, we haven't had time to discuss it yet.' His voice was so clipped every word shone with polished perfection.

Josephine flushed slightly but didn't turn round.

'By the way,' Hugo added, 'there was one question I forgot to ask you.' Somehow he made it sound as though it were Stephen's fault. 'Why exactly did you give up your glittering career in advertising?'

Stephen picked up a brush and flicked the fine bristle with his finger. 'I didn't give it up. I was fired because I was reluctant to design a ten-million-pound campaign for a new car that no one needed. I thought there were enough luxury cars on the market already.'

'A dangerous attitude.'

'Yes. But not as dangerous as going on doing something I'd stopped believing in.'

'Besides, Stephen wants to be a painter,' Josephine announced.

'You've come to the right place then.' Hugo watched Stephen's face carefully. 'Josephine adores painters, don't you, Jo? She likes to mine out their talent.'

Josephine looked at him angrily and Stephen felt a wash of relief when she glanced at her watch. 'You'd better go now if you want to miss the rush hour. Perhaps you could leave your designs for Hugo to see.' She held the door of the studio open for him to pass.

As they walked round to the front of the house she leaned towards him, her voice urgent. 'Look, whether the job thing works out or not, you should still go to the Bryant. Shall I call my friend?'

Stephen paused. 'Yes. Though I'd have to talk to my wife.'

'Of course. Well, goodbye. I enjoyed our lunch. We'll be in touch very soon. One of the advantages of only having two people on the board is that we can make decisions quickly.' She smiled suddenly. 'We used to have our board meetings in bed.' She turned away abruptly and Stephen wondered if she was angry with herself for having given something too personal away. 'Where's your car?' she asked brusquely.

'Actually I came by train.'

'Oh. I'd better give you a lift to the station then.'

'You don't need to. I can call a cab.' Stephen realized he'd prefer the anonymity of a taxi. His feelings about his first encounter with Richmond & Quinn were confused and he wanted time to think about them. At first he'd been enthusiastic and excited but now he sensed hidden undercurrents. He wanted to get away from this hothouse atmosphere. But Josephine had already disappeared into the house to get her car keys.

A couple of minutes later an open-topped white Mercedes purred silently into his vision. Stephen wasn't into cars and he didn't recognize the model but he dreaded to think what it must have cost. Bill would have known the maker's list price and what sort of discount you could hope to get.

They both sat silently on the brief journey to the station and Josephine shook his hand formally as they said goodbye.

As he hurried off to catch the train he could already see waiting at the platform, it struck Stephen that Josephine had given him most of her valuable day. Still, this US venture was a risky one. They had to make absolutely sure they found the right person.

On the journey back to London, he was even more conscious of mixed emotions. He felt strongly attracted to the philosophy and the atmosphere at Richmond & Quinn. And yet he also had a feeling of unease at the veiled hostility there seemed to be between Josephine and Hugo. But, harder to pin down than that, was an uncomfortable sense that although he'd only just met her, Josephine could in some subtle way have the power to influence his life.

Maybe it was all too intense and best avoided. If he was offered the job at all. And judging by Hugo Richmond's attitude he very much doubted he would be.

Tess, eager to know how Stephen's interview had gone, packed up her documents before five in the hope of getting home before he did. But life and Patricia were against her, and she found herself buttonholed and pulled into a discussion about a long and complicated case. So by the time she made it home to Chelsea Stephen was sitting in front of the television eating toast and Marmite with Luke and Ellie.

'So, what happened?' She sat down next to him. 'How was the legendary Josephine Quinn?'

'All right. A bit intense, actually.'

Tess sighed, exasperated at this typically male lack of detail. 'And what was the place like?'

'Terrific. The whole set-up is amazing. They have the most extraordinary philosophy. Real industrial democracy in action.'

Tess listened, amazed. This didn't quite tally with the tales she'd heard of Josephine Quinn. 'Really? I gathered from Phil she was a bit of a tartar.'

Stephen recalled the look on the face of the girl with the sandwich. 'I certainly get the impression Josephine's quite tough to work for.'

'So you liked the place.' At least that was encouraging. 'And what about the job. Did they offer it to you?'

'They're going to call me.'

For a moment Stephen looked as though he was going to add something, then clearly thought better of it.

'What?' Tess prompted. 'What were you going to say?'

'Just that I had this really weird experience there. She has this studio, you know, a real artists' studio, nothing to do with Richmond & Quinn, and I was standing there with Josephine and suddenly it was though I were back in my childhood, at my father's old studio in Northumberland Wharf. And I saw something clearly for the first time. I need to paint, Tessie, just like I need to breathe. I need to find out if I'm any good. Standing there I saw one thing for certain. I was right to get out of advertising. I'd rather be a bad painter than a good ad man.'

Tess sensed the excitement radiating out of him so strongly that she thought, if she just leaned forward, she could warm her hands by it. 'You mean you don't want the job after all?'

'Even if I get the job, it wouldn't start till September. And Josephine came up with this great suggestion. That I go to the Bryant Summer School. She's got a friend who's a tutor there and thinks she could swing it for me. Tess, that'd be brilliant. Then I could really find out if I had any talent.'

Tess tried not to wonder if their money would hold out that long, especially with the course to pay for.

Ellie pretended to be watching the television, but was actually listening to every word. She glanced at her parents, wondering if either of them had noticed that Stephen had mentioned Josephine Quinn's name three times.

Just as the familiar music of *EastEnders* filled the room, the phone rang and Ellie leaped up and ran into the kitchen to get it.

In seconds she was back. 'It's Josephine Quinn,' she announced, watching her father. 'She wants to speak to Dad.'

Chapter Twelve

Stephen listened, flattered that they had made up their minds so quickly, while Josephine outlined the terms on which they were offering him the job.

'Could I have a while to think about it?' Stephen asked when she'd finished. 'I'd just like to talk to my wife.'

Tess was already there, waiting.

'They've asked me to do it. Starting in September. For six months but with a rolling contract if they think it's working out and the project isn't finished.'

Tess nodded, not wanting to influence him. It had to be his choice.

'You want me to go for it, don't you?'

'Well,' smiled Tess, 'you seemed to like the place and the people. It'd certainly make life a damn sight easier if we can save up a bit before you decide to be Picasso.'

He took her hand. 'Yes. You're absolutely right. My wise virgin.'

'You don't have to take it if you don't want to, you know, Dad.' They turned to find Ellie in the doorway clutching a red plastic booklet. 'I've been putting all my birthday and Christmas presents from Gramps into a savings account. You can have it. There's nearly three thousand pounds.'

Stephen put his arms round her, incredibly moved, and lightly touched the pretty face shining above its shabby thrift-shop clothing. 'But I wouldn't want to deprive Oxfam of half its income. You can buy a lot of old clothes for three grand.'

He picked up the phone.

'Hello. Josephine. We've talked it through. Thanks for the offer. I'd be delighted to accept.'

'Good. By the way, I've talked to my friend at the Bryant. He's offering you an interview, if you want it. His name's Slouch Heyward.'

'Great.' Stephen felt a surge of excitement. 'I'll get in touch with him.'

Tess hummed as she gave the sitting room a quick tidy before following Stephen up to bed. She plumped up the cushions, laughing at herself as she remembered how she'd teased her mother for doing the same thing. Why was it we all became our mothers in the end, no matter how hard we tried to rebel? Just like her mother she faithfully kept butter papers in the fridge. Yet she never had time to bake. And she could hear her mother's shocked tones in her own when she scolded Luke for putting the milk bottle on the breakfast table.

Never mind. For the first time in weeks, Tess felt really relaxed. Her savings would just about last till September and then Stephen would be earning again. She didn't mind if they had to save. The knowledge that Ellie and Luke wouldn't have to change schools, and that they were safe here in the house she loved was quite enough.

She closed the curtains and turned to go to bed, not noticing that Luke must have moved a small table that usually stood by the sofa to put some of his wrestlers on. It crashed to the floor taking with it a little blue-and-white Chinese bowl. It had been rescued from the hold of a sunken tea clipper that had sunk three hundred years ago and was one of the few things her grandmother had left her.

She bent down to find it was smashed beyond repair.

As she picked up the broken pieces she found herself hoping it wasn't some kind of omen.

'So, I assume you're related to Julius Gilfillan, are you?' Stephen could feel the hostility leaking out of the man sitting opposite him like radiation. Slouch Heyward was clearly someone who didn't approve of the old boys' network.

The truth was Stephen admired him for it. The Son-in-law Also Rises had never been a dictum he'd had much time for. 'Only very distantly,' he lied.

Slouch cast his eye over the letter in front of him. He didn't like smartarses who'd worked in advertising, especially if they were related, no matter how distantly, to grand old men of painting. It tended to make them get above themselves. And the one thing Slouch liked in a student was humility. It was bad enough when he only had them for three years, but if it was a mere month of summer school they had to be prepared to unlearn everything they'd ever known and turn themselves into a blank page for Slouch to write on. Otherwise the whole thing was a waste of time.

Still, Jo Quinn had been very good to the school. He pictured her for a moment, the day she'd walked into this office on her very first day as a scholarship student at the Bryant, full of enthusiasm, fresh from Devon with her lustrous brown hair and country-girl freshness. That had disappeared years ago beneath the year-round tan, along with the West Country burr.

'All right then, Mr Gilfillan, you can have your place.'

Stephen looked in surprise at the tall angular man with the teddy boy sideburns and the lugubrious expression sitting the other side of the desk. 'Don't you want to even see my portfolio?'

'That's all right, you come highly recommended. See you in August.' Slouch smiled for the first time and shook Stephen's hand. After all, he'd promised to give him a place. But he hadn't said anything about giving him an easy ride. By the end of the month Stephen would probably be wishing he'd never left advertising.

It was only when he was halfway home that Stephen realized his course would fall right in the middle of the holiday Tess had been planning for them in Ireland. He just hoped she'd be understanding. She'd had to put up with a lot lately. He ducked into Marks & Spencer's and bought her a big bouquet of flowers to soften the blow. Screw the expense for once.

'How did you get on?' Tess was chopping onions for a spaghetti sauce. She eyed the bouquet 'Why the flowers? Have you done something you shouldn't?'

Stephen looked guilty. 'You'd better be the judge of that. Do you want the good news or the bad news? The good news is I got on the course.'

Tess put down her knife and kissed him. 'Stephen, that's terrific!'

'The bad news is it clashes with our summer holiday in Cork. So I wondered if maybe I could just join you for the last week?'

Tess was about to protest when she reminded herself Stephen was only really taking the Richmond & Quinn job for her sake. Painting was what he really wanted to do.

'OK.' She hid her disappointment by pushing her face into the flowers. 'Just keep away from the nude models.'

Stephen laughed, thinking of the wonderful old girl

who'd posed at his evening classes. 'I'll see what I can do.'

For the whole of June and July Stephen spent his every waking moment painting. He drove the rest of the household mad looking for people to pose for him. Tess refused point blank, saying she was far too busy. Luke agreed happily but wouldn't keep still for more than two consecutive minutes, and Ellie was going through a teenage 'I Hate My Body' phase and loathed the idea of being captured on canvas. The only person who was willing to pose for him was Inge. So she sat motionless for hours, dreamily staring out of the window and showing her best profile. It was driving Tess to distraction because no ironing, shopping or cleaning was getting done, and once Inge had been so deep in her artistic reverie that she'd forgotten to pick Luke up from his chess club and he'd fare-dodged to get home on the tube because he hadn't got any money with him. Then there was the question of Stephen's clothes, which were gradually getting absolutely ruined by oil paint.

It was Ellie who came to the rescue. Since the summer term was just ending she suggested she take him shopping to a brilliant place she knew called Laurence Corner.

In less than an hour she'd kitted him out from head to toe in army surplus. She stood back to admire her handiwork. It needed one final touch. She added an army baseball cap which she put on Stephen back-to-front in best rap fashion. Instantly he looked about twenty-five. Firmly Stephen turned it round the right way again.

'Coward,' she teased.

'Absolutely.'

'Come on. We promised we'd go and show Mum. She won't half be surprised.'

Out in the street they passed a steel-and-glass palace that Stephen had never noticed before. It wasn't quite Canary Wharf but pretty impressive all the same. Some workmen were busy putting the finishing touches to a sign outside it. Stephen watched, fascinated. And then he noticed the name. It was the advertising agency Raf Walensky had been leaving in favour of them. As he looked up two men came out of the building. To Stephen's amusement, one of them was Ted.

Stephen shouted a greeting. Ted looked over at them blankly before finally recognizing him.

'What are you doing dressed like that?' he asked, amazed. 'You look about sixteen. Have you sold your soul to the devil like Dorian whatsisname?'

'Bought it back, you mean. Actually I've become a painter.'

'Houses or pictures?'

'Pictures.'

'Pity,' remarked Ted. 'There's more money in houses. Fancy a bite?' He indicated a supremely smart French restaurant over the road.

'Sorry. We've got a prior engagement. At McDonald's. Tess is taking us out.'

Ted shook his head as he watched Stephen and Ellie walk away. 'I don't know how he can sponge off his wife like that.'

'Nah,' agreed the other man as they slipped into the 5-star restaurant where a meal cost twice the average national weekly wage. 'Is this on my lot or yours?'

Tess sat listening to a client and recognizing a lot of

what the woman was complaining about it in her own marriage.

'When we were first married he was a real high-flyer. Now he just coasts along and gets passed over. All my friends' husbands earn twice as much. They've all got country cottages or second homes in France and we're stuck in the same place we've been in for eighteen years. Frankly I've had enough. So I wondered what grounds for divorce you thought I should go for?'

Tess watched her client's pretty but dissatisfied face and thought how corrosive this kind of attitude was. And yet it reminded her, just slightly, of the whinge she'd had to Phil, comparing Stephen with Lyall Gibson. It wasn't an attractive thought.

'None,' answered Tess crisply, taking the woman by surprise. 'There's absolutely nothing wrong with your marriage. Look, life's a package. You get the bad bits along with the good. So he's not earning a hundred and fifty grand a year. Maybe he sees more of the kids than your friends' husbands. Have you ever asked them what they'd prefer? A highflying husband or one they actually *saw*?'

The woman shook her head somewhat reluctantly. Tess realized that all of this applied just as much to herself. What she'd loved about Stephen was his sense of fun, and his spontaneity, his capacity for feeling strongly and being passionate about things. She hadn't married him for his career prospects. She suddenly felt overwhelmingly cheerful. 'What you need is a romantic holiday, not a divorce. Get away somewhere on your own. It would do wonders for you.'

She shepherded the woman, who was still stunned, out of the office, only to find Stephen, looking ridiculously young and disconcertingly like someone who'd come to fix the plumbing, waiting with Ellie in reception.

Tess waved at them as she showed her client to the door. 'Thank you,' said the woman loudly just as Patricia appeared. 'I must say I never expected to consult a divorce lawyer and be told to stay married!'

Tess closed her eyes for an instant. She could imagine what Patricia was making of that. Actually discouraging clients from profitable legal action. Another black mark for Tess.

She decided not to think about it. 'So where is it for lunch?' she asked the plumber and the plumber's mate. 'McDonald's or Kentucky Fried?'

CHAPTER THIRTEEN

'Bag packed? Rubber, ruler, spare knickers?' Tess straightened the collar of Stephen's army surplus jacket and kissed him goodbye as he set off for his first day at the Bryant School of Art.

Although she'd passed it off by joking Tess couldn't stop herself feeling ambivalent about this new chapter in Stephen's life. To Stephen it was the beginning of a big adventure. But to Tess art and artists had always been distant and mysterious, suspect even. She knew Julius, of course, but Julius was simply himself. When he painted he disappeared into his own private world and no one, not even Stella, was allowed in. Stephen, she sensed, would be different. He would want her to understand and share his passion. But would she be able to? Was she up to it?

Pushing away any doubts, she turned back into the house to get her briefcase. After all, she had plenty of down-to-earth practical challenges of her own to meet. The big questions could wait.

Stephen got off the tube at Goodge Street and walked towards Fitzrovia and the Bryant. It was a part of London he knew hardly at all, and yet it had once been the city's cultural heart. The Bloomsbury set had all written, painted and swapped their bons mots within a few hundred yards. Dylan Thomas had drunk regularly in the Fitzroy Tavern. Almost every house had a blue plaque announcing that some distinguished painter, composer or writer had lived there. And the Bryant itself had a towering reputation. Stephen realized he was genuinely nervous for the first time since the night of the awards. That seemed a lifetime away and yet it was less than six months.

And then there it was, the Bryant School of Art, with its impressive portico. Stephen filed in with the other summer school students. To his relief only a handful were teenagers. He'd had a nightmare vision of being the only greybeard amongst a crowd of Doc Martened Ellies, but in fact at least half were mature students like himself, and one or two wouldn't see sixty again.

Noticing his slight hesitation, a steel-haired woman with a collapsible easel under one arm, wearing enormous corduroy trousers and a battered straw hat, decided to take him under her wing. 'New, are you?' she barked.

'Isn't everyone?' Stephen asked.

'Not at all. I come every year. This is my summer holiday. This and the Chelsea Flower Show. Never miss either.' She elbowed Stephen in the ribs with a ribald expression as she showed him which way they had to go. 'Leave the old boy in Somerset and enjoy myself for three weeks. It's a damn sight better than sweating it out in grotty Lanzarote or some such holiday hell-hole.'

Stephen grinned. He was clearly in for a few surprises.

'Welcome to the Bryant School of Fine Art, everyone. I'm Slouch Heyward, your guide and tormentor for the next four weeks.' Slouch unfurled his long body from the chair and stood at the front of the class. 'Now. Step One. If you think you know anything about art I'd like you to unlearn it. We only have a few weeks and I want a blank mental canvas from everyone. This week we're going back to the beginning. Any questions?'

'What if we've already done some work and we know we're happiest in one medium?' asked a middle-aged man at the back.

'You make yourself try some others,' Slouch replied crisply. 'For instance, Mr Gilfillan over there.' Stephen's head shot up at the unexpected mention of his name. 'He thinks he's pretty shit-hot at life drawing, don't you, Mr Gilfillan? So this week odds are he won't be doing any.' From the back of the class Stephen heard a titter. He couldn't believe what he was hearing. Slouch hadn't even bothered to look at his portfolio and now the man was pillorying him in front of the class. For a moment he was tempted to simply get up and leave. But that was exactly what Slouch was probably aiming for.

Stephen stayed his ground. It would be far more satisfying to fight back. After all, he wasn't some shrinking violet from the shires hanging on the lips of the master. If Slouch was going to be unpleasant, he'd just ignore him and plough his own furrow. He was going to make the most of his time here, Slouch or no Slouch.

'Don't worry,' hissed the steel-haired lady from Somerset, 'he always chooses someone. He obviously thinks you can stand the heat.'

Stephen shrugged. If this was flattery, he wondered what real criticism felt like. He had an uncomfortable feeling he might be going to find out.

'Hello, doll, how've you been keeping?' Phil recognized Terry's voice at once, but was damned if she was going to let on. It had been weeks ago that she'd had the roses and she'd decided he had a pretty funny way of showing his interest. As it happened she had a lot on at work, Hattie and Dan had broken up for the holidays and she didn't need any more aggro.

'Who is this, please?' she asked in her best "I'm A Very Busy Woman" voice.

'You know who it is,' insisted the other voice, coolly laughing at her.

'You've been a bloody long time deciding to call.' Screw sounding cool. One prerogative of being an independent, though admittedly manless, woman, was that you ought to be able to cut all that hard-to-get crap.

'I know. Business has been a tad preoccupying lately.' His tone implied he might have been doing a couple of bank heists.

'So, what do you want?'

'I wondered if maybe you might have dinner with me tonight?' He made it sound as though it were the most unsurprising request in the world.

'Tonight?' squawked Phil, half her brain outraged that he assumed she'd drop everything, the other half wildly calculating how to do exactly that. 'Did someone stand you up?'

Terry laughed, a deep, throaty, genuinely amused sound. 'No, no one stood me up. I just decided I couldn't wait any longer before seeing you again.'

Phil laughed too. This was such outrageous blarney that she might even choose to believe it.

'OK, then. Where are you taking me?'

Terry laughed again. 'Well, there's this nice little steak bar in Chigwell I'm very fond of. They have a cabaret and all. You can sing along, even go up on stage if you fancy.'

Phil was appalled. What on earth had she let herself in for? She'd never even been to Essex, let along Chigwell. The place was probably stuffed with fascist bores, all looking like they were auditioning for *Minder*.

But it was too late now.

'OK, pick me up from here at seven-thirty.' She was damned if she was going all the way home to change for a steak bar in Chigwell. After she'd said goodbye she paused a moment before putting the phone back in its cradle. Maybe she should have said no after all. She told herself to forget all about him and get stuck into the campaign she was launching. And to her surprise it worked. By the time seven-thirty came she'd achieved more than she had for days and only had time to refresh her lipstick and squirt on some Poison before the security man buzzed her that her guest was here.

When the lift doors opened she found Terry, standing only inches away from the lift shaft. She jumped, immediately losing her cool and forgetting to put on her haughty expression.

Outside the building his Rolls was parked unostentatiously right across the pavement. She jumped in before they got attacked by a militant member of Pedestrians' Rights.

'So,' Phil said tartly, 'Essex it is then.'

They drove in silence for a while as Terry headed down Shaftesbury Avenue towards Piccadilly, up St James's and then took the narrow turning into Arlington Street.

'This isn't the way to Chigwell,' pointed out Phil with towering perspicacity.

'No,' admitted Terry. 'I had a bit of a rethink on that one. I thought we might try this gaff instead.' He pointed to Le Caprice, which as Phil knew very well had a waiting list of two weeks and was possibly the most difficult restaurant in London to get a table at.

'Have you booked?' Phil jumped out of the car

before Terry had the chance to practise any old-fashioned charm and open her door.

'Nah. Doesn't look very crowded though, does it?'

Phil resisted the temptation to get straight back into the car, not least because it was locked. Well, this would serve him right for his arrogance in waiting weeks to phone her and then expecting her just to be available. In fact, she'd quite enjoy watching him taken down a notch or two.

But Terry, completely unabashed, was already inside the restaurant where, to her amazement, instead of being shown the door he was being greeted like a long-lost relative at a Sicilian wedding.

'Mr Worth! What a pleasure! No booking? Never mind, we'll squeeze you in. How are the children?'

Phil followed meekly as Terry was led past the black-and-white David Bailey photographs adorning the walls to one of the best tables in the house.

Another grinning waiter arrived with the menus, this time actually embracing Terry.

Terry waved them away and asked what was the best thing on tonight. The waiter reverentially ran through a couple of dishes.

'Fine,' nodded Terry. 'We'll have two fresh tomato and basil in pastry baskets, and after that the salmon and sole plait. Vegetables not salad. And none of your nouvelle stinginess with the spuds.'

The waiter laughed delightedly as Phil sat down, open-mouthed. Terry hadn't even bothered to ask her opinion.

Behind her she heard a smothered giggle. It was a trendy new assistant at Outrageous PR, gobsmacked at seeing Fearless Phil Doyle being bulldozed by a bloke.

'So.' Terry turned to Phil, smiling innocently. 'What would you like to drink. Wine or champagne?'

As the evening wore on Phil realized that it was almost as impossible to stay angry with Terry as it would be with Hattie or Dan. He simply disarmed you, with his good humour, his sheer nerve, his appetite for life as well as food, the way he singlemindedly pursued what he wanted. And clearly got it. She knew that to have made so much money he couldn't be as good-humoured and straightforward as he seemed, but compared to her ex, he was an open book. Greg had been so devious you needed a mindreader to find out what he wanted for breakfast.

By the time he held open the car door for her at the end of the evening, she'd forgotten why the gesture had so annoyed her a mere three hours before. Phil, who'd always found charm a highly suspect quality that usually masked manipulativeness and an over-developed sense of self, found herself lying down and surrendering in the face of Terry's.

When he dropped her off at her mansion flat in Holland Park there was only one thing she couldn't work out. Why on earth Tess seemed to think he could possibly be trouble.

Stephen woke and turned towards the clock-radio, conscious that he'd only been there a week but that today he didn't want to go into the Bryant. It had taken Slouch less than five days to knock his confidence and kill his enthusiasm. The man's drip, drip, drip of carping and criticism was like a Chinese water torture. And maybe he was right. Maybe Stephen had been been living on an illusion.

He turned to Tess, wondering whether to confide in her, but she was still asleep. Besides, she'd have every right to lose patience with him. First he'd shaken up their comfortable life and now he was losing his nerve.

This was one battle he'd have to fight alone.

Slouch distributed the charcoal to the twenty or so students so they could sketch a bare outline on their blank canvases. All round the room he could feel their hesitation at making the first mark. All except Stephen. Stephen, he noticed, had set up his easel in the furthest corner of the studio, almost out of sight from where Slouch stood at the front of the class, and was already sketching away.

'Right. Now. Look at the arrangement of the fruit in front of you and start sketching. Broad strokes are best. Be brave like Mr Gilfillan there.'

Everyone turned to look at Stephen. Stephen refused to look up. It was incredible that the man could make even what seemed on the surface to be a compliment sound like some kind of veiled put-down. Well, Stephen didn't need Slouch's opinion, good or bad. He'd decided in bed this morning that the only way to survive this course was to ignore Slouch and just get on with it.

When everyone was sketching quietly Slouch glanced at Stephen. He knew Stephen disliked him. But then, in his view it wouldn't do Stephen any harm to learn that, unlike in advertising, in painting there was no such thing as a free lunch. You had to do the graft, learn every skill. There was no point Stephen swanning in here thinking painting was in his genes or that, because he had powerful friends like Jo, things were going to be easy. He turned his back on Stephen and began to tour the room to check up on the other students.

Absorbed in mixing his oils for the next stage, Stephen forgot Slouch. The point of today's exercise was to try and finish the painting in a single sitting, without bothering with the finicky details, and Stephen found the technique wonderfully liberating. The subject of the still life was a bowl of plums in a ceramic bowl, some still with their leaves on, all with that wonderful dusty purple so peculiar to the fruit. As he painted Stephen remembered the plums and damsons he'd picked from the little row of trees Stella had planted in Northumberland Wharf: London plums, and they had been so ripe and sweet he could almost taste them now.

Smiling faintly he added a faint smudge of black to the bluish-purple oil paint on his palette.

'OK, everyone,' Slouch announced at the end of the day, 'you can leave your canvases where they are to dry over the weekend. Come in at nine sharp on Monday and we'll assess the masterpieces.' He grinned mercilessly. 'That should give you all a relaxing weekend.'

The students cleaned their brushes, each glancing surreptitiously at each other's work to see how it compared with their own.

'Have a nice weekend,' said Stephen's old lady friend cheerfully. 'At least you've got a family to go home to. They'll take your mind off things. Mine have all flown the coop. Just me and the old boy to bore each other to death.'

Stephen helped her out of the door. She was absolutely right. Feeling more cheerful he headed for home.

'God, Mum, have you seen Luke's zit?' Ellie delightedly demanded of her mother as Tess stood slicing vegetables in the kitchen. 'It's bigger than K2!'

'Ellie, really,' grimaced Tess, 'not when I'm making the supper.'

Luke sat at the kitchen table staring suicidally into Tess's make-up mirror which was propped on top of his physics homework. 'It's the school disco tomorrow,' he wailed, 'I'll be a social leper. Charlotte Johnson won't come near me.'

'I'll lend you my cover-up stick,' offered Tess. 'No one'll even notice, I promise.'

'Oh, Mum, don't be so dumb. Of course they will.'

Tess sighed with relief hearing the front door open, guessing it must be Stephen. He could deal with this family crisis. He came into the room and kissed her.

'What's up with Luke?' He gestured towards the tragic figure slumped over the breakfast table.

'He's got a spot as big as the Ritz,' Ellie supplied gleefully.

Stephen suppressed a grin, remembering how painful being an adolescent could be. 'Come on, old man, that's a magnifying mirror. Of course it looks big in that. Turn it over the other way and it'll look much smaller.'

Unfortunately for Stephen, Luke discovered he'd been looking in the plain side and that if he switched over it loomed like a peak in Darien. 'Oh God, that's even worse!'

'Ah ha. Only one thing for it then.' Stephen reached into the kitchen drawer and pulled out a fearsome skewer.

Luke jumped up from the table and backed towards the door. 'It's OK, Dad. I think I'll settle for Mum's make-up.' And he ran out of the room and dashed up-stairs to Tess's bathroom, leaving the others collapsing with laughter.

'Are you all right?' asked Tess, wiping her eyes. 'Only I thought you looked a bit fed up.'

'I was a bit,' admitted Stephen, 'but it was nothing a dose of family life couldn't sort out.'

Since the assessment was going to be so early on Monday Slouch decided to do a quick tour of the room before he left. He knew how annoyed May, the cleaner, got when he left the canvases out like this but then May and he had had a running battle for twenty years now. If he left the easels out it took her three times as long to polish the floor. So she retaliated by throwing away tubes of his most expensive cobalt violet. He must remember to put them away before she got the chance. She didn't bother with the cheaper ones, just contented herself with putting the students' sketches in the bin.

Slouch started his tour of inspection. He didn't like to spend too long on each painting, one's first impression, in his view, was usually right. This wasn't a bad bunch. Too timid, a lot of them, but that was to be expected with their first venture into oil. Others were too literal, allowing none of the sensuality of the ripe fruit to come through.

When he reached the final row he found that Stephen had deliberately turned his easel towards the wall as if to protect it. Slouch slewed it back round and considered it. To his grudging surprise it was by far the best painting in the room. The plums in their glazed ceramic bowl shone out from the dark cloth background, a difficult definition to achieve, reminding Slouch that he should have laid them out against a light background for beginners. The fruit was so real you could almost smell its ripeness and yet it retained a painterly quality that had nothing in common with a photograph.

Slouch contemplated it for a moment then strode

over to the portfolios of previous work all the students had had to leave. He opened Stephen's and turned over the drawings inside. There were about twenty in all. Other still lifes, some sketches of a young blonde woman in various poses, some flowery designs that seemed to be for some perfume or other, and two or three life drawings. All showed promise but it was the last drawing in the folder that trapped his attention and wouldn't let it go. It was of Olivia Darling. Thirty years ago she'd been the toast of the art world, the model everyone had wanted to paint and everyone had wanted to take to bed afterwards. Most had succeeded – even Slouch himself as a promising student of nineteen. He closed his eyes, remembering that night when Olivia, probably forty-five by then, battered but still beautiful, had let him make love to her and had gently shown him, without humiliating his tender pride, exactly how to give a woman pleasure.

He looked at the drawing again. He hadn't seen her for fifteen years and had heard she posed for evening classes now. Jesus, she must be over seventy! But he knew Stephen had captured her utterly. To his acute embarrassment Slouch felt a surge of tenderness and a tear of, what, recognition? well up in his eye. He'd have a word with Stephen on Monday. He owed the man an apology.

Tess hadn't even got her coat off on Monday morning before Jacqui pounced with the news that Will Kingsmill had been in looking for her and wanted to have a meeting this afternoon.

'Did he say what about?' Tess struggled out of her jacket. Why she'd worn one at all in August, she didn't know. Jacqui was far more sensibly dressed in linen shorts and top.

'As a matter of fact, he did,' Jacqui grinned infuriatingly.

'Well, what?'

'His exact words were, "I'd like a word with her about this partnership."'

Tess flopped down into her chair. 'He didn't!' Relief flooded through her. The timing was perfect. If she was made a partner her salary would go up significantly and their money worries would be wiped out.

'Why don't you give me a tenner,' said Jacqui, handing Tess her bag, 'and I'll nip over to the offie and pick up some sparkling wine. Sounds like we might be wanting to celebrate.'

'Absolutely!' Tess handed her twenty. This wasn't the moment for thinking small. 'Get two bottles!'

'Right, everyone,' Slouch announced as soon as the last student filed into the studio. 'I'm just coming round to have a quick word with each of you, but I'd like to say that the standard's pretty high.' There was a murmur of surprised pleasure from every corner. 'I'm not saying Stanley Spencer has to worry about his reputation yet, but at least there's been no painting by numbers. You're trying to paint what you feel as well as what you see. Congratulations.'

It took Slouch over an hour before he got to Stephen's row and even though he'd told himself he didn't give a stuff what Slouch thought, Stephen felt himself tensing up the nearer his tutor came. Finally he reached Stephen, who stood back to let him get closer to the painting.

'It's OK,' Slouch said. 'I had a look on Friday.' Without commenting he took Stephen by surprise by handing him a book. Stephen glanced at it. It was a memoir about the Welsh landscape painter Sir Griffiths

Williamson by his son, David Williamson, who became one of the great abstract painters of the twentieth century. Stephen looked at it in astonishment. 'I owe you a bit of an apology.' Slouch seemed entirely unabashed about admitting he'd been wrong, or about doing so in front of a room of fascinated students. 'You're a talented bloke. I like the still life. But not as much as your drawing of Olivia Darling.'

Stephen looked confused.

'The old girl at your evening class. I knew her once.'

Stephen glanced down at the gift again, its significance hitting him for the first time. Father and son, both painters.

Slouch looked at him impishly. 'I thought it might have a few resonances for you. They were both bloody brilliant in their different ways. I knew about Julius, you see. That's why I jumped to conclusions about you. I was wrong.'

Stephen opened the book. Slouch might be a cantankerous shitbag, but at least he knew how to make amends.

When Tess knocked on Will Kingsmill's door she expected an answering smile, but Will looked, if anything, a shade embarrassed as he let her in and settled her in the seat opposite his. Carefully she put her smile away. She wasn't sure she was going to need it again.

When he began to speak, Will's briskness reminded her of the matron at her school when she had some particularly unpleasant medicine to administer. 'Look, Tess, as you know we've been deliberating about creating a new partnership for some time. In fact we'd like to create several. But times are tough and we just can't afford it. We can only afford the one.' He stood up and began pacing so that she couldn't see his face. 'But unfortunately there are two outstanding candidates for it. You and Patricia Greene. The rest of the partners and I have thought about this long and hard and we've decided there's only one solution.' He stopped pacing and turned to face her. 'We're going to ask both of you to pitch for it. We want you to tell us how you see Kingsmill's in ten years' time.'

The unfairness of all this made Tess furious. So Patricia had been right after all. 'A couple of months ago you assured me the partnership was mine.'

'Under normal circumstances it would be. But these aren't normal circumstances. We're emerging from the biggest recession for thirty years. Law firms have been very hard hit.'

'You sound like a Tory about to announce a tax rise,' pointed out Tess cynically.

'Look, Tess, I'm behind you, but some of the other partners want to hear what Patricia's got to say too. The next ten years are going to be crucial for us and we have to make the right choice of partner.'

'And when will this momentous event take place?'

Will Kingsmill looked relieved. 'I knew you'd see the sense in it. Mid-September, when everyone's re-laxed after their holidays. That gives you five weeks.'

Five weeks, three of which were supposed to be spent relaxing on the beaches of Cork. Great.

'I'm sure the best person will prevail. Look on the bright side. At least you're both women.'

Feeling anything but sisterly at this patronizing com-ment Tess stumped back to her office. Jacqui was waiting with the sparkling wine and two glasses. She took one look at Tess's face and put the bottle down. 'What happened?'

'He didn't offer it to me. I've got to pitch for it, for God's sake, like bloody Portia in *The Merchant of Venice*. Against poxy Patricia Greene.'

'Oh Tess, so that's why she's been snooping round the accounts department.'

Tess had forgotten all about that. She suddenly felt overwhelmingly angry with Patricia. 'She's got a bloody nerve. We'll have to show her, won't we?' Tess pointed the cork of the fizzy wine at a photograph of Kingsmill's staff outing. Patricia was prominent in the front. The cork flew through the air, hitting her with satisfying accuracy.

But by the time she got home Tess was feeling less combative. She had nothing against taking on rich clients. She had her fair share herself. But she hadn't studied law for five years simply to help the well-heeled. There were plenty of lawyers who wanted to do that. It was vital the disadvantaged got good lawyers too. Tess sighed. She might have right on her side, but Patricia would have economics. And in these tough times economics often won. Her mood wasn't improved by falling over three blank canvases Stephen had just painted white to start work on, and ending up with paint on her suit. She stood in the hall swearing.

Stephen appeared, paint-smeared and eager, his hair pushed off his face in a peak like Tintin, brimming with excitement at seeing her and being able to tell her about Slouch's change of heart.

'Tess, love, I'm sorry, let me get you some turps.' He dashed off and returned to kneel at her feet, cleaning the white paint from her hem. As he did so a ludicrous tear, half anger, half discouragement, slid down her face.

'Tessie, what's the matter?'

To her fury and embarrassment another tear followed it. 'Just work. Will Kingsmill called me in today to talk about the partnership. I thought he was going to tell me it was mine. But he didn't.'

Stephen stood up and took her in his arms. 'So you're not getting it after all?'

'It's not as simple as that. I've got to pitch for it. Against Patricia Greene.'

'But that's all right!' He squeezed her encouragingly. 'You'll knock the socks off her. You're a terrific lawyer, and a brilliant advocate. You really care about your clients. You'll see Patricia Greene off in no time! Come on: remember the motto, don't get sad, get even! Let me tell you a joke. Why is Zsa Zsa Gabor such a good housekeeper?'

'I don't know. Why is Zsa Zsa Gabor such a good housekeeper?'

'Because every time she gets divorced she gets to keep the house.'

Tess laughed out loud at the delicious childishness of Stephen's joke and they hugged each other.

'Luke told me that one. Come on, he's been in the bathroom measuring his spot for an hour and Ellie's doing so-called homework. Inge'll look after them. Let's get away while the going's good and share a pizza. And don't say we can't afford it.'

Tess felt the happiness of family life lap around her. 'Tell you what! Let's push the boat out and have one each.'

'Congratulations, Jo, you've done it again.'

Josephine put down the bottle of wine she was opening. 'Done what again?'

Slouch breathed in the jasmine growing in profusion from a container on the roof garden of Josephine's London pied à terre. Below him Covent Garden bustled with office workers going home and theatre-goers just arriving. All the activity made Slouch feel at peace with the world. 'Picked another winner in Stephen Gilfillan. He'd go far even without the name. Having it certainly won't do him any harm.'

Josephine felt a small thrill of satisfaction. Slouch was right. She did have a good eye. She eased her way past the stephanotis and honeysuckle that scented her very own perfumed garden and handed him a glass of wine.

'How's he doing?'

'Fine. He passed the ego-breaking week with flying colours.'

'Slouch, why do that to people?'

'Because painting's a rough business. You need a strong ego to survive. I just test them a little to put them on their mettle.'

'You need to watch it with Stephen. I get the impression he's rather vulnerable at the moment.'

'Not your usual style then?' Slouch touched his glass to hers.

'Look,' Josephine said quickly, 'I think you've got the wrong idea about Stephen and me.'

'Ah.' Slouch's lips twitched maddeningly. 'I see. Your interest in him is simply altruistic.'

'Come on, Slouch, I help plenty of painters. You know that.'

'Yes, but they aren't all as attractive as Stephen Gilfillan, are they?'

Josephine's eyes narrowed. Really, Slouch could be very irritating sometimes. 'Tell me,' she said, firmly wrenching the subject on to a different track, 'who do you reckon will make the shortlist for the Turner Prize?'

After Slouch had gone Josephine had a long cooling

shower. She hated London in August. The nights were airless and heavy and she missed the river breezes that cooled her bedroom in Winchester.

As she got out and reached for a towel she felt another wave of satisfaction. She'd been the one who'd recognized the passion for painting latent in Stephen Gilfillan. She'd known who he was the moment she'd seen him, and what he was fighting against. His dull lawyer wife would probably have been quite happy if he'd gone on doing Flake commercials for ever as long as he pulled in the salary. She clearly had no idea of Stephen's depths. Artistically, Josephine sensed, all he needed was some careful nurturing. And in a month's time he'd be coming to work for her at Richmond & Quinn, so she would make sure he got it.

She stood in front of the steamy mirror drying herself. Then she let the towel drop and took a long look at her body. She smiled. Maybe one day she'd sit for him. Watching herself in the steam-streaked mirror she slowly put a hand to her breast and started stroking it. Then, as though the steam had suddenly cleared she snapped back into reality. Stephen Gilfillan was married to someone else and had a family. Soon he would be an employee. This was purely a business proposition. What the hell had she been thinking of?

CHAPTER FOURTEEN

Slouch Heyward peered over Stephen's shoulder and watched as he built up the colour in the landscape he was painting. It was unfinished as yet and had many of the hallmarks of the beginner about it. But something about it was giving Slouch an unfamiliar jolt of excitement. Its originality. The still life had been accomplished, but it was hard to stamp an individual imprint on a still life. This was different. And it wasn't simply the result of craft or technique. There was pure feeling in this painting.

'Not bad, Stephen, not bad at all. We might even make a painter out of you yet. *If* you don't get too cocky.'

Stephen smiled. 'Not much danger of that with you around. Tell you what.' A thought had just occurred to him. 'Can I take it home and show Tess? I'd like her to see how I'm getting on. I could probably finish it over the weekend.'

This wasn't the kind of request Slouch was used to. On the other hand he didn't see why not. 'OK,' he nodded, 'in fact I'll stand you a cab as far as the Chelsea Arts Club. Provided you buy me a drink. You can walk from there.'

Although he only lived a mile away down the King's Road, Stephen had never been to the Arts Club and found himself enchanted by its faded, raffish charm. He half expected to see Olivia Darling sitting in one corner, puffing at her untipped Gauloise and conning drinks from the yuppies who had begun to infiltrate the place.

Slouch led him through the big dining room. Every inch of its dark-green walls was packed with paintings from the nineteenth and early twentieth century. Above the large communal dining table a striking picture caught his eye. This one was earlier, done in the early nineteenth century perhaps, of a young woman, pale as milk, who appeared to be offering her naked body to a richly clad man, who was refusing it. Slouch smiled. 'They call that one "The Rent Collector". Typical capitalist, eh? Can't see the beauty. All he wants is his dosh.'

Slouch led him on out into the garden, a secret half-acre surrounded by high walls, rose-scented, with an arbour at one end hiding a single bench. Sitting at a white table in the middle of the lawn, a striking man in a vast black greatcoat, topped with a battered black felt hat, held court.

'Who's that?' Stephen whispered. 'He has to be a painter.'

'Oh, him.' Slouch sipped his Bushmills whiskey disdainfully. 'Actually he's a bookie.'

An hour or so later Stephen realized he ought to go. He picked up his painting and headed out to look for a cab just as the oppressiveness that had hung round all day began to turn itself into a thunderstorm. Worried about his picture he slipped back in and asked the friendly receptionist if he could leave it in the hall for a moment while he searched for a cab. He couldn't risk walking home with it in this weather.

Back in Old Church Street the rain began to bounce off the pavements. After five minutes of being soaked Stephen finally spied a cab and hailed it. In another minute every taxi in London would be taken. He rushed back into the club to find the greatcoated bookie holding his picture up to the light. 'What's your name?' demanded the man without the slightest attempt at apology.

Stephen, slightly annoyed because he feared the cab would abandon him, told him.

The old man looked up briefly as though Stephen had just cracked a very funny joke. 'Nice painting.' He put it down again. 'I'll look out for you.' He then swept out of the door Stephen was holding open and into Stephen's waiting cab.

Furious, Stephen realized it was too late to stop him as well as pick up the painting. He went back in and smiled resignedly at the receptionist.

'Well,' she congratulated him, 'you should be flattered. He doesn't often say he likes things. Thinks most painters are complete crap, as a matter of fact.'

Stephen looked confused. 'Who is he then?'

'I thought everyone knew *him*.' The girl seemed genuinely astonished. 'That's Ben Grainston.' Stephen forgot the rain and his irritation at losing his cab. Ben Grainston was the second most famous artist in Britain. After Julius Gilfillan.

It wasn't often that Tess took her mother's advice but, just for once, today she was doing so. As she sorted out her desk to apply herself to the challenge of what Kingsmill's should be doing in ten years' time, she counted her blessings. And, smiling ignobly, decided she had a lot more of them than Patricia Greene did.

She had just sat down, blank page in front of her, pen in hand, to plan her pitch when the phone went.

'I'm in love, I'm in love, I'm in love,' warbled an off-key voice, 'I'm in love, I'm in love with –'

'Thank you very much, Philomena,' Tess interrupted, 'and if I were you I'd stick to the day job.'

Phil pretended to be wounded. 'I just thought you

should be the first to know, but if you aren't interested . . .'

'Of course I'm interested, so who's the lucky man?'

'Ah ha. That I can't tell you. Yet.' Phil sounded infuriatingly smug.

This was certainly a first. Discretion came as easily to Phil as economizing did to Ivana Trump. For a dreadful moment it crossed her mind that it might be Terry Worth – after all, he had sent her roses. But Terry wasn't Phil's type. And besides, surely she wouldn't be that stupid.

'Just suffice it to say,' Phil simpered, 'that he's gorgeous. Sweet, kind, considerate; yet strong, independent, a real man . . .'

Tess giggled. 'You make him sound like Arnold Schwarzenegger.'

'Tess, you're not taking this seriously.'

'Sorry,' apologized Tess. 'He sounds divine. I hope you'll be very happy and that when you take his bandages off I'll be the first to meet him.'

'It won't be long, I promise. I just thought I'd keep the tender flower of our relationship out of the cruel beam of my friends' scrutiny just a little longer.'

'Very wise.' Tess wondered what was wrong with this one that Phil was hiding him away so thoroughly. No doubt time would tell. She said goodbye to Phil, glancing down at her watch. Damn. It was almost six o'clock. That had put paid to the only half-hour she'd managed to carve out of her day to think about the pitch. Now she'd have to try and do it later at home.

Her briefcase was half packed when Jacqui put her head round the door.

'Sorry to do this to you, Tess, but there's a lady out here' – she gestured with her head and Tess glimpsed a white-haired woman sitting in the waiting area – 'who says she's come all the way down from Manchester to look for a lawyer.'

Tess opened her mouth to protest that she couldn't possibly take on a new client just at the moment, that she was up to her ears in work, had to prepare her partnership pitch, and on top of that was about to go on holiday to Cork for three weeks when she noticed that Jacqui was struggling to keep a straight face.

'And?' she prompted.

'And she met your mother on the train,' replied Jacqui, trying to avoid Tess's eye, 'and your mother said she wasn't to settle for anyone else. She was to come straight to London and tell you your mother said you had to help her. That you would be just the lawyer she needed. So she did.'

Tess raised her eyes to heaven. She could just picture the scene now. How typical of her mother. Dymphna judged all train journeys by the quality of conversation she struck up with total strangers. While Tess liked to lurk behind a novel or a copy of *Marie-Claire*, a successful journey in her mother's book was one where her copy of *Woman's Realm* remained unopened. Like a gossip columnist at a society bash, she could cast her eyes over an entire carriage and pinpoint the two or three passengers who would happily bare their souls after five minutes' acquaintance.

No doubt the lady sitting in their waiting room had a troublesome neighbour on her posh estate, or perhaps a financial advisor who'd been dipping into the unit trusts. Anyway it was highly unlikely to be in Tess's field. Probably all she'd have to do was listen and point her in the direction of someone more appropriate.

Tess put down her briefcase. 'I suppose you'd better show her in. And Jacqui?'

'Yes, Tess?'

'Do try and stop sniggering.'

Jacqui ushered in the lady from the waiting room. 'Tess, this is Mrs Eileen McDonald.'

Tess stood up to shake hands. She put the woman at around sixty, smartly dressed in a silky aquamarine frock with a flowery hat more suited to the Henley Regatta than a visit to a solicitor. But as she began to talk to Tess, Tess noticed some giveaway details. Her clothes, though of good quality, were slightly shabby and in need of dry cleaning, her shoes hadn't seen a cobbler in a long time, and her handbag – one of those hideous little boxes so beloved of the Queen – revealed a split lining when she opened it to get out some papers. Mrs McDonald clearly wasn't wealthy, but was trying to keep up appearances.

As she sat and listened Tess heard a story that she'd been told a dozen times. Married to the same man for thirty years, with four children now grown up, her husband had upped and run off with a much younger woman and was in the process of divorcing her. Against her will.

'But since he found he'd have to wait two years he's asking me to divorce *him* on the grounds of adultery so that he can marry this woman now. But as I explained to him, I don't want to get divorced at all. And I have a standing in the community to think of. If I accuse him of adultery it'll be round the bridge club in ten minutes! I said why can't he accuse himself of adultery, but he says that's not possible. *I* have to do it. Is that really the case?'

Tess nodded. 'Yes, for adultery I'm afraid it is. But perhaps you could refuse to consent unless he agrees to a decent financial settlement.'

178

'You don't know my husband,' Eileen said grimly. 'He's already closed down the joint account, taken all the money out of the building society, and moved his business assets into God knows how many bank accounts in Geneva. He'd agree in principle then go back on it. He's a ruthless man, Miss Brien. Do you know how much he's left me to live on? Two hundred and forty pounds a year.'

Tess felt herself getting angrier and angrier at the levels to which some men would stoop when they wanted to get out of a marriage.

'And now' – Eileen's voice rose in indignation – 'he's taken on a smart new lawyer.' She reached in her bag and pulled out a letter. 'His name's Leonard Savoury. Have you ever heard of him?'

Tess tried not to wince. Leonard Savoury was the nastiest and most successful divorce lawyer in London.

'Do you know the man? Leonard Unsavoury would be a more appropriate name after the call I received from him yesterday.'

Tess was shocked. After all the man was a professional. 'What did he say, Mrs McDonald?'

'That since I would have to be on legal aid there was no chance I'd get a decent lawyer so I might as well give in now.'

Tess felt her temper rising unstoppably. How dare Savoury threaten an elderly woman in such a vulnerable position like that? And the worst thing of course was that it was true. On legal aid she could easily end up with someone inept or inexperienced.

Unless Tess took on the case.

Tess closed her eyes for a second. With Leonard Savoury on the other side this case could be a legal nightmare. The husband clearly had access to a lot of money and his wife had none. She could fight the good fight and still lose. And Kingsmill's would lose too. It would never be economical for them to take the case. And at this moment of all moments when Patricia was watching her every move.

She'd have to refuse.

And yet looking at the woman sitting opposite her, her seams fraying from lack of money, trying to keep her head above water while her husband was probably cruising around the Mediterranean, Tess couldn't rationalize her anger away. Most women got such a bad deal from divorce.

And yet to take the case would probably be professional suicide. What the hell was she going to do?

Much as it went against the grain Tess decided this was one occasion where she had to let rationality rule the day. 'Look, Mrs McDonald, I very much sympathize with your position, believe me –'

'It was so wonderful when your mother suggested you,' interrupted Mrs McDonald, 'a real life-saver. She said you always stick up for the underdog, always have, even when you were at school.' Her eyes softened. 'She's very proud of you, you know.'

Tess felt her logic drain away. She'd never had the feeling her mother was proud of her. All she'd ever sensed was her mother's unspoken criticism of her for leaving Liverpool. The image of her mother, busy and bustling in her no-frills council house, the hub of her little community, always concerned with the nitty gritty of life, with grandchildren and the wayward husbands of her other four daughters, suddenly filled Tess with tenderness and even regret. It was such a long time since she'd seen her.

And she knew, partnership or no partnership, she couldn't let her mother down.

'All right then, Mrs McDonald, I'll represent you.'

Mrs McDonald reached out a slightly grubby grey glove. 'I knew you would the moment I saw you!' She shook Tess's hand firmly, a lock of white hair escaping from its flowery hat. 'I'm an excellent judge of character. I knew you were a fighter.'

She stood up, Boadicea in Tricel. 'Let's show the bastards, shall we? They can't push us around just because we're women!' And as she strode towards the door, looking quite different from the droopy creature who'd come in fifteen minutes earlier, she added, 'By the way, please call me Eileen.'

Tess stood up too, laughing delightedly. She could see why her mother had warmed to Eileen McDonald. Maybe she'd enjoy the case after all.

Tess had hardly got inside the front door when Stephen jumped on her, confiscated her briefcase, and led her into the sitting room where Ellie, Luke and Inge were already sitting in a polite row ranged in front of an easel. On the easel was a painting draped in teatowels advertising the joys of EuroDisney, on whose account Stephen had briefly worked.

With a flourish Stephen removed the teatowels to reveal his landscape. 'OK, everyone. What do you think?'

'Oh, Dad, it's fabulous!' cried Ellie. 'The depth of colour's extraordinary. How did you do that?'

'Wet into wet. I just built it up gradually.'

Tess looked at her daughter, acutely aware that art was another world to her, one she knew frighteningly little about, far less than Ellie, certainly. At home in Liverpool art was a subject you did at school and usually dropped as soon as possible in favour of something more sensible. It definitely wasn't something people did for a living.

'It's great, Dad, maybe you'll even sell it!!' Luke agreed. 'Then I can have that new computer.'

'It is magnificent, Stephen.' Inge gazed at it reverently as though Stephen had just revealed another side to his already Renaissance nature.

'Tess?' he prompted eagerly. 'What do you think of it?'

'It's stunning, love,' replied Tess, uncomfortably aware that she had neither the instincts nor the language to express herself as Ellie had. 'Congratulations!'

She kissed him, obscurely aware that he'd been expecting something more from her. And that she had somehow let him down.

With the heat of a London August sweltering outside, Tess was deeply relieved that she and the children were decamping to Cork at the end of the week, even if she would have to spend some of the time while they were there preparing for her pitch. Three whole weeks away from marriage breakdowns and infidelity! No more clients weeping on her shoulder at the perfidy of husbands or the profligacy of wives. Bliss! It was only when she stopped doing it that Tess realized quite how emotionally exhausting her job was. Her only sadness was that she'd have to wait two whole weeks before Stephen could join them. But at least now he seemed to be enjoying his course. And clearly it was going very well. She just hoped she would be able to contain herself and not tell Julius.

'Have you got everything you need? Bikinis? Sweaters? Suncream? Wellies?'

Tess laughed at Stephen's run-down of the essentials

for an Irish summer holiday. Maybe it was because they had to be prepared for all weathers that they had *quite* so much luggage.

'I wouldn't mind something to read,' admitted Tess, 'to take my mind off all those lonely husbandless nights.'

They made their way to the bookstall and Stephen selected a copy of *The Lovers' Almanac*, complete with sticker promising it contained 'Sexually Explicit Material'.

'No thanks.' Tess put it firmly back on the shelf, much to Luke's disappointment, and picked up a magazine. A waft of disgustingly synthetic perfume drifted up from one of the scratch-'n-sniff scent ads that were all the rage now.

'I don't suppose you've got any odourless ones?' she asked the youth stacking piles of *Penthouse* on the top shelf.

'Nah. They all pong like cats' pee now. Enough to put you off scent for ever, innit?'

Over his left shoulder Tess caught sight of a glossy hardback entitled *Understanding Art*. That was more like it, but she felt a slight shudder of embarrassment about buying it in front of Ellie and Stephen. Fortunately Luke announced he wanted a Coke and the others decided to go with him.

Tess picked the book up. Nearly twenty quid. She quickly wrote a cheque only to find Ellie leaning over her shoulder.

'Really, Mum, why don't you just buy the *Bluffers' Guide* and be done with it?'

There was no point in trying to explain that she felt genuinely inadequate where art was concerned. Teenagers liked to tell you their problems, but they didn't expect you to have any of your own.

She shoved the book into her bag just as Stephen and Luke reappeared.

'Have you remembered to take that very expensive camera Father bought you?' Stephen quizzed Ellie, handing over four colour films. Ellie nodded. 'Good. Because you're official photographer and I want lots of shots of you all having fun. And take one of Mum, will you' – he winked at Tess – 'lying in the shells on Cowrie Beach.'

'Come on, you lot,' Tess said, ignoring Stephen's hand stroking her bottom in a most politically incorrect manner, 'they're calling our flight.'

As soon as they rose above cloud level the heaviness in the atmosphere lifted and Ireland revealed itself beneath them in a pristine blue sky. Ellie kept predicting that it would cloud over and grey set in by the time they landed, but it didn't.

Stella, who loathed driving, was waiting for them at Cork airport in a taxi and by the end of the afternoon Luke, fishing net in hand, was running down the beach for the first swim of his holiday. Ellie, whose only concession to country living was to remove the laces from her Doc Martens, sashayed after him in dark glasses and a black Lycra swimsuit, disappointed that her only audience was her own mother and a couple of heron gulls.

To Tess it was the closest she could imagine to heaven. She spread her towel on a small stretch of sand, surrounded by rocks and dunes, and sighed with happiness.

The weather lasted all that week and the next. They fell into a deeply relaxing routine of early swim, huge breakfast, sunbathing or in Luke's case rockpooling, a glass of very good champagne before lunch which

Julius opened to annoy Stella, rest, swim, more sun-bathing, drinks, dinner. Even Ellie was lulled by the rhythm of this until, just at the moment Tess could see the clouds of teenage boredom gathering, another invitation from Slane Castle arrived. This time actually to help organize a concert in three days' time. Ellie was ecstatic.

Julius proved to be the perfect host, simply getting on with his busy life but always pleased to see them when they wandered back into his consciousness. Stella remained, as ever, more remote with Tess, but after eighteen years of marriage to her son, Tess accepted this as absolutely natural. The only time any real warmth filtered through from Stella was when she was with Ellie.

Tess could hardly believe that ten days had already passed. She lay in her favourite place among the dunes, hidden from view, listening to a skylark high above her dipping up and down over the cornfields that stretched right down to the sea. And it struck her that Ireland in August with the sun blazing down was like nowhere else on earth. Unlike Spain or Greece it kept its softness. Accustomed to rain, people opened like flowers when the sun shone. Tess could feel it happening to herself.

There was only one shadow on the horizon and that was Julius and Stella's obvious disappointment that Stephen hadn't come. Unable to tell the truth, Tess knew her excuses about business commitments sounded slippery. They both thought he simply didn't want to be there and, more than once, when she saw the hurt in their eyes, Tess found herself on the brink of telling the truth. But just in time she'd pulled back. Stephen had to tell them in his own way.

And he'd be here soon. She thought of his long lean

body that day on Cowrie Beach and felt the sudden tightening of desire. A hoyden's vision came to her, not at all in keeping with Ireland's holy ground, of all the things she'd like to do to him, and even more, of what he might do to her. She had to roll on to her front and bury her face in the sand to stop the sudden hunger for him. How different from at home when sex became too much a part of their domestic routine, an item on their 'Things To Do' list sandwiched somewhere between the school run and the supermarket.

Smiling secretly Tess willed herself to go back to the ordered world of Jane Austen who seemed serenely untroubled by such base thoughts.

Usually Phil hated London in August and couldn't wait to jet off to some trendy sunspot. But this year it was different. London had a magic that made the dirty streets, the crowded tubes, the sweating tourists suddenly invisible to her. She saw only the good things. The restaurants you could suddenly get a table in since London, unlike Paris or Rome, didn't shut up shop and disappear to the seaside in August; the bright geraniums tumbling out of every window box; the empty taxis who would screech to a stop when you lifted so much as a finger instead of sailing by.

Since so many of her clients were away Phil took to bunking off mid-afternoon for picnics at Cookham on the banks of the Thames, or long lunches at the Waterside Inn, even a visit to Hampton Court, somewhere she'd never actually set eyes on even though she'd lived in London for more than twenty years.

And all because of Terry Worth.

With Hattie and Dan safely installed at their grandparents' and his children away with Angela, they had two whole weeks of freedom and they were spending every waking moment together they could.

Not to mention the nights. Phil lightly touched his face next to hers on the pillow. Its battered lived-in quality looked out of place on the white lace and she loved him for it. Until meeting him she'd firmly believed – and life had done nothing to disabuse her – that all men were bastards. But not Terry. He was so bloody *nice*! And Phil had never known that men could be nice without being weak or wimpish. The proof was lying next to her.

Grinning, as though he'd been aware of her gaze and of her thoughts, Terry's arm reached out to pull her to him.

For one moment she resisted. Holding him at arm's length she looked into his eyes. 'Go on' – her voice was serious with only a hint of teasing – 'tell me the catch. There has to be a catch. Life just isn't like this.'

Terry pulled away the sheet and stroked her soft body. 'Maybe it will be, now that you've met me.'

Slouch Heyward stood in the empty studio of the Bryant School of Art engaged in what could only be described as soul-searching. This was not an activity to which Slouch was accustomed. Nor did he want to become so. It was uncomfortable, had kept him awake last night, and generally disturbed the ebb and flow of his natural cynicism. The object of his soul-searching was Stephen Gilfillan. There were only three days left before the end of the course and he had invited Stephen to the Chelsea Arts Club in half an hour's time to try and talk him out of becoming a design consultant and into being a full-time painter. He had no idea how Stephen would react.

When Stephen arrived, Slouch fixed him with what

he hoped was a candid and unbiased expression. 'Don't go and work for Jo. You're a painter, for Christ's sake! She was the same. She was one of my best bloody students and she blew it all to start some sodding scent company.'

'And become a millionairess,' pointed out Stephen wryly. But he was fascinated all the same. 'I didn't know she'd studied art. I suppose that's why she's still so interested.'

Slouch eyed his whiskey sentimentally. 'You should have seen her. Like something out of *Cider with Rosie*. Just up from Devon, naïve as hell, no idea about theory. But she knew what she wanted to do and no one was going to stop her. Of course she was always too hard on herself, never quite happy with what she achieved.' Slouch's voice rang with a rare enthusiasm. 'So in her final year she met Hugo Richmond and he talked her into this scent shop idea.' Clearly, despite Richmond & Quinn's worldwide success, Slouch still found this decision hard to fathom. 'She missed her own degree show to go to some Godforsaken trade fair! Despite what she thought she'd have been the star of her year, press write-ups, gallery offers, the lot! But she was off in Lille talking about packaging. Lille!' This seemed to Slouch the ultimate insult. 'It's the arsehole of the world!'

'What kind of painter was she?' Stephen wasn't sure he could guess. Would Josephine have been drawn to figurative painting, as he was, or sophisticated abstracts?

'A colourist. Your stuff reminds me of hers now and then. She loved Matisse. And this was twenty years ago before all that stuff came back in. She was an original all right.'

Stephen was riveted. He'd had no idea they had so

much in common. He couldn't wait to talk to her about it.

Slouch stared up from his empty glass at Stephen accusingly. 'And now you're doing the same bloody thing. Don't do it, Stephen. Your future's as bright as hers was. They don't come along often, gifts like yours. Believe me, I see enough of the dross. Look . . .' Slouch hesitated as though he was about to say something that stuck in his throat. 'Why don't you talk to your old man? Julius'd agree with me.'

To Slouch's surprise Stephen stiffened and looked away. So that was the way it was. Not surprising, maybe. There wasn't always room for two talents in one family.

But Stephen realized there was no point losing his rag; Slouch meant things for the best. 'Slouch, I can't afford just to be a painter. I need to earn.'

'Look, sunshine, you've got to learn what matters in this life. You know what I wanted when I was twenty-one? A German car and a rich girlfriend.' He gestured to the barman for another round. 'And do you know what I've ended up with? A German girlfriend and a bicycle.' He poked a finger at Stephen. 'There's more important things in life than money. Money's all in the mind.'

Stephen laughed and drank the last of his wine. He had to get back home if he was going to finish the painting he was working on before going to Ireland. 'You obviously haven't heard of children. By the way, there's one other thing that fascinates me. What exactly is Jo's relationship with Hugo Richmond?'

Slouch, suddenly alert, looked at him foxily. 'Now why, Modigliani me old mate, would you want to know that?'

'Because I'm going to be working with them both,' Stephen said tartly.

'I see,' nodded Slouch. 'He's her business partner. He used to be more but Josephine changed her mind. Of course Hugo wants to play the old tune, but Josephine won't have it. She keeps him hanging on, though. Poor old Hugo, I often wonder if she lets him have a little sniff now and then just to keep him interested. He's very useful to her.'

'Poor old Hugo.'

'Rich old Hugo,' corrected Slouch. 'And before you go, mine's a Bushmills.'

Stephen went to get Slouch a final drink. The man could con a whiskey out of a temperance tea party, but he liked him.

From the darkness of his corner Slouch studied Stephen. He clearly wasn't going to be dissuaded. Slouch would just have to try Jo. The thought wasn't encouraging. Josephine didn't like interference in her life. She'd always played things exactly as she wanted them and anyone, Hugo included, who tried to get her to change her mind got short shrift. Still – he grinned his thanks as Stephen reappeared with his drink – he owed it to himself, and to Stephen, to have a go.

The first thing that hit Stephen when he opened the front door was the absolute total silence. And he knew that this kind of silence could only exist in a house that usually echoed with the sounds of a family. Yet he didn't feel lonely. In fact, he noted guiltily, there was a kind of freedom in being without them which, much as he loved his family, he couldn't help relishing. If he wanted to he could work all night.

Suddenly hungry, he made a sandwich and took half a bottle of whisky up to the room he was using as a temporary studio. He poured a couple of fingers into the nearest receptacle he could find without going downstairs again – a red tooth mug – and snapped a Delius tape into Luke's ghettoblaster. Then he started to paint.

As usual once he was painting Stephen lost all sense of time. The only way he could calculate it was by the declining level in the whisky bottle. Looking at that he reckoned it had to be well after midnight.

Somewhere between one and two there was a knock at the door. Stephen jumped. Then he remembered Inge. Of course, she was still here. Maybe she was concerned about the light being on or had decided to bring him a cup of cocoa. He opened the door. He was right. It was Inge.

She was standing outside the door with the Mona Lisa smile on her face he'd seen her perfecting. She carried a tray with two glasses of wine. And she was absolutely naked.

CHAPTER FIFTEEN

For a split second Stephen was lost for words. Then, without meaning to be unfair, he burst out laughing. It reminded him so precisely of a scene in an ancient X-rated film he'd been to see as a schoolboy, starring, if he remembered correctly, 'Lottie Tarp, the Danish pastry'.

'I'm sorry, Inge,' he apologized, seeing her anguished expression, 'it's just that you gave me a bit of a shock. You know how repressed we English are. And you see, well, I'm really very happy with Tess.'

Still standing at the door Inge burst into tears. Stephen gently took the tray from her and searched for something she could put on. The only thing to hand was one of Luke's old T-shirts featuring Freddy Krueger promising that he would be back. Stephen helped her to put it on.

'And now I must leave the family,' wailed Inge, her breasts wobbling under Freddy's bloodstained fingers.

'Of course you mustn't,' Stephen reassured her. 'We'd all be devastated if you left. Tess says you're the best au pair we've ever had.' It struck him that if Tess ever found out about this she might be forced to revise her opinion. 'And Luke would never recover. Let's forget it ever happened, shall we?'

'Oh, thank you, Stephen!' Inge grabbed his hand and kissed it fervently. 'And now I go and watch the lonely Sky TV.' Pulling herself up to her full statuesque height she padded off back to her room.

Stephen leaned on his easel and took a last swig of the whisky. He'd had enough emotion for one night.

Without even remembering to clean his brushes he stumbled up to their room where he stretched out on the bed and went to sleep fully clothed. And only partly for protection.

Tess woke up earlier than usual. She wanted to wash her hair and get ready for Stephen's arrival this afternoon. She jumped out of bed and threw open the curtains. It was another glorious day. Stripping off her nightdress she glanced at herself in the mirror. Her milky-white skin had tanned lightly and glowed with relaxed healthiness. Her hair was longer than usual, with a gypsyish look she rather liked. Tess Brien, efficient London lawyer, had been replaced, at least for the moment, by a genuine Irish Theresa.

She reached for the swimsuit lying on the chair where she'd flung it last night. The sea would be sunlit and cold and she would have it all to herself. Tomorrow Stephen could join her for her early morning ritual. She glanced at the four-poster bed with its lacy confection of sheets and smiled.

Maybe they'd have a lie-in instead.

Round about mid-morning Stephen drifted back into consciousness and looked down at himself in surprise. He was fully clothed and his head hurt like hell. And then it all started piecing itself painfully together. Slouch. Mixing the grape and the grain. Inge naked. From nowhere an intense feeling of panic gripped him. He was due to fly to Ireland this afternoon and he would finally have to tell his father about the painting.

And what would his reaction be? Julius would see it as a challenge, he was certain of that. His father was the most competitive man Stephen had ever met. Not about obvious things like exam results or sports, but about talents. As soon as Stephen had learned chess Julius had always made a point of beating him. The concept of letting his son win was entirely alien to him. And when Stephen had started the piano, Julius decided to have lessons from the same teacher. It had even stretched to Stephen's girlfriends. No matter how painful for Stephen, Julius had never been able to resist flirting with them.

That had been one of the reasons Stephen had loved Tess so. The very first time he'd brought her home Julius had virtually made a pass at her. But Tess came from a background where parents were parents, and the idea of a friend's father coming on to you was unthinkable. So she pretended nothing had happened and had persisted in referring to him respectfully as Mr Gilfillan no matter how many times he said, Call me Julius. Stephen could have kissed her.

He closed his eyes and imagined the look of scorn and disbelief that would cross Julius's face when Stephen told him his new ambition. Or maybe something worse. A kind of sympathetic humouring.

And he realized he couldn't face it. Not yet. Not until he was more confident of his talent. His abilities were still raw enough to fade in the face of his father's criticism. And he couldn't afford that. Not until he had fully discovered himself as a painter.

But how would Tess react? He knew she'd be disappointed and so would Ellie and Luke. But he'd make it up to them. And he was sure that when he really explained it to her, Tess would understand that coming to Ireland was something he just couldn't do at the moment.

'Josephine? How are you, lovey?' Slouch had already

phoned Winchester and been told she was still in town after a late meeting last night. 'Fancy a bite in a low-rent dive before you head off for Surrey?'

'Winchester is not in Surrey,' Josephine corrected him crisply, 'it's in Hampshire.'

'Silly me. I'm lost outside Soho. Anyway, remember what Uncle Aldous Huxley said. Better to be taken in adultery than in provincialism. I'll save you from it for another hour or two. How about it? My treat.'

Josephine, who'd been on the point of heading off, was intrigued. In all the years of their acquaintance she couldn't remember Slouch offering to pay for anything 'OK. When and where?'

'The Café Franca, just off Gower Street, halfway down. An hour suit you?'

'Fine.'

Slouch was already sitting behind a large grappa by the time Josephine parked her Mercedes outside the unassuming exterior. The Café Franca was one of those establishments that had acquired a reputation for being trendy, thanks to the students from the Bryant, despite having done nothing to change its image or its food since VE Day. However, to Slouch it had one overriding virtue. It was cheap.

Josephine took one look at it and shuddered. She could already picture the stodgy lasagne and glutinous carbonara. They probably didn't even know what pesto was. Without even going in she rapped on the window and signalled to Slouch.

Resignedly, but without surprise, Slouch got up.

Ten minutes later, settled amongst elegant shoppers and yuppie families taking their ghastly offspring to Baby Gap, Slouch and Josephine were handed the menu in Vitti, this year's trendy new Italian discovery. Slouch blenched when he saw the prices and hoped his one credit card had enough in it to avoid embarrassment.

They ordered their meal and Josephine eyed him over her wine glass with the direct stare that made her employees wish they could run for the door. 'So, what's all this about?'

Slouch decided this was as good a moment as any to plunge into the icy waters of her disapproval. 'What this is about is me trying to talk you out of employing Stephen Gilfillan as your design consultant and letting him become a painter full time.' Slouch returned her gaze unwaveringly. 'The man's got real potential. He's the best student I've had since you.'

'I'm glad to hear it.' Josephine dipped some focaccia bread into the scented olive oil the waiter had just brought. 'I wouldn't want to take on anyone mediocre. Look, it's only for six months or so. And Stephen needs the money. After that he can go and live in Polynesia or join an artistic community in St Ives for all I care. For God's sake, what do you expect me to do? The man starts with us next week and this launch is vital to our business.'

'And what if he turns out to be useful to you? Will you still let him go after six months?'

'Slouch, we've been friends for a long time but I don't like interference in the way I run my business.'

Slouch stared gloomily at the thin strips of pink liver that had just arrived on his plate, garnished with a slab of tomato-flavoured polenta. The lunch was proving a fiasco, as he'd known it would.

The rest of the meal passed in relative silence until Jo finally called for the bill and got out her gold card to settle it. Grandly, as though he bought seventy-quid lunches every day of the week, Slouch gestured her to put it away. And just in case his credit card didn't cover it he began to count out the total in grubby fivers. Josephine smiled and gathered up her belongings, grateful that at least the Bryant didn't give luncheon vouchers.

'So what's that layabout son of mine planning to do with his life?' Julius pulled up the knees of his ancient white trousers and sat down on a dry rock. 'Is he going to get a proper job one of these days or not?'

Tess stopped skipping stones across the calm water and turned to him. Her instincts told her that this was the moment to admit the truth. Knowing Julius, he wouldn't have asked unless he was already suspicious that he wasn't being given the whole story. And she couldn't lie again. Surely if she explained things – maybe as Stephen couldn't – she could prepare the ground for some kind of rapprochement between the two of them.

She sat down next to him running sand between her toes, searching for the right words. 'Julius, I'm afraid we haven't been entirely honest with you.' Julius nodded as though he'd suspected as much. 'The real reason Stephen couldn't come here with me was nothing to do with business. It's because he's been at the Bryant Summer School.'

She glanced at her father-in-law nervously, waiting for the reaction she knew Stephen was expecting. But Julius was looking out to sea, smiling.

'So he's finally admitted he needs to paint, has he?' Julius picked up a flat stone and skipped it across the water as Tess had done. 'I could have told him that years ago, but he's never wanted to hear anything from me. He used to do marvellous sketches when he was a boy, landscapes, people, anything. I always thought that he only took the job in advertising to spite me.' He glanced at Tess. 'It can be hard having a famous father, I know that. And I thought maybe that was his rebellion. But then I decided I was probably overestimating my own importance.'

Tess reached out a hand to him. 'I don't think you could overestimate your importance in Stephen's eyes. It's one of his problems. He needs your good opinion. And I don't think he ever feels he's earned it.'

'Tell me what his painting's like.' Tess could hear the excitement in Julius's voice.

'I'm not sure I'm a good enough judge. But his tutor seems to be very impressed.'

'Would you mind very much if I went to the airport to meet him? I think perhaps there's some things he and I should talk about.'

'Oh Julius, I know how much that would mean to him.' Tess, glowing with happiness and relief, threw her arms round him and hugged him until he almost overbalanced. This was going to be the best day of the holiday. 'Well' – Tess looked at her watch – 'I suppose you'd better go soon. His flight gets in at three.'

As she watched Julius's tall thin figure, miraculously energized and full of zest, walk briskly over the beach towards the house, Tess felt an overwhelming urge to run into the sea for another glorious swim. She just wished she could be there to watch Stephen's face when he found his father waiting to meet him, without a TV crew, for the very first time in his life.

The water was cold and blue and invigorating. Unlike the polluted waters of the Mediterranean you could see thirty feet down to the bottom. Forgetting she'd washed her hair Tess dived in and out like a playful dolphin, feeling the water rushing through her hair and the sun sparkling in her eyes.

So it was another ten minutes before she turned for

the shore and saw Luke standing there, waving, trying to catch her attention. She dipped her face into the water and did a fast crawl back to the empty beach, worried that this heralded some emergency.

'Don't worry,' Luke shouted as she walked through the last few feet of water. 'It was Dad on the phone. He can't come after all.' Luke was clearly trying to put a brave face on it. 'But he's promised to get me that computer though. He's going to call you tonight to explain.'

Tess stood stock still and felt herself start to shiver. She'd so longed to see him. This week was going to be magical. How could he do this to them? Letting them all down and buying Luke off with the promise of some expensive toy? Disappointment reverberated through her. And then the thought struck her. Julius would be halfway to the airport by now.

Julius drove his ancient Daimler twice round the periphery of the airport before he saw a sign to the short-stay car park and took a ticket. He hated the way everywhere was staffed by machines nowadays and wondered briefly what had happened to the army of bad-tempered old boys in satchels who used to take your money, then go back to their little huts and no doubt a warming nip of Jameson's.

The terminal building was bustling with Euro-golfers over for some tournament. Looking round him Julius suddenly felt inadequate. He travelled often but left all the arrangements to Stella. His sole contribution was to tell her she should have chosen another flight if planes were delayed or diverted. He looked around him, conscious of being in the way of speeding trolleys and Vodafoned businessmen. He attempted a helpless old man in distress look, hoping a charming Aer

Lingus stewardess might take pity on him. None did. Eventually he spotted an enquiry desk and joined the queue. In the end he was helped out with all the eyelash-batting and flirtatiousness he could hope for, but unfortunately by a man. Why was it only queers who gave you the full treatment these days? Women seemed to find charm demeaning. It wasn't the world he remembered.

Armed with Stephen's arrival time and flight number, Julius headed off for the bar. To his disgust, the claret they gave him was chilled and when he asked for a coffee it turned out to be cappuccino topped with whipped cream and chocolate like some children's party treat. You know what your trouble is, he mumbled to himself opening the *Cork Examiner*, you're turning into a cantankerous old sod. Julius smiled. The idea rather appealed to him.

Ten minutes before Stephen's flight was due he positioned himself next to the arrivals gate, trying to contain an overpowering sense of excitement. Ever since the party Julius had been forced to admit Stephen and he had wasted too many years in bitterness, and who knew how many more an old man like him was going to be allocated? Of course painters often lived to a great age. Julius grinned. Stella said it was because of their selfishness and that no doubt their wives died young. Mind you, she'd lasted. Probably stayed alive deliberately to stop him marrying some young totty who'd give him a good time. Bloody woman.

Already the efficient businessmen with hand baggage only were beginning to filter through. The flight must have come in early. Julius noted with surprise that he was feeling quite nervous.

The next wave was starting: holidaymakers in bright Bermuda shorts; Americans with enormous suitcases, looking for their roots. Then a lone child with a plastic ticket pinned to her cardigan like an evacuee, who ran into the arms of her doting grandparents. But no sign of Stephen.

Julius felt a bitter kick of disappointment. Perhaps these others were from another flight and Stephen's was still to come. He'd give him another few minutes anyway. Maybe he should ask his flirtatious friend at the enquiry desk if there'd been some delay.

And then he saw Tess walking towards him from the other side of the terminal building.

Even though the weather was as inviting as ever for their final week, for Tess the colour had drained out of the holiday. Ellie came back from her concert, bursting with news of amps and lasers and how many Porta-loos you needed per hundred guests, and announced she wanted to be a rock promoter. They were the ones, she announced with worldly wisdom, who made the real money. Tess smiled at having a mini-Madonna for a daughter and tried to suppress the wave of resentment she felt at Stephen's behaviour. He was missing so much. And she'd never forget the look of disappointment on Julius's face when she'd broken him the news. But then, wasn't it just the same disap-pointment Stephen had felt himself countless times as a child? *They fuck you up, your mum and dad* ... Families. Once again she wondered why people thought they were the cornerstone of all that was good and glorious. Maybe because they were all anyone had.

It was almost their last day before Tess remembered Stephen making Ellie promise to take photographs. Maybe he'd always suspected he wasn't going to come. Tess felt so angry with him she was tempted not to bother. But she herself wanted a memento of the first two happy weeks of the holiday so she asked Julius if he'd come down to the beach with them.

The one she wanted most was of her favourite spot, hidden among the dunes. She sat looking out to sea, her straw hat tied behind her head like a Fragonard shepherdess, with Ellie leaning on her shoulder and Luke half-lying in the sand, his head in her lap as she stroked it. Behind them the sky blazed, more Provençal than West Cork.

'That's wonderful,' Julius enthused, 'maybe one day I'll paint you all like that.' He clicked away, demanding small changes, but holding the pose until he was finally satisfied.

'Thanks a million, Gramps.' Ellie jumped up as soon as she was released. 'I'm sure they'll come out much better with you taking them.'

'Let's get these developed here, shall we?' Julius wound back the film. 'Then you can take a set home with you and we can keep some too. Stella can take them in this afternoon.'

He didn't notice Tess shaking her head at this classic Julius assumption.

'Maybe you could have a second career as David Bailey, Gramps,' said Luke.

'Except that Gramps earns more than him already,' Ellie retorted, kissing him.

'So I do,' nodded Julius smugly, 'so I do.'

The moment Ellie and Luke spotted Stephen waiting behind the barrier at Heathrow, they forgot any disappointment they'd been feeling and ran into his arms.

'I learned to jump, Dad,' Luke gushed. 'A five-bar gate!'

'Did you? That's brilliant!'

He ruffled Ellie's hair. 'Love the tan,' he teased, seeing her deathly pallor.

'I was at Slane Castle. Helping backstage at a rock festival.'

He glanced at Tess, who was hiding her anger by piling suitcases on to a trolley. 'Hello, love.' Noting the unbending lines of her body Stephen sent Ellie and Luke off to pay the car-park charge. 'Look, Tess, I'm really sorry –'

Tess cut him short, 'So why did you chicken out? You missed a brilliant holiday. The sun shone every single day. Even without you there.'

Stephen looked anguished. 'I just couldn't face Father. I knew I'd have to tell him about the art school and I just don't feel ready to have it all shot down in flames.'

In another mood, Tess might have tried to understand, but her own disappointment was still biting too deep. 'Grow up, Stephen, for God's sake!' She piled on the last of the bags furiously. 'I told your father all about the Bryant and you wanting to be a painter. And he didn't wail and gnash his teeth or say you'd be making a terrible fool of yourself. In fact he was absolutely thrilled; he said he'd always thought you would one day.'

Stephen listened, aghast. Her words made no sense to him. Surely all these crippling fears hadn't been for nothing? This had to be another of Julius's tricks.

Tess wondered for a moment whether to break the news that Julius had gone to meet him. Why the hell not? Why should she spare his feelings when he hadn't given a damn about hers?

'In fact he was so bloody delighted he went to meet you off your flight.' She saw Stephen flinch, the colour draining out of his face, and was glad. Maybe it would make him and his father see sense at last. 'He said it was about time you and he sorted things out.' And then her anger impelled her to turn the knife. 'But of course you weren't there, were you? I had to go to the airport and tell him you weren't coming. I've never seen him looking so disappointed. So you certainly got your own back, didn't you?'

Stephen looked at her unsteadily, as though he didn't quite recognize the Tess he knew in this strident woman.

And then Ellie and Luke were there, all bubbling gaiety. They each took one of Stephen's arms, leaving Tess to follow on with the trolley wondering if she hadn't just been unforgivably bitchy. But when they got home her mood wasn't improved by finding canvases all over the hall, unwashed dishes in the sink and that Stephen had finished the last of the milk.

He tried to make amends by opening a bottle of wine and handing her a glass. 'Come on, Tess, don't let's be angry with each other. This is my last day of freedom. Tomorrow I start gainful employment.'

Tess took a glass and delved in her bag for the photos. She handed them to him. 'OK,' she smiled grudgingly, 'there's a peace offering.'

Stephen opened the folder and pulled out the series of enlarged prints. Tess, Ellie and Luke smiled out from an impossibly blue sky, with rocks and sand and sea behind them rolling away into infinity. The scene was so evocative and alluring that Stephen felt regret wash over him, corrosive and shaming. This was what he'd sacrificed, out of fear.

Tess could see from his face that seeing what he'd missed was its own punishment. She raised her glass. 'To gainful employment.'

*

204

'Do you realize,' said Phil, stroking Terry's face as he cooked a fry-up for their breakfast, 'that this is our last day without the kids and I've never even seen your house?'

'That, you posh bird,' he replied, slapping her hand as she tried to pinch a fried potato, 'is because you've got an irrational prejudice against Essex.'

'Not now that I'm familiar with its inhabitants.' She slipped her hand into the pocket of his jeans and grabbed him. 'I realize it may have quite a lot to offer.'

Terry laughed, feeling himself stiffen. He turned off the gas and pulled Phil to him. 'Come on then, you shameless hussy, where's it to be?'

'What's wrong with the kitchen floor?' Phil dropped to her knees and began to unzip him. 'After all I cleaned it yesterday.' Very slowly she took him into her mouth until she heard him groan satisfactorily and grasp her hair. At the crucial moment she looked up at him, tantalizing. 'But tonight it's your bed or nowhere.'

'Anything, anything,' she heard him mumble, 'just for God's sake don't stop.'

Phil had meetings right up till six, so she didn't climb into Terry's car until well after seven, but at least it meant the traffic, always terrible going east in the rush hour, had eased a bit. She wondered what his house would be like. Terry was so full of surprises that she had no idea what to expect. If she assumed a neo-Georgian monstrosity, knowing him it would turn out to be a post-modern penthouse. The one thing she hadn't visualized was a red-brick Victorian rectory, perched on the edge of Epping Forest. But that was what it turned out to be.

When he opened the front door Phil was as nervous as a bride being carried over the threshold. Houses revealed so much about people. Inside, to her great relief, the place seemed cosy and comfortable without any great claims to luxury. Then she noticed the photographs. There must have been a hundred of them. They stood on every available surface, in every shape and size. Silver framed, tortoiseshell framed, gilt framed, sometimes just loose prints propped up. In Terry's study there were two of them, both huge, as big as family portraits in a stately home. And every single one was of his children.

For the first time in their two weeks together, Phil felt a flash of apprehension at what she had got herself into.

As Stephen drifted back into consciousness he was aware of a feeling he hadn't experienced since he'd left the agency. He didn't want to wake up, because when he did he had to go to work. He didn't want to get up, wear a suit, and go into an office. He wanted to put on his army surplus and paint.

He looked across at Tess. They hadn't made love last night even after an absence of three weeks. She looked gorgeous with her tan and freckles, about sixteen years old, but there was something about her, a kind of withholding, as though she were still angry with him, that had stopped him making the first move.

It would be silly to let this go on. There were things both of them resented about the other but they could get over them. He reached towards her, catching sight as he did of the clock-radio. He had to be at Waterloo in half an hour. The reconciliation would have to wait. He decided not to wake her.

At Waterloo Station Stephen bought a ticket, for a staggering amount of money, and understood for the first time why commuters were tempted to mutiny and commandeer the trains. He could buy an old banger for the same price. Maybe he would. Driving would give him a lot more freedom than being one of the poor lemmings tied to Network SouthEast's capricious schedules. He watched the ceaseless tide of people sweeping towards him, deeply relieved to be travelling in the opposite direction.

Settled in the carriage with a bacon sandwich and a cup of British Rail tea, things looked rosier. He looked out of the window as the landscape changed from city to suburb and gradually to countryside. At least if he had to go to an office it was in pleasant surroundings. An hour later, as Winchester's cathedral spires drifted into view, he was conscious of a pang of nervousness and realized it was nothing to do with the job. It was the thought of seeing Josephine Quinn again.

CHAPTER SIXTEEN

It wasn't in fact Josephine who appeared in Richmond & Quinn's reception to greet Stephen, but Hugo. He held out his hand, all suspicion apparently forgotten.

'Hello there. Josephine and I are both delighted you could join the firm.' He summoned the lift and took Stephen to the third floor and into an airy office looking out over the watermeadows.

Outside was an impressive mahogany work station, behind which a young girl sat trying to answer two phones at once.

'This is Lucy. She looks after Josephine and I, and she's agreed to take you on too.'

Stephen looked faintly surprised that the two most senior members of the firm should share a secretary, let alone consider she might have time to spare to look after him.

Hugo read his thoughts. 'Josephine and I believe in doing a lot of our own administration. It keeps the channels of communication open. At first we didn't even have an office and just used desks around the building.' He smiled a wintry smile. 'But it proved a little impractical. I expect you'll want to do most of your admin too' – indicating the spanking new word processor on Stephen's desk – 'Lucy will be happy to take messages and run your diary.'

Stephen smiled at the shy-looking girl who was now down to one phone, and she nodded back.

'We thought perhaps an introductory meeting late this afternoon when you might lay out your rough plan of attack.'

Stephen saw his relaxed, getting-to-know-you first day evaporate before him. 'Certainly. What time would suit you?'

'About five o'clock? Give you time to settle in.'

'Fine.' He could see Richmond & Quinn was the kind of place that didn't expect you to catch the five-thirty to Waterloo.

Stephen decided to go for a quick stroll to remind himself of the lie of the land, as well as the whereabouts of the photocopier, the canteen and the loos, then he unpacked his briefcase and sat down at his brand-new desk. It was too early to call New York so he made a list of the magazines and trade journals he'd need to keep himself up to date. Then he got out his notes and started reading, pausing only to wonder what Slouch would be getting up to with his new batch of students.

If he got too down maybe he'd have to hide a copy of *The Artist* in his briefcase and pore over the centre-fold like other commuters did over *Penthouse*.

At five on the dot Lucy put her head round the door to tell him they were ready for him. After all this talk of democracy their office turned out to be opulent enough to satisfy the megalomania of a Maxwell. It ran the whole length of one wing, with views of the grounds on one side and the river on the other, a vast ash desk stood at either end, presumably one for each of them, with two Biedermeier sofas and a large cabinet in the middle, subtly mixing old and new with great panache. Josephine sat on one sofa, her legs elegantly crossed, Hugo on the other. Stephen sat down next to Hugo.

'So, Stephen, fire away.' Josephine clearly didn't believe in wasting much time on smalltalk.

'The first thing we have to do is study the market in the US.' Stephen handed them both an initial report he'd prepared. 'Is there room for a new brand, and what will give ours impact in an already crowded market? How should it be packaged? I need to talk to buyers at Bloomies and the other big stores and some people from the big drugstore chains. That should keep me busy for a week or two. After that I'll look into advertising and marketing.'

Josephine and Hugo listened, asking occasional questions about timescale and whom he was thinking of approaching. From time to time Hugo threw in some imaginative idea of his own. He could really be quite helpful. Working with two such smart people who understood the business so completely and could make decisions fast might even be pure pleasure after the now-you're-up-now-you're-down world of advertising.

After an hour Hugo looked at his watch. 'You seem to have things well in hand, I must say.' He stood up. 'I must leave for another meeting.'

Stephen wondered whether he should leave too, but Josephine had already opened the vast cabinet and was pouring them both a drink. She hadn't bothered, he noticed, to ask if he had the time to stay. She handed him a glass of wine as Hugo closed the door behind him. 'How was the course? Slouch seemed impressed. He tried to talk me out of employing you.'

'Me too. He doesn't think much of filthy lucre.'

Josephine smiled. 'Only because he sponges royally off everyone. Even his students.'

'Especially his students,' Stephen corrected. 'I liked him though.'

'Clearly he liked you.'

'Once he'd decided I wasn't trading off my father's reputation.'

'You don't like people knowing about your father, do you?' Josephine looked at him curiously.

'No.' Stephen saw no reason to elaborate about how having a famous father made it almost impossible for you to compete. Especially in the same field.

'I won't tell anyone,' Josephine smiled, 'I promise.'

Deciding that he could just about leave without being insulting, Stephen stood up. 'I'd better go. There's a train at seven-thirty.'

'Stephen?' He wondered if Josephine were about to offer him another lift to the station but she made no move to get up. 'I know you're busy but you will keep up with the painting, won't you?' He was touched by the genuine concern in her voice. It was certainly more than Tess had shown. 'You could always use the studio here if you wanted.'

Stephen thanked her. Her studio was so fabulous it was a tempting offer, but some instinct told him to draw back. 'I'm all right where I am for the moment. But thanks anyway.' He waved goodbye and closed the door behind him.

Outside the office he saw Lucy sitting with her head down, her long hair dropping down round her face. She'd clearly been crying.

'What's the matter?' he asked gently, assuming it was boyfriend trouble. He'd seen Ellie like this when Mark in Lower VI ignored her in favour of Penny or Lil.

Lucy made a conscious effort to pull herself together, trying to decide whether he was trustworthy. She must have decided he was, for she confided: 'I made a cock-up over one of Josephine's meetings tomorrow. I'm just working up the nerve to tell her.'

'She won't kill you, surely?'

'She's fine about most things,' Lucy said apologetically, 'but the one thing she hates is inefficiency.'

Stephen nodded. This was the second time he'd glimpsed the steel beneath the silk.

A three-week-high pile of legal documents and unanswered correspondence leered at Tess from her in-tray, making her feel unseasonably depressed. Usually she came back from holidays full of energy, but not this time. Instead of getting down to it she kept staring out of the window and seeing not the unprepossessing drabness of the council estate next door but the coves and cornfields of West Cork. If Stephen had come and they'd had the glorious last week she'd planned, maybe it would have been easier to come home.

She shook herself. Self-indulgence like this wouldn't help.

Jacqui arrived bearing a cup of coffee and a broad grin. 'Hardly worth going away, was it?' She indicated the huge pile of work.

Tess laughed. 'You're only saying that because you've had your holiday already. Anything happen while I was away that I need to deal with?'

Jacqui reeled a list so long that Tess wished she hadn't asked. 'Oh, and rumour has it Patricia made a pass at Lyall Gibson.'

'No!' Tess bit her lip. 'And what did he do?'

'Told her he was into celibacy at the moment.'

'I don't believe you!'

'Well I wasn't there, was I? Anyway, they're avoiding each other so something must have happened.'

Tess shook her head. Offices were amazing. You only had to decide you fancied someone and the whole organization was taking bets on your chances.

The thought of Patricia brought her back to earth with a guilty bump. She was supposed to have done some work on her partnership pitch in Ireland, but the first two weeks had been so perfect and the last one so ghastly that she hadn't even opened her folder. There were less than two weeks left. Knowing Patricia she'd probably already typed out hers in triplicate and was practising it every morning in front of the bathroom mirror.

Sighing, she turned to the pile of work. Most of it was fairly routine, cases that needed to be resumed after the August recess, answers to financial questionnaires she'd sent out to clients' husbands, and the usual flood of post-summer-holiday divorce petitions. It was the same every year. People flocked off to Majorca or the Canary Isles for the make-or-break holiday that was supposed to save their marriage, only to find after two weeks alone together they ended up hating each other twice as much.

She thought for a moment of Stephen and had to admit she hadn't forgiven him yet. Maybe she ought to make an effort to patch things up.

By six-thirty she was belting round the Tesco's in Paddington Green picking up pasta and four-cheese sauce for a reconciliation dinner. It was expensive but about the only thing she had a chance of cooking before Stephen got home. She grabbed a lollo rosso lettuce which looked pretty and was relatively cheap to bulk out the meal and headed for the till.

By the time she got home Ellie and Luke had already grazed on various disgusting snacks so she laid the kitchen table for just her and Stephen. She'd long ago given up her dream of them all sitting round the table swapping civilized conversation about how their days had gone. Now she only insisted they appear for Sunday lunch or supper once a week. Even that was treated by Ellie and Luke as cruel and inhuman punishment.

She boiled the water ready to put in the pasta and prepared the salad. After the meal she'd slip up to the bedroom and do some work on her pitch. As she shook the vinaigrette in a jam jar the doorbell went. Stephen must have forgotten his key. She jumped up, forgiveness in her heart, at the thought of Stephen coming home after his first day at work. The mighty hunter returned.

But it was Phil who stood on her doorstep, beaming like an uninvited village idiot, and clutching two bottles of Asti Spumante which she dumped into Tess's arms.

'Sorry about those. They were all they had in your local.'

Ellie and Luke appeared at Tess's shoulder, thinking it was Stephen too. Phil turned to them with a dramatic flourish and held out her finger. 'Well, congratulate me, one and all, I've just got engaged.'

Luke and Ellie shook their heads and went back to the TV.

'Was it something I said?' Phil asked.

Tess giggled. 'Isn't getting engaged a little unusual when you've been married before?'

'Look, sweetie,' said Phil, waving her hand at Tess, 'if you don't get engaged, you don't get the ring. Right? Besides, I've never been engaged before. Greg gave me a week's notice before rushing me down to the registry office. This time I want the works. I wondered if you might be my maid of honour?'

'Oh, Phil, I'm far too old. So are you going to tell me who's the lucky man or not?'

'Well, actually you know him,' Phil confessed sheepishly. 'It's Terry Worth.'

Tess was dumbstruck.

'Terry,' repeated Phil helpfully. 'You know Terry. Terry Worth. Your client.'

Tess tried to take this in. Since Phil hadn't mentioned him lately she'd assumed he'd been long forgotten. Still, she'd always liked Terry. And maybe meeting Phil would cure him of his obsession with fighting Angela over their children. She realized Phil was, quite naturally, waiting for a reaction.

'Phil, that's terrific. Have you met his kids?'

'Not yet. And he hasn't met mine either. He's telling Angela this weekend and when he gets back he's going to meet my kids and I'm going to meet his. And if everything goes OK we're planning to announce our engagement as soon as poss.'

Tess could hear the happiness bubbling through Phil's voice and fervently hoped everything would work out for her.

'And how does he think Angela is going to take it?'

'He thinks she'll be fine if we do everything slowly.' A little of the confidence was beginning to drain out of Phil's voice. 'He says she's quite a reasonable woman really.'

Tess thought of Angela, whose behaviour had been mean and vengeful even without a tangible rival to her children's affections, and hoped he was right.

'We'd better have a toast.' Tess reached for the bottle of Asti Spumante and opened it. It went everywhere and Phil had to chase it with a glass trying to catch the foam.

'That looks nice,' Phil hinted, eyeing the pasta.

Tess decided to put in on. It was already eight-thirty and if Stephen didn't get back soon they'd better go ahead and eat first. She topped up their glasses, feeling lightheaded already.

After twenty minutes they'd finished the first bottle

215

and Tess put on the sauce, suddenly starving. As soon as it was cooked she and Phil fell on it, leaving Stephen's in the oven to keep warm. Phil opened the second bottle.

Stephen, standing at the bus-stop in Sloane Square, felt exhausted and ravenous in equal measures. What the hell had happened to the number 11? He decided to start walking, vaguely fantasizing that Tess, through the marital telepathy that sometimes worked between them, might suddenly appear in the car and give him a lift.

'So where's Stephen?' Phil asked as she and Tess attacked the salad bowl at the same time.

'First day at work.' Tess thought she could detect a slight slurring of her speech and decided to ignore it. 'Richmond & Quinn, remember?'

Phil poured them both another glass. 'Ah, yesss.' Tess decided Phil must have had much more of the wine than she had to be speaking like that. 'The lovely Josephine. How's he liking it?'

'How would I know, eejit? I just told you. He only started today.' Tess sniffed the air. There seemed to be a slight smell of burning. She'd investigate in a minute. 'Go on. Tell me. What's she really like?'

'Josephine Quinn . . .' Phil stared at the second bottle of fizz as though it had emptied itself spontaneously '. . . is the kind of woman who wears stockings instead of tights' – she picked up the bottle and turned it upside down – 'and then tells you about it. Especially if you're male.'

'Philomena Doyle!' Tess handed her last half-glass to her friend out of comradeship. 'How could you do this to me?'

They both collapsed in furious giggles so neither heard Stephen's key turning in the door.

He sniffed the air as he came into the kitchen and found Tess and Phil with tears running down their faces and two empty bottles of Italian fizz on the table. 'What's that funny smell?' he asked, heading for the oven.

Tess clapped her hand over her mouth. 'Oh my God, your spaghetti!'

Stephen grabbed a teacloth and removed a glutinous orange mess from the oven. All the strands had stuck together so it looked like a single solid lump.

Tess bit her lip, then collapsed with laughter again. 'Oh, love, I'm so sorry! We were celebrating Phil's engagement.'

All the petty resentments of the day, the early start, the train ride full of commuters, the wait at the bus-stop, the fact that he didn't want to be doing the job in the first place, welled up in Stephen and he slammed the plate into the sink, almost breaking it.

'Congratulations,' he snapped, grabbing a beer from the fridge and tearing at the ring pull angrily, 'and thanks for asking how it went today.' He turned to Phil and added acidly, 'I hope you'll be very happy. Just like we are.'

Her first week back at work seemed to pass in a dustcloud of meetings, court appearances and endless paperwork. Although she'd tried, Tess hadn't been able to claw back any free time to get on with preparing her pitch and she was beginning to panic. Tonight was Friday and she intended to start as soon as she got home and, if necessary, work through the night. Stephen would just have to cope with the domestic stuff.

As she packed her briefcase with the material she'd need she felt a flash of guilt about Stephen. They hadn't really made it up. She'd apologized and he'd accepted, but that was about it. She suspected under-currents were still swirling around. She blamed him for screwing up their holiday and he thought she was being a selfish cow who didn't appreciate his sacrificing the god Art. Still, everyone went through ups and downs like this. You could look across the room at the person you were married to and decide you didn't like them and still find in a week or two you'd forgotten all about it. At least she hoped so.

In the reception area Lyall Gibson was putting files into a cardboard box. She held the door open for him. Jacqui was right, he did have very nice brown eyes. She'd never noticed them before.

'Moving offices?' she joked.

'Just a bit of homework. How are you? You look a bit pale under that tan if you know what I mean. Not overdoing it?'

'Probably only lack of sleep. I had a heavy night the other night. Then there's the presentation next week.'

'Of course.' His voice rang with sympathy. 'How are you feeling about it? I'm sure you'll walk it.'

Tess smiled. It was nice to be reassured. Stephen seemed to have forgotten all about it. He'd just thrown himself into his painting as soon as he got home. Even Ellie and Luke had noticed.

'Thanks.' She gestured to her bulging briefcase. 'I'm going to do some boning up tonight.'

'Are we completely mad?' He shook his head at the craziness of them both going off for a weekend's work. 'Whatever happened to fun?'

The first thing Tess spotted in the hall was Stephen's briefcase. Good. Maybe he would have even put some supper on like he used to. But there were no giveaway cooking smells and she could hear Classic FM belting out from somewhere upstairs. Stephen was clearly painting as usual.

'Mum! Mum!' Luke flung himself on her before she'd even got her jacket off. 'Dad's taken down the Scalextric track and I wanted to play with it. He says he needs the space to paint.'

'God,' Ellie flopped down at the kitchen table, clutching her head, 'this smell of turps is giving me a headache. Why can't he find somewhere else to paint?'

Tess put her jacket on the back of a chair and looked at her briefcase longingly. If she didn't start soon she never would.

'Stephen!' she shouted up the stairs. 'Could you come down?'

She heard an answering sound of shoe on stair-carpet. But the face that appeared was Inge's. 'Tess, Luke's trainers fell apart today. The school said he must have some new ones by Monday.'

Tess closed her eyes. Next to her the hall phone rang. It was Terry Worth, of all people, and before she'd even had time to congratulate him he launched into a bitter recital of Angela's latest misdemeanour. She looked up to find Stephen gazing at her resentfully, holding one of their bone-china wedding present plates which he was clearly using as a palette. 'Could you get the supper?' she mouthed.

He banged into the kitchen.

Finally she extricated herself from Terry's complaints and joined him.

They ate their meal in silence.

'Look, love.' Tess reached out her hand to try and bridge the anger between them. 'Luke's been complaining about losing his Scalextric and we all keep tripping over your canvases' – she would let the matter of the dinner plate pass – 'so why don't you look for some studio space you can really spread yourself out in?' Almost as soon as she'd said it she saw this wasn't a good time to have chosen.

Stephen stood up angrily. 'What you really mean, is that you don't want me to paint at all. You think it's a rather self-indulgent hobby, something I should get out on Sundays and put away in a nice neat corner of the bedroom, don't you? Well, I've discovered painting's not like that. I took the bloody job for you, isn't that enough?'

'You did not take the bloody job for me!' Tess flared, her eyes sparking with matching anger. 'You took it for *us*. The family. Just like I'm going for this partnership for us, so you *can* paint if you want to.' She stood up and grabbed her briefcase. 'That's why I'm going up to work now and' – she gestured to the plates on the table – 'that's why you can load the sodding dishwasher, and' – catching sight of the paint-smeared bone china – 'you can put that plate in too. They were ten quid each.'

She ran upstairs to their bedroom, half wishing he'd follow her. But he didn't.

She got out all the facts and figures she needed for her pitch and tried to decide where to spread them out. She might as well use the bed. Not much else had been happening on it lately.

'Not searching for another job already, I hope?'

Stephen glanced up from the small ads in the *Evening Standard* to find Josephine standing in the doorway.

He grinned. 'I'm looking for a studio, as a matter of fact. Tess has been cutting up rough about my painting gear clogging up the happy home. It's driving the kids on to the streets, it seems. The thing is,' he confided suddenly, 'I don't know whether it's the gear under her feet or the fact I do it at all that's getting to her.'

Josephine sat down on the side of one of his chairs, watching him thoughtfully. 'Sometimes it can be hard for people who don't paint to understand the way it can take hold of you.'

Stephen nodded, grateful that Josephine at least understood. 'I used to think my father was simply a selfish bastard. Now I realize he was in the grip of a passion, an obsession almost.'

'And your mother understood that and Tess doesn't?'

'Tess is very different from my mother. She wouldn't put up with what my mother had to in the name of art.'

'Not even having a few canvases around the place?' Stephen was about to defend Tess but Josephine hadn't finished. 'Look, my offer still stands about the studio here. As a matter of fact the painter who's been borrowing it is just off to Tuscany. It seems a shame for it to be wasted.'

Stephen hesitated, thinking of the peaceful room with its glorious light, then pulled himself together. 'You're very kind. It's just that if I painted here as well as worked here, I'd never go home.'

Josephine smiled. 'I thought you said Tess was complaining about having you under her feet. Look, why don't you bring her here to see it. Let her decide. Then she can hardly complain afterwards. She'd probably like to see where you work anyway. Tell you what: why don't you bring the whole family to lunch here on Sunday?'

Stephen consulted his diary to see if they were doing anything. They weren't.

'I hope she likes the studio. It'd give me real pleasure to see it used again.'

'Oh God, Mum, surely I don't have to go all the way to Godforsaken Winchester just for lunch? There won't be anyone our age as usual,' moaned Ellie.

'Maybe you'll get a free sample of Richmond & Quinn perfume,' Tess coaxed her.

'Yuk! It's so flowery it reminds me of air freshener. I loathe the stuff.' And Ellie had a suspicion she was going to feel the same about its creator.

'Go away and have a bath, you truculent teenager,' Tess ordered, 'and don't snaffle all the best bits of the Sunday papers.'

To Tess's amazement Ellie appeared bang on time and looking astoundingly normal and it was Luke who kept them waiting by insisting he would only wear one T-shirt, which happened to be still in the washing machine so Tess had to extract and iron it dry while Luke searched for a missing trainer.

So, as usual, they were the statutory half an hour late starting and, as usual, Tess ended up shouting at Stephen for driving too fast in an attempt to make up lost time, and they had a thoroughly bad-tempered journey.

As they waited on the front steps of the Gothic fantasy and Luke pulled the Hammer House of Horror bell, Tess thought how odd it was to be about to meet someone whose face you already knew so well. She'd seen countless pictures of Josephine's high cheekbones and sleekly bobbed hair in the papers. What she hadn't expected, and discovered when the real Josephine answered the door, was how tall she was; three or four inches taller than Tess.

Tess, used to feeling perfectly normal, suddenly felt small and dwarflike.

'You must be Luke,' Josephine said as she gestured for him to go inside, 'and you're Ellie. Stephen's told me all about your painting. You want to go to art school, don't you?'

Ellie nodded her head, suddenly awed at the sight of the inside of the Lodge. 'What a fantastic house!'

'And Tess, how nice to meet you at last.' Josephine made it sound as though Tess were an old and valued friend who had, for some deeply hurtful reason, been avoiding her.

Tess stepped over the threshold and tried not to be impressed. It wasn't just the size and beauty of the place, filled with antiques from the right period, it was the calm and order. She tried not to think about the chaos of their own house: the bikes and rollerskates in the hall; the towels drying on the radiators (how *did* people get their towels dry if it was too wet outside and they loathed the way they went limp in the tumble dryer?); not to mention the plates piled high on top of the dishwasher because no one had bothered to put them inside and she was blowed if she was going to. But she noticed immediately that in Josephine's house there were no *things*, the sort of object you couldn't classify and therefore remained untidied for months on the coffee table or bookshelf.

'Right,' Josephine announced, 'I thought we might go straight in and have lunch.' Tess smiled and recognized this for what it was. A subtle reminder that they were three-quarters of an hour late.

The dining room was a dream. Yellow and blue, the colour of Monet's kitchen. A cold salmon was laid out garnished with slices of cucumber on the dresser surrounded by an array of delicious salads.

Josephine turned to Tess. 'I hope you don't mind a cold buffet. Only I hate keeping staff hanging round at weekends.'

I know exactly what you mean, Tess was tempted to reply; our au pair's so shagged out she just won't do a thing on Saturdays. But she didn't; instead she shot a look at Luke to forestall him asking if there was anything in breadcrumbs. Astonishingly he was quietly helping himself to a small slice of salmon and a vast dollop of hollandaise. For pudding he, who never let fruit pass his lips as a rule, woofed an apple and pear tartlet and a slice of strawberry shortcake.

During lunch, to Tess's surprise even Ellie, normally surly with strangers, chatted away animatedly with Josephine.

'So,' Josephine enquired after the last delicious mouthful was finished – Luke, class traitor, had even had seconds, little bugger – 'how about having a look at the studio?'

'What an amazing room,' Ellie enthused the moment she stepped inside. 'It gets natural light from every side. It must be fantastic to paint in. Did you know, Mum, that Josephine really meant to be a painter? She studied art under the same tutor Dad did.'

Tess, who had heard all she wanted to about Josephine's mutifaceted personality, smiled neutrally.

Josephine turned to her. 'So, Tess, do you share Stephen's passion for painting?' Tess had a pretty good idea she already knew the answer to that one. 'Who're your favourite painters?'

Tess's mind went blank. She could hardly say van Gogh and Cézanne. Far too Athena Reproductions.

'God,' laughed Ellie, jumping into the silence, 'don't ask Mum. She doesn't know her Matisse from her Picasso, do you, Ma?' She grabbed her mother's arm affectionately. 'Not unless you've been reading that book you bought.'

Josephine smiled, all eager interest. 'What book's that? Robert Hughes?'

Tess blushed. 'Oh,' she murmured, wanting to kill Ellie, 'I can't remember the exact title.'

'I can,' Ellie supplied helpfully. 'It was one of those teach yourself books. *Understanding Art*. You have got a bad memory, Mum. Must be all those brain cells you've destroyed through alcohol.'

'How marvellous,' smiled Josephine, 'you're clearly taking it all very seriously.'

Stephen missed the patronizing undertones, but Ellie didn't. She shot a look of surprise at Josephine.

'Tessie.' Stephen put his arm round her, genuinely touched. 'I didn't know you were boning up. How sweet you are.'

'Fine,' Josephine said briskly, 'we're all agreed then, are we? That Stephen can use the studio for his painting.'

'Maybe I should come with you?' Phil had already half opened the car door, delighted with her spur of the moment plan to join Terry on his delicate mission. He was about to drive to Cheltenham to break the news of their engagement to Angela. 'You could probably do with some moral support.' She registered Terry's horrified expression. 'I could always stay in the car.'

Terry glanced at her shocking-pink leggings and 'SAVE THE WORLD, KILL A TORY' T-shirt and concluded that neither Cheltenham nor Angela would be able to cope with Phil.

As usual the sight of Angela's small and faceless house on the outskirts of Cheltenham irritated the hell out of Terry. It wasn't as though he hadn't given her a very generous settlement. He had. Sometimes he thought it wasn't so much out of principle that she was bringing his kids up in this depressing place but just to spite him.

Then he saw Lianne and Johnny tearing out of the front door and he forgot his irritation with their mother in his joy at seeing them. They threw themselves into his arms and dragged him towards the house where Angela stood in the doorway looking like a librarian who'd caught someone shouting in the Reference section.

The house was even worse inside. Instead of sofas or chairs Angela preferred beanbags. There was scratchy sisal matting everywhere and a Buddhist shrine in the corner where Angela chanted twice a day. The whole place had about as much warmth and hominess as a dentist's waiting room. Lianne and Johnny sat on the floor good as gold. Too good in Terry's view. He thought of Phil's chaotic existence and her two bubbly children who often looked after her as though she were the wayward child and they the long-suffering adults. And he realized quite how difficult it was going to be to break the news about Phil. He'd have to do it later.

For now he just wanted to get out of this lifeless, poky house. 'Tell you what,' he suggested, picking Lianne up in one arm and Johnny in the other, 'why don't I take us all out to a cream tea?'

Lianne and Johnny whooped in unison.

'Terry, what are you thinking of?' Angela's voice rang with disapproval at such wanton extravagance. 'I've already made tea here.' She disappeared into the kitchen and came back in with a tray of camomile tea, two small glasses of apple juice and four Mr Kipling's almond slices.

*

226

Terry had known he ought to leave for at least an hour now, but he didn't want to say goodbye to Lianne and Johnny. And, more than that, he didn't want to tell Angela about Phil. So far everything had gone well. Angela had apologized for the misunderstandings about dates and had even put some future ones in her diary. In fact he'd rarely seen her so friendly, a fact that in itself was making him feel that something was brewing.

The children were out in the garden playing with the cat from next door and Angela had just given him a small sherry. It was now or never.

'Angela, there's something I need to talk to you about.'

She smiled at him so sweetly, with an air almost of having expected this, that he hoped to God she wasn't still fantasizing about some kind of reconciliation. For the first year after their divorce she'd treated it as though it were some kind of temporary separation and that Terry would appear at any moment with a giant Pickford's van and carry them off home.

'The thing is . . .' All Terry's ebullient confidence felt as though it were trickling down his neck into a pool of water at his feet. 'I'm thinking of re-marrying.'

Angela's face froze and her back, already straight as a ballet dancer's, stiffened. 'You're what?'

'You heard me, Ange.' Terry struggled to keep his voice friendly and neutral. 'She's called Philomena Doyle and she's divorced too, with two kids of her own, a bit younger than Lianne and Johnny.'

Angela paused as the reality of the situation finally got through to her. Then she said slowly, 'You do what you want . . .' The reasonableness of her words made Terry's heart sing with relief. Angela smiled again. 'But just remember this. I'm not having some London tart anywhere near my children.'

Josephine stood and waved from the front steps as they all piled into the car. For once Ellie and Luke didn't quarrel about which seats to take or whether Luke was going to play with his infuriating computer game all the way home.

Despite the oldness of the car and the ordinariness of the sight – a mother, father and their 2.2 children – Josephine felt a sudden pang of envy. Yet that kind of ordinariness was something she'd never wanted. Children had always seemed simply to be a tie, sapping your energy and diverting your talents into the kind of domesticity that in her view was little short of slavery, even in these days. The truth was she'd always seen children as vaguely irritating, not as intelligent people who might be interested in art and culture as Ellie clearly was. She'd actually been good company.

Pulling herself together she waved one last time and went inside. She'd have a glass of champagne and a long, cooling bath, much better than a journey back to London with two bickering teenagers. Then, for the rest of the evening she could be exactly what she wanted. But the thought didn't have the capacity to cheer her that it usually did.

'I think I'll have to work tonight,' Tess announced on the way home. She'd been hoping the glory of the evening might distract her from the thought of her ordeal ahead. But it hadn't. 'I've only got four days till my pitch and I'm nowhere near ready.'

'OK. Why don't I do supper then?' Stephen took a hand off the steering wheel and squeezed hers. 'Look, I'm sorry I've been a pain lately. The humourless husband getting at you because you and Phil were getting pleasantly pissed.'

'We weren't pissed,' protested Tess, 'just a little jolly.'

'So jolly you put the empty wine bottles out for the milkman,' reminded Ellie from the back, 'with a note in one asking for four pints.'

Tess laughed.

'So what did you think of her?' asked Stephen.

Neither of them had to ask who. 'She seemed very . . .' Tess paused, searching for the right word.

'Bossy?' suggested Ellie.

'Confident,' supplied Tess, 'and just a little bit lonely.'

'Lonely?' Stephen was surprised. 'Do you really think so?'

'Maybe even more than she realizes.' Tess looked out of the window, contemplating the inescapable truth that a lonely woman was a dangerous woman.

'Mum,' piped up Luke suddenly from the back, 'I've got a sore throat.'

'Oh Luke, you always get something on Sunday nights,' chipped in Ellie unsympathetically, 'and you always have to go to school in the end. I don't know why you bother.'

Tess turned and stroked his head. He did look a bit fishy. 'Try and have a sleep,' she said, handing him her jacket to use as a pillow, 'you'll probably feel better then.'

But by the time they got home, his glands were visibly swollen.

'You look just like a gopher!' hooted Ellie. 'I bet he's been scratching his head to make them swell up.'

'Oh, no,' Tess muttered, cursing God for so disapproving of working mothers as to do this to her. 'I think he's got mumps!'

By the next morning Luke was worse and they had to call the doctor. Both Inge and Stephen offered to stay with him but there was only one person he wanted. Tess.

The trouble was Tess had endless meetings so, consumed with guilt, she went off to work promising to leave as soon as she could. By eleven she took an anguished call from Inge informing her that Luke was refusing to swallow even the antiobiotics the doctor had left. So, carrying armloads of files, she cancelled all her appointments and dashed home, whereupon Luke managed to force down Lemon Barley water and even some Ambrosia creamed rice with a spoon of jam in it.

The vigil in the sickroom turned out to be an unexpected boon. Sitting in the dim light with no phone calls to disturb her, Tess's brain functioned better than it had for weeks and she managed the first solid work on her presentation.

By Wednesday afternoon she was finally happy with it and, utterly exhausted, fell into so deep a sleep that Luke couldn't rouse her to turn on the telly and had to go and fetch Inge.

'I think you'd better take over for a bit,' he croaked indignantly, 'Mum's snoring's keeping me awake.'

The first thing Tess noticed when she woke up on the day of her Big Pitch was that she had a raging sore throat. Oh God, she muttered to herself diving back under the duvet, not mumps, today of all days!

Twenty minutes later there was a loud fanfare outside the bedroom door and Luke appeared, astonishingly recovered and carrying a tray, closely followed by Ellie proudly holding out Tess's best suit which she'd obviously just ironed. New to the art of pressing, Ellie had obviously done it right side up without even using a damp cloth and all the seams were shiny. But who cared? It was a lovely thought.

Stephen followed with a bunch of white heather he'd bought from a gypsy. This on close study turned out to be something completely different, dyed white, but Tess said nothing and smiled. All three of them squashed into bed just as they used to when they were small and Luke, suddenly ravenous after days of starvation, started eating her croissant. Tess felt incredibly loved and blessed.

An hour later Stephen loaded all his painting gear into the old banger he'd bought through *Exchange & Mart* to take to the new studio, then shoehorned Ellie and Luke into the back to drop them at school. They all waved and shouted good luck.

'I won't be late,' Stephen shouted, blowing her a kiss. 'You'll be amazing. Just remember: "The quality of mercy is not strained . . ."'

Tess waved back. Her throat was feeling better already.

At work she was determined to get through the day and behave perfectly normally until the dreaded moment arrived. This worked up to a point though twice during quiet moments she found herself nipping into the Ladies to mug up her notes.

Then finally, at about four p.m., the summons came.

Stephen sat at his spanking new desk waiting for his call to New York to come through.

'Jack! Great to hear from you!' Jack Palazzo had been the dazzling success story of the eighties, taking the fragrance world by storm. He'd bypassed the great perfume houses and the giant multinationals and produced from his own small company the most successful scent of the decade. When he'd come to launch it in England, Stephen had worked on the commercial and they'd stayed friends. 'Look, Jack, I'm working for a firm of British perfumiers and they want to launch in the US. So I'm looking for a little advice.'

'You've come to the right place then, Stevie boy!' From the far side of the Atlantic Stephen could picture the great bear-frame of Jack Palazzo shaking with laughter. Jack had immensely enjoyed upsetting the fragrance establishment with his own success and clearly looked forward to stirring it up a little on behalf of his British pal.

After they'd finished speaking Stephen mulled over the conversation. It had been fascinating. Months of research couldn't have told him what Jack had imparted in ten minutes. And basically the response had been good. The US market was a crowded one but hadn't been as hard hit as many. When people were too broke to buy a car or a new bedroom suite they bought a lipstick or a bottle of perfume to cheer themselves up. Jack thought their project sounded OK, provided they packaged and marketed it right.

And by that, Jack had explained, he meant they should Go Nostalgic and play the Olde Englishe card for all it was worth. And this, Stephen smiled to himself, from the man who'd launched the most modern and ultra-sophisticated scent to hit America in decades.

Tess smoothed out her suit and combed her hair, adding a dash of ginger lipstick to make her feel jauntier than she actually felt. The tan had faded and there were shadows under her eyes from sitting up with Luke. She only hoped the shiny seams on her suit didn't show too much. She had so much riding on today: the partnership she'd always dreamed of, as well as the financial security to let Stephen do what he wanted without crippling them with money worries.

She turned to Jacqui. 'How do I look?'

'Like a woman who's not too hung up on her appearance.' Jacqui pulled a bit of fluff off her shoulder. 'And who has a home to go to when she leaves this place.'

Tess put her hand on her hip in mock protest. 'Roughly translated,' she grinned, 'you mean I look a mess!'

Jacqui held the door open, smiling back at her. 'Shame on you. You look great.'

Tess walked as calmly as possible towards the boardroom where Kingsmill's existing partners were waiting to grill her, glad that at least none of the other staff seemed to know what was going on. She couldn't bear to have everyone from the receptionist to Suzanne in accounts wishing her good luck.

Paul, the acned postroom boy, suddenly swooped out and screeched to a halt. 'Hi, Tess. Just thought you'd like to know. We're running a sweep on who'll get the partnership.' He smiled, the light reflecting off the heads of his pimples. 'The smart money's on Patricia, but I'm backing you.' He leaned towards her confidentially. 'You see, you always remind me of my mum.'

Her confidence zinging after this exchange, Tess walked into the boardroom. Ten partners got to their feet. Patricia, she noted, stayed seated. As Tess sat down, holding her hands in her lap and realizing they were cold and clammy with nerves, Lyall Gibson almost imperceptibly winked. It was such an inappropriate gesture that it cheered her up.

She had no idea what would happen next. Which of them would be asked to do their presentation first? And would the other be allowed to stay and listen to it?

Will Kingsmill fiddled with his papers, looking surprisingly nervous. 'Tess.' He turned towards her, smiling stiffly. 'You're the senior candidate and I know we'd all be fascinated to hear your ideas about what you could bring to the firm. So perhaps you could begin?'

CHAPTER SEVENTEEN

Tess stood up, her back straight as a squaddie's, and hoped to God that no one else could hear the thundering in her chest.

She looked round to make sure she had their attention before starting. 'When Will Kingsmill founded Kingsmill's back in the 1960s he did it because he had a vision . . .' Tess glanced at Will, noting that he looked less proud than apprehensive about what she was going to say. 'What Will found then was that there was one law for the rich and another for the poor, so he did his damnedest to even up the balance. It wasn't, of course, the recipe to get rich.' Laughter from all round reminded her of the truth of this. 'No doubt there were times, when he saw his fatcat friends in City law firms buying a manor house or adding a swimming pool, that Will may have asked himself if he was mad.'

Will nodded, acknowledging that this was true.

'But you weren't mad, Will,' she reassured him, 'you were right. And there are even more people at the bottom of the heap who need us now. So we must maintain that commitment to the underprivileged before the law follows education and health – and becomes something that can only be bought by the rich.'

Tess knew she had to hold their attention. It was vital she appealed to their emotions, not their logic. She was being too general, she needed some telling examples – like Eileen McDonald's case. One or two partners were already doodling or glancing at their watches.

'Three weeks ago a grey-haired woman of sixty came into my office. She'd been married for thirty years to a rich businessman, had four grown-up children and her husband wanted to divorce her. He'd run off, closed down all their bank accounts, siphoned his fortune off to Switzerland and left her with two hundred and forty pounds a year.'

She could hear the odd tut from their number, but they were, after all, used to seeing the seamier side of human nature. She had to make them sit up. 'So imagine when this nice frail lady gets a call from her husband's lawyer – one of the best-known solicitors in London, by the way – who says, "You might as well give up because all you'll get on legal aid is some rubbishy lawyer who knows damn all about divorce." And she nearly did. As her last chance she came to us instead. And I took her on.' She smiled around the table at the other partners. 'So Will Kingsmill, as well as the rest of the partners, still has something to be proud of thirty years on. As I'm sure it will have in the next thirty. Thank you.'

Tess sat down, feeling wrung out, to the unexpected sound of applause. Listening to it she felt dizzy with relief. It was over and she'd done her best. Maybe, after all, her best would be good enough.

And then it was Patricia's turn.

The moment Patricia began to speak, Tess realized she'd underestimated her. Patricia was far too subtle to say what she really believed, that they should dump the poor and get themselves as many corporate clients as possible. Instead she praised Tess's speech and claimed to be right behind her. But only if the firm was making healthy profits. Which at the moment it wasn't. With terrifying clarity Patricia outlined the changes needed to put that right. A clear vision, better marketing of their services, more emphasis on new clients. And each partner bringing in profits of at least fifty thousand pounds.

And then came the final putting-in of the boot. The case of Eileen McDonald. To Tess's horror Patricia handed out a sheet of figures outlining exactly how much money the McDonald case was likely to cost the firm.

'Helping people like Eileen McDonald may be a worthy gesture,' Patricia concluded, 'but it's one that, at the moment, Kingsmill's can't afford to make.'

Tess listened, her spirits taking a nosedive. It was a brilliant speech and one the partners would find it very hard to resist.

As Patricia sat down there was no clapping as there had been for Tess, but this seemed to Tess simply an acknowledgement of her speech's power. This time Lyall didn't catch her eye. He was looking straight ahead.

Will stood up. 'Thank you both. Now if you could leave us so that we can discuss your two excellent proposals, one from the heart and the other from the head . . .'

As she walked past the postroom on the way back to her office Tess caught sight of the odds against her marked in Pentel on the back of the year-planner. She suspected they'd got it right.

Jacqui was waiting in the office desperate to hear how it had gone.

'I think you can take it Patricia will be the new partner.'

'Come on, Tess,' encouraged Jacqui, 'it's not over yet.'

Tess looked at her watch. After six already. She felt

a sudden longing to be held by Stephen and to see her children. They wouldn't tell her their decision tonight anyway.

She might as well go home.

Stephen cleared his desk at five, feeling good. He was beginning to get somewhere at last. This afternoon he'd sketched out some more designs for the packaging using a nostalgic theme and he was pleased with the results. Tomorrow he'd try some different colourways and present the whole thing to Josephine and Hugo some time in the next week.

On his way to the car he decided to drop in at the studio. With about fifteen of his canvases propped up around the place, it already looked busy and used. He ran his fingers over the neat row of brushes he'd laid out on the work surface and sniffed the linseed oil as though it were perfume.

He'd set up an easel by the long windows and put a blank canvas there this morning. He knew the picture he wanted to paint: it was of a couple he'd seen on the beach in Cork when they'd been there in April. But he couldn't work out the right composition.

He stood leaning on the polished wood of the door frame for a moment, his eyes closed in concentration, trying to conjure up the image that had so transfixed him. And then he had it. The woman had been lying in the foreground examining a shell while the man, ten yards behind her, stared out to sea. They had seemed disconnected, yet connected.

Tearing off his coat in his excitement, Stephen found some charcoal and began to sketch the two figures boldly.

He became so absorbed that he had no idea how

long had passed until he became aware of the light fading and that someone was standing behind him.

He wheeled round to find Josephine in the doorway watching him sketch. He thought for a moment that he might have minded. That this might be precisely the kind of invasion of privacy he'd find irksome. But he didn't. Instinctively, perhaps because Slouch thought so highly of her talent, he knew he could trust her judgement. What he felt was a wary excitement.

He stood back, as if seeing it through her eyes, then turned to her. 'Well? What do you think?'

'Mum!' Ellie leapt on her. 'How did it go? Did you knock the socks off Perry Mason?'

Tess put down her briefcase and hugged her daughter, saying nothing. Who gave a stuff about partnerships when you had a fabulous family and a husband you loved?

'As bad as that, eh?' Ellie asked perceptively. 'Look, you go and sit down. Luke and I'll make supper.'

'Where's Dad?'

Ellie deftly changed the subject. 'Now, what would you like, white wine or a G & T?'

Tess settled down with her feet up and the gossip column of the *Daily Mail* and wondered what the fascination was that caused otherwise sane and sensible people like herself gleefully to follow the antics of disgraced race horse trainers, ageing bimbettes, and naughty majors caught out in massage parlours.

Ten minutes later no drink seemed to be forthcoming and coming from the kitchen was a distinctive burning smell suspiciously like the Bakelite handle of one of her brand-new matching saucepans. Tess jumped up to inspect the damage just as the phone rang.

She picked it up, half expecting it to be Stephen ringing from the car to explain his absence, then remembered the carphone had been in the company BMW.

'Hello, Tess. Will Kingsmill here. I thought you'd want to know that we've come to a decision.'

Tess's heart lurched as wildly as the gearbox during her first driving lesson. Was this a good sign? Was she going to be offered the job after all?

'I would have liked to tell you in person, as we did Patricia.'

Typical Patricia still to be there when Tess had run away.

'But I thought it important to tell you tonight . . .'

There was a pause in which Tess thought she could detect a glimmer of guilt.

'Look, Tess . . .'

Did you say, Look, Tess to people you were about to give jobs to? She doubted it.

'Look, Tess, I'm very sorry but the consensus was that we offer the partnership to Patricia.'

Tess stood, stiff and shivery, in the darkness of the hall. Funny how expecting something didn't make it hurt less.

'Why don't you come and see me tomorrow and we'll talk about it? If it's any consolation it was a very hard decision to come to.'

Tess summoned what dignity she could. 'Thanks for letting me know so quickly.' Very carefully, as though the receiver were made of something breakable, she replaced it. Then she ran upstairs to lock herself in the bathroom, the only place in the house she could be sure of some privacy.

She turned on the taps full blast and poured in half a bottle of her favourite bath foam. All she needed was a little time alone, then she'd be fine. But more than that she wanted Stephen to hold her and love her. Where the hell was he?

'Mum?' There was a gentle knock at the door. 'Mum!'

Tess closed her eyes. Couldn't she get even a moment's peace? She opened the bathroom door.

Luke stood there, a glass of wine in his hand. 'We thought you might like this.'

Tess took the glass and hugged him. He'd always had a sixth sense for other people's pain. Even when only five years old he'd come and put his small hand in hers whenever she looked sad. And it had helped. Just as it was helping now.

'You didn't get the job, did you?' he asked her shoulder.

'No.' Tess stroked his soft hair. 'Someone else did.'

He looked up at her, anxiety in his eyes. 'It wasn't because of my mumps, was it?'

'No, darling.' Tess held him even tighter. 'It was nothing to do with your mumps.'

Looking relieved he slipped quietly away, closing the door behind him.

Tess dropped her towel on the floor. With love like that how could she possibly be miserable? It was only a job, after all. And she still had everything else. They'd manage. She hopped into the welcoming waters of the bath and gasped. It was freezing cold. On top of everything else the boiler must have stopped working.

Tess jumped out, wet and shivering, and threw herself on the floor, weeping unstoppably. She could cope with the big things. It was the little things that really got to you.

★

Stephen busied himself with cleaning his brushes as he waited for Josephine's comments.

'Are you sure you want my opinion?' She went on looking at the sketch. 'It doesn't come with the studio, you know.'

Stephen smiled, grateful that she was being so sensitive, but conscious of how much he did want it. 'I know, and thanks. But I'd like to hear it all the same.'

She surveyed it for a moment longer. 'The composition's wrong. It'd be stronger without the second figure. It draws attention away from the real centre of the picture, the woman.'

He stepped back, fascinated, and saw immediately that she was right. 'But they were both there, in the scene I was painting from life.'

'Tch, tch.' Josephine shook her head, her voice teasing. 'Painting isn't about reality, it's about imagination. But the woman's wonderful.' Her smile widened. 'And you seem to be able to take advice.'

He caught her smile and returned it. 'I wouldn't be too sure about that. Tess says I take criticism about as well as the Pope.'

Josephine's face changed subtly at the mention of Tess. And using her name suddenly reminded Stephen of his promise to be home. He glanced at the clock. It was almost eight p.m. Jesus, he'd been here nearly three hours and it'd be another hour and a half before he got home. Tonight of all nights.

It was almost ten before he opened the front door, clutching champagne and a bunch of slightly wilting roses he'd picked up at a late-night supermarket. The house was silent and unnaturally cold.

He ran up the stairs pausing only to drop a kiss on to Luke's sleeping face before heading for their own bedroom. Tess was sitting up in bed reading. Her eyes were puffy and red.

He held out the flowers but she made no attempt to take them. 'Tess, what happened?'

All evening she'd wanted to hold him, but now that he was finally here all she felt was resentment. 'I would have thought that was obvious. I didn't get the job. Patricia did.'

'Oh, Tess, I'm so sorry. And even more that I wasn't here. I got stuck into a painting and had no idea how late it was.' Even as he offered it, Stephen was aware how feeble the excuse must sound. He put the flowers down and reached for her, but she shook him off.

'Maybe being sorry isn't enough.' Cold and miserable, she turned away, burying herself in the warmth of the duvet. 'Sometimes just being there's what counts. Not buying roses.'

Stephen sat on the bed in silence. Of course she was right.

A moment later she heard him walk to the door and out of the room, leaving the roses by the bedside. For a moment she was tempted to call out to him, to say it was all right. But was it? A few months ago he would never have done this, his acute sense of what she would be feeling would have brought him back like a homing device. But something had happened to that precious empathy.

She lay there, dog tired yet completely awake, trying not to listen out for the sounds he was making downstairs. How strange marriage was. One moment it could seem as strong as a fortress, built of a thousand bricks, each one a different moment, a happy memory, a pain lessened by being shared, the birth of a child, the death of a loved one, jokes laughed at, friends loved together. And then, a moment later, it seemed as fragile as a house of straw.

Half an hour later everything had gone completely quiet. Stephen must be spending the night in the spare room. It was the only time he'd done so in their marriage.

'So,' said Ellie, breezing into the silent and uncomfortable atmosphere of the kitchen next morning, 'who spent the night in the spare room then? Haven't you heard all that stuff about not letting the sun go down on your wrath?'

Tess looked up from her newspaper and caught Stephen's eye. Ellie was offering them a chance to make it up.

But before either of them could answer Luke jumped in. 'Look, Mum, is it money that's worrying you? Ellie and I could always change schools and go to a comprehensive, you know.'

'Speak for yourself,' Ellie protested. 'I'm not mixing with oiks and drug pushers.'

'No,' Luke nodded innocently, 'I suppose you've had enough of them at Chelsea Collegiate.'

Stephen decided the conversation had gone far enough. 'Hang on a minute, no one's going to have to change schools. We'd move house first. Anyway, I've just had an idea that might make me a few quid.'

'I hope it hasn't got four legs,' snapped Tess.

Stephen looked at her as though she was vaguely unfamiliar. 'Tess, for God's sake, it was your father who couldn't keep out of a betting shop, not me.'

'No. But then you're full of surprises these days, aren't you?'

Losing patience with both of them, Ellie stood up and grabbed her backpack. 'Look, if you two aren't

244

going to make it up, can you at least get us to our expensive fee-paying school on time for once?'

Still angry at Stephen and smarting from the rejection over her partnership, Tess was deeply grateful for work. It meant she could hide in her office away from all the sympathetic glances and the 'Better luck next times'.

She attacked the pile in her in-tray with rare gusto. Halfway down she came across the questionnaire just sent back by Eileen McDonald's husband. It made fascinating reading, but the interest lay mainly in what was left out. According to Ted McDonald he was a victim of the recession whose businesses had not fared well. Tess smiled. This wasn't the picture Eileen had painted. She'd better ask Eileen to do some digging.

Tess started to feel more cheerful. She'd just have to prove to Patricia and to the other partners what a mistake they'd made about Eileen McDonald's case. It struck her that this was just the sort of case the media liked to highlight. She might even call one of her old college friends who worked on *The Times* and get her to write an article. After all, there were plenty of other middle-aged women like Eileen, divorced against their will after thirty years of marriage, victims of our liberal views on divorce. It wasn't a bad angle.

'So, what do you reckon our plan of campaign should be?' Stephen had come to his afternoon meeting with Hugo and Josephine bang on time, but Hugo was barking questions at him before he'd even sat down.

'I think we should go ahead in the spring.' Stephen had spent the last few days researching and was confident of his position. 'The US market seems ready for us, providing we package and market ourselves right.

I think we should play the nostalgia card to the hilt. In fact,' he said, reaching down and picking up his folder, 'I've done some preliminary artwork for the packaging.' He handed round some pieces of paper.

Josephine studied the intricate floral designs, impressed that they managed to be both detailed yet dramatic. The style had an almost photographic quality which would shout its individuality from the perfumier's shelves. 'Stephen, these are beautiful . . .'

'They're pretty enough, I grant you,' cut in Hugo, 'but we're aiming for mass-market America and this approach strikes me as lunatic. Surely what we need is something sophisticated, in tune with the times. American women work. They don't sit about in shady nooks sniffing tea roses. All this nostalgic crap is the wrong approach.'

'I disagree.' Josephine was still studying the designs. 'I think Stephen's on the right track. A career woman in Pittsburgh may have nothing in common with an Edwardian lady, but she likes to dream. To feel feminine while she chews off balls. What we're selling isn't reality, it's fantasy. We need to be as English as Anne Hathaway's cottage.'

'As a matter of fact,' Stephen threw in neutrally, realizing he had a difficult game to play here, 'I didn't dream this up on my own. I consulted a friend who understands the American psyche pretty well.'

'Oh yes?' Hugo raised an eyebrow scathingly. 'And who was that? Dr Ruth?'

Stephen grinned. 'No, but I'm sure she'd be very useful. In fact his name's Jack Palazzo.' Hugo shot Stephen a look of disbelief. 'I faxed the designs to him last night and he got back to me straightaway. He thought they were great.'

'How the hell do you know Jack Palazzo?'

'I worked on his British launch and we hit it off. We've stayed in touch.' Stephen realized he was enjoying himself. 'I thought that was why you hired me – for for my US contacts?'

Josephine laughed. 'Then we've got our money's worth.' Despite Hugo's surliness, she was clearly impressed. 'Contacts don't come much better than Jack Palazzo. I think we should listen to him.'

'I suppose so,' Hugo conceded grudgingly, 'but I think we should do some market research too.'

'Of course,' Stephen agreed. 'I've already put some feelers out.'

Hugo stood up, announcing that he'd got another meeting, a tactic Stephen was beginning to recognize as inevitable whenever Hugo felt outmanoeuvred.

'Round one to you, I think.' Josephine seemed almost pleased as she handed the designs back to Stephen.

Stephen wondered if this were a good moment to broach his scheme. 'Josephine . . .?' He paused, wondering if he had the nerve to go on. 'I know this probably sounds a bit ambitious, but do you think any of my paintings are good enough to sell?'

'To sell?' Josephine looked at him in surprise. 'But you shouldn't be thinking about selling. You should be building up a body of work so you can show it.'

'Yes . . .' Stephen hesitated. 'It's just that . . .' He realized Josephine was the last person to whom he could explain their financial position. She'd probably offer him a loan backed by some tactful rationale about how she liked to invest in the future. 'Forget I mentioned it.' It would be better to find another moment.

'Of course, if you needed to make some money, there's a much better way. Have an exhibition.'

'An exhibition?' Stephen sounded astonished. 'But I'm a complete unknown.'

But your father isn't, thought Josephine, though she was far too subtle to say it. 'You may have done enough at least to hook a gallery. You wouldn't get a full-scale show, just a week or two when they've got a gap. If someone took you on you'd just have to work like crazy to get enough done.'

Stephen started to feel excited. 'Do you really think so?'

Josephine shrugged. 'I could put some feelers out if you want. And we'll find out.'

'That would be absolutely great.' Stephen picked up his folder and began to pack away his designs, then stopped for a moment. 'Josephine, you wouldn't have to use my name to try and swing it, would you? I'm only interested in getting somewhere for what I do, not because of who my father happens to be.'

Josephine raised a dismissive eyebrow. 'Stephen, would I?'

As soon as she was alone in her office, Josephine picked up the phone and called Slouch Heyward.

'You know that gallery friend of yours, the one who runs the Zora Gallery and likes appearing in *Tatler*?' Slouch and Tad Zora had met on a painting week in Turkey and had shared so many bottles of Raki they had had to abandon the paintbrush and recuperate on a bare-bottomed boat. 'How do you think he'd like to put on a show by the son of the most famous portrait painter in the world? You could tell him what a PR dream it'd be. Julius is bound to come for the opening. Think of all those father and son pieces in the press. He won't be able to resist. Especially if you tell him someone else will be paying for the champagne and making sure every leading light from the art world shows up for the private view.'

'I imagine he'd jump at the chance.' Slouch smiled slyly. 'But who would be foolish enough to do all that for an unknown artist?'

'Slouch, sweet,' purred Josephine, 'don't act naïve. It doesn't suit you.'

CHAPTER EIGHTEEN

'Tess, this is Eileen McDonald speaking.' Tess picked up her pen, eager to hear what Eileen had to say. 'I think I might have found something rather useful. It's a bank statement.'

'Great, Eileen, where from?'

'From the Grundesbank of Zurich.'

Tess's heart raced. This was what they'd been looking for, the breakthrough they needed. Proof that while Ted McDonald pleaded poverty he was salting away funds in Switzerland. There was only one more thing she needed to know.

'When's it dated?' If it was years old then Ted could try and pretend the account had been closed down and had no bearing on the case.

She could sense Eileen grinning broadly. She knew she'd landed him. 'It's dated two months ago. Just before he left.'

'Fan-tastic!' Tess's smile was as broad as Eileen's. 'I think we've got him!'

She did some fast thinking about the other information they'd dug up and came to a decision. 'Do you know, Eileen, I think it's time we briefed a barrister?'

'This one's fine, but that one' – Josephine stacked the two paintings she was happy with against the windows of the studio – 'could do with some more work.' She put the latter against the other corner and lifted up his life drawing of the artists' model. 'Why don't you do an oil from this? It could be incredibly powerful. What was her name?'

'Olivia Darling, would you believe?' Stephen laughed, watching the autumn sunlight filtering through and picking up red lights in Josephine's hair that he'd never noticed before. 'Do you know, I think Slouch had an affair with her when she was younger. He got positively misty eyed at the sight of this.'

Josephine sat back on her heels. 'Slouch tends to dip his nib in any inkwell he can find. Sometimes when they're still under age.' She looked back at the drawing. 'Not a problem in this case, however.' They both laughed. 'You should get her to sit for you again. You could make her famous. Want a cup of coffee?'

Stephen looked surprised. It was the middle of the afternoon, usually Josephine's busiest time. Yet here she was sorting through his canvases to see which would be good enough for an exhibition. 'Have you got time?'

'Absolutely.' She unwound her long legs and got up, sinuous as a cat after a sleep. 'I love it over here. The light, the peace, all the smells of a studio.'

'So do I. It took me right back to childhood when I walked in here the first time, just like stepping into my father's studio in Chiswick.'

'What was it like, growing up as his son? Were you surrounded by famous artists?'

'Only the drunk ones. Of course some of them are famous now. When I was about six I remember Gregor Bailey coming into my room and raiding the piggy bank. "It's only for mixer drinks, dear boy," he assured me, "not for alcohol." To Gregor there was clearly a fine moral distinction.' Stephen smiled at the memory of his father's best friend, with his vast fur-lined cape and lion's mane of white hair. He'd always liked Gregor. 'He'd be appalled to know how much his work fetches now. He never had the money for a packet of Capstan when he was alive.'

'It sounds wonderful.'

'Not always. It was bloody freezing in winter and no one paid the slightest attention to me. I just had to fit in. How about you? Slouch said you come from Devon and had red cheeks and looked like something from *Cider with Rosie*.'

Josephine threw back her head and laughed noisily. Stephen could see her pink tongue and some fillings in the back of her mouth. It was such an uncharacteristic gesture that he laughed too. 'Absolute balls. I come from Tiverton. A boring little country town. Fine till you're twelve and then hell on earth with nothing to do except bonk in the bus shelters.'

'So that's what you got up to, was it?'

'With some spotty boy from the secondary mod? Absolutely not. I knew my price, kind sir. I saved myself for someone who'd know what to do with me.'

Stephen realized with a shock that they were flirting and that he was hugely enjoying it. Tess and he never talked like this any more, dipping into the past and pulling out pieces of themselves they'd long forgotten. Maybe they already knew everything there was to know about each other. Or perhaps when you were married you didn't have time. There were just too many domestic details to discuss.

'Now I really do have to get back.' Josephine stood up and looked for her shoes. Her feet were so long and narrow that she probably had to have special fittings. Stephen watched her ease them back into their soft leather pumps. It suddenly seemed an act of great intimacy. For a fraction of a second she touched his arm. 'I'm sorry, you never did get that cup of coffee.'

'Never mind, you can always come and make it for me another day.' Afterwards he was faintly shocked at his own tone.

They both smiled. The kind of secret, loaded smile that both knew they would have to wipe away as soon as they left the room.

'How do I look?' Phil asked nervously. Tonight she'd finally had the nerve to ask Terry round to meet her children and was already wondering if it was a good idea.

Hattie and Dan, familiar with their mother's panics, were calming her down. Hattie had taken over the cooking and Dan had poured her a glass of wine.

'You are going to like him, aren't you?' demanded Phil. 'At least promise me that.'

Dan rolled his eyes and went on putting out salted almonds in dainty little dishes and trying to stop his mother giving in to the urge to smoke. 'How can we possibly know? We haven't even met him yet.'

'What am I going to do if you hate him?'

'Probably ignore what we think and go ahead like you usually do.'

'Thanks a lot.'

The doorbell rang and Phil jumped, spilling her wine down her dress.

'Don't worry,' sighed Dan, handing her some of the kitchen roll he kept behind the sofa for his mother's clumsiness. 'I'll go.'

Terry, standing on the doorstep, was equally nervous but knew that to admit it was death. 'Hi. You must be Dan. You support QPR, have just sold your Nintendo and would like to be on the *Crystal Maze*.' He grinned and held out his hand. 'Your mother talks about you occasionally.'

Dan stood back but wasn't offering up a smile this early in the game. 'Hi. Come in. Mum's having kittens in case we don't like you.'

'Quite right.' Terry strolled across the room, sat next to Phil on the sofa and kissed her on the cheek. 'How could you possibly know if you like me. You don't know me.'

'That's what I told Mum.'

'Tell you what, why don't you ask me a few questions to speed things up? You know, the really important things. Do I like football, how much do I earn, do I usually wear ridiculous suits like this?'

Dan giggled. 'All right then. Do you like football?'

'Lifelong Spurs fan. Season ticket. Next question?'

'How late do you let your kids stay up?'

'As late as they like if they're not a bloody nuisance. Are you a bloody nuisance?'

'What sort of pocket money do you give them?'

'Really, Daniel . . .' interrupted Phil.

'It's OK, Phil, I'd rather he asked.' Terry patted her hand then turned back to Dan. 'A tenner a week. They have the choice of spending it all or giving me a fiver to invest for them. I'm very good at making money so they usually do the latter.' He winked at Dan, who was still struggling to look disapproving. 'And, yes, I am hoping to marry your mother. Any objection?'

For once Dan was lost for words.

'Now, Dan, I've got a question for you.' He patted the seat on the sofa next to him. Dan sat down tentatively. 'What do you think of boarding school? One of those really posh ones where they wear tail coats. Eton is it? Or Harrow?'

Terry burst out laughing at the horror written on Dan's face. Slowly Dan returned his smile, realizing that Terry was simply winding him up. 'You're OK. At least you've got a sense of humour, which is more than my dad had. You only have to look at his girlfriend to see that.'

Waiting on Stephen's desk at Richmond & Quinn two days later was the first sample of the packaging based on his design. The small firm of manufacturers he'd discovered had done a brilliant job with amazing speed and efficiency. He picked it up and examined it. It was a really classy product, the colour register clear and defined, without losing any of the vibrancy that he'd feared might be reduced in the production process. It had style as well as individuality. And although it was unashamedly nostalgic it had a kind of chic that rescued it from being cloying or pretty-pretty. Even Hugo might quite like it.

He picked it up and went to see if Josephine was free so that he could show her. As he knocked on their door he looked so pleased with himself that even Lucy remarked on it.

Josephine was standing reading a report by the long windows, her tweed suit in shades that echoed the autumnal scene beyond.

'Stephen, hello. What can I do for you?'

He held out the box.

'Good God, is that a sample already?'

'I didn't think you could really tell just from a design so I had a local firm knock those up. Pretty, isn't it?'

Josephine picked it up. 'It's more than pretty, it's absolutely stunning.' Her eyes held his for a moment. 'Well, Stephen Gilfillan, is there no end to your talents?'

Stephen looked away. There was an unmistakable

challenge in her tone that excited him too much to be able to return her gaze.

'Right,' he said matter of factly, 'I'll leave it with you to show Hugo.'

'So, Miss Brien, you believe your client's husband has been guilty of omission in the matter of his financial position?'

Tess looked at Michael Ellworthy, the eminent barrister sitting opposite her. What made men at the bar so bloody pompous? Michael Ellworthy was probably not much older than she was yet he talked like an eighty-year-old high court judge. 'If you mean is my client's husband lying through his teeth, then yes.'

Ellworthy flinched. 'We have yet to prove that, Miss Brien.'

'Well then,' Tess reached into her briefcase and pulled out the sheaf of Swiss bank statements, 'these should help.'

Men like Ellworthy drove Tess mad. He seemed to have so little enthusiasm for his work she wondered how on earth he got up in the morning. Probably only the thought of the enormous sums he made. Yet he'd come very highly recommended. Tess told herself to give the man a chance.

He looked up from studying the papers. 'By the way, do you know who we've got on the other side?'

'Leonard Savoury,' she announced, watching for his reaction. Would he be cowed at the thought of London's sharpest lawyer opposing them?

Unexpectedly Ellworthy smiled. 'Ah, dear Leonard. He and I play tennis together.'

Tess's eyes narrowed. She was going to have to watch this Michael Ellworthy.

*

256

As Stephen packed up for the day he put the other sample in his bag to show Tess. He'd be interested to know what she thought. Perfume was a weakness of hers. Having to wear all that black to work, she often said it was the only way she could rebel.

She was already sitting at the kitchen table when he got in, so absorbed in some paperwork that she didn't even look up. He kissed her cheek. 'Doing your homework?'

'Mmmm.' She reached a hand up and stroked his face, her eyes still on the papers in front of her. 'I feel like Sam Spade digging up the dirt. It's incredibly exciting.'

'You'd make a great private eye, except you're not patient enough,' Stephen delved into his briefcase. 'I had an exciting day too. Look at this.' He held out the sample perfume box.

Just as Tess was about to look up an inspiration suddenly struck her. Ted McDonald hadn't even mentioned his pension scheme and Eileen should be entitled to at least a share!

Stephen watched Tess taking notes furiously and put the sample back in his bag. She'd been keen enough for him to get the job, but that was where her interest had clearly ended. She didn't care what the hell he did as long as he brought home the bacon. Angrily he turned away and helped himself to a beer from the fridge.

Tess finally looked up and smiled. 'Sorry. What was that you were about to show me?'

'Nothing,' Stephen shrugged, 'nothing of any interest whatsoever.'

Tess watched him walk out, puzzled. She'd only been a second. How typical of a man that his work had to matter more than hers. Well, too bloody bad. She picked up her pen again, but her line of thought had disintegrated. A small flicker of concern lit itself in the back of her mind. She and Stephen still seemed to be going through a bad patch.

'Guess what?' Josephine put her head round the door of Stephen's office, her smile sly and catlike.

'Hugo loves the designs so much,' Stephen hazarded, 'that he's decided in view of my extraordinary talent I can run the launch myself?'

'Not quite. But the Zora Gallery in Cork Street has agreed to give you a show.'

Stephen jumped out of his chair. 'Josephine, you're a marvel! When?'

'They're not sure yet. But you'd better start painting because you might not get much notice.'

Stephen imagined his father's face when he told him. A one-man show! 'This could be an incredible break for me.'

'I know.' Josephine came into the office and closed the door behind her, serious for a moment. 'But you deserve it, you know. I'm not sure you realize just how talented you are. If, and I mean if, you work hard and don't turn into a prima donna.' She sounded almost like Slouch but Stephen knew it was because, like Slouch, she really cared about painting. 'I've seen plenty of promising artists blow it because they start thinking they're Picasso before they've even mastered all the techniques.'

'Yes, Josephine,' Stephen said mock contritely, glowing with pleasure that she thought he was worth all this effort, and even better, that he had real talent. 'I don't know how to thank you for all this.'

'Just don't get so excited you forget about your day job or Hugo will kill me.' She headed for the door. 'Oh. And you can buy me a thank-you drink in a good old British pubbe. Winchester's packed with them. I'll see you at six.'

After she'd gone Stephen thought about Tess. But going for an after-work drink was hardly a betrayal, and anyway, it was her late night tonight. He sat down at his desk and made some calls to perfume buyers in the US, trying to repress the sense of anticipation that kept coming back to him all through the afternoon. But he still noticed the minutes ticking away until it was finally six o'clock.

'We'll drive into the centre and walk the rest of the way,' Josephine said, holding the car door open for him. 'It's a fabulous night.'

And of course it was. Somehow Josephine wasn't the kind of person whose plans got rained on. She'd been sent precisely the kind of evening she'd ordered. Cold and sharp, with air you could almost drink it was so clear. They parked in Little Minster Street and walked, their footsteps ringing satisfyingly on the pavement, past rows of smart shops towards the cathedral. Josephine took his arm in a way that seemed entirely natural, and said, 'When I came to live here, the first thing I noticed was that nobody's poor. Do you think they take people out and shoot them if they earn less than twenty grand a year?'

Stephen grinned. Tonight, away from the business, he was seeing another side of Josephine. Less controlled, more human.

'Hi, Jo, how's it going?' shouted a voice as they passed a bunch of kids draped over the Butter Cross. Stephen looked at the group of bedraggled youths, their heads half-shaved and ponytailed, in tattered jeans with holes at the knees, each of them with a mangy dog on a lead. A hat with a few coins was at their feet. How on earth did Josephine know them?

The boy who'd called out detached himself from the others and walked towards them, juggling five illuminated skittles that glowed magically in the dark. In the narrow medieval street it was almost like being transported suddenly to the middle ages. In the crowd someone strummed a guitar and another played maracas. The boy who was juggling put on a virtuoso performance for Josephine. She clapped delightedly and flung a pound in their hat.

'Beggars?' asked Stephen.

'Buskers. There's a world of difference in my book,' corrected Josephine, 'or rather Crusties, they're called here. They live in teepees outside the town. I think they're rather charming, but the locals don't. Especially the parents. They see Nick there as the pied piper on ecstasy.'

Stephen shook his head. 'You're a very surprising woman.'

'I know.' Again she gave the throaty infectious laugh that seemed so out of character with her sophisticated image.

Stephen laughed too, feeling suddenly elated, almost ridiculously youthful after the encounter with the Crusties, as though some of their carefree irresponsibility had rubbed off on him. On impulse he grabbed her hand and started running. Nick the Crusty watched them and raised an eyebrow at his friend. 'Looks like Jo's got herself fixed up. Lucky man.'

When they were both out of breath, Josephine led him down a narrow back street behind the cathedral and into the Wykeham Arms. It was like walking into a stage set, the precise version of what an English pub should be. Roaring fire, candles on the tables, ancient graffitied schoolboy desks instead of tables, the smell of spiced ale and mulled wine.

They chose mulled wine and sat at a desk in which some former pupil of nearby Winchester College had carved 'Manners Makyth Man' with a penknife. It was almost too perfect to be true.

And Stephen sensed, watching Josephine's eyes sparkle in the firelight, that he must be careful, that he was fooling himself if he thought an occasion like this was entirely innocent. Perhaps he should have made some excuse after all. Yet he couldn't bring himself to get up and leave. Maybe the excitement he was feeling simply came from seeing Josephine out of context.

Tomorrow things would be back on the old footing.

'Gosh, Dad,' Luke enquired unflatteringly at breakfast the next morning, when Stephen announced he was to have an exhibition, 'you mean people are actually going to *buy* your paintings?'

'Amazing though that may seem, yes. At least that's the idea.' He glanced across the breakfast table at Tess, the remnants of guilt still hanging about him from last night. 'Look, why don't we all go out and celebrate tonight?'

'I can't, love,' Tess apologized. 'I'm in court first thing for the final day and I'm going to have to work tonight. Let's go tomorrow.'

'Tomorrow it is then.' But she could see he was disappointed. 'Aren't you going to congratulate me anyway?'

She leaned over and kissed him. 'Of course I am. You're a very clever boy.' Even to her it sounded as though she were talking to Luke.

She gathered up her things for work just as Stephen was disappearing through the front door. Why was it that when women stuck to their guns when they had something important to do, they came out sounding like selfish cows? Yet men did it habitually without so much as twinge of guilt. But then, what if this were some kind of olive branch? Maybe she'd better go after all.

She picked up her briefcase and ran after him. But by the time she'd found her coat and scarf he'd already disappeared round the corner. Tess unlocked her car, telling herself she was damned if she was going to feel guilty. But she felt guilty all the same.

Outside the courtroom where the judge was about to hear her case, Eileen McDonald stood, her silk-effect suit fluttering in the cold wind, wearing a flowery hat more suitable for Ascot.

'Hello, Eileen, you look glorious.' Tess greeted her. 'The only thing is' – leading her tactfully towards the ladies loo, 'the hearing's informal, no wigs or Perry Mason stuff, and it'd probably be better if you looked as ordinary as possible.'

Eileen removed her hat, stripped off the white gloves, and popped her costume jewellery into her handbag. 'Better now?'

'Much better.'

'Pity. It was doing wonders for my confidence.'

Tess squeezed her hand. 'You've got plenty of that anyway.' They headed back towards the court. Outside a small group of people was standing, including both Leonard Savoury and Michael Ellworthy, who were swapping tennis anecdotes.

Eileen stiffened and grabbed Tess's hand. A little way beyond the group stood a perfectly mild-mannered man, peering amiably down the corridor in his bi-focals.

'Oh my God, there's Ted! I haven't seen him since he ran off.'

'Better to get it over with.' Tess shot a glance in his direction. He didn't look the cruel type. But then, she ought to know by now that bastards came in all shapes and sizes. Often the most charming were the worst. If her job had taught her one thing it was to distrust charming men.

And then they were summoned into the courtroom where Mr Justice Martin reminded them that they were here today to discuss the financial settlement not the divorce itself.

The first thing Michael Ellworthy did was to ask Eileen for exact details of her own financial position. Then he moved on to her husband, asking him a few deliberately dull and routine questions about the nature of his assets. Only when he was looking calm and relaxed did Ellworthy move on to more pointed questioning. Tess had to admit, the man was skilled.

'How would you estimate your income, Mr McDonald?' asked Michael Ellworthy.

'About twenty thousand a year,' he replied, looking at the judge over the top of his bi-focals. Tess could hear Eileen sucking in her breath in disbelief.

'Mr McDonald, you say in your questionnaire that you hold the following bank or building society accounts.' Ellworthy read out a list.

Ted McDonald nodded. Ellworthy paused for a moment and Ted took this as a cue that he could sit down. At the last minute Ellworthy stopped him.

'Mr McDonald, there was one further point I'd like to query. Perhaps you thought you only had to declare your assets in the UK? Do you in fact have a Swiss bank account at all?'

'No, sir, I do not.' Ted McDonald managed to look both innocent and shocked.

Michael Ellworthy paused as if searching through

his papers. Then turned to Eileen. 'Mrs McDonald, hold up the piece of paper in your hand, if you would?'

Feeling more confident, Eileen did so.

'Could you tell us what it is, Mrs McDonald?'

'It's a bank statement from the Grundesbank of Zurich,' Eileen stated clearly, 'I found it in my husband's study.'

Ted McDonald visibly started and got a quelling look from Leonard Savoury.

'And what is the date on the statement?'

'Two months ago.'

'And how much is the balance on the account?'

This time it was Eileen's turn to keep them hanging on. She looked her husband in the eye. 'Over six hundred thousand pounds.'

'And exactly how much has your husband left at your disposal to support yourself?'

'Two hundred and forty pounds a year.'

Tess tried not to smile. They were almost home and dry.

Mr Justice Martin chose this moment to adjourn for lunch and Tess felt like taking Eileen out to a celebration drink. But she'd learned that in this business it was better not to count your chickens until you'd seen them safely back into the hen house. You never knew who would turn out to be a fox in sheep's clothing.

'How's it going?' whispered Eileen as they sat down in the coffee shop round the corner to grab a quick sandwich.

Tess crossed her fingers. 'Pretty well, I think. But we've still got this afternoon, and Leonard Savoury's been suspiciously quiet.'

As they walked back towards the chambers Tess glanced in at the open door of the Black Cap, a favourite pub for local lawyers. Michael Ellworthy and Leonard Savoury were leaning against the bar drinking whisky, pally as old school chums.

From then on things got worse. To Tess's fury Ellworthy seemed to be softening every blow, despite the flurry of notes she kept sending him. As the afternoon drew on Tess knew her suspicions were right. Ellworthy and Savoury had come to some kind of locker-room deal. They'd agreed to compromise. It was common enough – the lawyers would get the case neatly wrapped up in a day – but Tess hated it. Despite all the information they'd dug out about how much money Ted McDonald really had and exactly where he was keeping it, Eileen would end up with a much smaller settlement than she deserved.

By three-forty-five Tess decided she'd had enough and sent a note to their barrister demanding an adjournment on the grounds that she'd just had access to further information.

Michael Ellworthy turned furiously in her direction. They both knew it was bollocks but Tess smiled sweetly all the same.

Twenty minutes later the judge emerged from the robing room to witness Miss Tess Brien tearing several strips off learned counsel in the shape of Michael Ellworthy, QC, an ambitious man Mr Justice Martin had never much liked. He smiled as he passed. That young woman was very impressive. And what's more she was right. It was obvious to anyone with half a brain that McDonald was concealing assets simply to keep them from his wife.

He smiled and nodded to them both as he passed.

Tess, mid-acrimonious sentence, stopped and smiled back, a wave of excitement flooding through her. Was it too much to hope or did she get the impression the judge was on their side?

CHAPTER NINETEEN

It was Ellie who noticed that Stephen seemed to be coming back later and later these days. At first she decided not to mention it, at least to Tess. After all, now that he was having an exhibition there was always the chance he really was painting.

Tess, still immersed in her precious case, hardly seemed to notice.

'Where's Dad?' Tess asked a couple of nights later when she was back particularly late herself, putting down her bulging briefcase, feeling shattered after a gruelling day. Ellie raised an ironic eyebrow. 'Stuck on the M25, or so he says.' Her voice dripped sarcasm. 'Roadworks apparently. They seem to have a lot of those, don't they? He rang half an hour ago.' She looked up at her mother, her eyes challenging, 'He's hardly home, is he, these days?'

Suddenly the accuracy and obviousness of this statement hit home. It was true. Stephen was getting back later and later. 'Come on, Ellie,' Tess coaxed, reassuring herself as much as her daughter, 'he's trying to work *and* paint. There probably aren't enough hours in the day.'

That night in bed her worry made Tess reach for him, hoping that making love might bring them closer to each other. But for once Stephen, usually ever eager, made an excuse.

'Look, love,' she murmured, 'what's the matter? I know we're both tired but is that all it really is?'

'Yes,' lied Stephen, hoping as much as she did that this was true. 'That's all it is. Really.'

And within seconds he was deeply sleep. Often in the past she'd envied him this capacity to fall totally and utterly asleep as soon as his head hit the pillow. But tonight she resented it. It seemed somehow an act of aggression, of closing her firmly out.

When she woke he was already up and downstairs. Tess lay in bed listlessly. Something was going wrong between them. They hardly ever seemed just to sit down and spend time together. One of them, or often both, was always rushing somewhere. It was time she did something about it. Tonight she'd come home early and cook a proper supper for them. Roast pork, his favourite, with roast potatoes and apple sauce. What was it her mother always advised friends who were worried about their husbands? Turn up the central heating and make him a nice casserole. Very politically incorrect and probably deadly accurate.

'What time do you think you'll be home tonight?' Tess asked when she went downstairs, kissing the top of his head.

But to her amazement Stephen exploded. 'For Christ's sake, Tess, I don't *know*! You want it both ways, don't you? You can't cope if I don't earn enough, and then when I try to make some money you get at me for not being home. What is it you *want* from me?'

Luke jumped up from the breakfast table, spilling his cereal bowl. 'Stop fighting!' he yelled. 'This is our home too! And we never see either of you. Why don't you think about us for a change?'

He ran out of the room, leaving Tess and Stephen staring at each other, wondering if either of them should follow him.

Ellie stood up first. 'He's right, you know. It isn't

267

much fun round here lately. You two used to quite like each other. Now you're just like everyone else's parents.' She followed Luke out of the room.

'I think maybe it's time we saw a bit more of our children,' Tess said ruefully, 'and maybe each other too. What are you doing this weekend?'

Stephen, who'd been looking forward all week to finishing a big landscape, knew when he was beaten. 'I rather thought Hamleys with Luke, then lunch at Ellie's favourite Chinese? Maybe that new Spielberg film Luke keeps talking about? With lots of popcorn? Rounded off by dinner with my wife.'

Tess grinned. 'Sounds good to me.'

Tess woke bright and early on Monday morning, buoyed up by the fun of the first weekend they'd all spent together in months. Hamleys had been hell, as expected, but Luke had at least decided what he wanted for Christmas. Elsie had pigged out on dim sum. There had been the usual arguments about sweet v. salty popcorn and Ellie had put up a ritual howl of disdain at being dragged off to a kids' film, then sat gripped throughout, hiding her face in Stephen's jacket at the scary bits. To Tess's intense embarrassment she had felt tears slip down her face at the happy ending. If only life were like that. After that Inge had babysat while they went out to their local Italian, drank too much Chianti, came back and made satisfying, if a little automatic, love.

Tess smiled to herself. They'd just lost sight of each other for a moment, that was all. It was frighteningly easy to do, and she'd just have to keep an eye out that it didn't happen again.

Gently she leaned over to Stephen and touched his lips with her finger. She could see why Ellie's friends fancied him despite his great age. They were right. He didn't look like other fathers.

Quietly, so as not to wake him, she got dressed, brushing out her long red hair and putting in her bold new earrings instead of her usual tiny seed pearls. They might make you wear sober black in court but they couldn't do anything about your earrings.

She pulled the curtains and stood watching the pink dawn come up over the sleeping rooves of London. Today was a big day for her. They were back in court with Eileen and she had high hopes of winning a really big settlement. She crept downstairs and made herself a pot of coffee, luxuriating in the thought that she had at least half an hour before anyone else invaded her peace.

As it turned out it was more like twenty minutes before Luke and Ellie thundered down the stairs and burst into the kitchen.

'I don't want to go to school today, Mum,' announced Luke, 'Spencer in 5b says I've got BO.'

'Well, tell him to get lost,' advised Tess unperturbed.

'But do I, Mum?' Luke attempted to sniff his own armpit.

Tess, who had in fact noticed a faint hum given off by Luke's T-shirts, asked, 'Why don't you get some deodorant? Then you won't have to worry what Spencer in 5b says.'

'Yes,' seconded Ellie, 'why don't you? Buy some Brut. Then you can smell like a poofter instead of a gorilla on heat.'

When she finally got away Tess decided to go straight to the court rather than via the office as she'd planned. It was an easier journey anyway.

By half past nine there was already a small knot of

269

people outside the judge's chambers. Among them Tess recognized John Finch, a young lawyer from Kingsmill's. She wondered briefly who'd been considerate enough to send her some back-up on this important final day. It'd be nice to have him there to witness her triumph.

Tess smiled and stretched out her hand to him in welcome. 'Hello, John, I didn't expect to see you here.'

Instead of returning her smile, John, new to the firm and all of twenty-five, looked hideously embarrassed.

'What on earth's the matter?' asked Tess.

'I'm really sorry, Tess,' he replied in strangulated tones, 'but I assumed you knew all about this. Patricia Greene sent me down to replace you. They want you back in the office.'

Tess stormed straight past the Kingsmill's reception desk and into Patricia's office without even bothering to find out if she was interrupting anything. She was burning with a fine Celtic fire and knew that if she stopped to question it she would lose the sense of outrage she needed to insist on an answer.

'Patricia,' she demanded, ignoring the flustered Suzanne who was in mid-discussion of billing procedures, 'perhaps you could tell me exactly why I've been replaced on the Eileen McDonald case?' She flung her briefcase down on the spare chair with such force it rocked. 'And the answer had better be a bloody good one!'

To Tess's horror Patricia smiled, as though this were a scene she had been expecting and was more than prepared for. 'I'd be delighted. Though perhaps Suzanne might like to leave us first.'

Suzanne gathered up her papers, looking disappointed. She'd hoped to be a witness to the drama and be able to spread it all round the office.

'Why don't you have a seat?' Patricia gestured to the chair Suzanne had just vacated.

'I don't want a seat,' Tess flashed, 'I want an answer.'

'The answer's quite simple,' Patricia looked up at her with infuriating cool. 'Will Kingsmill asked me to look at ways of cutting costs. An obvious solution was allocating junior rather than senior staff to badly paid legal aid work. Your case was the obvious choice.'

'Then why the hell wasn't I told?' Tess's eyes still glinted with fury. 'How do you think I felt arriving in court this morning to be told by some spotty law graduate that I'd been taken off the case?'

'Rather embarrassed, I assume,' Patricia agreed smoothly, 'but if you'd either come into the office as your diary said you were going to or checked your answering machine you would have already known about it.'

'We were on the point of winning that case. As you probably know.'

'Then I'm sure John Finch will carry on the good work. No one's trying to steal your glory.'

This was too much for Tess. 'This isn't about my glory. It's about getting a fair deal for an old woman.' She stalked towards the door. 'Look, I'm not prepared to leave this here. I'm going to talk to Will Kingsmill about it.'

'Why don't you do that?' Patricia's smile held a hint of smugness. Tess's heart sank. There was only one reason she would react like that.

If she and Will Kingsmill had already talked the whole thing through already.

'What do you mean, Miss Brien has had to return to the office?' Eileen McDonald had a flinty gleam in her eyes which the other ladies from her bridge club would have instantly recognized. They would have advised the young man standing opposite her to give in now. 'I saw her here five minutes ago. Tess would never have gone off at this point. She's a fighter.' She looked across at their barrister for confirmation, but Michael Ellworthy was simply looking relieved.

'I understand there was some urgent matter to attend to,' soothed John Finch in an attempt to pacify her.

'Urgent matter, my arse,' announced Eileen, causing the men in the group to look shocked. 'there's something funny going on here.'

In court Eileen decided her only course of action was to be as disruptive as possible. She was damned if she was going to be palmed off with some pimply youth. She wanted Tess back.

'Now, Mrs McDonald.' Michael Ellworthy leaned towards her at his most pompous. 'Could you tell us exactly what assets you have in addition to the two hundred and forty pounds per annum your husband is transferring to you?'

'Do you know, Mr Ellworthy,' Eileen simpered, suddenly the picture of a helpless white-haired old lady, 'the figures have completely slipped my memory.'

Michael Ellworthy raised his eyes to the ceiling. 'And do you not have them written down anywhere, Mrs McDonald?'

'I thought that's what legal advisers were for, Mr Ellworthy.' Eileen beamed. 'I'm sure Miss Brien would have them.'

'Do you have the figures, Mr Finch?' enquired the

judge, equally aware that something odd was taking place.

'I'm afraid I don't, your honour.' John Finch thumbed through the pile of papers Tess had handed him, flustered. He'd thought the substance of the case was already over and he'd only been sent to oversee the settlement.

'I think, Mrs McDonald,' Mr Justice Martin was hugely enjoying himself by now, 'that we had better wait until your learned representatives have sorted out what they're doing, don't you?'

Eileen smiled in triumph, every sign of the vulnerable old dear of five minutes ago forgotten, as the case was adjourned once again.

Tess almost ran into the Ladies and splashed cold water on her scalding face. She could not remember feeling this angry ever before. She glanced in the mirror to see tears glittering in her eyes, just below the surface. She'd always been like this. Tears only moments away from extreme anger. Once before, when she'd lost her temper with a stupid motorist who'd almost run down six-year-old Luke, she'd bellowed at him only to find tears beginning to well up in her eyes. And the man, whom she had actually wanted to kill, had said, *There, there, you'll feel better in a minute*.

Leaning over the basin, feeling almost physically sick, she knew what she wanted to do. Not to walk into Will Kingsmill's office and listen to his sensible justifications of why things had to be this way. What she wanted to do more than anything in the world was to stride in there and tell him to forget his stupid job, just as he'd forgotten all the principles his firm had been founded to enshrine. And then to walk out of the building.

Willing herself to calm down she tidied her unruly red hair, and put on some make-up to cover the streaks where she'd been crying. She applied some confident red lipstick, smoothed down her suit, and shook her head once so that her Celtic crosses jangled assertively in her ears; ready to walk out of the Ladies and straight in to Will Kingsmill. Outside his door she paused to listen for voices. As she stood there, grasping the doorhandle, it struck her that this was precisely the position Stephen had been in only six months before. And she had accused him of an entirely male response, thinking only of himself and not of his family. And the same was even more true of her. Her income was vital to all of them.

Slowly she turned round and walked back to her office.

Jacqui was waiting for her just inside the door. Clearly word had got round already.

'Hot news from the courtroom.' Tactful as ever, Jacqui made no mention of the scene in Patricia's office. 'John Finch didn't have the right facts with him, and neither did Pompous Eldridge. So the judge postponed it all till they could get their act together. The case has been adjourned. Patricia's absolutely furious.'

'Do you know,' Tess said, 'that makes me feel a whole lot better.'

'Yes. I thought it might.'

The phone rang on Tess's desk and before Jacqui had time to reach for it, Tess picked it up herself.

'Hello,' said a plummy voice she didn't recognize, 'is this Miss Tess Brien?'

'Yes, this is Tess Brien.'

'Good. Sorry to call you out of the blue, only it is rather urgent. My name's Anne Salisbury. I'm a partner at Hanover's.' Tess wondered what on earth one of the poshest legal firms in London could possibly want with her. When royals decided their marriages had reached rock-bottom they called Hanover's, whereas Tess's clients called the police. No doubt the woman wanted to co-opt Tess on to some dull committee designed to bring more women into the profession. 'The thing is, we're looking for a solicitor who's experienced in family law. And you come highly recommended.'

'Really?' Tess tried not to sound too surprised and racked her brains to think whom she knew in Hanover's circles. No one. 'Who by?'

'As a matter of fact' – the woman dropped her voice confidentially – 'Mr Justice Martin. He seems to think very highly of you. So I wondered, would you be free to come and have a chat?'

Tess felt she could have kissed the man. This'd be one in the eye for Patricia Greene all right.

'Certainly.'

'Would tomorrow suit you?'

Tess stood in the middle of Grays Inn and stared up at the sweeping steps and colonnaded façade of the Hanover's building, designed in the seventeenth century by Inigo Jones. Nothing could be more different from Kingsmill's tatty paintwork and smart though still functional interior. But then, one look at a place like this and half of Tess's clients would have done a bunk.

Inside, the reception area reminded her less of a law firm than a plush museum, with a hint of West End hotel. The carpet she was walking on was deepest pile in a warm shade of claret, everywhere marble busts of eminent legal figures gazed down at her. Even the receptionist looked like she'd been to Finishing School and when Tess gave her name she had to struggle not to whisper, as though they were in church.

She sat and waited, noticing the piles of *Country Life* and *The Connoisseur*, spiced up by the occasional brand-new copy of *Vogue*. There was no sign of the tattered copies of *Woman's Realm* and *Bella* she kept outside her own office, with all the recipes and tips and hints for curing herpes ripped out by the clients.

Tess was just in the middle of a fascinating article on the hazards of stud farming in *The Field* when Anne Salisbury arrived to fetch her. She'd had no idea how hard it was. No wonder the aristos looked so long faced. As if Lloyds hadn't been enough.

'Miss Brien, how nice to meet you. I'm Mrs Salisbury. Perhaps you'd like to follow me?'

No Christian names here, Tess noted, following Mrs Salisbury up another swoop of claret staircase. Maybe they were cosier when they got to know you. After ten years or so.

They followed the welcoming smell of fresh coffee into a large meeting room, where four men in dark suits were already seated round a polished mahogany table. On a matching sideboard stood a cafetière, surrounded by six bone-china cups and a plate of Belgian biscuits, the kind they sold in Marks and Spencer that she was always telling Luke he couldn't have because they were too expensive.

'Sorry about the five thousand' – Mrs Salisbury gestured at the group round the table – 'the thing is we were rather badly let down at the last moment by a partner who went on maternity leave and Got Motherhood.' She wrinkled her nose as though it were a rather unpleasant social disease. 'And we need to find a replacement rather quickly. So I thought it would save time if you met some of the other partners today.'

'You've just been appearing before Mr Justice Martin, I understand,' threw in one of the pin-striped partners sitting opposite her. 'He seems very impressed. In fact he described you as the Joan of Arc of the Family Division.'

Tess laughed. 'Or the Joan Rivers, perhaps.'

Four faces looked back at her blankly. They probably listened to Mahler instead of watching television.

'Richard Martin is very friendly with our Senior Partner,' confided Anne Salisbury.

'I see.' Tess sipped her coffee. 'So what exactly does the job involve?'

Tess listened as Anne Salisbury outlined a job that was in essence not so very different from the one she already did. Except for the clientele. For twenty minutes or so they discussed her experience and how soon she might be available.

Finally the partner opposite smiled coyly. 'Well, Miss Brien, I expect you'd like to know about the remuneration?'

When he told her Tess was deeply grateful she didn't have a mouthful of coffee because it would certainly have ended up down her smart lace blouse. If she got this job all their money worries would be over. Stephen could give up Richmond & Quinn and paint full time.

'Well, Miss Brien,' Anne Salisbury rounded off briskly, 'is there anything else you'd like to know?'

There was. And Tess knew she'd been putting off asking about it.

'Just one thing,' Tess smiled affably. 'Do you do any legal aid at all?'

The partners exchanged small smiles as though she'd just cracked a rather daring joke.

'To tell you the truth, Miss Brien, we're rather at the other end of the market.'

'So how did it go?' Ellie demanded the moment Tess walked in the door. 'Are you going to be a high-powered lady lawyer with Armani suits and a company Porsche like they have on the telly?'

Tess ruffled her daughter's disgraceful haircut. 'Highly unlikely. Especially if they ever see you. They'd ban me at once for lack of parental control.' She looked round for Stephen. She'd seen his car as she was coming in. 'Where's Dad?'

'Playing with Luke and those appalling plastic wrestlers of his. Can't he see,' she said, shaking her head with all the worldly wisdom of a sixteen-year-old, 'that they're just Barbie dolls in drag?'

'No, I don't suppose he can.' Tess smiled at the memory of how much Ellie had loved her own Barbie, dressing and redressing it endlessly for hours, only able to sleep if it was next to her on the pillow.

The sitting room carpet was almost invisible under Luke's wrestling ring and a virtual army of hideous plastic fighters, while Stephen operated a machine that made them go 'Unnnh!' or 'Ugggh!' whenever they fell over. When he saw Tess, he looked up a shade guiltily, clutching a figure of Bulk Brogan, the man who dared to suggest wrestling might be fixed.

'Hello, love.' He waved Bulk's arm at her in greeting. 'How was it?'

'I'll tell you later when we get some peace.' She clapped her hands. 'Come on, put Bulk Brogan away. Time for bath and you can read in bed.'

'Oh, Mum,' yelped Luke. 'We're at a really interesting bit. Bulk's got British Bulldog in a double neck-throttle. Can't I have five more minutes?' The age-old cry of every child told it's bedtime ensured it was after ten when Stephen and Tess finally sat down with a glass of wine. She described the set-up at Hanover's carefully to him, keeping the salary till last.

'So.' She rested her head briefly on his shoulder. 'What do you reckon?'

Stephen topped up their glasses. 'What I think is that you shouldn't touch it with a ten-foot pole.' He jumped up and started pacing between Luke's wrestlers. 'For God's sake, Tess, it'd be a betrayal of everything you've ever believed in. I don't know why you're even thinking about it!'

Tess looked him in the eye. 'For two reasons. One is that I'd love to tell Patricia Greene that they can stuff their bloody job. And the other thing I was thinking of was you. If I earned all that dosh you could stop working for Josephine Quinn.'

Stephen put his finger to her cheek, touched. 'Don't worry about me. I'm going to have an exhibition, remember?'

Stephen had never painted on a Saturday in Winchester before but since Ellie and Luke were both out all day and Tess wanted to go shopping, he decided to drive down. There was an idea he'd been wanting to have a crack at for weeks now. Today he'd give it a go.

The motorway was wonderfully empty with only a few late-starting weekenders, their cars packed with bikes and duvets, and he made the journey in record time. He turned into the drive with almost the whole day ahead, pleased with himself that he'd even managed to remember to bring some milk.

He glanced up at the Lodge windows as he parked, wondering what Josephine did with her weekends. Maybe she was still in bed, breakfasting on brioche brought to her by one of those mysterious servants you never saw, reading the Saturday supplements undisturbed by loud music or children. He wondered for a moment what her bedroom would be like. How extraordinary to have the money and the freedom to choose precisely what you wanted, without even compromising your taste to that of a budget or another person. No unseemly arguments over duvet covers in John Lewis for her. Would it be unashamedly romantic with swathes of lace and piles of broderie anglaise pillows? Surely Josephine was more the exotic type. He could see her lying back in a tent of fabric, all jewel-like colours, yet somehow subtle and original like she was.

Stephen willed himself back to the present. What on earth was he thinking about? He'd come to paint, not to fantasize about Josephine's boudoir.

Ten minutes later he sat in the middle of the studio floor, warmed by invisible heating designed to chase away the chillest November air, nursing his cup of coffee. His eyes were closed as he tried to picture in his mind's eye what he wanted to paint. Until now he'd mostly confined himself to still lifes and to people. Now he wanted to try a landscape. But none of that gentle Sunday-painter stuff. What was in his mind was something altogether starker. He willed himself back to Cork where, as a boy, he'd stood on the beach or the nearby jetty hearing the winds lashing, chasing the fishing boats back to harbour in the face of a sudden squall.

When the memories came back so vividly that he could almost smell the sea and hear the waves, Stephen began to paint.

'What time do you think they'll be here, love?' Phil

asked Terry anxiously. He put his arm round her, loving her for her excitement.

'In about half an hour, I should think.'

Hattie and Dan appeared at her shoulder, surveying the table she'd just laid with a Winnie-the-Pooh tablecloth, plus matching plates and cups, crackers and hats, funny noses, a little present on each plate, and party bags.

'You don't think you've gone a bit over the top, Mum?' Dan blew a squeaker and a feather jumped out at the end. 'I mean, they are nine and eleven.'

Phil, with her usual panache, ignored him. This was the first time she'd ever met Terry's children and she was going to make it an occasion to remember.

An hour later they still hadn't arrived. 'How much longer do we have to wait?' Hattie demanded. 'I'm starving.'

'We'll give them another half-hour, shall we?' said Phil, trying to hide her worry that they weren't coming at all. Terry lobbed a couple of sandwiches in the children's direction.

By two-thirty he came and put his arm round her. 'We might as well face it, Phil, they're not coming. We'd better go ahead without them.'

Phil uncharacteristically burst into tears.

Terry jumped up. 'I'll ring her. I'll ring the selfish cow.'

Angrily he dialled Angela's number. After only a couple of rings her voice came on the line.

'For God's sake, Ange, where are the kids?' demanded Terry. 'We've been sitting here at a table decked out like Christmas for two sodding hours.'

'Oh Terry, how awful for you,' purred Angela. 'You didn't mean *this* weekend, did you? I thought you meant next. So sorry.' And she put the phone down.

'She knew.' Terry dropped his head in his hands, thinking of his children creased up with disappointment, used once again by Angela to get at him. 'She knew which weekend we meant, all right. Phil, she's done this deliberately.'

Terrified of hating what he'd painted if he stopped to look at it, Stephen worked on until his arms ached and the light began to fade outside. Finally he stood back and surveyed his canvas. It was far more ambitious than anything else he'd tried. And so far it was only the bones. But he'd established the shapes he wanted and the streaks of colour, which were brighter and more outlandish than any he'd ever used before.

Looking at it he felt excitement fighting with uncertainty. It had emotion, certainly, yet he had no idea whether it was brilliant or absolute rubbish.

Behind him he heard the door open and he felt a wave of pleasure and relief. She'd come. And he realized that all day he'd been hoping she might. She would know if it was any good and she was the one person he could trust to tell him the truth.

He turned, his face alight with anticipation, to find not Josephine but Hugo standing in the doorway.

'Working weekends now, are you?' Hugo's voice held its usual undercurrent of innuendo. 'How very keen you are. You haven't seen Josephine, I suppose?'

'I came here to paint. I haven't seen anyone.'

Sceptically Hugo watched Stephen begin to clean his brushes. Stephen knew he suspected there was something going on between him and Josephine, but he was wrong. Their relationship was perfectly innocent. Then why had he felt such intense disappointment when it hadn't been her standing in the doorway?

Perhaps it was time he faced an uncomfortable truth. He was deeply attracted to her, and in the most dangerous kind of way, to her mind as much as her body. During office hours it was perfectly containable, but spending so much time here was clearly asking for trouble. He was going to have to find a studio somewhere else.

'Tess, I made up my mind about something this afternoon.'

Tess was sitting at the kitchen table reading a letter from her friend Catherine in the country. Apparently there were a few problems in paradise after all. Josh, her husband, had been behaving very oddly. She looked up, taken aback by the determination in Stephen's tone.

'I've decided to look for a studio somewhere round here. I think I'm spending too much time at the other end of the M3. I'll go and nose about in Lots Road tomorrow. There used to be some old lock-up studios round there.'

Tess smiled, delighted he'd thought up the idea himself. She too had been getting worried at the amount of time he was away from home.

'Whoopee.' Ellie abandoned the peanut butter sandwich she was making and threw her arms round him. 'I knew you'd see sense in the end. Why eat hamburger out, as Blessed Paul Newman said, when you can have steak at home?'

Stephen knew she couldn't possibly mean what it sounded as though she meant. 'Ellie, what on earth are you on about?'

'Oh, nothing.' she smiled innocently, then reached out a hand and stroked his hair. 'I love you, Dad.'

Whatever Ellie's implication Tess didn't seem to have picked it up, thank God.

'I love you too, Eleanor,' he said. And their eyes held each other's for a moment. It was he who was the first to look away.

'Hiya, Lucy. Is Josephine about?' He might as well tell her his decision now in case he started back-tracking.

'In London all day, I'm afraid.' Lucy returned his cheerful smile. She liked Stephen. Hugo talked about doing his own admin but that didn't seem to include a million demeaning little jobs, from buying his pana-tellas to picking up his dry cleaning. Stephen actually did his own fetching and carrying. 'Do you want me to try and find her for you?'

Stephen shook his head. 'No, no. It's not important. I'll catch her sometime.' He disappeared into his office to make some calls. If Josephine and Hugo OK'd it he'd probably nip over to New York to talk to some of the key buyers pretty soon.

After work he couldn't wait to get down to his landscape. It was Tess's late night and he might as well make the most of the studio space. He wouldn't have it much longer.

By nine p.m. he was exhausted and told himself that if he was intending to drive home he'd better do it now. He was just cleaning his brushes when he heard the crunch of a car turning into the gravel of the drive. It was probably Josephine. For the first time he felt a shock of panic at the idea of being alone with her. If she saw the lights she might well come over. He turned them all off apart from one small spotlight over the workbench and quickly finished the brushes.

Then he remembered his car was in the drive. Of course she would know he was here. A streak of light suddenly lit up the studio from the kitchen door.

'You're working late. Can I see it?' Josephine was about to put on all the lights.

'Not tonight, I'm shattered. I was just leaving as a matter of fact.' He picked up his jacket. 'Look, Josephine, there's something I need to mention. It's fabulous here but I feel I need to find somewhere to paint nearer home.'

Josephine's face betrayed no emotion. 'Of course. How sensible of you. Maybe Slouch knows somewhere.'

Stephen felt a pin-prick of rebellion that Josephine was once again taking over his decisions. 'It's fine. I'll find somewhere.'

Then she noticed his hands, which in his hurry to get away were still covered in paint. 'You can't go home like that,' she insisted with nurselike briskness, 'you may not have any turps at home. Clean them here.' She led him, mildly protesting, to the counter where the turpentine was kept. Pouring some on to a rag, she took one of his hands in hers and began to clean it.

Despite himself Stephen closed his eyes. In some strange way her action brought visions of Mary Magdalene. And Stephen wondered sacrilegiously if having his feet cleaned gave Jesus the same guilty sexual charge as he was feeling now.

CHAPTER TWENTY

Josephine lay in her luxurious French bed watching the dawn light up the sky and panicking. She'd taken Stephen's news about the studio calmly but she hadn't felt calm. Until then she'd felt so confident that, slowly but surely, she was winning. She was the one who appreciated him and understood the artistic temperament while all he ever seemed to get from Tess was vague resentment. She could offer him so much. And she'd thought he was starting to see that. But tonight, when he'd told her about the studio, she'd seen everything slipping away. Stephen wasn't like her other conquests. He had a conscience. And yet, in a contradictory way, that was one of the things she liked about him.

What if the studio was only the beginning and soon he'd leave the job too? Perhaps he'd seen the light in her eyes and decided it was too dangerous. She'd tried to be subtle, to become friends first. Or maybe she hadn't been obvious enough?

For a brief moment she wondered if her behaviour was justified. Of course it was. No one was unfaithful if their marriage was really working. And if it wasn't, then why was what she had in mind so terrible?

Everyone got divorced these days. Almost every couple she knew was on their second marriage. It was unrealistic to think you could stick with one person all your life. Tess of all people ought to know that. And the children were hardly babes in arms. She remembered what a New Yorker friend had said to her about her own marriage split. 'We made it for ten years. Ten years is a long marriage in the US.'

And, after all, it wasn't as though she were trying to seduce him into some casual affair. Her intentions towards him were serious, if not honourable. She wanted him for keeps. She hadn't planned it that way, but over the months of working together it had just happened. She was in love with him. And – she smiled to herself in the glowing softness of the dawn – love justified anything, didn't it? It was time she took decisive action. Before it was too late. She needed to find ways of making herself essential to him. The exhibition was one. Without her it wouldn't happen. She'd better lean on Tad Zora for a firmer commitment.

Phil had come into the office early, but sat gloomily staring at the photograph of Terry on her desk instead of working. She did not feel her outrageous, bouncy, motivated self at all. This business with his children was beginning to affect their relationship. Terry knew Angela was using the kids to string him along, but as long as she went on claiming it was an accident there seemed to be nothing he could do. Poor Terry, Angela really had him by the balls. If he gave up trying that would be the end of his relationship with his own kids. And Angela knew it. Maybe that was what she was trying to achieve.

Phil began to feel a wave of healthy restorative anger. She wasn't going to let the cow get away with it. Or wreck her and Terry's relationship on the way. Maybe Tess would have some ideas. There must be *something* they could do about Angela.

'Mum, have you seen my clarinet music anywhere?'

Tess, just about to go out of the front door, swore under her breath. 'Can't Inge find it, or Dad?'

'He's already left and Inge's looked everywhere. She said to ask you.'

Tess put down her briefcase and spent the next twenty minutes feverishly searching for the missing music until Luke came into the sitting room holding it up triumphantly.

'Where was it?' Tess asked wearily.

'Do you know what?' Luke marvelled at his own efficiency, 'I'd put it into my schoolbag already!'

Tess jumped up with eye-defying speed. 'Come here, you horrible little squirt, so that I can wring your neck for you!'

By the time she got to the office she was twenty minutes late for her meeting. Wonderful Jacqui stood with the appropriate file held out ready.

'Children,' Tess muttered darkly, 'put them off as long as possible. Till you're seventy or eighty at least.'

'I will,' nodded Jacqui. 'By the way, I nearly forgot. That Mrs Salisbury rang again from Hanover's. She said it was quite urgent that you call her back. Now what does a posh firm like Hanover's want with us again? Go on, tell me. The Queen's getting divorced, and we're acting for Prince Philip?'

Tess pushed a reluctant Jacqui towards the door. 'Be a love, go and make some excuse for me. I'll only be a couple of minutes.'

Jacqui looked at her suspiciously. This wasn't like Tess, who was normally so conscientious. 'OK,' she agreed. 'What shall I tell them? That you've been offered a big-time job and they're lucky to be seeing you at all, being such small potatoes?'

'Jacqui' – Tess gave her one last push – 'wash your mouth out with soap.'

'Yes, Miss ex-Radical Lawyer,' nodded Jacqui humbly, 'I surely will.'

Tess got straight through to Hanover's and asked the receptionist for Mrs Salisbury. But there was no answer on her line. Tess swore quietly and said she'd hold on for a moment. After another three rings the phone was picked up.

'Thanks for calling back, Miss Brien.' Anne Salisbury's voice was warmer and friendlier than she'd remembered it. 'I wonder if you could call in and see us this evening at about six p.m.?'

'Stephen, are you free at lunchtime?' Josephine buzzed his office just as he'd finished faxing the perfume buyer from Bloomingdale's, the Queen Bee of the scent world according to Jack Palazzo. 'It's just that Tadeus Zora, who owns the Zora Gallery, would like to talk a bit more about your exhibition.' She neglected to add that she'd had to lean heavily on Tad to get him to have the meeting.

They arrived at the Ritz at one-fifteen and walked through the lavishly carpeted lobby towards the restaurant. Even though Stephen had lived in London for so long, he'd never eaten here and was enchanted. 'This is a bit grand, isn't it?' He gestured at the goldleafed cornicing and the gilded swags that decorated even the corridor. 'Who's buying, us or him?'

'He is.' Josephine steered him away from the pillar he was about to bump into. 'But don't be fooled. The gallery's only over the road so it saves Tad a taxi and he'll make a point of ordering the set menu, so we'll have to follow. It'll cost him less than an à la carte Italian.'

Stephen laughed, impressed at her grasp of the politics of the business lunch and, while they waited for Zora to arrive, looked around, his artist's eyes taking in the painted rococo ceilings and the elaborate plasterwork. There was even a gypsy violinist playing 'Greensleeves', for God's sake.

And then he noticed something that took all the pleasure out of the luxurious scene around him. In the far corner Catherine's husband Josh was lunching alone with a woman. Of course there were a thousand explanations. It could be his publisher. Josh wrote trendy books on sociology which got him interviewed in the posh papers. Or perhaps his agent. Or an enthusiastic TV researcher. Then he took in the champagne bucket next to the table. His publicist? They were given to extravagances, it was a well-known fact.

Assuming that the Ritz restaurant was the last place he was likely to meet anyone he knew, Josh lifted the woman's hand and kissed it.

Stephen looked away in horror, genuinely shocked. The thought of Catherine and their four children, their Queen Anne house and their apparently happy life flashed into his mind. Tess was always going on about them having a perfect marriage. Only a few months ago he'd envied Josh his stability. To his surprise he felt a strong streak of disapproval. Then the hypocrisy of his position hit him so hard that he kept his back firmly turned throughout the whole lunch, in the hope that Josh wouldn't see him. When he got back to the office he'd start looking for a studio at once.

'The only studios we have, mate,' the young Jack-the-lad in the estate agent's ofice cheerily informed him when he phoned later that afternoon, 'are the ones we used to call bedsits. Eight by six with a single bed you pull out of the wall, and double the price. Not enough room to swing a paintbrush in. If I was you

I'd try newsagents' windows or ask around in Finch's.'

'Finch's?' Stephen echoed. 'I thought that was a pub.'

'It is. Boozer in Chelsea, full of writers and down-and-out artist types. They might know of somewhere.'

Stephen made a mental note to look in on the way home.

Tess was grateful that, as usual, her day was so busy that she didn't have too much time to worry. Once or twice she tried to phone Stephen to tell him the news that she'd been summoned back, but Lucy said he was out at lunch.

At half past five on the dot she tidied herself up and debated whether to take the car. Would it be less stressful not to have to look for a parking space? She decided to take a chance and drive herself. And everything seemed to be going her way, she found the route easily, and there was a space right in the square outside Hanover's building.

By six o'clock precisely she was walking up the steps to her appointment.

Stephen fought his way towards the crowded bar in Finch's, trying to grab the attention of the young Irish barman and ask him to point out who might know about studios. After the third attempt it struck him that immediately after work clearly wasn't the ideal time to try and chat up the bar staff.

'What are you doing in here, Matisse old lad?' enquired a voice behind him.

Stephen turned to discover Slouch Heyward an inch away. 'Trying to find anyone who might know of some studio space to rent.'

'I thought you were all fixed up at Josephine's gaff.'

'I was. But it meant spending my entire life in Winchester. My children were starting not to recognize me.'

Slouch smiled to himself like a malicious leprechaun. 'Poor Stephen. What it is to be handsome and talented. Everybody wants a bit of you, eh? Well, as it happens I might know someone. I'll introduce you to him in a minute. He's taking early retirement on the grounds of good health. He thought he was dying and the doc's just given him another year to live so he's decided to spend it in the pub. His studio's too lonely. By the way, since you're buying, mine's a Bushmills.'

As Slouch felt the golden liquid bite at the back of his throat he wondered how Josephine was taking this little rebellion.

Tess walked into the familiar room at Hanover's to find not six but ten people, clearly the firm's bigwigs, waiting to put her through her paces. To her astonishment they even had cuttings about her cases that had appeared in the papers and asked her to explain her decisions.

At the end of half an hour the senior partner took off his very expensive horn-rimmed spectacles and asked her if she'd leave the room for a moment.

Tess sat outside and waited, trying not to bite her nails or tap her feet but to behave like a grown-up lawyer.

Ten minutes later she was summoned back.

The senior partner immediately apologized for giving her such a hard time. 'You see, we like to be absolutely certain when we take on someone new. Hanover's doesn't care to make mistakes.' He smiled

ponderously. 'And with you we know that's most unlikely. Miss Brien, the job is yours.'

'Thank you all very much.' Tess smiled engagingly.
'Could I possibly have a day or two to think about it?'
She stood up, noticing the surprise on everyone's face.
When God the father made you an offer he didn't
expect you to sleep on it.

She walked away from the meeting room fast, her
feet silent on the deep pile of the carpet, along the
wide corridor and down the sweep of staircase towards
the front door. She was feeling a sense of freedom, and
suddenly she realized what this place reminded her of.
Not a museum as she'd thought, but the convent
school she'd spent the first eighteen years of her life
trying to get away from.

She stood in the road and looked back at its beautiful
but utterly anachronistic exterior. It reminded her of
those strange people who bought Georgian houses and
refused to use electric light because it wasn't in period.
They forgot they were living in the 1990s. Stephen
was right. This wasn't her world, no matter how much
money they were offering her.

By the time Stephen got away from Slouch, Tess was
already home, changed into jeans, and listening to
Luke's shaky clarinet practice.

'So what happened?' he demanded.

'I got the job,' replied Tess glumly.

'So that's why you're looking suicidal. Did you take
it?'

'I asked for forty-eight hours to make up my mind.'

Stephen grinned. 'That must have floored them.
They offer you a hundred grand and you ask to think
about it.'

'Stephen?'

'Yes?'

'I couldn't work there.'

'Of course you couldn't,' he agreed, 'I told you that last week. You'd only last five minutes before they discovered you were a dangerous radical and called in the security men. But it's still the best thing that could have happened to you.'

'Why?' asked Tess, puzzled.

'Because now, my love, you're going to march straight in to Will Kingsmill and hold it to his head until he abjectly surrenders to everything you demand.'

'You know, Stephen, that's a really good idea.'

Stephen nodded. 'I didn't survive nearly twenty years in the advertising jungle for nothing, you know.'

Instead of going straight to work, Stephen decided he'd quickly check out the studio Slouch's friend was offering to rent a room just off Lots Road. After three whiskies the old boy had very trustingly handed over the key and now that Stephen had let himself in he could see why. There was certainly nothing to steal. And any self-respecting squatter would turn up their nose at the cold and the mess. Everywhere there were piles of newspapers and paint-stained rags, old enamel plates covered in hardened oils and copious empties of Harvey's Nutbrown Ale, which looked as though they'd been there since before the war. Jars of half-cleaned brushes were crammed on every ledge next to corks cut in half for use as makeshift rubbers. Unfinished canvases were piled against the grubby paintwork. It was a far cry from the warmth and perfect light of Winchester. But it had atmosphere. There was a large window which looked out on to a junkyard, then on to a railway line and beyond to the smart reaches of Chelsea Harbour on the dim and distant horizon. And the light, if the window were cleaned for the first time in living memory, would be terrific. He would move his stuff in on Sunday.

He locked the shabby but somehow likeable studio and skipped down the front steps, picking his way through the black bags of rubbish. He'd taken a step towards breaking away from Josephine. He knew that was the right thing to do, especially after Ellie's remark the other night. But if he were honest with himself he was experiencing another, equally powerful feeling. A sense of loss.

Tess strode assertively towards Will Kingsmill's office without even stopping to take off her coat. 'Good morning, Lilian. I need to see Will as soon as possible, please.'

Will's bossy secretary opened his desk diary deliberately two days ahead, but Tess wasn't going to take any nonsense.

'Today, Lilian. In fact this morning would be ideal.'

'Well, I don't know,' began Lilian, 'he's extremely busy.'

'Just tell him I want to see him, Lilian. Now.'

Lilian was so startled she actually did what she was asked.

'He says he'll see you in half an hour.' Lilian put the phone down with a hint of satisfaction. At least he hadn't said send her straight in.

Thirty-eight minutes later she rang Tess and told her Mr Kingsmill was now free. She made it sound like an enormous favour.

'So, Tess.' Will Kingsmill leaned back in his swivel chair patting his watchchain like some fusty lawyer out of *Bleak House*. 'What can I do for you?' Ever since her unsuccessful pitch Will had adopted this tone of patronizing affability towards her, which drove her wild.

But today Tess didn't care. Today she was the one with the upper hand – it was just that he didn't know it yet. She fixed him with her best Don't Mess with Tess smile. 'I'm sure you remember, Will, I was very cut up about the partnership business, but I told myself it had been a fair fight and I knuckled down. Then, when I was taken off the Eileen McDonald case, I couldn't believe it.'

Will Kingsmill reached for a pen to twirl, his face already settling down into avuncular tolerance. This was just going to be another whinge and he could handle that.

'So when I got an invitation last week, to come and talk to Hanover's about a job with a salary of a hundred thousand a year, you can imagine I listened.'

Tess noticed that she suddenly had Will's full attention. She was beginning to enjoy herself hugely.

'How much did you say?' he repeated.

'I think you heard, Will.' She watched him beadily. 'A couple of months ago I wouldn't have even considered their offer. I believed in this firm and what it stood for. I was prepared to earn a fraction of what they're offering because I was doing what I felt was right. But things have changed, haven't they, Will?' To her immense satisfaction he was beginning to look rosy and uncomfortable. 'You didn't value me enough to give me a partnership and I was unceremoniously dragged off a case which I was on the point of winning. So I have no option but to take this offer very, very seriously.' She stood up, relishing the change in Will's patronizing manner. 'Hanover's have given me until tomorrow evening to make up my mind. So I'll give you the same. Do you want me to go to Hanover's, or are you prepared to offer me the partnership you promised?'

'Look, Tess,' Will protested, his face now a picture of liberal concern at this commercial outrage, 'even if we made you a partner we could never match a salary like that.'

'No, Will, I appreciate that. But money isn't everything, is it?' She smiled winningly. 'Or so I used to believe. There are plenty of other things you could offer, aren't there?'

And she swept out, brimming with confidence. Stephen had been right. Will Kingsmill was a worried man.

Stephen put the phone down and smiled to himself. Betsey Bronowski had taken the bait. Bloomingdale's perfume buyer, known throughout the industry as the hardest nut to crack, had actually confessed to liking his marketing concept.

Now he just hoped Josephine and Hugo would like it too. He knew he'd jumped the gun by putting it to Betsey before selling it to his own bosses, but sometimes you had to take a risk. The way you put together any deal was to tell each party that the other had already agreed even if they were only thinking about it. The best deals were always an edifice of exaggeration and daring that at some stage, often scarily close to your deadline, hardened into reality.

He picked up his folder and decided it was time to convince them.

'What on earth's this?' asked Hugo rudely when Stephen handed him a glossy cut-out card with pictures of various celebrities and members of the royal family on it.

'It's a Scratch 'N' Sniff quiz on which of those people buys which Richmond & Quinn perfume. Behind each panel there's a pad of perfume. Try it.'

Josephine laughed. 'I'd forgotten Fergie likes Royal Romance. She would. It's the only really brash one we do. And Di's a Spring Bluebell fan. Mrs Thatcher and Lily of the Dell! I'd forgotten that one. Our most feminine scent. I suppose every woman has a hidden side.' She handed it back. 'Stephen, that's really fun.'

'What precisely are you thinking of doing with it?' Hugo handed his over without comment. 'I mean this is privileged information. You can't just slap it out to everyone. We might lose these people's custom.'

'Oh, Hugo, don't sound so pompous.' Josephine's irritation wasn't lost on Stephen. Or Hugo. 'I think it's a brilliant idea. And so will the press.' She turned to Stephen. 'What are you planning to do with it?'

'So far I've just sent it to a few key buyers in the US.'

'You've what?' Hugo demanded furiously. 'Without even OK-ing it with us?'

'I made it perfectly clear it's only a teaser, not the official material.'

'That's not the point. You do not make crucial decisions like that without consulting us. What if they loathe the whole concept? We'd be screwed before we even started.'

Stephen wasn't going to lose his cool. 'Just as well they seem to like it then. I had a fax this morning from Betsey Bronowski of Bloomingale's –'

'I know who Betsey is, for Christ's sake,' cut in Hugo impatiently, 'I have been in the fragrance business a little longer than you.'

'Leave it out, Hugo.' Josephine didn't even bother

to look in his direction. 'And what did dear Betsey have to say?'

'That she loved the concept and wondered when I'd be coming over with samples.'

'That's brilliant! This is the break we've been waiting for. If Betsey takes it everyone will. Maybe we'd better bring the launch date forward in case we lose momentum. Of course you must go over. Hugo, we need the samples now. Then if we go ahead with the packaging Stephen's come up with . . . but maybe we should test that out on the buyers too.'

'I've already punted it at five or six. They seem pretty positive about it.' Stephen handed her a sheaf of faxes he'd had in reply. 'So now all we need is a name. We can't go on calling it Richmond & Quinn's new perfume for ever.' He stopped, struck by the word he'd just used. Everyone said they needed a name that was romantic and timeless. 'I know this is a bit off the wall. But what about calling it "Forever"?'

Hugo stood up and, as Stephen guessed he would, claimed a pressing meeting. Josephine watched him go, making no attempt to stop him. When the door closed behind him, she changed sofas so that she was sitting only inches away from Stephen and crossed her legs. Stephen was aware of the faint, erotic sound of her stockinged legs rubbing against each other and tried to blot it out of his thoughts.

'Sorry about Hugo. I suspect we ought to be thanking you and he knows it.' She leaned forward, exposing a few more inches of caramel skin. 'You really are quite an operator, aren't you?'

Stephen fought against a sudden desire to slip his hand inside the silk of her blouse. What the hell was he thinking of? He pulled himself back to reality, his tone harsher than he meant it to be. 'It struck me that if we didn't act soon my contract would be up. It's only for six months, after all.'

'But you'll extend it, surely?' Josephine hoped the edge of anxiety she was suddenly feeling hadn't crept into her voice.

'For a while, obviously. But you know I want to paint. And there's the exhibition to think of. I know I have you to thank for that, but I can't stay indefinitely. So I thought maybe I should get moving.'

Josephine nodded. For the moment there was little she could do to stop him anyway.

Both sat silent, the intensity of the moment hanging between them, unacknowledged, until Stephen felt he must burst the bubble. 'By the way, I've found a studio. In Fulham. A friend of Slouch's. I'll be moving my stuff this weekend.' He stood up. 'I'd better get back. The fax machine calls.'

Josephine sat silently for a moment. How had she let this happen? For the first time in her life she'd let a man make all the running. It was time she took back the initiative. Soon.

Will Kingsmill sat in his office, panicking. The truth was that although Tess could be spiky on the question of principles, she was a brilliant lawyer. Personally he would have given her the partnership and so would three or four of the others. But what he'd overlooked was Patricia Greene's lobbying skills. No government whip could have done a better job than Patricia in inviting the other partners for quiet drinks and persuading them of the superiority of her case. Tess wasn't that type. But even so, the battle had been more evenly weighted than Tess probably suspected. And he didn't want to lose her. This damned McDonald case proved how strong a loyalty she could inspire in her clients for a start. He'd been furious with Patricia over the inept handling of all that.

He'd better call an emergency partners' meeting for tonight at six-thirty p.m.

Just before six Jacqui put her head round the door. 'What's going on? Everyone's scuttling round the place looking purposeful. Is there something I should know that's bypassed the secretaries' bush telegraph?'

Tess felt a glow of satisfaction. 'I haven't the slightest idea,' she lied smugly.

Tonight she wasn't going to make the mistake of going home on time. She'd wait and see if anything developed.

But as she sat in her office trying to keep her mind off what was being said next door and get on with her paperwork she felt her certainty ebb away. Maybe she'd overplayed her hand. What if the partners decided to call her bluff and let her go after all?

Unaware of all the excitement at Tess's office, Stephen packed up and headed for the studio. He'd had a good day on the campaign and felt invigorated at the thought of two or three hours of solid painting. If he felt energetic enough he might pack everything up tonight.

He changed from his business clothes into jeans and a sweatshirt and put some oils on his palette. If he had a real spurt tonight the painting would almost be finished.

It was an hour and a half before the meeting broke up at Kingsmill's. Tess, listening intently behind her closed office door, tried to pick up some hint of the outcome but couldn't. The only positive clue was that Lyall Gibson had been whistling as he left, and she knew he'd been her chief champion at the previous pitch. There was no sign of Patricia. As the last of them got their coats and left she opened her door again, guessing that Will Kingsmill would be the last.

Five minutes later he appeared at her door. 'Ah, Tess. You're still here. Good. Perhaps you'd like to come into my office for a moment?'

Stephen added a small touch of viridian to the green of a field and cursed. He'd made the classic mistake of putting on too much oil paint and muddying the colours. Now it'd take him half an hour to correct it. He picked up his palette knife and painstakingly began to scrape off the paint.

One of the problems he'd discovered about painting was knowing exactly when a picture was finished. You might think it was, leave it for a few days then walk past it again, irresistibly drawn to fiddling with one more little detail. Only to discover, as he just had – sod it – that the thing would have been better left untouched. He looked at his watch. Seven o'clock. He'd give himself two hours and that, whether he was creatively satisfied or not, would be it.

Tess sat in the chair opposite Will's and waited. She still had no idea from his expression which way they'd jumped.

Will fumbled in his drawer for the very odd Gauloise he allowed himself on stressful occasions, and lit it, and said, 'What we've decided, Tess, is that we would very much like you to stay. We understand your resentment at what's happened lately, and we'd like to make some amends. The consensus is . . .' He paused and dragged on his cigarette, leaving Tess to imagine who was *not* part of the consensus, 'that we should now offer you a partnership and put you back on the Eileen McDonald case.'

Tess almost kissed him. It was everything she could have wanted! 'Thanks, Will, that's wonderful.' To his surprise she asked for a drag on his Gauloise.

'I didn't know you smoked.'

Tess breathed in the evocative fumes, held her breath, then exhaled. 'I don't.' Turning round, her smile spreading from ear to ear, she strode back to her own office.

Behind the closed door she raised a fist and shouted, 'Yes!'

Then, brimming over with desire to tell Stephen that his ploy couldn't have been more successful, she tried his number in Winchester. The phone rang eight or ten times in his office. She felt a bitter kick of disappointment as she realized he must have left. She so wanted to tell him her news.

Just as she was about to try him at home a woman's voice answered with a clipped, 'Yes?'

She recognized Josephine's cool, vaguely irritated tones at once.

'Hello, Josephine. This is Tess Brien, Stephen's wife. Is he still there, do you know?'

'I've no idea.' Josephine clearly wasn't offering to find out.

Tess felt her excitement dip then fought back. She was damned if she was going to let Josephine spoil the moment. 'Could you check? He's not in his office but I wondered about the studio.'

Josephine leaned back so that she could see out of the window. A light shone from beyond the kitchen. He must still be there. She buzzed the studio on the internal buzzer but there was no reply.

'I'm afraid he doesn't seem to be answering.' Josephine's voice held the slightest tinge of smugness. 'Maybe he's stuck into a painting.'

Her tone infuriated Tess. 'Well, could you give him a message?' she demanded rashly. 'Tell him I got my partnership and the champagne's waiting on ice.'

'Congratulations.' Josephine's tone now somehow managed to belittle her achievement. 'I'll make a point of telling him.'

Tess packed up her briefcase, humming. Even Josephine couldn't dim the brilliance of her excitement. She'd stop on the way and buy the champagne. It'd be nice and cool by the time Stephen got home.

Josephine stood for a moment looking out of the window. Then she came to a decision. She walked swiftly towards her bathroom, touched up her already perfect make-up and sprayed on the perfume she had individually mixed for her. She hadn't liked the sound of that cosy little celebration waiting for Stephen at home. If she was going to act, then this seemed to be her moment.

He was almost there, Stephen knew it. He could feel the excitement creeping up on him as he tinkered with the strong, dominating colours until they had the exact luminosity he was looking for.

At last he stood back and surveyed it nervously. It was huge. The biggest canvas he'd ever attempted. Standing back he scraped the oils off his palette knife and looked at it for a long minute. It was certainly different from his usual style. Yet he still had no idea whether it was the worst thing he'd ever done, or the best. He decided not to try moving the painting tonight but to leave it where it was and come and study it again in the morning.

Picking up his jacket, he took one last glance at the

picture before snapping off the light. Then, cursing himself, he realized he'd left his brushes covered in oils. For a moment he thought of leaving them overnight, but rule one of painting was that you always had to clean your brushes before they hardened into boardlike tufts. He poured turpentine into a jam jar and swirled them in it.

Behind him a small noise made him jump.

'Josephine,' he breathed, 'you gave me a shock. I've finally finished the picture. Turn on the light and see what you think.'

'No, leave the light off,' she replied quickly, still standing in the doorway, part lit, part in shadow with that familiar half-enticing smile. Even from across the room he could smell her perfume, as distinctive as a signature. 'I'd prefer to look at it in the moonlight.'

The house was warm and dark when Tess got home. Only Ellie was downstairs, curled up on the sofa watching television.

'What's that?' asked Ellie, noticing the bottle of champagne.

'I got my partnership.'

'Mum, that's great!' Ellie hugged her mother, eyeing the bottle. 'So aren't you going to open it?'

'Not now. I'm keeping it for Dad and me. To have in bed.'

'Fab. I can just picture it. You naked as nature intended with just a dash of Chanel No 5 to get his pulses racing, and Dad stuck in roadworks on the M3, as usual.'

'Haven't you got any homework to do?' asked Tess, picking up the champagne and heading upstairs with what little dignity she could muster.

She put her head round Luke's door but he was already fast asleep.

Singing to herself, she went into the bathroom and turned on the bath. Not too hot or she'd end up like a lobster rather than an inviting peach. She took off her work clothes and hung them on the back of the door and slipped into the inviting water. Lying back she closed her eyes and almost felt like shouting for joy. She'd finally done it. And it was thanks to Stephen for encouraging her to take a stand. Tonight could be a new beginning. In the last few months she knew they'd drifted apart. They didn't seem to share things the way they used to. Even the sex had to be prompted more by duty than desire. But they could change all that.

Eager to set the stage before he got back, she pulled herself out of the bath, wrapped herself in the biggest bathsheet she could find and went back to the bedroom.

Somehow the Chanel-only approach didn't appeal. Anyway, if she got into bed at all she'd probably fall asleep and miss the whole event. And tonight she felt powerful and sexy. Clothes would be more fun. Then he could undress her. Slowly.

She went over to the chest of drawers and dug out the new briefs and pale stockings she'd bought for a weekend away a couple of years ago. They'd be perfect with her ivory satin bra. Who could wear tarty black or obvious red when ivory was so much more subtly seductive?

She slipped on the stockings, pulling them up sensuously, inch by inch, then put on the rest of the underwear and surveyed herself in the mirror. The trouble with their marriage was that in the demands of the everyday they'd forgotten to be sexy for one another. She'd put that right, starting tonight.

The question was, should she lie down and wait just as she was? But then a little fantasy of her own crept in. She kept on the bra and stockings and removed the ivory knickers. Then she put on her favourite suit, caramel linen with an ivory blouse that made her breasts look like Charlotte Rampling's, and added some smart court shoes with heels high enough to suggest pleasure rather than work.

Finally ready, she sat on a high-backed chair and poured herself a glass of champagne. Stephen had to be back soon. Closing her eyes she sipped it and imagined him coming into the room. He would see her there and stop for a moment, surprised. Then he'd come slowly towards her and kneel at her feet. Without being told he would push aside her skirt and know what was waiting underneath. Smiling maddeningly he would pull her towards him and she would feel his tongue burying itself between her legs, inflaming her until she cried out his name never, never to stop.

Tess opened her eyes and smiled a slow, secret smile. Even thinking about it had almost made her come.

From the other side of the studio Josephine looked at the picture. Then, very slowly, she moved nearer and surveyed it from one angle, then from another.

Stephen knew the tension in the room was about more than his painting. It crackled between them, dangerous and alluring. 'Well,' he demanded, watching her. 'For God's sake, Josephine, what do you think?'

Josephine walked over to him until they were standing eye to eye with only inches between them. Her voice was low and sensual. 'I've seen a lot of paintings I thought were good, a few that were wonderful. But that work's inspired. Stephen, it has a touch of genius.'

Stephen felt light-headed as though he'd drunk too much too fast and suddenly hit cold air.

Unlike Tess, she didn't see it as a bit of canvas cluttering up the hallway or the fruits of a vaguely irresponsible hobby. She thought his painting was amazing. Stephen closed his eyes and let the warmth of her admiration flow over him, heady and irresistible.

Josephine looked up at him, her eyes dark and liquid, and moved so close he could feel the warmth of her body. And then she stepped even closer so that her breasts were pressed against him, the nipples already hardened with desire. All he could smell was her perfume, all he could see was the dazzle of her skin in the moonlight. And even though he knew in every inch of his body that he shouldn't, he had to resist, that it was to avoid this he'd found somewhere else to paint, he felt himself stiffening in response, until he melted against her and her mouth opened under his lips.

And slowly they slipped together down on to the Turkish-rug-strewn floor of the studio and tore at each other's clothes like teenagers discovering sex for the very first time.

CHAPTER TWENTY-ONE

Tess sat in the semi-darkness feeling the fizz drain out of her just as it had from the champagne she was holding. Across the room the luminous green numbers of their bedside clock told her it was after midnight. Where the hell was he? He'd never been this late before, even when he was painting. Surely Josephine must have given him her message?

Angrily she began to undo her suit and kick off her shoes. If he walked in now she'd want to kill him, not seduce him. She stripped off her skirt and silk blouse, and marched to the bathroom leaving a trail of discarded underwear. She reached for her cleanser and scrubbed her face clean of the carefully applied make-up, then splashed it with cold water until it glowed. From the back of the door her old towelling dressing gown beckoned comfortingly and she put it on, as scrubbed and asexual as a nun, all traces of desire forgotten.

So much for a new beginning.

Outside in the street she heard the familiar chugging of a black cab, a sound that drew you irresistibly to the window even when you weren't expecting anyone. Stephen had taken the train this morning; this could be the cab bringing him from Waterloo. She peered out, but it was her neighbour's husband from across the road – a persistent philanderer. His wife had long given up trying to trace his movements. Another car appeared at the end of the road, a sleek white Mercedes which certainly didn't belong to any of their neighbours. It double parked a few houses away, under a street light, even though there were plenty of spaces opposite their own house. Tess was about to close the curtains when someone got out. Shaken by a cold shiver of suspicion, she realized it was Stephen. Desperately her mind looked for a way out. Maybe it was Hugo's car and he was dropping Stephen back after some business dinner or a long evening's painting.

She watched, motionless, as Stephen walked round to the driver's side of the car. The driver rolled down the window and leaned out, dark hair gleaming in the pinkish artificial light. It was unmistakably Josephine. As Tess watched, frozen in horror, Stephen bent down and kissed her long and hard on the lips.

Moments later, as though everything was perfectly normal, instead of changed for ever by that one chance look out of the window, she heard Stephen's key turn in the door and his ordinary treacherous footsteps coming up the stairs. She half expected to hear him whistle. And then there was silence and she realized he must have gone into Luke's room. The bastard! How dare he go and kiss their children when he'd just kissed *her*?

When he came in she was still standing by the window.

'Hello.' He smiled in surprise to see her still up. 'I thought you'd be asleep by now. I'm sorry I'm so late. As I'm moving studios at the weekend I wanted to finish a painting.' She noticed with almost clinical interest that the register of his voice altered slightly as he lied. Prompted by her silence he added lamely, 'I should have rung, I know.'

Tess didn't move but simply looked at him. 'I know about you and Josephine.'

Stephen flinched. 'How could you? We only . . .'

His voice trailed off, conscious that he'd already said too much.

'I was waiting up. I got my partnership after all, just like you said. I wanted to celebrate. I saw you out of the window.'

He looked beyond her to the empty champagne bottle and the pathetic trail of satin underwear.

'Oh, Tess.' He closed his eyes. When he opened them she could see that they were clouded with pain. 'I'm so sorry.'

At least he wasn't denying it like those husbands who blustered and said I don't know what you're talking about, or passed a year-long affair off as a one-night stand. But suddenly she was overwhelmingly, blazingly angry.

'It's a bit bloody late for that, isn't it? I suppose she massaged your precious ego and said you were the best thing since Picasso! God, Stephen, and you fell for it.' She could see the barb hurt and was pleased. 'And all boring Tess could go on about was the mortgage and the bills and push you into getting a job. But that's reality, Stephen. Though you always did have a slender hold on that, didn't you?' She kicked furiously at the underwear lying there reminding her of her pathetic fantasy. 'Maybe Josephine's just what you need. A rich woman who can support you and mop your fevered brow until the world recognizes your true genius.' She could hear her own voice, shrill and shrewish, but didn't care. 'And that lovely house! So much less messy than a real home, with real children, and real responsibility.' She began picking up books and newspapers from the untidy pile by his bed and throwing them at him. 'Well, if that's your idea of reality, you'd better bloody well go back to her! After all, our marriage isn't up to much, is it?'

Stephen turned round without another word and walked from the room. Moments later she heard the front door bang, and then nothing. Except the heavy rain that began to beat down a depressing rhythm on the skylight above the bed.

Stephen slammed the door of his car and started to drive much too fast back towards the M3 and Winchester. How dare Tess accuse him of wanting to sponge off Josephine? But then money mattered to Tess. When he'd been fired she'd made him feel he was sponging off *her* too. And then that stuff about falling for Josephine because she flattered him. He knew, God he knew, that he shouldn't have made love to her tonight. But it hadn't been because she flattered him. Understood him, maybe, when Tess never seemed interested, but surely that wasn't the same thing?

The road were empty and he got to the turn-off for Winchester in record time. Angrily he gunned the engine and took the bend too fast, forgetting that it was November and there was black ice about. He felt the car go into a skid. Unable to believe his own stupidity, he panicked and tried to right it. Instead the car slewed right across the broken white line and straight into the path of any oncoming traffic.

Josephine lay in bed reading the same page over and over without taking anything in. She'd tried to get to sleep but it had been impossible. What was going to happen next? Would Stephen turn up for work, not meeting her eyes, and behave as though nothing had happened? Or would he see Josephine as a bit on the side, a nice sexy but uninvolving affair that wouldn't risk his marriage?

She closed her eyes and remembered the hard feel of him against her, the blissful moment when she had

had him inside her. And she realized how desperately she wanted him to come back to her. She certainly wasn't going to let go of him now. The question was, how could she get him away from his family?

Stephen willed himself to calm down and began to drive into the skid as he'd always been told you must. Thank God there were no cars in his path, but a telegraph pole was fast coming up to his right. Within a hair's breadth of hitting it, he felt the car finally begin to respond to the steering wheel and veer back on to its own side, slowing down until it slowly crashed into a signpost with a picture of a car skidding on a bend.

Stephen dropped his head down on to the steering wheel, trying to hold himself together and only just succeeding. He wanted to shout and scream, to rail at how unfair it was, and most of all to blame Tess. But a streak of honesty prevented him. There was no getting away from it. What Tess had said might have been grossly unfair but this whole mess was still his fault.

Finally he dragged himself out of the car to inspect the damage. One wing was bashed in and a tyre slashed. Wearily he got out the jack and changed the wheel in the bitterly cold rain. It was only when he got back in that he realized how much his shoulder and cheekbone hurt.

Josephine sat up, convinced she could hear tyres on the gravel at the front of the house. She pulled on her dressing gown and ran downstairs. Stephen stood on the doorstep, soaked and bleeding.

She understood at once that he was near exhaustion and didn't need any more emotional scenes, so she led him to her spare bedroom and tucked him in like a sick child. At least he had come back. She had no idea why, but she knew she'd won the first round at least. There would be plenty of time for explanations in the morning.

It was still dark when Tess felt cold skin touch hers and woke with a start. She couldn't believe she'd actually slept. All she could remember was an awful, dull, aching pain which had seemed to flow over her like freezing water, paralysing her body yet leaving mind raw and alert.

She reached out and snapped on the bedside light. It was Ellie, her eyes red from crying. How strange that Ellie had cried when she hadn't been able to.

'Was that Dad storming out last night?'

Tess nodded.

'For good?'

Tess held out her arms and Ellie pressed herself into them, suddenly looking more six than sixteen. 'I don't know.'

'To Josephine?'

Tess shivered at the mention of her name. 'How did you know about that?'

'Oh, Mum, she's been after him ever since that lunch we went to. But I just thought Dad was bigger than that. And that he loved us a bit.'

The pain in Ellie's voice was more than Tess could stand. 'Ellie, he does love you. It's just us that's the problem.'

Ellie pulled herself away. 'So you're splitting up? Aren't you even going to ask Luke and me what we think and then ignore it?' The sudden bitterness in Ellie's tone cut Tess to the quick. 'I thought that was what parents did in this situation.'

Tess looked down at her daughter's sad, lovely face.

Ellie was right. In the white heat of their anger and hurt neither of them had spared a thought for their children. 'What *do* you think we should do, then?'

Ellie looked at her mother hard. 'I think you should try to stay together. For our sakes. I suppose that sounds corny but Luke and I love you both and we want you to be together. We don't want to spend three days with you and three with Dad, never knowing where our home is, just settling into one place when it's time to go to the other. We don't want to have to listen to you slag each other off and enlist us in your fights. We just want two ordinary parents who live with each other.'

Tess was silenced by the grimly realistic picture her daughter had just painted.

'Mum, I'm sorry. It must be hell for you. It's just that it's all so awful. I know it's not your fault.'

'Isn't it?' Tess remembered the accusations she'd flung at him. Not all of them had been fair.

Without warning Ellie jumped out of bed and grabbed the phone. 'Oh, Mum, I know you probably shouldn't, but give him one more chance.'

Tess took it from her and before she could think about it dialled Josephine's number. After two rings an answering machine picked up the call and Josephine's voice invited her to leave a message.

Tess knew what kind of message she'd like to leave, but after a moment's struggle, she simply asked Stephen to call her, then put down the receiver, instantly regretting that she'd made the call at all.

Ellie buried her head in the duvet, unable to be brave any longer. 'Why did you let him go? Surely you could have stopped him?'

Tess lost her temper. 'Because I was bloody hurt! Because it seemed the right thing to do. Ellie, we both need time to think about what's best for you as well as for us.'

Ellie's eyes sparked with an answering anger. 'Come off it, Mum, at least be honest. You're not doing this for us, you're doing it for you!'

Tess watched as her daughter flung herself from the room, feeling that the agony was too much to bear. Why shouldn't she be doing it for herself? Was she supposed to overlook Stephen's infidelity just because she had children? All the clichés flooded into her mind – that affairs were the symptom not the cause, that strong marriages should be able to survive the odd indiscretion, that they could even grow. She'd actually said it to her own clients, for God's sake. Lying here, it felt like absolute balls. She was never, ever, going to say it again.

At the other end of the line Josephine listened to Tess's message and debated whether to pass it on to Stephen or not. It would be so easy to press Erase Incoming Messages. As her finger hovered over the button, Josephine was struck by a rare flash of conscience. Maybe instead of wiping it she should leave it to fate. She wouldn't draw it to his attention but if he asked, she'd feel obliged to tell him it was there.

By twelve Stephen still hadn't woken and Josephine decided to take his breakfast up on a tray. She hummed as she smoothed out a lace tablecloth, warmed some croissants, and turned on her gadget that made freshly squeezed orange juice. Thank God it was Saturday and she didn't have to do any explaining to Hugo or the other staff. By Monday they could get their story sorted out.

Stephen was just emerging from a dark tunnel into what seemed like blinding light, but in fact was a narrow crack in the tightly closed curtains. He struggled to sit up when he heard the knock. The sight of Josephine, carrying a tray and smiling as though everything were hunky dory instead of a Godawful mess, struck him as almost surreal.

He pulled himself up on to his good shoulder. 'Has anyone rung for me?' They both knew whom he was talking about.

Josephine, her good mood evaporating, slammed the tray down so that the orange juice stained the perfect white lace of the traycloth. 'There's a garbled message of some kind on the machine.'

He reached out and took her hand, forcing her to look at him. 'I'm sorry, Jo. I seem to be hurting everyone at the moment. But I can't just walk out. Not after eighteen years of marriage. You'd think I was a shit if I did.'

'Would I?' Josephine mopped up the spilt orange juice aggressively.

'Yes. You would. If I did that to Tess' – he held her hand to his lips and kissed it – 'what guarantee would you have that I wouldn't do the same to you?'

Tess stood in front of the mirror trying to put the pieces of herself back together. What the hell was she going to do? The thought of the mortgage and the bills and the school fees, not to mention facing life alone, snapped at her ankles. For today at least she decided to kick all such thoughts away. She couldn't face them yet. Women, she knew, even abandoned ones, were expected to be strong, to hold things together. She remembered a holy picture she'd had at primary school of the Virgin Mary standing on a cloud, her feet crushing vipers, while a dagger pierced her heart. That was how you were supposed to be. But what about all the poor cows who weren't up to it? She'd had enough of them in her office, the ones who couldn't cope, whose kids were taken into care.

Tess did what was expected of her, and pulled herself together. She even put on her make-up and washed her hair, dressing up for normality.

Downstairs Luke was watching a video of his precious wrestlers, unaware of the storm that was tearing his world apart. Tess stroked his hair, putting off the evil moment when she had to break it to him that everything had changed, and went into the kitchen to make a cup of coffee.

In the din of the electric coffee grinder she missed the sound of the front door opening, and when she heard someone in the hall, she assumed it was Inge back from her Saturday fitness class.

So when she turned round the last person she was expecting to see was Stephen.

CHAPTER TWENTY-TWO

'Hello, Tess.'

Tess and Stephen stood looking at each other, as awkward as ex-lovers meeting again for the first time. For a brief second it was possible that one of them might have opened their arms and the gap between them been breached by the healing power of touch. Then the moment passed.

'Hiya, Dad,' Luke called from the next room, reaching out his hand without even looking away from the TV screen. The trust and innocence of his gesture turned Tess's heart over.

Stephen kissed him briefly then closed the connecting doors between the kitchen and sitting room.

'Josephine said you rang.' Tess winced at the mention of her name and Stephen cursed himself for his tactlessness. 'Look, Tess, I wanted you to know. Last night was the first and only time. I know that's no excuse. It's still a betrayal. But I wanted you to know it wasn't a full-scale affair . . .'

'Yet,' cut in Tess angrily. 'But what if I hadn't found out? Wouldn't it have become a full-scale affair then? And even if you hadn't done anything, you'd have wanted to!'

'Tess, the reason I was moving studios – it was to avoid this.'

'Then you should have moved a bit earlier, shouldn't you?'

Stephen looked away, as though any argument he came up with would just sound hypocritical. 'If you feel like that, why did you ring?'

'It was Ellie's idea. She thinks we're only thinking of ourselves and should have consulted them.'

'I suppose there's some justice in that.' Stephen showed the ghost of a wry smile. 'And what would their advice be?'

'According to Ellie we should try again for their sakes.'

'And what do you think?'

'I don't know, Stephen. It depends on you and Josephine. Are you prepared to give her up?'

'I wouldn't be here if I wasn't.'

'It'll be hard seeing her every day.'

'Not as hard as losing my family.' There was an appeal in his eyes but she refused to look at him. 'I realize how close I came to that, Tess.'

'Yes, you did.' Tess went on making her coffee, the hurt slicing into her, realizing that far from a joyful reunion the most they could probably expect was an uneasy truce. But for Ellie and Luke's sakes maybe it was worth trying.

'Tess . . .' Stephen hesitated, nervous of her reaction.

'Yes?'

'It won't work if we're just doing it for them. It has to be for us too.'

Tess didn't look up. 'I know,' she said in a voice so low that he had to strain to catch it.

'And do you want to?'

'Yes, Stephen, I want to. But I can't pretend yesterday didn't happen.'

Stephen wondered if he should try and put his arms round her but the stiffness of her back shut him firmly out. And anyway, maybe asking for her forgiveness was simply a way of letting himself off the hook.

'Look, why don't we all go out tonight to some

wildly expensive hamburger joint and celebrate your partnership?'

'Since we didn't do it yesterday?' she flashed.

Stephen shrugged. 'Tess, we can't go on like that.'

'No,' Tess agreed, guilt setting in already. Either this reunion was serious or they might as well forget it. 'The Hard Rock it is then.'

Both of them turned at the sound of the interconnecting door opening. Ellie emerged, her eyes puffy, still in the oversized T-shirt she slept in.

'Dad,' she shrieked, expressing all the joy and delight Tess couldn't feel. 'Thank God you're back!'

Josephine stood at the island unit in her vast and immaculate kitchen slicing tomatoes. Even though they were the ripe imported Italian ones the greengrocer got specially for her, she took none of her usual pleasure in the act. A plate of Brie and crisp French bread stood waiting for her on the counter.

Suddenly she stopped, mid-slice, and abandoned the thought of lunch. Instead she grabbed a bottle of white wine from the fridge and poured herself a glass. What she needed was some repetitive, mind-numbing task. Her Christmas card list caught her eye and she sat down to start it. But after writing out six cards and addresses from her enormous list of acquaintances, she gave that up too.

Instead she grabbed the whole bottle and went into the empty sitting room to do something she'd never done before. Bury herself in the cushions and watch the afternoon weepie on the television.

'Hello, Inge.' Tess realized she hadn't seen her au pair for days. 'We're off celebrating my new partnership at the Hard Rock Café. Want to join us?'

Inge looked thrown. 'Oh, no.' She shook her head vehemently, 'This is a family occasion. You should be on your own. It is good for families to be together.'

Tess looked at Inge in surprise. She wasn't usually one for homespun philosophy. And then to her horror she understood. Inge knew about Stephen too. Maybe she should just take an ad in the paper and be done with it.

As usual the queue for the Hard Rock went right round the block and by the time they got inside they needed something to warm them up. As they sat hugging their coffees waiting for their order to arrive, Tess was grateful for the deafening rock music which blotted out the embarrassing silence that suddenly fell on them. Instantly sensitive to it, Ellie did her best to keep up a flow of bright chatter, and Stephen joined in. Turning to Luke with uncharacteristic heartiness, he said, 'So, how's science this term? Doing any interesting projects at the moment?'

Luke looked at him as though he'd been asked to name the constituent parts of DNA. 'God, Dad, you sound just like Jack's father. And he only sees him every other Sunday. You know how much I loathe science.'

At that point to Tess's relief the wine arrived and Stephen poured a glass for each of them.

'Wow, Dad, even me?' Luke's eyes widened in glee. Normally he was only allowed a sip of theirs.

Stephen caught Tess's eye. 'This is rather a special occasion.'

'A toast,' insisted Ellie, raising her glass. 'To Mum and Dad. I know you love each other really.'

Stephen and Tess exchanged a softer look.

'Of course they do,' chimed in Luke, mystified.

What was the matter with everyone tonight? 'They're married to each other, aren't they?'

It was almost midnight when they got home. Tess tried to talk Ellie out of watching *Buffy The Vampire Slayer* for the nineteenth time but failed. Then she went up to bed, conscious that on her and Stephen's first night back together she couldn't bear the idea of making love.

Instead of her usual silk nightdress she put on her Marks and Spencer's tartan pyjamas in anti-erotic flannelette.

Stephen arrived a few minutes later. The message clearly wasn't lost on him.

'Don't worry,' he said, sitting down on the bed, 'I wasn't going to try anything. We're both a bit too bruised for that.' He held out a hand towards her. 'But I do think we ought to talk.'

'What about?' Tess busied herself at the dressing table, irrationally furious that Stephen was the one who was being calm and sensible while she still seethed with hurt and rejection.

'About why it happened.'

'Oh yes. And why did it happen? Apart from the fact that you were too weak to resist Josephine's wiles?' Tess knew she was being a bitch, but anger was important. She needed anger to maintain her self-respect. He had to know he couldn't cheat on her and get away with it. Only then could she afford to be understanding.

'It wasn't all me.'

'No,' Tess conceded, resisting a desire to hit him. 'I don't suppose it was. Fire away then.'

'It all started when I left advertising. We were happy until then. Then you made it clear you resented me. To you I was one step up from a wino and two down from a dole scrounger.'

'Stephen, that's ridiculous.'

'But that's how it felt to me. I know your old man was a compulsive gambler, I understand your need for security. But security can be stifling. It was to me, anyway. I needed to break out. But you couldn't cope with that, so you pushed me into the job at Josephine's.'

Tess closed her eyes. Maybe it was true. If she hadn't rooted for him to take the job, none of this would have happened.

'But it was only short-term. Just so that we could save up.' *And I could hardly guess you'd end up screwing her*, Tess almost added, but thought better of it.

'I know. Look, I don't mean to sound accusing. In a lot of ways you've been very tolerant. I just want you to understand.'

Tess nodded. 'And then there was Art,' she added ominously.

Stephen smiled. 'And then there was Art, as you say.' He reached for her hand. 'I know you think it's an eccentricity of mine, even a kind of male selfishness, like spending every weekend on the golf course or down at the pub. But it isn't, you know. It's a passion. I wish you could enter into it with me.'

Tess returned his smile. 'I might find golf easier. At least it's concrete. I have tried, you know.'

Stephen squeezed her hand. 'Maybe we should have some ground rules. Rule One. We both work less hard and try and make time for each other.'

Tess decided she'd better enter into the spirit of the thing. 'Rule Two. We go out together at least once a week. And we aren't allowed to mention the children.'

'Rule Three. More sex.' He said it with all the briskness of a Freudian analyst. 'You're such a sexy lady, but we always seem to be too tired. Rule Four. I don't spend every weekend painting.'

Tess felt a flash of guilt. Only a few days ago she'd been telling herself she ought to make more room for his painting. He was clearly making an effort.

Downstairs the phone rang. Tess glanced at the clock. Who on earth could be ringing at this hour? She felt a shudder of apprehension that it might be Josephine. What if she turned out to be the *Fatal Attraction* type?

'Mum!' Ellie's voice called up the stairs. 'It's for you. Says he's called Terry Worth!'

Stephen raised his eyes to heaven and laughed.

'Rule 5.' Tess smiled back at the perfection of the timing. 'I stop giving clients my home phone number.'

Tess ran downstairs, ready to blast Terry out for calling her at this time, but he sounded close to tears. 'It's bloody Angela again; I've driven half the night to pick the kids up first thing tomorrow and she's not even here. The bloody answering machine says they're away. I'm going to strangle her one of these days, Tess!'

'Why don't you come in and see me next week and we'll write her a letter, OK? And, Terry, I hope you're not driving any more tonight.' His speech was distinctly slurred.

'Don't worry, gel. It's a temperance hotel. The Lips That Touch Liquor Shall Never Touch Mine and all that. I'm thinking of suing the guidebook for not mentioning it.' Tess stifled a giggle at the thought of Terry in a non-alcoholic establishment. 'I had to go out to the pub to get pissed. On foot.'

By the time she got back upstairs Stephen was

under the duvet on his side of the bed, firmly asleep. Rule Three wouldn't be starting tonight, thank God. She wasn't ready for that hurdle yet.

In the usual Monday morning rush there wasn't time for Tess to have misgivings about Stephen going back into the jaws of death – or rather the jaws of something more dangerous entirely – at Richmond & Quinn. But through the morning, even though she was as busy as ever, Tess found it hard to banish the thought of Josephine.

In the end she gave Phil a ring, both to find out how Terry was and to get her advice. What Phil advised was an immediate and lengthy lunch.

Tucked into a booth at a small Greek restaurant, Tess opened her heart and told her best friend everything that had been happening between Stephen and Josephine.

Phil listened, appalled, not least because she had been the one to bring them together. 'And you've forgiven him? Just like that? Without even insisting he moves out?'

Tess nodded. 'We've agreed to have another go. For the sake of the children.'

'You're absolutely raving starkers.'

'Why?'

'I just don't think this staying together for the children crap works.'

'Why not? Didn't you and Greg ever think of doing it?'

Phil shook her head. 'The children were quite relieved when he moved out. The tension was too much for them. We did think of staying together for the sake of the mortgage, but I suppose that's different. Greg was a lousy father anyway. So you've actually let him trot back to Josephine's tender loving care? At least during the daytime?'

'That's what I'm worried about. I'm not sure I shouldn't have insisted he jack in the job.'

'Absolutely. I mean how do you know he's not still carrying on with her? Or do you intend to put up with that for the sake of the children too? Turn a blind eye to the late nights and the not wanting to make love, and the fact that everyone knows? Come on, Tess, you've got too much pride.'

'Of course not. But I don't think he will. I've got to trust him, Phil, or we might as well give up now. Besides, maybe pride isn't the only issue.'

'Am I hearing you right? Is this my best friend Tess Brien, brave and fearless champion of underdogs everywhere?' Phil took a large sip of retsina. 'You can't do it, Tess. Not in this day and age. Not when women don't need to depend on men to live. You're earning enough to survive on your own.' Tess listened, taken aback by Phil's hectoring tone. Maybe it was the retsina talking. But then Phil had always been someone who knew her own mind – providing it was about what other people should do. 'You shouldn't take this shit. Men will go as far as you let them. And you're letting him. You should chuck the bastard out. What's happened to your self-respect?'

'Maybe my self-respect isn't such a big deal to Ellie and Luke. Maybe they'd just rather have parents who live together. Besides, he only made love to her once. Isn't everyone entitled to one mistake?'

'You sound like your mother. I'm sure she'd tell you to give him one more chance.'

'Maybe she'd be right. And maybe their generation was right about not getting divorced.'

'Oh, come on, Tess. Look at all those miserable

couples chipping away at each other behind the net curtains.'

'All right. Some of them were unhappy. But maybe they were more realistic about marriage then. They didn't expect it to be perfect. And they didn't even know each other before they settled down. They didn't live together like we all do and have trial marriages and long-term relationships. They just got married and stuck with the consequences.'

'And look what they did to each other.' Phil waved a bread stick to underline her point, her voice rising in indignation. 'Women put up with shitty lives and lived through their children. Oh, Tessie, why is it always the same old story with men? Sex or family? It's such a cliché. You'd think they'd be ashamed of being part of an endless repetitive bloody pattern, wouldn't you?'

Tess sipped her wine. It was one thing to dismiss divorce. But what Stephen had done to her that night was to kill her trust. And rebuilding it was going to be a very slow process.

She decided it was time to change the subject, 'Anyway, enough of me, what's the latest chapter in that other long-running saga, Terry and Angela?'

Stephen was deeply grateful that his first encounter with Josephine was at a large meeting to present his progress to the rest of their marketing and research and development people. Josephine, professional to the tips of her shining bob, gave no sign that there was anything different from any other meeting.

To Stephen's surprise it was Hugo whose behaviour had altered. Instead of pouring cold water on Stephen's ideas, he positively supported them. And on more than one occasion he noticed Hugo watching him with a tolerant interest that Stephen found deeply disconcerting. Had Hugo known, then? And had Josephine told him it was all over? It was extraordinary that someone at Hugo's level of success could let a personal issue cloud his judgement, as Hugo had clearly been doing until now. But then Josephine was a woman with the power to cloud anyone's judgement.

He watched her for a moment. If anything, she looked more startling than ever. She had all her usual chic, but the suggestion of dark shadows under her eyes gave her a fragility she didn't usually display. Stephen wrenched his mind away from her back to the safer ground of the facts and figures in front of him. From now on their relationship had to be strictly professional.

'So, Stephen.' Josephine turned in his direction for the first time. 'I assume you're planning a trip to New York sometime soon?'

'Yes.' He hoped his voice was steadier than it sounded to him. 'As soon as we have some finished samples.'

When the meeting broke up he made a point of leaving with all the others, but Josephine called him back.

'Well,' she asked, looking down at some papers on her desk, 'how was the touching reunion scene?'

'Edgy. It'll take a while, I suppose.'

'You mean you didn't sweep her into your arms and renounce me and all my evil works?'

'No. We talked about why it happened and tried to set up some ground rules for the future.' God, he sounded pompous, even to himself.

'How very liberated. What were they? Never being alone in a room with me?'

'Look, Jo, you don't want to hear all this. We're trying again, that's all.'

But Josephine couldn't help picking at the wound. 'No, tell me, I'm fascinated by the mechanics of the modern marriage.'

'We just agreed to spend more time together. Less work for her and a bit less painting for me.'

'Oh, Stephen' – Josephine's tone lost its sneering quality and sounded genuinely shocked – 'you mustn't paint less. Don't let her do that to you!'

Stephen got up. In future he'd more careful to avoid intimacy between them. 'It isn't like that, Jo. She didn't ask me to give up painting. I volunteered to cut down, that's all. I don't want to turn into my father.'

'Maybe artists have to be selfish.'

Stephen laughed as he opened the door. 'Very handy for artists.'

As he left the image of her body, lithe and smooth, opening up to him like a ripe fig, darted suddenly into his mind. He made himself blot it out. All that was in the past.

'I thought I'd make a start on cleaning up the studio today,' Stephen announced the following Saturday as he and Tess sat in their dressing gowns in the cosy kitchen, working their way through the huge pile of Saturday papers, which now threatened to overtake Sundays for sheer volume of newsprint. 'If that's OK with you,' he added carefully.

Tess smiled at the conscious consideration in his tone. 'Fine. Tell you what, I might even help you. There's nothing like a good clean-out to make you feel optimistic.'

He took her hand. 'Do you need to make yourself feel optimistic then?'

Tess felt a faint shadow of depression. This new phase between them was like walking on eggshells.

She changed the subject. 'Come on, let's go and put on some old clothes. Is there a kettle there?'

'I doubt it. Slouch's friend was keener on Nutbrown Ale.'

Tess packed a carrier bag with tea-making things, threw in a packet of biscuits and a radio and went to change into an aged tracksuit.

As it turned out a dose of physical work, side by side, was just what they needed. Clearing the studio was a manageable task, which looked much worse than it turned out to be, and even by lunchtime their efforts were visibly showing.

'Come on.' Stephen picked up two of the black bags filled with rubbish. 'Let's chuck these out and zip down the road to Finch's. You might even meet the owner of this rapidly improving studio property.'

They sat down in the pub, with plates loaded with Ploughman's lunches and a glass of cool lager and watched the clientele. Not by any means the smart set. Most of them looked as though they'd either slept in their clothes or rolled out of bed five minutes earlier and got dressed in pitch darkness. The fug of cigarette smoke was amazing in these puritanical times, though fortunately dominated by the blue haze of Gauloises. 'It's a writers' haunt too,' Stephen pointed out, 'of the old school. The ones who can't put pen to paper without a full pack of something untipped and full strength next to them. You won't see any Silk Cut in here. Or single measures. They take their drink seriously. Everyone wants to be Dylan Thomas. The trouble is they're forty years too late.'

'Not to mention not having any talent,' said a voice behind them. Stephen turned. 'Slouch!' he grinned, standing up and making room for him. 'Tess, this is Slouch Heyward, my tutor at the Bryant.'

'I've heard all about you,' Tess said, holding out a hand.

'Nothing good, I hope.'

'Absolutely not,' Tess smiled in agreement. 'Fancy a pickled onion?'

Slouch gave her a swift glance. Even with her red hair tied back he could see that she had that creamy fieriness he so loved in Irish girls, and those fabulous light-green eyes that he guessed would flash whenever she lost her temper. He could see Tess was a fighter. He smiled back at her with a sense of relief. Very different from Jo's cool sophistication, but at least her match if he was any judge of character. Lucky Stephen, having two women who wanted him. He sensed the slight awkwardness between them and guessed something had come to a head. Maybe not so lucky Stephen after all.

'Well then.' He sipped the Bushmills that had miraculously appeared at his elbow. 'How's the new studio?'

'Ask us a bit later,' Stephen replied, looking at his watch. 'We'd better get back to work, Tessie.'

The afternoon seemed to disappear in minutes and by four the studio was looking tidy and even characterful and inviting. Twelve bags of rubbish were stacked in the hall. Jam jars with clean turpentine lined the shelves soaking years of impacted oil paint off brushes, the floor was swept and Tess had thrown down some old rugs she'd found outside in a skip. One of the previous occupant's more attractive landscapes was propped up on the mantelpiece and Tess had even black-leaded the fireplace. Next time Stephen could bring some coal and have a real fire. They both stood back and surveyed their handiwork. Instead of filtering through dirty panes as it had earlier, the late afternoon

332

sunshine streamed in, giving the room a satisfyingly rosy glow.

'Not bad,' admitted Stephen, noticing a black streak on Tess's nose, 'not bad at all.' He stepped closer and rubbed it off, then gently put his arms round her. 'Thank you, Tess.'

'It was nothing,' she smiled. 'I like a good clear-out.'

'That's not what I meant. I meant thank you for taking me back, for letting me have a second chance.' Very gently, almost like a young boy on his first date, not sure of the reaction he was going to get, he kissed her.

Tess closed her eyes. But she felt no passion. It felt almost like being kissed by a brother. Still, it was a start.

One of the nicest things about the next few days was how pleased a lot of the partners seemed to be that Tess was joining them. Patricia had decided to be gracious in defeat, and Lyall Gibson was positively effusive.

'So how did the royal solicitors react when you refused their pot of gold?' he asked as he held the door open for her one morning.

Tess laughed. 'I don't think gobsmacked is putting it too strongly. Let's say I got the impression Hanover's aren't that used to being turned down.'

'I bet they're not. Well, anyway –' there was genuine warmth in his voice – 'I'm really glad you got the partnership. As a matter of fact I thought it was crazy you didn't get it last time round.' He glanced at Patricia Greene who was standing at the reception desk giving orders to some hapless messenger. 'Unlike some people.'

Patricia turned as she saw them walking towards her. 'The very people I'm looking for.' Tess felt Lyall's elbow dig gently into her ribs and couldn't help smiling. 'I wanted to invite you both to dinner on the fifteenth of December. Nothing fancy, just a few close friends. Plus other halves, of course.' She beamed her attention to Lyall. 'Would you like to bring anyone, Lyall?'

'Not unless Michelle Pfeiffer's available.' He turned to Tess. 'I take it you'll be bringing Stephen?'

'If he can come,' agreed Tess, mildly surprised at the question.

'It'd be better if *you* came alone, then the numbers'd be even.' Patricia put Lyall's arm through hers and drew him away from Tess. She hadn't liked the way he had seemed so comfortable with her.

Tess pushed open the door of her office with her foot, calculating that December 15 was only a couple of weeks away, and that she and Stephen hadn't even thought about what they were going to do for Christmas. They usually went to his parents one year and her mother the next. This was Dymphna's year. Could she face it? But Christmas alone with just the four of them might be even more stressful. And she of all people knew that Christmas was often the final blow that sent fragile marriages reeling towards the divorce courts.

She sat at her desk and worked through her post, stopping with excitement when she came across a document from the Family Division. The Eileen McDonald hearing had been reconvened for next week. And this time she wasn't going to make the mistake of briefing Michael Ellworthy. Now solicitors had been given the right of audience in court, she was going to represent Eileen herself.

*

When Tess walked into the courtroom the following week she longed to have a camera. Capturing the look on Leonard Savoury's face for eternity would have given her the greatest possible pleasure. She could have looked at it whenever she felt down or discouraged about being a lawyer and known that it was all worth it.

Leonard Savoury was livid. No one had told him that Tess was back on the case. If they had done he would have taken his preparation a tad more seriously and come home a little earlier from last night's jolly at the golf club. As it was he was feeling distinctly dyspeptic. And the beaming faces all round him weren't helping. Eileen McDonald looked as though it were her birthday, and even the bloody judge seemed more cheerful. Only his own client looked like a dog that had had its day.

Tess took up her position next to Eileen and smiled. It had been obvious from the paperwork that Savoury had let down his guard during her absence and left gaping holes in his client's case.

Tess took to her feet and outlined in damning detail the full extent of Ted McDonald's deception. As she spoke she felt the power running through her. She knew she had them on the run and it was a glorious sensation.

When they broke for lunch she even invited Leonard Savoury for a celebration drink. He simply swept by and ignored her.

'How can you be sure we're going to win?' asked Eileen nervously.

Tess smiled. 'Sixth sense. The judge has been on our side from the start. A lot of them wouldn't have adjourned no matter how right they thought we were. Too much hassle.'

'To Mr Justice Martin then,' Eileen raised her small sherry.

'To Mr Justice Martin,' echoed Tess. 'As a matter of fact I owe him a lot.'

By mid-afternoon the judge had come to his decision. 'Mr McDonald, I'd like to remind you that even in this throwaway society thirty-year marriages still count for something. Your wife helped you build up your business with her own time and effort as well as bringing up your four children. And you rewarded her with a pittance while you tried to mislead us about the actual size of your assets. You did not succeed. Consequently I am awarding Mrs McDonald a lump sum of a hundred thousand pounds plus an annual income of forty thousand.'

Ted McDonald gasped and blenched. Tess tried not to smile. Mr Justice Martin stood up and left the court.

Eileen and Tess embraced. 'Thank heavens I met your mother on that train!' Tears of relief that the awful strain was finally over swept down her face as Leonard Savoury and Ted McDonald left without a word.

Tess hugged Eileen harder. She knew if Eileen had had one kind word from her ex-husband it would have meant nearly as much as the money. When marriages ended like this it was so bloody sad. But she wasn't going to let that spoil their victory.

Outside the chambers Savoury stood in consultation with his client, who was clearly asking whether there was anything he could do. Behind them the judge appeared and walked towards Tess and Eileen. 'Congratulations, Miss Brien. An excellently presented argument.'

Tess smiled. 'By the way, I'd like to thank you for

336

suggesting me to Hanover's,' Tess said quietly. 'I'm sorry I turned down the job but it did help me get my partnership at Kingsmill's.'

'Ah, well,' shrugged the judge, 'that's the way the world works. I'm not sure Hanover's would have been your style, but I do like to see talent rewarded and I'm not sure you're entirely happy at Kingsmill's. Tell me, Miss Brien, have you ever thought of starting up on your own?'

Behind them Eileen was opening a bottle of champagne she'd pulled from an M&S bag. The cork came out with a loud pop, soaking both her husband and Leonard Savoury who were standing only feet away.

'Never mind' – Eileen pulled out some British Rail paper cups she'd removed from the Ladies on the train – 'serve the buggers right. He was mean all through our marriage' – she raised her paper cup in salute – 'and he's still bloody mean. To ex-husbands everywhere! Sod the lot of them!'

'So how did it go?' Stephen had got back before her and was chopping onions for pasta.

'Great. We won. A hundred grand lump sum and forty thou a year.'

'That's terrific. Congratulations.'

'She deserved it. She'd stood by him throughout his working life and then he ups and leaves with a newer model without giving her a penny. Sad, though. Thirty years of marriage and four kids together ending like that.'

Stephen looked up from the chopping board. They both knew she wasn't just talking about Eileen's marriage.

After supper they watched television until Tess's eyes began to close. 'Why don't you go up and have a bath before Ellie steals all the hot water?' suggested Stephen.

'Hey!' Ellie threw a cushion at him. 'I was just about to go up myself.'

'Exactly. Let your mother have a hot bath for once. She's looking knackered.'

Tess said goodnight and took her mug of decaffeinated coffee upstairs to a deep scented bath in which she stayed for twenty minutes. It was bliss. She emerged pleasantly drowsy and wrapped herself in a towel. Then she quickly brushed her teeth and turned to find Stephen standing in the connecting door to their bedroom watching her. He stepped towards her and began gently to undo the bathtowel.

A wave of panic swept over her. They hadn't made love once since she'd found out about Josephine, and she knew they needed to break the cycle, that the old intimacy had no chance of returning till they did. Marriages needed sex like a machine needed oil.

With one hand he began to stroke her breast, then dipped his mouth to kiss the other. Tess tried to will herself to respond. This was Stephen, her husband, the man she'd loved for nearly twenty years. And yet it felt like a stranger.

Her panic intensified. If she went ahead it would be under false pretences and she might simply end up resenting him more. This wasn't what they needed. Only a spontaneous coming together could heal their wounds, with both of them willing and wanting. And yet if she refused it might put even more distance between them.

She tried desperately to summon up remembered desire. Cowrie Beach. Or the night when she'd listened out for him, warm and wet, waiting for his tongue to inflame her most secret place. But what came instead was the memory of him kissing Josephine, and worse, her imagined picture of what had gone before it, two bodies locked in animal passion.

And then Stephen resolved it for her. He felt the clenching of her body and knew at once it was closing itself against him. Unlocking his lips from her breast he stepped back and let her go, a look of pain in his eyes. He turned and quietly closed the door. Staring into the mirror at her naked body, Tess felt a sob begin to tear at her.

She knew she had to get over this for both their sakes. But she had no idea how.

CHAPTER TWENTY-THREE

'I'm sorry about last night.' Tess rolled into the middle of the bed to press her body against Stephen's and bury her head in his shoulder. The alarm hadn't gone off yet and it was cold in the room, with icy streaks on the windows, yet Stephen's body was warm as an electric blanket. They often joked about his hot-blooded nature, how he slept naked even in winter.

'It's all right.' But the pain was still there. 'It was probably too soon.'

She smiled a small smile. 'So much for Rule Three.'

'Rule Three?'

She held him tighter, feeling his warmth flow into her sadness. 'More sex.'

He turned round so that he was facing her. 'Look, why don't we go away together. A weekend somewhere. Just us. To one of those no-kids places where the carpet comes up to your knees and there's a chocolate on your pillow. There's a time for extravagance and maybe this is it.'

'Sounds wonderful.'

'It'd have to be after Christmas.' He paused, wandering how she was going to take this. 'I may have to go to New York for a day or two.'

Tess's body stiffened. 'With Josephine?'

'No. Not with Josephine. On my own. Or, if I'm very unlucky, with Hugo.' He stroked her face. 'I'm sorry about the timing. So near Christmas.'

Tess caught his hand and kissed it. 'It's not the timing that worried me. More the staffing.'

'She's not going. Really.'

'OK. By the way, I've been meaning to ask you. Could you bear Christmas at my mother's?'

Stephen, who rather liked Dymphna, pretended to look appalled. 'You really do want your pound of flesh, don't you? Of course I don't mind. As long as she doesn't try and convert me to Catholicism.'

'She's given you up as a lost cause. She just prays for your soul instead.'

'Does she now? That's nice. Nothing wrong with taking out an insurance policy.'

'I'll ring her today. And you haven't forgotten Patricia's dinner party next week?'

'I wouldn't miss it for the world.' The alarm went off and Stephen leaned over her to switch it off. 'Your turn to make the tea, I think.'

'Tess, what a lovely little present!' With what perfect inflection, Tess marvelled, Patricia managed to stress the 'little' as she took their coats and deposited the small but expensive box of chocolates Tess and Stephen had brought on her hall table.

Tess glanced around her in amazement. From the outside Patricia's block just off Sloane Square looked like any other dreary service flats, the kind inhabited by countless old ladies on fixed incomes reduced to living in a shoe box but still dreaming of colonial grandeur. But Patricia had transformed the small space into a vision of country house extravagance. Every window had ruched blinds as well as frilled curtains with matching tie-backs. A bow graced each picture frame, silk flowers bloomed in artificial profusion on skirted occasional tables. It was as if Peter Jones had been given a free hand in redecorating the stately homes of England.

341

Tess sat cautiously on the edge of a chintz sofa and accepted a glass of Blush wine while Patricia introduced them to the other guests, a pompous barrister cut from the mould of Michael Ellworthy and a tax consultant called Peter who was in the middle of insisting he was a socialist, and their wives.

Tess listened, intrigued. He didn't look like any leftie she knew.

'Come on, Peter,' Patricia protested, refilling his glass, 'you can't be a socialist. You earn too much.'

'Ah,' twinkled Peter, tucking his thumbs into the waistcoat of his pinstripe suit, 'but I earn a lot more under Labour. They always try and make the tax laws fairer. Then no one understands them. So I get richer translating them. Long live socialism, say I.' Peter laughed heartily at his own witticism while Tess wondered how to steer the conversation away before she hit him. But London dinner party topics were all minefields. Private education, private health care, off-season holiday destinations, nannies and how much you paid them. Fortunately the arrival of Lyall provided a welcome distraction and soon it was time for dinner.

Even though the flat was tiny and the table took up half the sitting room, the lavishness of the place settings wouldn't have shamed the Palace – though whether the Queen favoured turning her table napkins into water lilies with a chocolate hidden inside was an open question.

Tess was seated between the barrister and Peter the tax lawyer, while Lyall and Stephen sat each side of Patricia.

'You work full time, don't you, Tess?' asked Peter's wife Henrietta, a toothy blonde in a black velvet hairband covered in seed pearls. 'What do you have, a nanny or an au pair?'

'An au pair.' Tess undid her napkin, wondering how long they'd taken Patricia to fold.

'Let me give you a tip. Get a Filipino. They work all the hours God gives and you only pay them tuppence ha'penny. It's changed my life.'

Tess choked down a retort and tried to change the subject. She looked down at the tomato and mozzarella salad on her plate. She leaned forward to breathe in the basil. 'How delicious, Patricia. Basil's my favourite herb.'

'Ah.' Patricia broke off her conversation and turned to Tess. 'But the basil isn't the key.'

'What is the key then?' Tess asked dutifully.

'The cheese. You must use *mozzarella di bufalo*. Of course, the buffalo can only be milked during certain months. I had this flown in from Italy. It costs a fortune but it's really the only way.'

'I didn't know you made mozzarella from buffalo milk.' Tess tried to catch Stephen's eye, knowing how much he'd be savouring the pretentiousness of the conversation. 'I buy mine in Safeway's.'

But Stephen wasn't listening. In fact he hardly seemed to be taking in where he was at all. He just sat there with a polite, remote smile. Instead it was Lyall who was watching her reaction, his napkin in front of his face, shaking with suppressed laughter. Very subtly he winked.

Tess felt a cloud of depression settle on her as she tried to join in the ludicrous banter. Once Stephen would have enjoyed every absurdity of these awful people as much as she did. They would have laughed together on the way home, swapping hilarious details.

Tess looked straight ahead of her and turned up her collar against the freezing night. Sharing the absurd had always been a bond between them. What had happened to the old telepathy? The way they always knew what would make each other laugh? Tess felt a finger of fear reaching out to her. Maybe they were drifting apart in more things than sex.

'Guess who Luke's got a Christmas card from, Mum?' Ellie bounded into the kitchen with Luke only inches behind her trying to grab the card from her. It was one of those huge three-pound jobs with two Teddies kissing on the front. 'Yuk! Look at that, will you?' Ellie handed it to Tess in disgust.

'I don't think Luke should have to tell me who it's from unless he wants to.'

'It's from Laura in my class,' Luke said, mustering his dignity.

'The fattest girl in the school,' Ellie translated meanly. 'She has a desk of her own because she's too gross to share one.'

'Ellie,' Tess chastised her, 'I'm ashamed of you. You're supposed to be a new woman in the making. Looks aren't everything.'

'No,' conceded Ellie ungenerously, 'but she's dumb as two short planks as well, otherwise why would she like Luke?'

The Christmas rush had just set in with its endless list of activities. School plays, report nights, carol services and Christmas fairs, even the annual moment of guilt when she bought a pudding from M&S for the Parents' Supper instead of making one herself like all the other mothers. It was frenetic and not at all geared to the needs of working mothers, but Tess enjoyed it. It was comforting and helped her to feel things were gradually getting back to normal.

In three days Stephen would be flying to New York.

344

And after that they'd have Christmas to look forward to. It might even be quite good fun.

'Tickets, schedule, faxes confirming your meetings.' Lucy handed Stephen a neat folder. 'You've got your passport with you, presumably?'

'Yes, Lucy.'

'Visa?'

'Yes, Lucy.'

'Your meeting with Betsey Bronowski's at eleven tomorrow.'

'Thank you, Lucy. What about the hotel? The Gramercy Park, wasn't it?'

'Oh!' Lucy looked guiltstricken. 'I forgot to mention it. Josephine changed it to the Pierre.'

'How very grand. Why did she do that?'

'She prefers it. It's the only hotel with decent closet space.'

Stephen looked mystified. 'But I don't need closet space. I'm only going for two days. And Josephine isn't coming.'

Lucy shrugged. 'Maybe she wasn't before, but she is now.'

Stephen calmly put down his folder and walked down the corridor to Josephine's office. To his great relief Hugo wasn't there. She was alone.

'What's all this about you coming to New York?'

'Stephen, this is a big deal for us. I'm not coming to spy on you or breathe down your neck. It's just that I'm the figurehead of Richmond & Quinn and people may think it's odd if I'm not around. I'll keep out of your hair and you can just call me in for PR purposes. Or not at all. It's up to you.'

'And leave you kicking your heels in a hotel room for two days?' Stephen was convinced there was more to this than she was letting on. 'Jo, what's all this about?'

'Precisely what I've said.' Josephine let a shade of irritation slip into her voice. 'I'm not after your virtue, if that's what you think.'

Stephen looked embarrassed. 'I didn't imagine you were. But I think I should stay at the Gramercy Park as planned.'

'For the sake of dear Tess's sensibilities?'

'And mine. I'll rebook the Gramercy Park.'

'Have it your own way. Anyway you'd better go and get sorted out. The cab'll be here in half an hour.'

'So you're a friend of Eileen McDonald's?' Tess smiled at the friendly woman sitting opposite her wrapped in a cosy fur coat and hat that reminded Tess of a toy bear she'd had as a child. 'Eileen's a wonderful lady. I was so glad we were able to get her a decent settlement in the end.'

'All thanks to you, Eileen says.'

Tess smiled. 'I hope she hasn't told everyone she knows I can do the same for them.'

Eileen's friend took another sip of coffee and finished her custard cream. 'Oh no. Anyway my case is very different. I'm the one who wants to divorce my husband. My youngest is just going off to university and Gerald and I really have nothing in common. We just irritate each other.'

'Is there anything specific that's brought this on?' Tess smiled across the desk encouragingly. 'Sorry to ask you such a question, but he hasn't been unfaithful or anything, has he? I mean it does make the divorce procedure a lot simpler.'

'Good heavens, no!' She seemed to find the idea of

Gerald being unfaithful highly amusing. 'We would have split up years ago but there were the children to think of. We decided to stay together till they were off our hands. But now the youngest's leaving and I thought I might as well get on with it.'

'Do you mind if I ask you something? I mean, not strictly a legal question?' Tess leaned forward fractionally in her seat.

Eileen's friend smiled. 'I think I know what it's going to be. Has it all been worth it? Shouldn't I have admitted the truth and given myself a chance of real happiness?'

Tess nodded, feeling a tiny chill of apprehension.

She leaned across Tess's desk and squeezed her hand lightly. 'My dear, the answer is: I don't know. All I know is that I feel I did the right thing.'

Tess returned the pressure of her hand. But somehow it seemed a high price for twenty years without real love or passion.

Hamleys the week before Christmas reminded Tess of Dante's Inferno without the light relief. Everywhere she looked parents fought over the last set of Meccano, or the final Polly Pocket. Tills pinged more often than a Nevada casino and the shop assistants looked as though they'd be happier doing a stint in Pentonville. The season of goodwill was here again.

Tess elbowed her way to the enquiries desk as politely as she could and asked for Bulk Brogan's Super Wrestling Ring with bounce-back ropes, which they'd ordered for Luke's Christmas present.

After a ten-minute wait the young girl returned. 'I'm very sorry, madam, but there seems to have been some mix-up. We have no Wrestling Rings.'

'But we ordered it weeks ago,' she protested,

imagining Luke's anguished face. It was the only thing he'd asked for as his Christmas present.

'I'm really very sorry but there's nothing we can do, I'm afraid.' The girl was beginning to look like a dog who expected to be beaten. 'We're right out of stock.'

Swearing under her breath Tess fought her way back out of the shop. She had ten minutes before her next meeting and finding an empty cab in Regent Street was about as likely as bumping into the real Father Christmas in Selfridges. All she'd achieved so far was wasting an hour and a half.

When she broke the news to Luke he looked close to tears. 'But, Mum, it's the only thing I wanted. I've invited all my friends round to play with it. We're having a wrestling superchallenge.'

'I'm sure we could make a ring ourselves if we put our minds to it,' Tess offered hopefully.

'Absolutely.' Ellie giggled. 'Why do you want to waste £34.99 on some crappy plastic thing when you can have one Mum made with a cardboard box and four Squeezy bottles?'

Tess pushed her towards the door. 'Ellie, I'd really rather you stayed out of this. I remember having to cross London several times in a snowstorm to find a four-poster for your Sindy doll.'

'I know.' Ellie grinned, trying to make amends. 'Tell you what, why don't you call Dad and ask him to get it? He's in New York and F.A.O. Schwarz is the best toy shop in the world.'

Against the advice of the cab driver Stephen rolled down his window and leaned out as they crossed the East River so he could get the best possible view of the Manhattan skyline. It was clear and very cold and the driver said snow was forecast. Stephen breathed in the

348

air, urban though it might be, the prospect of New York near Christmas filling him with breathless excitement. It was one of those givens that Americans didn't take Christmas as seriously as the Brits did; they only stopped for Christmas Day and not even Boxing Day; but a single visit to the big stores told you what utter nonsense that was. He couldn't wait to see their window displays tomorrow morning.

He also felt a breath of relief that Josephine had been met at the airport by a courtesy limo and carried off to the Pierre, leaving him to make his own way to the Gramercy Park. He'd spent half the flight resisting all her arguments that his hotel was inconveniently located for his appointments, and not really a businessman's hotel anyway. That, Stephen had explained, was exactly why he liked it. Plus the fact that it was near his favourite haunts of SoHo and Greenwich Village. What he didn't add, though they both knew it was firmly lodged in the subtext, was that it would also be safer that way.

Phil couldn't help smiling gleefully as she made the final booking with the travel agent. Christmas in Spain! After weeks of persuasion she'd talked Terry into coming with her and the children for a warm and relaxing Christmas near Malaga.

She'd known exactly what would happen if they didn't get away. The whole event would be dominated by wondering if Lianne and Johnny would really be allowed to come as agreed, and then vast disppoint-ment when they didn't turn up. She'd had enough of it. No way was Phil prepared to have their first Christmas together wrecked by Angela. Phil was beginning to understand her game, even if Terry didn't want to face up to quite what a bitch she was.

Phil closed her eyes and imagined pale golden sunshine, warm enough to sit out in, if not to swim, breakfast on the patio of *medialunas* and strawberry jam, walks in the orange groves, sunsets over the sea. But there was a hell of a lot to do before then. Presents for the rest of her family, her secretary, Tess, all to be bought and wrapped, work to get sorted out. The thought was horrendous, but then ... She sighed deeply, mentally packing her suitcase. Sod you, Angela love!

In vain Tess looked for Jacqui to ask her to phone Richmond & Quinn for Stephen's number in New York. She had solid meetings all day long, and realized she hadn't bothered to ask him where he was staying. He'd simply said Lucy had the details if she really needed to contact him. It was one of those little differences between men and women, she'd noted, that when she went away on business she rang home every morning, but if he was away only for a day or two, he didn't ring at all. Unless he was lonely.

She smiled at her next client whose small child was contentedly ripping apart this week's copy of *Hello!* magazine in the waiting area outside her office and assured her she wouldn't be a moment. She slipped back into her office and rang Richmond & Quinn. Nice Lucy was only too happy to give her the number.

Tess looked at it and shook her head. All right for some. She'd only dimly heard of the Pierre but knew one thing about it: it was a byword for the lap of luxury. She glanced at her watch. Two-thirty. In New York they'd be five hours behind. If she phoned now she might catch him before he left for Bloomingdale's. Ellie had said the toy shop was only a few blocks away.

As she dialled the number she marvelled that she'd

managed to produce a daughter who knew so much about toy shops in New York without even having been there. The global village was clearly a reality.

The reception desk at the Pierre answered within seconds with the kind of courtesy you encounter only in the upmarket US.

'Hello,' said Tess. 'I'm calling from London. Could you put me through to Mr Stephen Gilfillian's room? He's with a company called Richmond & Quinn.'

There was a pause of several seconds before the ultra-helpful voice returned. 'Their original booking was for two rooms,' it explained, sounding desolated at having to disappoint her, 'but they cancelled one of them. Would you like me to try Miss Quinn's room instead?'

'Miss Quinn's room?' Tess repeated. She clutched the phone as though it were her only solid link with reality. 'No, thank you,' she whispered, 'that won't be necessary.' When she put down the receiver the room looked exactly the same, but Tess saw it through a haze of threatening hysteria.

He'd lied to her. Josephine was there after all. And they were sharing a room.

She sat down and tried to fend off a terrifying sense of panic. She wanted to trust him, but she couldn't see any other possible explanation.

The only one that shone out clearly through the mists of pain was that she had been a gullible fool.

The meeting with Betsey Bronowski went off brilliantly, Stephen instantly hit it off with her. The seventy-plus native New Yorker, who sounded as though her lines came courtesy of Billy Wilder, liked the fragrance and the concept. The phone call she'd had from Jack Palazzo hadn't exactly harmed his cause either, although it was perhaps just as well he didn't know Jack had pointed out that Stephen was just Betsey's type: cool on the surface and passionate when it counted.

Stephen could have kissed her when she promised not only a large order, but a display too, maybe even a window depending on the competition and how good their point of sale material was.

Next stops were Bergdorf's and then Macy's, where the reception, though less breathtaking, was nevertheless encouraging. They were definitely on to something.

On his way to find a cab he took a deliberate detour through Macy's toy department, and the powerful appeal of family Christmas – even at Dymphna's – made him realize how close he'd come to losing everything. The thought had him heading quickly for the lingerie department where he scandalized the sales staff by refusing all offers of scanty underwear in favour of a brushed wool tartan dressing gown that almost exactly matched Tess's pyjamas. Whatever skimpy fantasy he might be tempted by, he knew Tess would prefer this. As the salesgirl handed it over, exquisitely gift-wrapped as only American stores knew how, he imagined Tess's face as she opened it on Christmas morning and felt a glow of anticipatory pleasure.

It was almost six before he got back to the Gramercy Park, longing for a shower and a beer, to find that Betsey had invited him and Josephine to her apartment for dinner.

He picked up the phone and called the Pierre. Josephine, already in the bath, took the phone off the hook next to her. 'Great, isn't it? And in her home too, that's amazing. A restaurant would have been fine, but home's much more of a compliment. You'll see all the family photographs and be able to memorize the name of her grandchildren.'

Stephen laughed. 'I'll try and do that.'

'Good. I'll pick you up at seven-thirty.'

Stephen had been about to make the same offer and felt a pinprick of resentment that Josephine took over so automatically. But then, he supposed, she was the boss. Anyway, only one more night and he'd be home again. The thought cheered him.

On some impulse Stephen phoned Lucy and asked her to fax Tess the details of his return flight. He was arriving at seven p.m., UK time, and couldn't help thinking, though he made no mention of it, how nice it would be if they came to meet him.

'You go on ahead, I'll only hold you up.' Stephen stood by the carousel at Heathrow waiting for their flight number to come up while Josephine, the ultimate business traveller, shouldered her olive-green leather overnight bag, designed to the last millimetre to fit into the overhead locker so she never had to stand in line waiting for her luggage with package holidaymakers or visiting relatives from Omaha.

'I've got a cab waiting.' Josephine knew perfectly well Stephen had been holding her at arm's length, but felt strangely loath to part company with him. Even a cab ride seemed better than nothing.

'Actually,' Stephen said carefully, making a show of doing up his hand luggage, 'I think Tess may be picking me up.'

'Oh.' Josephine could have kicked herself for walking into that one. She changed her bag from one shoulder to the other, smoothed her already immaculate suit, and picked up her briefcase. She'd almost

353

forgotten it was Christmas. A whole week without seeing him. How would she get through it? 'Well, see you after Christmas then. Congratulations. It was a very successful trip.'

As she walked away it struck Stephen for the first time that if Tess had come to meet him Josephine would be walking straight past her in about thirty seconds. He really should have told her about Jo's change of plans.

The carousel next to him jolted into action and the suitcases from their flight began to circulate slowly in his direction.

Five minutes later he walked through the green customs channel and out on to the Heathrow concourse, past the crowd waiting behind the barrier for their loved ones. He scanned the two-deep line of people, realizing quite how much he was hoping her face would be among them. He'd never sent her his flight details before and she must have understood the hint behind the act. But there was no one there. He put down his bag and waited for another ten minutes, watching joyous reunions enacted all round him as relatives arrived from the other side of the world for the Christmas celebrations. Then he picked up his bag again and headed for the tube station, fighting off a ludicrously strong sense of disappointment.

Tess clearly wasn't coming.

CHAPTER TWENTY-FOUR

In spite of everything Tess felt an almost irresistible desire to go and meet Stephen at the airport and give him a chance to explain. She knew, just as he did, that the fax of his flight number amounted to a request. And it was a request she was confused by. Why should he want her to meet him when he'd been away with Josephine? In the end, though, she couldn't stomach the thought of seeing them walk out together and have to listen to the pretence that it had all been in the cause of business which would no doubt follow. She'd been forgiving enough. The question was: what were she and Stephen going to do next?

She didn't have long to think about it. A few seconds later she heard Luke whooping a welcome as he threw himself into his father's arms and Ellie paying him the supreme compliment of voluntarily turning off the television. Then they all traipsed upstairs to find Tess herself.

'Hello, Stephen.' Tess looked up from making the bed, which, as usual, Inge had failed to do, but made no move to embrace him. 'Did you have a good trip?'

Luke, not sure whether it would be politic to ask if he'd been brought a present, decided to get back to *The Wonder Years* and hope for the best. Ellie, picking up the nuances between them with her usual deadly perceptiveness, realized with dismay that things were not going well. She followed Luke and shut the door.

Stephen stood, suitcase still in hand, watching Tess across the wide empty bed as she smoothed the sheets. Somehow it seemed symbolic.

'I hoped you might come and meet me at the airport,' Stephen said finally.

'So that I could be humiliated by Josephine as you walked off the plane together?'

Stephen closed his eyes. 'I knew I should have told you. She suddenly insisted on coming at the last minute. Since we were staying at different hotels I decided to chance it. How did you find out?'

'I phoned you at the Pierre. Lucy told me you were staying there.' Tess was beginning to feel extremely confused. 'And they said you'd cancelled your room because you only needed one.'

'And you thought that was because I had moved into Josephine's? Oh Tess.' Stephen strode across the room to her, looking as pained as she did. 'The truth was I was staying the other end of the city at the Gramercy Park. At my own insistence. You can ring and check if you like.' He smiled at her tenderly. 'There were forty blocks between us. Even you couldn't ask more than that.'

Tess smiled weakly. She wanted to hold him and say how sorry she was for distrusting him. But she couldn't. Because Phil had been right. As long as he went on seeing Josephine day in day out she could never really relax. What she really wanted, she saw now, was for him to give up the job. But it was the one thing she couldn't ask. She'd virtually forced him to take it, after all. The idea had to come from him.

'Is that everything to go in the boot?' Stephen eyed the enormous pile of luggage they were taking to Dymphna's. Christmas Eve and the whole of London would be taking to the road, turning a five-hour journey into a minimum of twelve hours, with the only thing to look forward to being a fry-up in a Little Chef

356

so they could truthfully tell Dymphna they'd eaten and thus be saved from one of her killer three-course meals at midnight.

Upstairs Tess tried to prise Luke and Ellie from their nice warm beds and out on to the black and freezing pavement.

'I never wanted to go anyway,' Luke protested, tugging a tracksuit over his pyjamas. 'I can't stand our cousins. All they're interested in is football and girls.' He uttered this last word with blank incomprehension. 'They don't even have Nintendo.'

'Just as well you can play with someone you really love then' – Tess shoved his Game Boy into his hand unsympathetically and pushed him towards the stairs – 'yourself.'

'But, Mum.' Ellie tried to pull her duvet back over her head. 'It'll be murder on the roads. We should be starting out late tonight and it'd take half the time.'

'I'm sure you're right,' agreed Tess, stripping off her bedcovers pitilessly, 'but then you aren't driving. Me and Dad are. You're the lucky one who can go to sleep in the back.'

Stephen packed the boot methodically with suitcases, Christmas presents and Trivial Pursuit. They'd played it so often they knew the answers backwards but Tess always brought it on the grounds it was something they could do as a family. Stephen sighed. He'd hoped that since they'd cleared up the misunderstanding over Josephine the tension between them would evaporate, but it was still there. Not all the time. Sometimes things were almost back to normal. Then, like a ghost, it would materialize out of nowhere to haunt them. And he kept sensing Ellie's eyes on them, monitoring them like a spy satellite with an inbuilt happiness-counter. He knew she was doing it for the best but it only made things harder.

He'd just finished packing the boot and was congratulating himself on his handiwork, everything in and he could still see out – just – when Ellie and Luke appeared, wrapped up as though they were about to walk to the Pole with Sir Ranulph Fiennes. They shoehorned themselves grumpily into the back.

Tess followed them and stood on the top step, with a large Selfridges bag full of Christmas presents for her sisters' families. 'Stephen, I forgot this lot. Can you shove it in the back?'

'For Christ's sake,' he shouted, all his sense of injury that she still didn't trust him exploding into his voice, 'why didn't you put them out before? You'll have to keep them on your knee.'

'Don't be so ridiculous,' Tess snapped back. She'd been up since five sorting everything out and was shattered already. 'I did all the bloody shopping. The least you can do is pack the bloody boot!'

'What's the matter with Mum and Dad these days?' Luke looked from one angry parent to the other in surprise. 'They always seem so bad tempered with each other.'

'Don't you notice anything, you dumb boy?' flashed Ellie. 'Can't you see they're trying to work out whether to stay together?' She buried her head in the cushion she'd propped against the cold, damp window. 'And frankly they're not doing too well at the moment.'

Luke sank back into his sleeping bag, hoping no one could see his face. He'd known something was wrong, but not that wrong. Silently he felt his tears wetting the soft cotton of the cushion he was leaning on. He hoped she was winding him up but he had an awful feeling she was telling the truth.

★

'Tess, love, how smashing to see you all.' Tess had rarely been quite so relieved at the sight of her mother, bright and cheerful, with the special Christmas perm she had every year with her pensioner's discount, standing outside her house waiting for them.

'Hello, Mum.' Tess tumbled out of the car, her legs stiff and her back numb. She kissed her mother as Stephen parked in the driveway next to the house, leaving Ellie and Luke asleep in the back.

'Hello, Dymphna,' called Stephen as he began to unload the boot.

'Hello, Stephen love,' Dymphna replied. She peered in at her grandchildren fondly. 'Like babes in the wood.'

Tess and Stephen exchanged a weary smile. 'More like something nasty in the woodshed. They've been bickering solidly since we hit the M1.'

'I've got a nice cup of tea just made,' Dymphna said. 'Why don't you leave the boot for five minutes, Stephen?'

Stephen shook his head. 'I'd rather get it done, then I can relax. By the way, Dymphna' – he hugged his tiny mother-in-law affectionately – 'remind your daughter to book a removal van next time we come.'

Tess ignored him and followed her mother inside the house, noting the look of slight anxiety on her face. 'Don't worry. We just had a shitty journey, that's all. Ten solid hours of traffic jams and Christmas spirit with everyone at the end of their tethers crawling along at fifteen miles an hour. What was that about a cup of tea?'

Half an hour later they were all gathered round Dymphna's living-flame gas fire drinking tea and eating homemade biscuits. The TV muttered to itself quietly in the background. Dymphna never turned it off, but treated it as a family friend with whom she had perfectly rational and sane conversations. Occasionally she even enjoyed throwing a cushion at a politician.

After tea Tess produced a bottle of Bristol Cream and they all had a pleasantly quiet evening criticizing the rubbish that was on TV over the Christmas period, knowing full well they would watch most of it. Ellie rearranged the presents under the tree and added theirs while Luke, unnaturally quiet, sat on the floor eating biscuit after biscuit and playing with his wrestlers as if he were six or seven instead of a strapping twelve. At ten Stephen announced he was off to bed, while Tess and Dymphna withdrew to the kitchen for some serious discussions on cooking the turkey. Turkey, Tess decided, must have become the universal Christmas fare because it was almost impossible for anyone, even her mother, to ruin. Almost, though not quite impossible.

She put an affectionate arm round Dymphna. 'Do you remember the time Dad made rum punch and you had so many you stuffed the turkey with a J-cloth?'

'Now, Theresa, that was all a misunderstanding,' Dymphna said, pulling herself up to her full five feet two. 'I was just cleaning the bird out and forgot to remove it.' A giggle escaped her, throaty and disarming. 'Though maybe you'd better deal with the wretched thing tomorrow. Just in case.'

By eleven they'd just about finished organizing the food and the presents to their joint satisfaction.

'Now.' Dymphna turned to her daughter. 'How about coming to midnight mass with me. It starts in half an hour.'

And Tess, who hadn't been inside a Catholic church for a decade, found herself agreeing.

Stepping over the threshold, Tess almost thought twice about the wisdom of the venture. This was the church where she'd been baptized, made her First Communion dressed like a little bride, and had come every Sunday, willingly and then unwillingly, until finally at the age of seventeen she'd rebelled and declared herself an atheist.

Like most Catholic churches it was an ugly nineteenth-century building, with none of the comforting golden stone and Perpendicular architecture of the Anglican tradition. Everything it had came from the atmosphere. Tess was taken aback at how crowded it was. Every pew was filled, and people stood six deep at the back and in the side-aisles. To her embarrassment they had to walk right down the main nave to a side-chapel, past the garish life-size crib and the plaster saints, with everyone watching.

Tess dropped to her knees and closed her eyes. The smell of candles mixed with incense transported her instantly back into her childhood world where things had been simple, and decisions made for her. At moments of uncertainty like this you could see why the teaching of the Catholic Church was at its most seductive. Accept my word in all things and I will give you rules to live by, from which no deviation is permitted.

All around people shuffled to their feet and began to sing 'Good King Wenceslas'. To her horror Tess found tears beginning to run down her cheeks. She remained seated, scrabbling in the pocket of her coat for a tissue. Why was this happening to her? Was it the powerful message of the carol? The kindness of the king making sure his serf didn't die of cold or hunger on a harsh winter's night? Or simply the regression into childhood of being in this place after so long an absence? And then she saw the truth. The powerful atmosphere had broken through her defences. She was weeping for herself because she was frightened and unhappy. The pleasure and spontaneity had gone from her marriage. They were both working hard to make it natural, but most of the time it was more of a strain than a comfort. It didn't really matter whose fault that was.

A chill shivered through her even though it was hot and stuffy in the church. Maybe it was too late for them already. She dropped to her knees, hardly noticing that she was out of synch with the other worshippers who had just been instructed to sit. *Let it not be too late; don't let us have failed when we had so much love.*

Tess sat up, aware again of where she was and of her mother pretending not to notice, but showing her anxiety in the way she clutched her handbag on her knee and looked forwards with rigid attention.

The congregation kneeled reverently as the bread and wine were turned into the body and blood of Christ according to ritual. People filed up for communion.

And then it was all over. The organ struck up 'O Little Town of Bethlehem' and everyone began to file out. Dymphna got to her feet and led the way, past a small altar to the Virgin Mary. Drawn to this image of a mother in pain, Tess put a restraining hand on Dymphna's shoulder and knelt down. A row of candles guttered in the wind from the open side door. Tess lit one. There was something magical about a candle, its perfect symbolism, that the Anglican church had overlooked by dismissing it as Popery. And Tess knew exactly what this one represented to her. The future of their marriage. Unconsciously she made the sign of the cross and stood up. She felt better. But as she and Dymphna walked, arm in arm, Tess was seized by a vivid picture of her symbolic candle suddenly snuffed out by the wind. Anxiously she turned. The candle burned as brightly as ever.

The courtyard outside the church was emptying. A few people called out 'Happy Christmas' to them. Tess held on to her mother, smiling at the friendliness of the people and the beauty of the night. They walked through the deserted streets towards Dymphna's home.

For a few minutes neither of them spoke, Tess unsure of how much intimacy she wanted to re-establish with her mother, and Dymphna wary of interfering in her deeply independent daughter's life.

Eventually it was Tess who made the first move. 'Sorry about all that. I've been under a bit of strain lately and the carols got to me.'

'Is it you and Stephen? I noticed you seemed a bit short with each other.'

They crossed the deserted main road and headed down an orderly side street, past houses with fairy lights in their trees and Christmas trees in their front windows that winked at them as they passed, all speaking of order and security within.

'We're going through a bad patch. I hope that's all it is, anyway. Sometimes I worry it might be more.'

'Poor Tessie.' Dymphna patted her hand. 'Marriage is so much harder for people now. You expect so much from each other. In my day if a man was a good provider and a woman kept a nice house that was enough to keep them together. Now you expect your husband to be everything. Lover, friend, husband, father, and to do the washing up. It was easier for us.'

'Why?'

'We didn't have choices like you. Choices always make things harder. Women don't put up with marriage like they used to; they're not prepared to do all the gluing back together, the smoothing over of the cracks like we used to do. They just get out. They can earn, so why shouldn't they? And no one disapproves any more. When my friend Lou divorced her husband thirty years ago – because he beat her, mind – no one would speak to her but me. Now people don't give a toss who gets divorced. And the funny thing is, all that makes it harder for people. They have to decide for themselves how much they'll put up with.' Dymphna speeded up her steps a little. Her feet were beginning to get cold. 'How are Ellie and Luke taking it? They seemed a bit anxious to me.'

'But it's because of them we're trying to make it work,' Tess protested.

'Maybe they realize that. It's a lot to carry.'

Tess glanced at her mother, amazed. Was she saying it wasn't good for the children for her and Stephen to be staying together?

'It's none of my business, but what brought all this on? You seemed so happy when I last saw you.'

Tess hesitated, wondering if she would regret what she was about to say. After all, her mother was passionately against divorce.

'He had an affair with the woman he works for. It was only brief but it might have lasted a lot longer if I hadn't found out. It wrecked my trust in him and I'm finding it hard to build it again.'

She waited for her mother to come up with her usual homespun advice about it taking two to tango, and why didn't she make sure he had a home he wanted to come home to. But she didn't. Instead she stopped and hugged her. 'Poor Tess. What a lot for you to carry round. No wonder you're stressed. I've always liked Stephen, but you can only do your best.

If it's too much strain maybe you should agree to part.'

Tess stared at her, horrified. What had she been expecting? To be told to pull herself together? That there was nothing wrong with her marriage really? She realized, shamefacedly, that part of her had actually *wanted* that response.

They had reached the driveway of her mother's house.

'Come on, let's go in. If it's going to happen, it'll happen. Worrying won't help. Let's just concentrate on having a happy Christmas.'

Tess hugged her for a moment and they stood under the starlight. 'Happy Christmas, Mum.'

'Happy Christmas, Theresa. Now go on in or you'll be knackered in the morning and driving us all mad with your temper.'

Tess put her coat on the bottom of the banisters and went straight up to bed. The room was pitch dark and she could only just make out Stephen's shape in the bed. She sat down on his foot.

'Ow!' he protested as she quickly undressed, shivering in the cold of the bedroom. 'Where've you been all this time?'

'To midnight mass with Mum.' She waited for a nasty crack.

'Once a Catholic, eh . . .?' he commented, but his tone was friendly and affectionate. Before she had time to put on her pyjamas he reached out and swiftly pulled her to him. 'Your tiny hand is frozen. And I know just how to warm it.' He enveloped her in the blissful folds of the duvet and guided her hand to his burgeoning prick, kissing her neck at the same time. Very gently his own hand worked its way down her body and began to stroke the soft hair between her legs. Despite all the tension between them lately, Tess began to respond. She closed her eyes and surrendered to the waves of pleasure that radiated out from his touch and tried not to cry out, wanting the intense feeling of delight to never end.

And then, without warning, the door was flung open and Stephen froze under the bedclothes. It was Ellie. 'Sorry to disturb you, but it's Luke. He's just been sick all over the bedroom. Too many of Gran's home-made biscuits.'

'When can we open our presents, Mum?' Luke's head appeared round the door looking disgustingly sprightly considering that he'd spent most of the night being sick and sabotaging his parents' sex life.

'What time is it, for God's sake? It's still dark outside.'

'After seven already.'

Tess groaned and burrowed down under the covers.

'And what happened to my stocking this year?' Luke managed to look both energetic and aggrieved at the same time. 'I couldn't believe it when I woke up and there was nothing there.'

'You wanted the money last year. You told me. For computer games.'

'That was last year.'

'Anyway, don't you think you're a bit old for a stocking?'

'You're never too old for a stocking. The things in it just get more expensive, that's all.'

'Go away and watch *Driller Killer* or something then,' mumbled his exhausted mother.

'Gran hasn't got a video.' Tess threw a pillow at him. 'OK, OK. I know when I'm not wanted.'

Tess snuggled against Stephen's sleeping form.

Maybe they could go on where they left off last night. Then she remembered she'd promised Dymphna to put the turkey in. Sometimes life seemed like a conspiracy.

By breakfast everything was under control, the turkey stuffed and stowed in the oven, the Christmas pudding bubbling gently on the hob, the vegetables prepared. All that was left to worry about was the serious dilemma of how on earth you cooked roast potatoes, which crisped nicely at gas six, when the turkey needed to be cooked at two. This was a mystery she was never to penetrate as Stephen arrived and began to bustle about making coffee.

Dymphna appeared next, looking like Mrs Tiggy-winkle in a flowery quilted dressing gown and marvelling at how much Tess had done, then went off to have a bath.

'Presents in half an hour, Dymphna,' Stephen shouted after her. Then he dropped his voice to a whisper. 'She was watching me like she was David Attenborough and I was Guy the Gorilla. Have you been swapping secrets about Our Marriage and My Part In Its Downfall?'

Tess looked guilty.

'Come on.' He held his arms out to her. 'It's nothing a weekend away from spewing teenagers won't fix. Happy Christmas.'

Tess sat down on his knee and kissed him. 'Happy Christmas.'

'That's better,' Ellie congratulated them, appearing in the doorway. 'Season's greetings one and all.'

'Did I say Guy the Gorilla?' said Stephen, burying his face in Tess's pyjamas. 'I meant Chi Chi the panda. Now I know why the poor beasts can't breed in captivity. They never get any peace.'

Three-quarters of an hour later everyone was finally dressed and assembled in Dymphna's cosy front room, and Stephen began giving out the presents. In a blatant abuse of power he distributed the ones he'd bought first, dying to see everyone's reactions.

'Dad!' Luke shrieked. 'You got it! You got my Wrestling Ring!'

Stephen grinned, unaware of the irony of the situation. 'I picked it up in New York.'

Ellie was unwrapping hers. She chortled with laughter and held up a sweatshirt proclaiming 'MY FATHER WENT TO NEW YORK AND ALL I GOT WAS THIS LOUSY BLOOMINGDALE'S CHARGECARD'. 'Penny and Lil will love it!'

For Dymphna there was a large box of embroidery silks in every colour of the rainbow. 'They're wonderful! How did you know I was thinking of taking it up again?'

'I didn't know you liked embroidery,' Tess said in surprise.

'You should be more observant, my love. There are lots of examples of your mother's stitching upstairs. Now, here's your present.' He handed over a beautifully gift-wrapped box with a subtle Bergdorf's sticker on it. She hoped it wasn't going to be silk underwear. Just at the moment that would seem an ironic symbol. She tore off the embossed fleur de lys paper, opened the box inside and unwrapped the layers of tissue paper. Inside was a beautiful tartan dressing gown in brushed wool with a red satin collar. A pair of matching tartan slippers decorated with red satin bows fell out. A perfect mix of warmth and frivolity.

'Oh, Stephen, they're fabulous!' She hugged him so tightly that he had to halt distribution for a second.

As she sat down, admiring her present and thinking

368

how exactly it would go with her tartan pyjamas, Dymphna leaned over. 'I shouldn't worry too much about your marriage, Tess love,' she whispered. 'I know a lot of folk'd change places with you and feel they'd got the best of the bargain.'

Afterwards everyone helped get the lunch, falling over each other in the tiny kitchen, even Luke, and they all sat down to a contented Christmas dinner with only the smallest scuffle between Dymphna who insisted that God didn't intend sprouts to be eaten raw and Tess who said He didn't intend them to be overcooked and fart-inducing either.

Boxing Day passed uneventfully enough with a visit from three of her sisters and their children, and there were times when the old closeness and ease between her and Stephen seemed to be back. Apart from having the uncomfortable sense that he was right. Her mother was indeed watching them, which had the unfortunate effect of magnifying every normal outbreak of irritability into something more ominous. By the time they packed up to go home it was a relief all round.

'Bye, Mum, thanks a million for having us!' Tess gave her mother a last embrace and got into the car. Luke and Ellie had their windows down and were waving madly from the back. Dymphna waved too as they disappeared off down the road, dabbing back a tear. It had been a lovely Christmas. It had even gone with a swing yesterday when they'd got together with her other daughters and their boisterous children. She'd felt like a matriarch, Rose Kennedy in a council house. She laughed at the daftness of the comparison. But then, why not? Life hadn't dealt her many moments when she could feel proud and happy. And one of the nicest things was how close she'd felt to Tess for once.

Sad, though, that it had to be anxiety over her marriage which had brought them together.

Walking back into the house Dymphna felt some of her newfound happiness draining away. What was going to happen to those two? They had so much materially, so many opportunities and choices and it just seemed to make things harder for them. She'd never admit it beyond these four walls, but she liked Stephen more than any of her other sons-in-law. He was man enough to show emotion and tenderness, and he was the best father out of the lot of them.

Dymphna sighed deeply. The truth was, she wasn't quite as optimistic about their future as she'd pretended to be. She'd noticed too many gaps between them, too much distance that they were trying too hard to fill. And, in her view, poor little Luke was taking it worse than anyone realized. Ellie, with her big mouth, would just come out and say what she felt, but Luke was different. People said splitting up hurt small children most but Dymnpha wasn't so sure. At Luke's age you needed security more than ever so you could rebel against it.

She went into the hall to put on her coat. She'd just pop down to the church and light another candle to replace the one Tess had lit, which must have burned down by now. Those two could do with all the divine help they could get.

'You're looking very glum,' Tess pointed out to Jacqui, emptying the bulging briefcase of paperwork she'd failed to look at over Christmas on to her desk. Jacqui sat at her post outside Tess's office, but with none of the usual gaiety about her. 'Didn't Santa bring you what you wanted?'

'He brought me what I wanted all right.' Jacqui

waved a piece of paper in Tess's direction. 'And now he's sent the Visa bill.' She tore it up and put it in the bin. 'God, how I hate New Year.'

'Tell you what, why don't you pop over to the pâtisserie and get us both something with enough calories to see us through January?' She handed over her purse.

Jacqui opened it. 'We won't get many calories for 42p.'

Tess looked puzzled. 'I could have sworn there was a tenner in there. Here's my cash card.' She got out her filofax and flipped through to the Bs for Bank. 'The number's 1892. Get out fifty, would you?'

'Tsk, tsk. You're not supposed to write your PIN number down. You're meant to memorize it and eat the paper.'

'I did memorize it and eat the paper. Then I forgot it and had to ask for a new one. *Then* I wrote it down. Now geddouta here and stop lecturing!'

Jacqui laughed, feeling more cheerful.

Stephen felt a rush of excitement as he opened his post. New Yorkers had been back at work since Boxing Day and the responses to his approaches were still pouring in. At this rate, if the manufacturing process was up to it, they could launch even earlier than planned. It was funny, his interest in perfume had until this venture been a purely sensuous one and he'd never really expected to enjoy the job of launching one himself. But he *was* enjoying it. In fact he felt quite proprietorial. Soon they'd be ready for a really big push.

He reached in his drawer for the copy of *Romantic Retreats*, a paperback he'd spotted at Waterloo Station and bought to find somewhere for him and Tess to go and stay, and flicked through the pages. There were three possibles, but the first two were booked up with weddings or conferences. He quickly reread the entry for the third: *Melchett Manor, Gloucestershire. Perfect getaway for lovers and second honeymooners. Secluded setting in miles of woodland. Stunning views. Jacuzzis in every room. Five-course gourmet dinners.* Stephen got on the phone at once. The hotel-keeper who answered made it sound like the Garden of Eden, only better catered.

'One last question,' Stephen enquired. 'Do you take children?'

'I'm afraid not.' The man's tone changed subtly. 'You see, we have to think of our other guests. A lot of them come to us to get away from their children.'

'Perfect. I'd like your best room for Friday and Saturday night.'

'And will you be having dinner both nights?'

'Absolutely.'

'Listen to this.' Stephen read Tess the entry from the guidebook.

'Oooh, Mum,' Ellie pointed out gleefully, 'you can't take your tartan jimjams on this one. It's the silk scanties for you and no mistake.'

'I don't possess any silk scanties, as it happens.'

'I'm with Ellie on this one.' Stephen smiled lecherously. 'You'd better get some, hadn't you?'

Tess turned right off Shaftesbury Avenue realizing she had over an hour till her next meeting. She could sit quietly over a coffee in Pâtisserie Valerie or hop on a bus to Selfridges and check out the lingerie department. Instinct told her that Marks and Spencer's wouldn't be an adequate response to the occasion. She was just crossing Wardour Street when she noticed an intriguing shop called Secret Fantasy. She could just pop in there for five minutes and see if there was anything suitable.

Before she was over the threshold, she realized her mistake. It was a good old-fashioned sex shop. The kind she'd spent her training as a lawyer trying to prosecute as they opened up in nice suburban areas.

She was about to turn round when a young woman in a French maid's outfit stepped between her and the door. 'Hello, madam, can I help at all?' She had the kind of relentless cheeriness usually encountered in geriatric nursing staff.

'Well, I . . .'

The assistant was clearly used to this reaction. 'I'll just show you where things are and leave you to browse, shall I?' She closed the door behind Tess to bar any thought of escape. 'Brass monkey weather out there, ain't it? And I can tell you it's nippy in this get-up. Now where shall we start? Naughty nighties over here, keyhole bras, crotchless knickers. This is our top seller.' She took a red satin basque off the rail, edged with black lace and suspenders. 'Just got a new lot in. All the fellas bought it for their ladies for Christmas.' She put the garment back. 'Next, vibrators. This one's very popular. You'll soon see why.' She held up a brown rubber object carved to resemble a tree. On the side towards the root was a tiny squirrel. The girl switched it on. The squirrel started gnawing away. 'The man pops it on over his willie and the squirrel does the business for the lady. Clever, eh? We're very clitoral here.' She turned to her fellow maid. 'That's what counts, ain't it, Dor?'

Tess giggled in spite of herself.

This was all the encouragement the girl needed.

'Course, if you get bored with the sex, they've got plenty of other talents.' She took two vibrators off the shelf, put them side by side on the floor and switched them on. They raced drunkenly across the carpet like a pair of animated sausages.

'I don't think so, thank you.' Tess shook her head, smiling.

'No? Suit yourself. There's crinkly condoms, French ticklers, little balls you stuff up your fanny and they roll around apparently giving you orgasmic bliss but personally I think they're crap. I prefer my balls on the outside, thank you very much.'

Temporarily tired out by this burst of candour, the girl leaned on the counter. 'I don't suppose leather and chains would interest you? No,' she answered that one for herself.

Tess looked at her watch. This deviation into fantasy-land had taken much longer than expected. She wouldn't have time for Selfridges after all. She retraced her steps and took down the satin basque. No doubt deep down men preferred sexy sleaze to silk sophistication anyway.

'Very nice too,' commented the girl, wrapping it in tissue paper. 'You'll wow him in that. He'll keep it up for hours. And if he doesn't, rub a bit of this on him.' She added a small bottle of Black Stallion Performance Enhancer. 'Just remember. You owe it to yourself, gel.'

CHAPTER TWENTY-FIVE

'It should be the next on the left.' Tess squinted at the mapbook in the darkness. 'I think.'

'Come on, give it here.' Stephen took the map from her. They'd already taken two wrong turns which she knew he considered her fault and was forbearing to say so because of the occasion.

'That's a right turn, sweetheart,' he pointed out in the special voice he reserved for commenting on her mapreading. 'This left hand' – he held out his left hand patronizingly – 'this right hand. OK?'

Tess took back the mapbook, barely resisting the temptation to assault him with it.

A sudden right turn appeared out of nowhere and he swerved into it, sending a two-foot fan of gravel up behind him. Ahead, down a short drive, was a Georgian manor house surrounded by a small paddock. It was startlingly near to the main road. Taking refuge in superiority, Tess refrained from pointing this out.

Stephen's hand tightened on the steering wheel. Bloody guidebook. There'd been no mention of 'handy proximity to main trunk route'. He hoped to God they had double glazing.

He parked in the circular drive and took their bags out of the boot. The reception area, with its fetching flock wallpaper, was empty and silent apart from the piped music. Stephen felt a distinct temptation to get back in the car and head back towards the M40.

'Mr and Mrs Gilfillan?' They turned to find a woman in a fussy cocktail dress coming downstairs towards them. 'I'm Fleur Phillips. My husband and I own the manor and I know you're going to enjoy your stay.' She eased herself behind the desk and searched for the signing-in book. 'Second honeymoon, is it? We specialize in second honeymoons.' She turned the book in their direction. 'You'll find plenty of other not-so-young lovers here. It has been known for guests never to emerge from their room all weekend. So romantic.

'Now' – Mrs Phillips shook her tiny blonde head so that her costume jewellery tinkled – 'it's six-forty-five and dinner is at seven-thirty so you've got nice time for a wash and brush up. Ties and jackets for the gentlemen, and something nice for the ladies. We do like our guests to make an effort. We find they enjoy it more that way.'

'We'd prefer to eat at nine, thank you.' Stephen abhorred early dinners and was looking forward to a pre-prandial bath and maybe something more.

'Didn't my husband tell you? There's only one sitting. We like our guests to eat together, at one big table. Then Mr Phillips and I can sit at either end and keep the conversation going. We find our guests . . .'

'. . . enjoy it more that way,' finished Stephen.

'One more thing. I expect my husband mentioned we don't have a licence, so perhaps you could note down whether you want red or white with your dinner and Teddy will pop out and get it for you from the pub at no extra charge.'

Stephen looked at the woman in disbelief. His first question was going to be Where's the bar? He couldn't credit this. There wouldn't even be a minibar in the room.

'Teddy'll take your bags up now. By the way, Mr Gilfillan, could you move your car round to the back of the hotel? We find cars parked in front spoils people's view of the manor.'

*

'Jesus!' Stephen flopped down on the bed half expecting it to break under him. 'This place is awful. How are we going to survive a whole weekend?'

Tess stood looking out over the paddock towards the woods. The views were quite pleasant, as long as you didn't feel the need to open a window. 'Come on,' she coaxed, turning back to Stephen, 'look at it this way. It's going to make a very funny story.'

She swiftly unpacked her bag and turned on the gold taps to fill the vast shit-coloured jacuzzi. 'Let's be second honeymooners and have a bath together.'

He smiled reluctantly. 'OK, you're on.' Tess laughed as he did a quick striptease and ran across the room to the jacuzzi and jumped in. 'Bloody hell!' he squealed. 'The bath water's cold.' He grabbed the nearest towel – small and cheap, he noticed – and ran to the phone.

'Mrs Phillips, this really is too much. The water in our bath is stone-cold.'

'That's hardly surprising, Mr Gilfillan.' No hint of apology registered in her tinkly voice. 'Everyone in the hotel must be having one now. Besides, the dinner gong's about to go and you wouldn't want to miss that, would you?' Her who's-a-naughty-boy tone made him want to strangle her.

Stephen stood, dripping and speechless, staring at the phone. He slammed it back into its cradle. 'It may make a funny story when we get home, but it isn't bloody funny now, is it?' He slumped on to the bed. 'You go down to dinner. I couldn't face any. It's bound to be disgusting anyway.' Reaching for the remote control, he snapped on the television and began to watch *Family Fortunes*, a programme he loathed, at full volume.

Tess sat down next to him on the edge of the bed,

unsure what to do. Once he would have seen the funny side of all this. He would have got dressed in his jacket and tie and sat with the other guests, playing it to the hilt. But there was too much tension between them for that. It really was going to be a great weekend.

Ellie and Luke tucked into the takeaway pizza ordered with the money Tess had left for them and rewound the video of *A Nightmare on Elm Street 27*. They weren't really allowed to get out this shocker after Tess had seen an extract of it on television, but what was the point of your parents going away for the weekend if you couldn't do things they'd told you not to?

Feeling faintly guilty despite her bravado, Ellie put the video on pause and proceeded to lock all the doors and switch on the burglar alarm as Tess had told her to do. Then she settled down to enjoy being terrified out of her wits by Freddy Krueger, the spine-tingling villain who seemed to be dead at the end of *Elm Streets 1–26* but always came back to life in the final frame.

Stephen was woken up the next day by the encouraging signs of sun streaming in the window and the delicious smell of bacon frying.

He rolled towards Tess and kissed her nose. 'Sorry about last night. I probably overreacted. It's just that I wanted it to be perfect. Tell you what, why don't we have breakfast and do a runner from this five-star Colditz till dinner?'

'Suits me.' The thing about Stephen was that he lost his temper but he didn't sulk for days like some men. 'Stanton St Michael's got some nice antique shops; we could go and explore them.'

'And this from the woman who says she's got too much clutter in her life.' He jumped out of bed and beat his chest with Tarzan-like enthusiasm, then flung open the curtains. 'I suppose it's too much to hope there'll be any hot water this morning?'

By the time they made it down to breakfast everyone else had gone out. 'Twenty to ten,' announced Teddy from behind the reception desk, leering at them as though they'd broken some kind of Olympic record. 'Had a bit of a lie-in, did we?' Stephen half expected to be asked how many times they'd done it.

They ate their bacon and eggs, sausages and mushrooms, all clinically laid out by Fleur as if each had been individually weighed with no chance of an extra gram creeping past her vigilant housekeeping. When they asked for more toast Tess noted a distinct cluck of disapproval.

'Quick,' hissed Tess as Stephen finished his cup of coffee, 'let's get out of here.' And they half ran, laughing like children truanting from school, out to the car.

'I say,' Teddy shouted after them, 'you will be back for dinner, won't you?'

'Absolutely,' Stephen replied in his most charming voice, 'we wouldn't miss it for the world.'

Even though it was mid-January Stanton St Michael was bustling with Saturday morning shoppers eager to catch the morning market and a smattering of tourists doing the sights of the classically pretty Cotswold town. They spent the morning exploring the mellow stone colonnade of the old Wool Market, source of the area's medieval prosperity; took it in turns to climb the Market Cross; and wandered round the parish church reading out to one another the plaques commemorating long-dead knights and ladies. Tess window-shopped at an embroidery emporium and nearly bought a cushion-cover kit, then decided she'd never finish it and it would only live to haunt her, eternally reminding her of the lifestyle she sometimes wished she had, but didn't.

'Fancy lunch?'

Tess shook her head. 'It's only two hours since breakfast.'

'How about a drink then? You remember alcohol? Amazing stuff, makes you loosen up and relax no matter how trying the circumstances.'

'Lead me to it then.' They ran across the frosty square to a pub still lit up by fairy lights. Inside it was packed and noisy with a blazing fire at one end, and they sat and drank two Whisky Macs apiece before reeling out again into the cold afternoon air.

'I know,' Tess suggested, 'let's go for a walk.'

Stephen looked at his watch dubiously. 'It's two already. Another hour and it'll be starting to get dark.'

'Cissy. You're just lazy, that's all.'

'OK, you're on. Where do you want to go?'

'Down by the river then back across the fields. I love fields in winter.'

'Will you be all right in those shoes?' He looked down at the light leather casuals she wore with her jeans.

'I'll be fine,' insisted Tess. She liked walking and anything would be better than an afternoon at that ghastly hotel.

They set off down the narrow path by the edge of the river, watching the swans coming in to land elegantly among the rushes. The branches of every bush seemed to be woven together with intricate lacy patterns of ice. They thought for a moment it might snow but Tess, wishing she hadn't left her gloves in the car, decided it was too cold. There was no sign of that overhanging feeling you got before snow fell. The sky was crisp and clear, though darkening now into pink towards the horizon as the sun dipped lower and lower over the river.

After half an hour or so they climbed a stile and started to walk round the edge of one vast field, then another, listening to the echoing caw of the crows warning each other of the intruders below from the leafless tops of the trees. The heavy clay had frozen solid in the furrows, twisting your ankle painfully if you didn't watch your step. *Earth stood hard as iron*, Tess hummed the words of her favourite carol, *water like a stone. In the bleak midwinter, Long ago.*

'Tess,' Stephen cut into her thoughts, 'I think we've come the wrong way.'

'You always think we've come the wrong way, especially if I've suggested it.' She stopped for a moment. 'We came along the river bank then turned left, so the car has to be in that direction.' She pointed across the huge stretch of field.

'Obviously,' he agreed testily, scanning the horizon which was getting darker by the minute, 'but how the hell do we get there? You can't tramp straight across in those shoes and God knows how far it'll be if we go round the edge.'

'Why don't we turn back and walk along the river then? Maybe that'd be safer.' Her toes were dying quietly in her ridiculous shoes but she was damned if she was going to say so.

'Fine, but which way is the river?'

'That's easy.' Tess had always had much greater faith in her sense of direction than Stephen had. 'It's behind us.' She turned on her heel and struck out in the direction she was convinced the river lay. How stupid of her to have refused lunch. She was absolutely ravenous now. She delved into the pockets of her Barbour, praying for a stray polo mint or two among the used tissues, but no such luck.

To her dismay the edge of the field simply led to another and yet another with no sign or smell of the river. She glanced back at Stephen. From the rigid set of his shoulders she could tell he was furious.

It was after five before they met not the river but a country road and turned, exhausted and freezing, in the direction of the car, just as a light but penetrating rain set in.

Stephen still said nothing, but it was a hostile, angry silence. It had nothing in common with the easy, companionable one down by the river.

'Go on, say it. It's all my fault.'

'It's all your fault.'

'I hope that makes you feel better.'

'Nothing will make me feel better except finding the bloody car and getting some circulation back into my fingers and toes. I thought you said you knew the way!'

Tess stopped running away from it and let her anger catch up with her. 'Typically male reaction. Everything always has to be somebody's fault.' Her voice rang out in the echoing blackness. There was a time when he wouldn't have blamed her, when he would turned it into an exciting adventure. A Dungeons and Dragons tale of battling knights chasing a trail of good and evil through the tangled paths of the greenwood. It would have been scary, but fun.

Stephen turned on her. 'Forget all this male/female stuff and face it for once. It *is* your fault! You suggested the sodding walk. I told you it was too late.'

'*Why* does it always have to be someone's fault? We got lost, that's all.'

This was too much for Stephen. 'That's so bloody typical. You never take responsibility for your own actions. If you run out of petrol, it's just bad luck; if Inge breaks something, that's life. Well I *am* angry. And starving. And cold. And this weekend is rapidly turning into a nightmare.' Even the car finally looming into sight didn't have the power to cheer them. 'And now I suppose you've lost the car keys and that won't be your fault either.'

Tess delved in her shoulder bag and furiously yanked them out. 'You don't need to remind me the weekend's turning into a nightmare. I had noticed all by myself.'

Dinner, as it happened, was much better than either of them expected. The food was surprisingly good and the hosts' idea of an interesting seating plan meant that Tess and Stephen were at opposite ends of the huge table, which suited them both perfectly. Tess had been put between a shy man who'd made a killing in computers and clearly didn't know how to spend it if he came to places like this and a hearty matron who'd left six boys behind and was clearly savouring every moment of her freedom.

Stephen had a moustachioed Wing Commander to his left and the wife of a stockbroker who'd come with her husband to celebrate their silver wedding anniversary on his right. Fleur, Tess noted with malicious pleasure, seemed to have taken quite a shine to Stephen. Serve him right.

After coffee the Wingco sidled up and whispered that he had a bottle of port if anyone fancied joining him in the lounge. Tess got the distinct feeling she'd wandered into a *Carry On* film and glanced up to see if Stephen shared the joke. He didn't.

'Just a quick one.' Tess followed in the Wingco's

blazered wake. Before she could sit down she felt a hand grasp her elbow and lead her out of the thick of the crowd. It was Stephen. 'I'm sorry, Tessie, I was just cold and tired and hungry. I behaved unforgivably.'

Tess was about to point out that it was when you were cold and tired and hungry that love mattered most, but after all, she'd given as good as she got. 'OK. Apology accepted.' And as she said it, it struck her that these days they seemed to be apologizing to each other all the time.

It was hot in the lounge with its huge log fire and as she added a glass of port to the wine at dinner and her lunchtime Whisky Macs, Tess found herself nodding off. She decided it was time for bed before she started snoring.

'Good night all.' She raised an eyebrow at Stephen sitting the other side of the fire deep in conversation with the stockbroker. 'Are you coming up now or later?'

'I'll be up in five minutes, love. As soon as I've finished my drink.'

Tess walked alone up the empty staircase away from the laughter below, realizing that the weekend, on to which they'd pinned so many hopes, was lying around them in ruins. It seemed to her that she had two choices. She could admit that the whole thing had been a mistake, or she could make a last ditch stand to rescue it. She tossed her red hair as she turned the key in the lock. She'd just decided which option to go for.

In the lounge Stephen was just beginning to grasp the difference between a bull and a bear market as he settled into his second glass of port. After this he'd join Tess. He leaned towards his new stockbroker friend, aware that he was making conversation but at least it was something he actually wanted to know. 'Tell me, what is a bond dealer? These Masters of the Universe we hear so much about?'

The stockbroker looked delighted and launched into a detailed history of Salomon Brothers while his wife dozed quietly by the fireside, grateful that she could put off for another hour the celebratory coupling they'd come here to achieve.

Tess lazed in the vast jacuzzi, filled to the brim with steaming water. Clearly the only time you could get hot water here was in the middle of dinner and she was going to make the most of it. Afterwards she dried herself carefully and anointed herself with body lotion. She brushed her pubic hair so that it curled gently like inviting fluff, the undeniable proof she was a natural redhead. Then she stood by the wardrobe debating. Hesitantly, feeling a little knot of tension building up in her stomach, she put on the red satin basque, snapped on some black silk stockings and slipped her feet into the only pair of high-heeled shoes she owned. She let down her long hair and brushed it too, touched up her make-up and dabbed perfume on her neck, between her breasts and on the soft part of her inner thigh. She gave herself a long look in the mirror just as she heard the handle turning on the door.

Did she look sexy or just ridiculous? Pouting slightly, she licked her lips so that they shone and repeated the words of the cheery sales assistant to herself: 'Just remember. You owe it to yourself, gel.'

She left it another minute until she knew Stephen was safely inside the room then, very slowly, she opened the interconnecting door to the bedroom and waited until he saw her.

CHAPTER TWENTY-SIX

Stephen took off his jacket and went to the wardrobe to reach for a hanger. As the door swung open he caught sight of Tess in the long mirror. Never before in their marriage had she shown the slightest inclination to dress up as Penthouse Man's idea of a sex siren. From her tarty high heels to her underwired breasts she looked like a total stranger.

Stephen never knew whether it was from nerves or alcohol or just plain ineptitude, all he knew was that his automatic reaction was to burst out laughing.

Instantly Tess slammed the bathroom door and crashed the bolt across, fighting back tears of humiliation. Here she was trying to dream up ways of saving their marriage and all he could do was laugh. What was she doing in this ridiculous outfit anyway? She couldn't keep up this charade much longer. All the spontaneity had gone from their life together, leaving them feeling like actors in a play. She turned the tap on full blast and shoved her burning face under its cold soothing water as Stephen banged on the door apologizing and telling her to open it up so that he could show her what he really thought of her sexy get-up.

But it was too late. Tess's already delicate pride was shattered. She stripped off her black silk stockings, ripped them to shreds, and stuffed them tearfully into the bin.

'Did you hear the rain in the night?' Teddy enquired cheerily as they stood at the reception desk to settle their bill. 'Came down in buckets. Farmers are in a terrible tizz. Worried about their early lambs. Get snow at this time of year generally. But not floods. You'd best be careful driving to Stanton St Michael. It's a water-trap, that road. One giant puddle, I expect. Did you enjoy your weekend?'

For a mad moment Stephen felt like telling him the truth. That it had been amongst the worst few days of his life, from the time they'd arrived to the dreadful moment last night when he'd thought he was going to have to break down the bathroom door. At the last minute Tess had emerged, livid, and lain down stiff-backed on her side of the bed refusing to talk until she fell asleep. But, 'Fine, thank you,' he replied with perfect English understatement.

In the car the silences were deeper than the sheets of water that lay all over the road. Miles passed without either of them speaking a word. Somewhere around Woodstock Stephen came to a decision.

'Tess, I've been thinking. This trouble between us seemed to start when I left the agency. But it got a lot worse when I went to work for Richmond & Quinn. I realize it must be hard for you, me seeing Josephine every day. So I was wondering if it might be better for us if I gave up the job.'

He was looking straight ahead, his voice steady and deliberately neutral, yet Tess knew that he was enjoying working there, and how much this offer must be costing him. 'Oh, Stephen. I couldn't ask you because it was my idea you took the job in the first place, but I do think it could make a difference. In fact it could make all the difference in the world.'

The relief in her voice took him by surprise. He'd no idea she felt this intensely about it. Without taking his eyes from the road he raised his hand from the gearstick and squeezed hers, dismissing a small sense of disappointment. Somehow he hadn't thought she'd actually want him to do it.

Ellie climbed up the ladder into the loft and looked around her helplessly. There was water everywhere and for the last half-hour it had been pouring through the ceiling into her parents' bedroom. She'd heard slates falling in the high winds during the night and hadn't felt brave enough to do anything about it. She'd just wished that she hadn't been so offhand with her parents after all, insisting that she was old enough to look after Luke and the house and blackmailing them, against their better judgement, into leaving her in charge. And now look what had happened. Not that anyone could possibly say it was her fault, but she didn't know how to deal with it, as a babysitter would have done. Should she call the fire brigade? Or an emergency plumber? She realized she had no idea. She'd just have to ring her parents at their hotel. She didn't want to disrupt their romantic weekend, but this was a full-blown emergency.

When Fleur Phillips told her that Stephen and Tess had already left she almost burst into tears. Heaven knows where they were then. They might be driving back slowly and doing some sightseeing on the way. She sat on the bottom stair and dropped her head in her hands. Luke came and sat next to her. 'Don't worry. Why don't we phone Phil and Terry? He's a practical type of bloke. They'll know what to do.'

Ellie could have kissed him. Phil would sort things out. And with luck she'd have someone else here to break the news to Mum and Dad when they got back.

'What the hell is Terry Worth doing up a ladder

looking at our roof?' asked Stephen, stunned. 'Surely your bills aren't so steep he's taken to moonlighting?'

Tess laughed. 'It'd take a lot more than my bills to affect Terry's bank balance. My God, Phil's there too. What on earth is going on?'

They were hardly out of the car before Phil bounded over the road, unseasonably dressed in leggings and a baseball jacket, her face a mixture of concern and bustling self-importance. 'Hi, kids, nice weekend? It'd better have been to prepare you for the shock. To put it bluntly, your roof's fucked.' Three pairs of eyes shot roofwards to where Terry and a bobble-hatted man were looking grave at the top of a ladder. 'You should have had it done yonks ago, apparently, and last night was the final straw. Half your slates came down; Alf says it was lucky no passers-by got topped. Water's been pouring into your bedroom. Alf says you'll need a whole new roof. But don't worry, he says the insurance'll probably pay. You'd better check your policy.'

Relief washed over Stephen. He couldn't cope with another disaster this weekend. He ran up the front steps into the sitting room where he kept a box file with their insurance policies in it. The file was just where he'd left it. He opened it up then stopped dead, remembering the reminder they'd had a couple of months ago that the premium needed paying.

He was almost certain he'd forgotten to do it.

'Take a look at that.' Stephen pushed the estimate for the new roof across the table to Tess.

'Eight thousand quid! Do you think he's right about us needing a new one? Couldn't it just be patched up?'

'I got the survey out last night. They said it needed a new one then, that it'd already been patched. And that was years ago.'

'We'll have to do it then?'

'Unless we want water pouring in on our bed every time it rains.'

'But how on earth are we going to pay for it?'

Luke, munching his Golden Crackles and forgotten by both of them, looked anxiously from one parent to the other.

'God knows. Borrow, I suppose. Tess . . .' he hesitated.

'Yes I know. I've got there already. You won't be able to stop working at Richmond & Quinn now.'

'It's going to be difficult enough even with me working. Look, I'm really sorry.'

'Yes. Well. I don't suppose Josephine Quinn has divine powers and can cause rainstorms. Though she might have the power to distract people so they forget about renewing insurance policies.' Tess couldn't resist a dig.

'That's not fair. I feel bad enough about it as it is.'

'Maybe I'm not in the mood to be fair.'

'This is silly.' He stood up. 'I promised Ellie and Luke I'd drop them off this morning so I've got to go.'

By the time they arrived at Chelsea Collegiate there was a teeming mass of pupils fighting to get in and the bell was already ringing for assembly. Luke and Ellie scrambled out of the car and joined the thronging mass.

'Do you think the weekend worked?' Luke whispered to Ellie as soon as his father had driven off.

'Doesn't look like it to me. If anything they're worse with this roof business.'

'Ellie?' Luke's voice wobbled in his effort to hold back the tears. 'You don't really think they're going to split up, do you?'

Ellie hugged him quickly. 'Of course not. Don't

390

worry. They'll get over it. It's just a bad patch. I expect all marriages have them.'

Luke watched her run off to her friends. He didn't feel like assembly. He might just go and sit in the cubby hole by the gym. He wouldn't mind being on his own for five minutes. Just in case he did something silly like crying.

'Have you got my shopping money, Tess?' Inge asked just as Tess, wrapped up against the cold morning, was about to leave for work. Inge usually did the shopping on Monday mornings to replenish everything they'd run out of over the weekend, but this business with the roof had put everything else out of Tess's mind. She took her purse out of her handbag and counted out some notes. That was funny. She could have sworn there were another ten pounds in there. She happened to have counted it last night in the car to see if she needed to stop at the cash machine on the way home.

'Inge, you didn't happen to . . .' But she could already see the look of outrage appearing in Inge's face. 'No, of course you didn't.' She handed over forty pounds. 'Thank you very much, Inge.'

'You are very welcome, I'm sure,' Inge replied huffily and banged out of the room. But if Inge hadn't taken that ten pounds, who had?

'So how was the romantic weekend?' Josephine sat, disgracefully elegant as usual, on the Biedermeier sofa opposite him, her eyes shining with wicked amusement at her indiscretion in asking such a question.

Stephen looked appalled. Did everyone in the whole of the South-east know about his private life?

'Lucy told me. I asked where you were on Friday

afternoon. She didn't mean to rat on you, she just let it slip.' Josephine picked up a bone-china cup and sipped her coffee without messing up her perfect lipstick. 'So, you haven't answered my question.'

'Absolutely bloody awful, if you must know. A disaster from start to finish. The place was dreadful. All flock wallpaper and non-iron sheets, the owners were dreadful, we had to eat together with Mine Hosts, and to cap it all, it didn't have a licence.'

'Poor Stephen, you should have asked me for some suggestions. I'm quite good at romantic weekends.'

Stephen ignored the implications of this remark. 'It would hardly have been appropriate, would it?'

'Better than two days of hell. So how did you both cope? Did love triumph over adversity?'

'We quarrelled three times, as a matter of fact.' He knew he shouldn't be talking like this to Josephine but he needed to talk to someone or he'd go mad. 'It was incredibly depressing. I really thought things would be better if we just got away.'

'Have they been bad, then?' Josephine tried to keep the intense interest out of her voice.

'Pretty terrible, yes. Then on the way home I offered to give up working here. I know, I know.' He caught Josephine's horrified expression. 'But I think it's a real problem for Tess that I go on seeing you every day.'

'And what did she say? Surely she didn't ask you to do that?'

'She perked up at once. Then we got home and found the roof had fallen in and I'd forgotten to renew the insurance. So here I am in your continued employ.'

Josephine was still looking shocked. 'Surely you wouldn't have gone at a crucial moment like this?'

'Not at once, no. I'd have stayed until you found someone else, obviously. Look, I shouldn't be telling you any of this. You of all people. It's just that it's all getting a bit difficult to handle.'

'Look,' Josephine's voice was warm and low and reassuring. Stephen felt if he closed his eyes he could listen to it for ever. 'You mustn't let all this get on top of you. If you ever need a break, if it gets to be too much, remember there's a futon in the studio and it's warm in there. You've got a key. I won't even know you're there.' She almost added, 'Unless you want me to,' but managed to stop herself. She had to be subtle. Things were going quite well enough already without her jumping in with size eleven feet. If anything was going to happen it had to be because Stephen wanted it to. She had to stay firmly out of the arena.

'Well,' she said, suddenly brisk, 'perhaps we'd better get on with our Monday meeting?'

Tess sat in her office reading through the notes she'd written during her session with Eileen McDonald's friend. It was sad, really. There were no obvious grounds for divorce. No infidelity, no drunkenness, neither of them was outrageously mean or wilfully spendthrift. In Tess's experience there were three causes for marriage breakdown: sex, money or disagreement over children, and none of these applied in this case. They were a couple who had simply grown apart and no longer shared any interests. It fascinated Tess that it was nearly always women who started divorce proceedings. Maybe men still had more to gain from even a bad marriage than a woman did. And yet, no matter what men might protest when they married again and still had to support their first family, it was usually women who got screwed by divorce. Left holding the children, and very often broke or reduced to state benefits.

Yet this didn't put them off. And neither did the evidence that children of divorced parents probably had a harder time than other kids and seemed to repeat the pattern in their own marriages.

Why was the instinct to divorce so strong? Was it the sense that we had a right to personal satisfaction which outweighed all other factors, even the best interests of our children? Yet if she had to make the choice, would she do any better for all her knowledge and experience of the havoc divorce caused?

Tess put away the notes. This would be a rare case. The parties wanted to divorce by mutual consent and without acrimony. In nearly every case Tess had dealt with, one of the parties had felt it was the other person's fault.

A knock on the door interrupted her thoughts. Expecting it to be Jacqui, she picked up her mug, about to ask for a cup of coffee. But it was Lyall Gibson, bringing a memo about the next partners' meeting which had wrongly come to him.

'Good weekend? Jacqui said you'd gone off early to the wilds of Gloucestershire.'

'In parts,' replied Tess guardedly, noticing that his springy hair was refusing to lie flat, as though he'd slept on it.

'Well, I won't ask which parts.' His grey-blue eyes twinkled in a rare outbreak of flirtatiousness. Usually Lyall was rather serious. And as he stood smiling down at her, to her shocked surprise Tess found herself wondering how he would have reacted to the sight of her in a red satin basque, black silk stockings and very high heels.

Chapter Twenty-seven

Tess loved the comforting warmth of the Provençal tiles under her bare feet as she made the early morning tea. The kitchen, which also housed the central heating boiler, was the cosiest room in the house. As she warmed the pot she heard the postman push their letters through the door. He was earlier than usual. She pulled back the big yellow curtains on the French window that led to the garden and went to fetch the post while the tea brewed. There was a postcard from her mother from a day out to the Tate Gallery of the North, several bills and a bank statement. She was about to put the bank statement away till she felt stronger, but that wouldn't help anything. Instead she opened it.

Her eyes were immediately drawn to the bottom line, which was overdrawn as usual. But then something odd caught her eye. Three withdrawals of £10 each over the month. She never took out £10. It wouldn't last five minutes.

She put it on the tea tray and took it upstairs to see if Stephen had any inspirations. On the way up she noticed Luke's door open and decided to stop off and give him a good morning kiss. He was rarely awake at this time. Usually it was a mad dash to get him into his clothes, breakfasted and through the door in time for school.

He was out of bed and already dressed, sitting at the desk unit they'd bought him at Christmas so he could do his homework in peace. He was playing his hand-held computer game, completely absorbed. Tess came up behind him. For once it wasn't his precious Nintendo but some gadget she didn't recognize.

'What's this?' she asked, ruffling his hair and kissing the top of his dark head. 'I've never seen this one before. Is it new?'

To her surprise his instinct was to try and hide it.

Tess picked it up. It still had the price sticker on it: £69.99. Far more than he'd saved from his pocket money. A shockwave of premonition flooded through her.

'Luke, is this yours?'

'They were half price. I bought it with my pocket money. It wasn't nearly as much as it says on the label. Honestly.'

Tess gave him back the toy and walked over to the chest of drawers where his Three Wise Monkeys moneybox stood. It was still full.

'Luke, tell me the truth. How did you pay for it?'

Luke flushed. He'd always been a terrible liar even when he was tiny and tried to say it wasn't him who'd broken another child's toy.

'Luke, tell me the truth: did you take money from my purse and use my cash card?'

Luke shook his head miserably.

'Please, Luke, tell the truth. I know I didn't take that money out myself. I'll have to go and ask Dad and Ellie if they did.'

Luke burst into tears. 'I took it. I'm so sorry. I thought you wouldn't notice.'

'But that's dishonest. It's stealing, Luke.'

'What's dishonest?' Stephen had come in search of Tess and the tea.

Luke's eyes flew to hers, beseeching her not to tell his father. But she had to. This was something so serious she and Stephen would have to deal with it together.

'Luke's been taking money from my purse to buy a computer game.'

Stephen looked horrified. 'Luke, is this true?'

'Only a few times.'

'The number of times you did it is irrelevant,' Stephen snapped angrily, 'it's still just as dishonest if you do it once.'

'It's your fault too,' flashed back Luke with a rebelliousness in his tone Tess had never heard before. 'You've both been so caught up with your own problems you haven't had time for us. I didn't think you cared much what we did as long as we kept out of your way.'

His words opened the floodgates of her maternal guilt. She was already smarting from having left them alone the weekend the roof caved in. Without even knowing she was doing it she reached out her arms and he ran into them.

'For God's sake, Tess, don't encourage him. That's just a feeble excuse from someone who knows he hasn't got a leg to stand on.'

But Tess had seen the fear and vulnerability under his bravado and it had twisted her heart like lemon on an oyster. What he'd said was true. All her attention had been focused on trying to sort things out with Stephen.

'Don't think you're getting away with this because your mother's too soft on you. You'll take it back to the shop and tell them how you acquired it. Then you'll ask for a refund. If they won't give it to you, it'll be stopped from your pocket money. Is that clear? You'll go today after school. And you won't be allowed to go to Ben or Tom's house for the next month either.'

'Stephen, hang on a minute.' Tess put a restraining

arm on his shoulder. 'Of course he must take it back, but surely he doesn't have to tell them why?'

Stephen shook her hand off. 'You can stay up here till school-time. I want to talk to your mother.'

Back up in their bedroom Stephen turned on her angrily. 'You might at least back me up, Tess. This is serious. You never know where it'll end.'

'I agree. But I think we should also see that it may be a cry for help.'

'For God's sake, Tess, don't give me that do-gooding claptrap. You're always too soft on him. Look, if you're so sure your way's right, fine. You deal with it. I won't interfere. Then at least we'll have a united front.'

He dressed quickly and banged out of the room. She knew Stephen felt she was soft with the children, that she saw things too much from their point of view instead of disciplining them. Maybe it was an extension of her natural sympathy with the underdog. To him it looked like weakness.

As she lay in bed she remembered the three things that broke up marriages. Sex, money and children. Three out of three. That was pretty good going.

When Stephen went down to make the tea the next morning he found Luke lying on the sofa watching television as he did every Saturday. Stephen sat down on the arm.

'So,' he asked gently, all his fury of yesterday evaporated, 'did you take back the game?'

Luke didn't look up. 'Yes, Dad.'

'And did they give you a refund?'

'Yes, Dad. It's in an envelope on the dresser.'

Stephen had the tact not to ask if Luke had given the real reason for the return. Instead he sat down on the sofa and put his arms round his son.

'Why did you do it, Luke?'

Luke snuggled in like a small child. 'I don't know, Dad, I really don't. Maybe I wanted you to notice me. Perhaps I was scared. We don't seem to be as much of a family as we used to be.' He looked up at his father anxiously. 'Do you think I'm making an excuse?'

Stephen stroked the dark head, feeling a shiver of inadequacy and pain. Luke didn't deserve this. The one thing you needed from your parents was security, and that was the one thing they hadn't been giving him. But how could you give it to another person when you didn't feel it yourself?

Tess dressed quickly, suppressing a blast of irritation that Stephen hadn't reappeared with the tea. Probably waylaid by some fascinating article in the paper. Sometimes she thought newspapers were the enemy of family life. She even knew one couple who'd stopped getting them altogether because they never talked to their children.

Downstairs in the kitchen she touched the kettle. It was cold. Stephen hadn't even got as far as boiling it. In the sitting room next door she could hear the TV and she opened the connecting door to protest. The sight of Stephen and Luke, their two dark heads together, stopped her. Her heart twisted inside her at the complexity of love, perfect one moment, spoiled the next.

'Hello, you two. Fancy getting dressed while I make the breakfast?' And then some instinct prompted her to add: 'Luke, love, why don't you think of something you'd like to do with Dad and me today?'

'How do you fancy coming to a private view next Friday?' Josephine leaned on the door of Stephen's office, giving him the full benefit of her long legs.

'Hugo can't make it and it'll give you a taste of what it's like when you have one yourself.'

Stephen had been sitting at his desk trying to concentrate on his marketing plan, but kept seeing Luke's anxious face looking up at him. At least they'd had a fun day together on Saturday. It had been touching how seeing some mediocre film and eating a Big Mac together had clearly meant so much to him.

Josephine was waiting for an answer. Sometimes it seemed to Stephen that she came from another planet where everyone was well dressed and behaved properly, and where everything was shiny and serene. Money couldn't be the whole answer. It had to be an attitude of mind. 'Sounds interesting, but I'd have to check with Tess.'

A shadow of irritation crossed Josephine's elegant features. Tess, always bloody Tess.

'Why don't you invite her too?' Josephine suggested. She was fairly convinced Tess would be well out of her depth in the heavyweight gathering that would be attending. 'I'm sure she'd find it fascinating.'

'All right. Maybe I'll do that.'

'What kind of painter is this Stefan Grodzzyk then?' Tess asked, sipping her coffee. Her first instinct had been to say no, but she rightly identified this as cowardly. Besides, she knew the invitation was something of an olive branch and that Stephen was probably consciously trying to include her in his interests. On that basis alone she really ought to go.

'I don't know much about him, except that he's been shortlisted for the Turner Prize.'

'And what does that mean, exactly?'

'That he's young. They have to be under fifty, I

think.' Tess smiled at this redefinition of youth. Ellie thought you were old at twenty-one. 'And fairly experimental. Sharks through the roof and that sort of thing. Bits of old building. Preserved entrails.'

'I read about an artist,' offered Ellie, 'who used to preserve her own turds.'

'Thank you, Eleanor,' reprimanded Tess, 'not at the breakfast table.'

'Not quite as experimental as that,' Stephen reassured her.

Tess stood up. 'I can hardly wait. Where and when?'

'Six to nine, Semprini Gallery, Cork Street.'

'Oooh, Mum,' Ellie pointed out, 'the epicentre of the art world. Mind you don't buy anything.'

'I couldn't afford to. Mind you, a shark in our roof might look quite fetching. We've got just the place for it.'

Tess looked at her watch as she walked down Cork Street. It was just after six-thirty. Since she probably wouldn't know anyone she didn't want to be too early. Finally she psyched herself up to go in. She was greeted at the door by two willowy blondes who looked like sisters from the same aristocratic family. Of course, working in art galleries was one of those OK jobs for upper-class girls who hadn't found Lord Right yet. One of them scanned her list. 'What did you say your name was?'

'Tess Brien.' She hoped to God Stephen had mentioned she was coming. 'Or maybe Gilfillan.'

The girl looked at her dubiously. 'Have you by any chance got your invitation with you?'

Tess cursed. She'd half known this was going to happen. Now what was she going to do? Get shirty or disappear and have a drink for half an hour till Stephen got here?

As it happened she had to do neither.

'Tess, dear! How lovely to see you!'

She swung round to find her mother-in-law Stella standing behind her, in an unusually jovial mood too. 'Come and join us old lags over here. It's perfectly all right, dears' – she gave the girls on the door the benefit of her most patrician smile – 'Tess is with us.'

Stella took a drink from a passing tray and handed it to Tess.

'I didn't know you were in London,' Tess said, easing herself into a comfortable corner, slightly away from the thronging mass that had shoehorned itself into the smallish gallery. 'Is Julius here too?'

'No, still at home. I came over because an old schoolfriend's ill. At our age reading the obituary column's rather like flipping through your address book. You know everyone in it. So I thought I'd better come, just in case. And then I bumped into dear Duncan at Brown's' – she indicated a man in the group – 'and he talked me into coming here. Now let me introduce you to a few faces.' She turned to the raffish crew of assorted painters and sculptors gathered round her and reeled off their names. One or two even sounded vaguely familiar. 'We've just been complaining about the absurd rule for this silly Turner Prize. Under fifty indeed. As if talent stopped with age. Look at Julius.'

'Ah,' threw in a small Scot with a wonderfully irreverent grin, 'but that's because we're all old fogeys. Someone's got to encourage the young blood. Otherwise who would discover geniuses like Mr Grodzzyk?' He threw his arm out expansively, almost knocking Tess's glass from her hand. They all looked round at the examples of the artist's work. These seemed to be unidentifiable parts of vast machines, things which looked like ships' doors and portholes, the odd drain cover all painted in subtly different shades of industrial grey.

'So, what do you think of Mr Grodzzyk's prodigious capacities?' Tess realized the satirical Scot was talking to her. 'I'm Duncan McShane, by the way.'

'Scotland's leading colourist,' Stella filled in helpfully.

'Thank you, Stella, I'll do my own PR. Anyway, how can I compete with talent like this?' He sipped his sparkling wine. 'God, I hate this stuff. Why can't they have some decent spirits at these poncy occasions? Mr Grodzzyk trained at Glasgow School of Art, you know. He's not an English Pole, he's a Scottish Pole. I had better look to my laurels.'

Tess sipped her wine, grateful that he seemed to have forgotten his question in the flow of his own loquacity. But she was wrong. He turned to her again, eyes twinkling wickedly. 'Come on, young lady, what's the verdict?'

'I'm no expert, I'm afraid. They look like the Emperor's new manhole covers to me.'

Duncan McShane spluttered into his wine. 'A woman of taste and judgement!' He put an arm round Stella, undiscouraged by the fact she towered over him by a good six inches. 'Do you know, Stella, she reminds me of you in the old days at Northumberland Wharf. Stella used to keep our feet on the ground. If we talked about Art for too long she'd stand up and announce she was off to give the kitchen table a good scrub. It kept us in our place, I can tell you.'

Stella pealed with laughter at the memory. 'Only when you were all getting too pompous.'

Tess grinned. This was a side to her mother-in-law she'd never glimpsed before.

Outside on the pavement Josephine put a restraining hand on Stephen's arm before they went in. 'There'll be a lot of critics and buyers here tonight but there's only one who really counts. Ronald Wyman from the *Sunday Leader*. He's got the power to establish an artist with a single review. I'll make sure you get to talk to him, and mind what you say. He's an abstract fan and is pretty suspicious of anything figurative. If he asks about your style just be vague.'

Stephen nodded, pushing open the door to let her go in first. Even in a gallery crowded with famous faces from the art world, the sight of Josephine Quinn, tall and startling in a tailored black beaded jacket, was enough to turn heads.

But to her irritated surprise the first person she cast eyes on was Tess, laughing delightedly and looking utterly relaxed in a noisy group by the door.

A slim, elegant woman detached herself from the group and came towards them.

'Mother!' Stephen kissed her warmly on the cheek. 'What on earth are you doing here? Hardly your kind of bash.'

'Oh, we're having a great time, aren't we, Tess?'

Tess joined them, nodding. 'Hello, love, I was expecting you ages ago.'

'Josephine didn't think we ought to arrive too early, did you, Jo?'

Thanks so much, Josephine, Tess muttered into her drink. For a moment they all stood together in a vaguely embarrassed knot until Josephine spotted Ronald Wyman, pinned in a corner. The eyebrow he raised in her direction told her he needed rescuing.

'I hope you won't mind if I borrow Stephen for a

second. There's someone I very much want him to meet.'

Stella watched them go, her eyes narrowed. 'Who is that frightful woman?'

'That's Stephen's employer, the famous Josephine Quinn.'

'I don't like her proprietorial air.' Stella watched them beadily. 'And neither should you, dear.'

If only you knew the half of it, thought Tess, as Duncan McShane pounced on them again. 'Come on, Stella old girl. Time for our dinner booking.' He turned to Tess. 'Are you coming too? I do hope so.'

'Stephen's only just arrived. I think he'll want to circulate for a while. Perhaps we could come on later?'

'Why don't you do that.' Stella smiled. 'We're only at Brown's. Just down the road.'

As they left Tess realized that now she really didn't know a soul. A waiter passed with a tray of drinks. She'd really had enough but what the hell? One more wouldn't matter. She helped herself to another glass of sparkling wine and headed off towards Stephen and Josephine who were talking to a man in claret corduroy with a droopy moustache and long hair, who looked like he wanted to be mistaken for Salvador Dali.

Stephen was standing with his back to her and didn't see her approach, though she'd bet a tenner Josephine did. But instead of making room Josephine pretended not to notice her, so Tess found herself standing like a lemon firmly outside the group. She began to feel very unsisterly towards Josephine Quinn. She took another sip and plunged in.

'Hello, all. Everyone enjoying the party? How do you tell whether a bash like this is a success or not?'

Josephine turned and smiled at her with patronizing

tolerance. 'It's a success if the artist gets a chance to talk to Ronald Wyman here.' Her tone managed to imply that Tess had just screwed up Stephen's opportunity to do just this.

'Sorry, Ronald,' Stephen apologized, 'I don't think you've met my wife. Tess, this is Ronald Wyman.'

'So, Mrs Gilfillan, have you had a chance to look around? We were just saying how impressed we were, that by taking something industrial and putting it in a neutral setting he makes you notice the power and significance of the objects. What do you think of Mr Grodzzyk's work?'

Tess recalled Duncan McShane's story about Stella. 'To tell you the truth, it makes me want to go and give the kitchen table a good scrub.'

Wyman smiled dismissively. 'The hausfrau perspective. An interesting angle.'

Tess decided she didn't like Ronald Wyman or his immediate assumption she was an appendage with nothing of value to contribute. 'And of course housewives' opinions don't count, do they, in the company of important art critics?'

'Tess,' interrupted Stephen, 'I think it's time we left . . .'

But Tess was going to have her say. 'The truth is, I think it's a heap of garbage. But then I'm only a housewife so what does it matter what I think?'

Stephen led her firmly towards the door as Josephine watched, the tiniest glow of satisfaction apparent in her eyes.

'What a curious woman,' remarked Wyman before changing the subject to the impact his latest review had had on an unknown artist. 'Since my write-up the man's gone from chip butties at art school to five grand a painting in the space of three months. Really,

Josephine, I almost feel I should get a cut.' They both laughed at the ridiculousness of the great Ronald Wyman being bribed.

Stephen slammed the car door almost before Tess was inside and marched round to the driver's side. 'Well, you certainly made a fool of yourself then, didn't you. And me.'

'Oh come on, Stephen, the man was a pompous git.'

'A useful pompous git.'

Tess felt suddenly sober. 'You never used to think that. You always admired Julius for putting up two fingers to the art establishment.'

Stephen gunned the engine, causing an old man to jump off a zebra crossing. 'Yes, well perhaps I've changed. I've got an exhibition coming up, remember.'

Tess stared ahead of her. She'd been going to suggest they join Stella and the others at Brown's. Now she didn't feel like it.

The drive home was silent and tense. Tess stared miserably out of the window. Maybe it was time they both faced the truth. That they'd become different people over the eighteen years of their marriage. Perhaps spending your life with one person was too much to ask in an age when choice guided our lives, not duty. No one could say they hadn't tried. And yet, would it be a mistake to split? How many women of her generation sat there in their single-parent families envying their parents and grandparents for staying together, wondering if compromise wasn't after all a better solution than choice, if choice left them alone and broke?

She was about to speak when they turned the corner from the King's Road into their street and noticed a police car parked outside their front door. The door was open and a young constable lounged on their balustrade speaking into a walkie-talkie.

Tess scrambled for the door handle. 'My God, they're in our house. What the hell's happened?'

But before she even got the chance to get out of the car Ellie ran down the front steps, her face whiter than her T-shirt. 'Oh, Mum, thank God you're back. It's Luke. He's been caught shoplifting.'

Stephen slammed the door of the car. 'What the bloody hell is he playing at? He promised me he was sorry about the money business, that he wouldn't do it again!'

'I don't know,' Tess shouted back from halfway up the front steps, 'let's just find out what actually happened, shall we, before you go jumping in with both feet?'

Any anger evaporated at the sight of Luke, sitting dejectedly on the sofa, arms round his knees, refusing to meet anyone's eyes. Tess had never seen him look so unhappy.

She sat down beside him. 'Could you tell us what happened exactly?' she asked the WPC sitting opposite.

'He and some other lads were playing the slot machines at the Arndale Centre in Wandsworth. Two or three of them went into First Foot shoe shop and while the others distracted the assistant's attention I'm afraid your son stole these.' She held up a transparent plastic bag containing a pair of Nike trainers with an £84.99 price ticket on them.

Tess took the trainers from the policewoman and studied them. 'But these aren't even his size,' she blurted out in the sudden hope that there'd been some stupid mix-up. 'He takes a five and these are a three. He wouldn't even be able to get his feet into them.'

'Mr and Mrs Gilfillan, I wonder if I could have a word in private.' The WPC gently took the trainers from Tess's hand.

'Of course. Ellie, you stay with Luke for a moment.' She led the way into the kitchen and shut the door.

'The thing about shoplifting,' explained the young woman, 'is that it isn't always about getting something you'd normally go in and buy. They do it for the thrill. Often it's just an act of bravado for their mates. I've seen flats like Aladdin's caves where people haven't even bothered to take the things out of their wrappers.'

'Yes, yes, I'm sure you're right. But this is so completely out of character.' She glanced at Stephen. 'At least it was till very recently.'

'Has something changed, then?'

'Yes.' Tess looked directly at Stephen, deciding that if ever there was a moment to face the truth, this was it. 'My husband and I haven't been getting along very well lately and Luke's noticed.' Stephen's eyes held hers for a moment, then looked away. 'As it happens, I'm a lawyer. But I don't have much experience of juveniles. What's going to happen to Luke?'

'That depends on the shop. They usually insist on prosecuting. But as far as I can see your son's not the usual type; perhaps you should have a word with the shop manager. Obviously the fact that he's never done anything like this before will make a difference. I don't want to raise your hopes but it's possible he'll just get cautioned.'

'Who were the other boys he was with?' She longed to be able to phone another anguished mother and discover it was nothing to do with her and Stephen after all.

The policewoman consulted her notebook and read out three other names.

'But they aren't even friends of his.'

'Maybe he's made some new friends. It sounds as though they haven't been having too good an influence either.'

'No. Look, thanks for all your help. I'll go and see the manager as soon as possible.'

'You do that. I'll be off now. We'll be in touch soon, I'm afraid.'

Tess showed the woman out, leaving Stephen sitting at the kitchen table staring ahead. Then, as if Tess wasn't even there, he jumped up and ran into the sitting room, grabbing Luke by the shoulders and shaking him. 'For Christ's sake, Luke, why did you go and do a stupid thing like that? I thought we'd talked about all this!'

Tess watched horrified as Luke began to sob. 'Stephen, this is pointless. Leave him alone. It's too late to come the heavy father.'

But Stephen ignored her. 'First you steal from your mother, now from a shop. Are you trying to ruin your life? What the hell's the matter with you? Answer me, for God's sake, when I'm talking to you!' For a split second he raised his hand as though to hit Luke.

Tess grabbed it and Luke ran sobbing from the room. Ellie glared at them both as she jumped up to follow him. 'I must say, you're both doing a grand job at being parents lately.'

Stephen flopped on to the sofa and picked up a cushion in which he buried his head for a moment. When he looked up his face was composed again. 'I think it's time we faced up to it, Tess.' His dark-blue eyes were shadowed with pain and for the first time she could remember he actually looked his age. 'It isn't working out between us, is it?'

Tess woke the next morning knowing in some deep part of herself that she didn't want to open her eyes. It was Saturday, usually their favourite. As a rule one of them would make tea and they would spend a leisurely half hour in bed reading the papers before Luke or Ellie invaded the bedroom to remind them of a hastily given promise to give them a lift to some inaccessible part of town or other. Then they'd toss for who would drag themselves up while the other had a bath and a peaceful morning.

She turned fractionally towards Stephen. With his extraordinary capacity for giving off heat he wore no pyjamas or even a T-shirt despite the fact that in a couple of days it would be February. He lay facing away from her, clutching his pillow, so that his lightly tanned shoulders were exposed. She felt a brief temptation to reach out and touch him. To stroke the smooth skin until he turned with a lazy smile, still half asleep, and lifted the duvet so that she could glimpse his erect penis, always faster to wake than the rest of him. Then she'd laugh and snuggle back down under the duvet, opening herself to him as she'd done so many times before.

But not today.

As if sensing her eyes on him, he rolled over and returned her gaze. But there was no spark of fun or lust in his eyes this morning, only the same dull pain of last night. He reached out a hand, but not in invitation. 'We tried, Tess. No one could say we didn't try. For the last two months we've done nothing but try. And maybe it wouldn't have mattered so much that we aren't making each other happy if Luke and

Ellie felt secure. But they don't. We've had enough evidence of that lately. I think I should move to the studio for a while.'

'The studio? In Lots Road, you mean?' At least he wouldn't be far away.

He touched her face briefly, before replying. 'No, in Winchester.'

Tess flinched. 'I see.'

Stephen took his hand away. 'I doubt it. But it doesn't really matter.'

He jumped out of bed. Tess turned away, not wanting her mind to be filled with the image of his body. He pulled on jeans and an old paint-stained sweatshirt and a pair of Nikes which made her think instantly of Luke.

She watched, seized by a dreamlike paralysis as he took down his biggest suitcase and packed it quickly. 'I'll get this into the car.'

Downstairs he grabbed his Barbour, winter overcoat, and a scarf, the yellow Rupert Bear replica Luke had given him for Christmas. He took one swift glance round the sitting room, as though imprinting it on his memory, and noticed the photograph, not yet framed, of Tess and the children on the beach in Cork, looking happy and carefree as though no clouds could ever threaten the contentment of their lives. He put it in between the pages of a magazine to protect it and slipped it into the pocket of his suitcase.

Tess lay in bed, stock still, and listened as he knocked gently on Ellie's and then Luke's door. Ten minutes later he came back. 'Goodbye Tess.' He sat on the edge of the bed but didn't touch her this time. 'We did try, remember that. No one could do more. I've said goodbye to Ellie and Luke and that I love them and will be in touch very soon.'

Tess nodded, torn by conflicts that told her that what he was doing was right, and the temptation to make him stay.

'Don't come down. It'd be easier if you didn't. You know where to get me.' Stephen walked fast out of the room, down the stairs and out of the front door without looking behind him.

If he had he would have seen Luke's pinched face watching for a brief moment between the curtains, stiff and solemn and too wounded even to cry.

CHAPTER TWENTY-EIGHT

Josephine, still in her white silk kimono, put down her copy of the *Daily Mail* and listened to the sound of a car turning too fast into her drive and spraying up gravel. Irritated, she looked out of her bedroom window. If it was that cowboy window cleaner she would send him packing. He had left drip marks running down her windows last time that had annoyed her for weeks.

The car was now out of sight, but there were distinct bald patches tracing its progress across the drive. She opened the window of her bathroom and leaned out, her breath quickening when she saw that the driver wasn't the window cleaner but Stephen and that he was in the act of unloading a suitcase and carrying it into the studio. It had happened then.

Quietly she closed the window and began to get dressed, ignoring the fragrant bath she'd run for herself. Five minutes later she stood in her Saturday outfit of jodphurs and a pale silk-knit sweater, excitement rushing through her. She brushed her dark hair till it gleamed and put on some tawny lipstick, nothing too overdone, eager to run to him, to tell him he'd made the right decision, that Tess had only held him back and that it was she, Josephine, who understood what it was to be a painter.

Then she remembered her own words when she'd suggested he move into the studio. That she wouldn't even know he was there. And her instincts shouted to her that she must leave him alone, that he had to come to her, and not she to him.

She sat down on the bed, fighting back her disappointment. The game wasn't won yet. She would just have to console herself with the thought that the tide had clearly turned in her direction.

In the studio Stephen shoved his suitcase into one corner, unopened. All the way down he had been seized by guilt and uncertainty until he no longer knew what was for the best. The only answer was to throw himself into his work until he acquired some sense of detachment.

He laid out his oils and placed a huge blank canvas on his easel. Its emptiness was somehow reassuring. And then he began to paint furiously until the outside world gradually became unreal compared with the truth and immediacy within.

Tess sat at the kitchen table and listened to the silence enveloping her. It was fanciful, she knew, to sense a dead feeling around her like a phone ringing in an empty house, but that was how it felt. Damp and cold and echoey even though it was light and bright and warm. She knew she should go upstairs and check up on Ellie and Luke but she felt totally unable to move, even to make a cup of coffee. Every rational thought in her brain told her that this was the right thing they were doing, that, as Stephen had pointed out, they really had tried their best. So why did it hurt so bloody much?

Inge, dressed as usual like a rich housewife in one of her pale-blue designer tracksuits, paused on the way out to her fitness class and wondered what to do. She, too, had been picking up the tension in the house and had seen Stephen leaving with his suitcase. It moved her to see Tess, usually such a tower of strength, sitting immobile at the table.

Inge, among whose virtues tact was not numbered, decided to cheer Tess up by telling her about that night in last summer when she'd attempted to seduce Stephen and been rejected. Surely that would show he was a good man really?

Fortunately the phone rang before she had time to recount this unfortunate episode. 'Tess,' she called, 'Tess! It's your mother.'

Tess hesitated. Her mother was the last person she felt like talking to. She wanted to be able to lick her wounds in peace without being spoonfed with advice, no matter how concerned or caring. And yet Inge had quite clearly admitted she was in. Reluctantly she picked up the receiver.

'Hello, love. How are you? Everyone fine?'

'Yes,' Tess answered automatically, 'everyone's fine.'

'Are you sure, dear?' The warmth of Dymphna's concern radiated down the line from Merseyside as clearly as if she were sitting in the room. 'Only you sound a bit strange.'

'Oh, Mum, it's so awful,' Tess heard a voice saying. Surely it couldn't be hers? 'The roof's fallen in, Luke may be done for shoplifting and Stephen's just walked out and gone to Josephine.'

For once, Dymphna had the sense not to offer any advice, no matter how good.

'Tess, love, would you like me to come down?'

And Tess, having kept her mother at arm's length for years, heard herself saying 'Oh, that would be wonderful. Do you really think you could?'

Luke didn't even look up from his computer when Tess opened the door of his bedroom but stared with renewed concentration at the green glowing digits flashing in front of him. Despite his determination to seem unconcerned Tess saw that his bed was crumpled and that Ted, the ancient bear she hadn't seen for years, had mysteriously reappeared as a companion.

'He's gone, hasn't he?' Luke's voice was completely toneless. 'Was it because of the trainers?'

Tess flew across the room and put her arms round him. 'No, it wasn't because of the trainers.'

But Luke's slight body remained rigid, not responding to Tess's longing to console him. Then suddenly his whole frame seemed to sag at the effort of pretending to be tough.

'Do you think he'll come back this time, Mum?' His eyes pleaded with her for a reassuring lie. 'Or has he gone for ever?'

All Tess could do was hold him, hoping she could at least restrain her own tears. 'I don't know, darling. But whatever happens, he still loves you, you know that.'

'But how could he?' At last Luke looked up at her. She could see the red rims round his eyes where he'd been crying. 'There's nothing about me *to* love. Don't worry. I knew it anyway. All this does is prove it.'

Ellie simply stayed in her room with the door locked all day, not even giving Tess the chance to try to explain. When she finally emerged she was silent, refusing to mention her father's departure at all. She simply put on an outrageous outfit and piles of make-up and disappeared out until Tess had gone to bed.

All Saturday Stephen worked. There was an exhaustion, both physical and mental, about painting so intensely which was just what he craved. It meant that for long periods he felt no pain at all, just concentration. So it wasn't till far into the night, when he finally fell into bed, that the fear and the doubt and the fervent hope that he'd done the right thing crowded into his brain.

By early morning he was awake and painting again. If he managed to get plenty done today it might even be finished by tomorrow morning.

The other side of the drive, Josephine watched. She saw the lights burning long into the night and was grateful that tomorrow was Monday. It might bring some normality back instead of this torture of watching and waiting. And she knew that, whether it was sane and sensible or not, if he didn't make a move soon she would have to do it herself.

By Monday Tess was deeply grateful for the lifesaving predictability of work. Its simple demands, whether dull and repetitive or challenging and stressful, had the miraculous effect of making her forget about her own situation and just get on with it. But even before she'd sat down at her desk she'd come to one decision. She wasn't, for the moment at least, going to tell anyone about the split. Sympathy, she'd discovered, whether phony or genuine, was very hard to take.

'Good weekend?' Jacqui asked brightly, dumping a huge pile of correspondence in front of her.

'Better than last weekend.' Tess attempted a smile. 'At least the roof didn't fall in.' Even as she said it she wondered if it was strictly true.

'Which reminds me. Your friend Phil rang first thing. Something about the roofing man being able to start immediately.'

Tess waited for Jacqui to leave, then dropped her head into her hands. She'd forgotten all about Alf and his estimate. Where the hell was she going to find eight thousand pounds? She'd just have to get Stephen to pay half and borrow the rest. For the first time since he'd gone she managed to feel some healthy anger. She felt tempted simply to send him the bill at Richmond & Quinn. After all, it was his bloody fault they had to pay it at all.

In a moment, when she felt calm again, she'd ring Phil and tell her what had happened.

As he arrived for work, Hugo noticed that Stephen's car was parked in a different spot from usual. Instead of in the front drive near the reception area it was almost tucked out of sight, over by the studio. Curious, he strolled over, buttoning his coat against the intense cold of the morning. How he loathed February, the most depressing month of the year. It was obviously warm and cosy in the studio because the condensation on the inside of the enormous windows was as disguising as blinds or curtains. Only a small patch of glass was transparent where someone must have cleared it to look out at the day. Feeling a little like a voyeur, Hugo peeped in.

The studio was empty. But in one corner the futon was unfurled and a sleeping bag lay on top of it. Next to it was a clock radio, beeping irritatingly as there was no one in the room to stop it. Several suits hung suspended from an easel along with a couple of brightly coloured ties, which he instantly identified as Stephen's. A suitcase, with shirts and socks dripping out of it, lay at the foot of the futon.

Stephen had clearly moved out of the marital home. But not into Josephine's. Interesting.

Up in their office Josephine was already sitting at her desk transferring engagements from the large desk diary Lucy kept to the small one she carried around with her.

'So,' Hugo observed, helping himself to a cup of coffee, 'I see you've got him where you want him at last.'

Josephine looked up. 'Got who? Hugo, what are you talking about?'

Hugo smiled maliciously. 'Stephen, of course.'

'Ah.' Josephine went back to her diary. 'Not quite where I want him,' she said, in a voice so soft that Hugo couldn't hear it.

Having Dymphna around turned out to be a mixed blessing. Tess had agreed to it because with Stephen gone she wanted to try extra hard to create a sense of welcome, so that Ellie and Luke would at least feel there was something to come home *to*. And her mother's presence certainly added to that. A stockpot permanently bubbled at the back of the hob for Irish stew; she knocked up Toad in the Hole in a jiffy with her famous Yorkshire pudding. Delicious baking smells hung permanently in the air. Dymphna also struck up an immediate understanding with Alf the roofer who accepted her foremanlike vigilance in exchange for endless cups of tea and homemade biscuits. She wouldn't put it past her mother to get up on the roof after he'd gone and have a good look at the quality of his workmanship.

But while Tess realized that it was their way of dealing with the situation, what Dymphna didn't understand was Luke and Ellie's sudden need to be free. Despite all Dymphna's and Tess's efforts both of them seemed to want to spend as little time at home as possible. Ellie stayed on hour after hour in the art room at school and Luke seemed practically to have moved in to Ben's house two streets away. When he was at home he was silent and withdrawn and got out of the house again as quickly as he came in.

'It is because without Stephen the house is no longer living,' pronounced Inge one evening with a show of Nordic wisdom.

'Nonsense,' snapped Dymphna, who didn't approve of Inge or her foreign ways. 'In my view the role of men in marriage is highly overrated.'

Tess smiled. 'Luke, darling, do you have to go straight to Ben's? Why don't you stay and watch TV with Gran and me?' Luke sat there looking mutinous. 'What's so special about Ben's these days anyway?'

'What's so special about Ben's,' Luke answered reproachfully, 'is that they're a real family. Like we used to be.'

After work Tess drove to the Arndale Centre car park, thinking as she did so what depressing places shopping centres like this were. First Foot was right in the middle, with rows of tempting displays of trainers lined up in racks in their open foyer. Tess glanced at the prices. The most expensive was nearly a hundred pounds; there wasn't a single pair for under forty. No wonder people nicked the things.

Reminding herself that this might not be the best spirit in which to approach the situation, Tess went in and asked for the manager.

He turned out to be half her age and clearly didn't relish meeting her. Like the postroom boy at Kingsmill's she probably reminded him of his mum. Since his tiny office was being used for stocktaking they had the added embarrassment of having to talk in the shop.

Tess sat down in the most discreet position she could find and proceeded to explain that Luke had never been involved in anything like this before.

The manager nodded as if he had already been

appraised of this fact. 'And I understand from the police things had been difficult at home between you and your husband.'

'Yes,' she confirmed, surprised. She hadn't been expecting such thoroughness on the part of the police in putting her case for her. 'And now he's gone altogether.'

To her eternal shame, for the very first time since Stephen's departure, Tess burst into tears. And once she'd started she couldn't stop. As the young manager looked on in horror and the customers tried to keep their eyes to themselves, Tess sobbed unstoppably. All the hurt and the sense of failure and the tension of having to cope alone flowed out of her in great wells of tears, making her eye make-up run until a black runnel marked each cheek.

The manager signalled desperately to the one motherly woman in his employ who was at that moment up a ladder stickering prices. She, who'd been watching the fascinating scene unfolding below, eager to get her own back for the uppity attitude he'd been taking with the staff lately, climbed slowly down the ladder.

'Well, well, Mr Watts, what have you been saying to upset this poor lady?' she enquired loudly, putting a comforting arm round Tess.

'Just tell her I'll do my best, Susan, and get her some paper hankies, would you?'

Susan handed Tess a packet of Handy Andies and helped her up. At the door of the shop she turned towards the unfortunate Mr Watts once more. 'I'll just see her to her car. And next time you would a woo-ing go, Mr Watts, perhaps you'd better stick to someone your own age.'

Catching sight of Mr Watts's indignation, Tess couldn't help stifling a giggle.

'That's better,' said the indomitable Susan, squeezing her shoulder reassuringly. 'Don't worry about him. I'll nag him till he lets your boy off.' She helped Tess open the door of her car and get in. 'I'm sorry to hear about your hubby. Most women think men are bastards, but I think we're being too kind to them, don't you?'

'I see you've moved into the studio,' Josephine commented to Stephen as neutrally as she could manage. She had spent the whole weekend feeling like a spider who'd caught a fly in its web, but had to understand the fly's psychology instead of just eating it. 'So what happened? Did everything come to a head?'

Stephen nodded. 'After the exhibition. We quarrelled on the way home and then when we got there, there was a policewoman waiting to tell us Luke had been caught shoplifting. It was the last straw. We'd been trying to make it work for the children's sakes, and obviously if Luke was behaving like that we were failing.' He looked away and she saw there were tears in the corner of his eyes. 'We couldn't even agree on how to react to the shoplifting.'

Hearing the pain in his voice, she reached out and touched his hand. 'Poor Stephen. What a terrible time you've been having.' Watching him carefully, she sensed that the moment was right. If she took the initiative now, she would probably win. As long as she was subtle about it. 'Look, Stephen, you did everything you could. You went back. For two months you tried everything and so did Tess. And now you've just spent the weekend alone to make sure you've no regrets.' She got up from the sofa she was sitting on and came across to him. Very gently she took his head in both her hands so that his eyes looked into hers. 'You've done all you can, Stephen. It's time to start looking forward, not back. It's our turn now, and it's going to be wonderful.'

Gently at first, but then with a passion that surprised herself, she began to kiss him, oblivious to the danger that Hugo or Lucy or anyone else could walk in at any moment.

The next few weeks passed in a blur of misery for Tess. No matter how often she told herself it was for the best, that there was no advantage to either of them, or Luke and Ellie, in staying in a dead marriage, she still felt unendurably lonely.

She was fast learning what every single mother knows – that no matter how miserable you feel you are still the one who has to hold things together.

But when Luke and Ellie had gone to bed she was finally able to give in and sit leafing through old photo albums and weeping into her wine.

At least, thank God, her mother had gone home. It had been lovely having her there, but Tess felt she had to deal with the situation her own way and she could do that better unobserved.

She pulled herself out of bed. Now that Stephen had gone she'd stopped bothering with early morning tea, it had been too much a part of their ritual together. She started to run a bath then turned off the taps, convinced she could hear the sound of crying. On the landing she stopped and listened again. It was coming from Luke's room.

Gently she opened the door. He was still in bed, buried under the duvet. She knelt next to him and pulled it back till she could see his tear-stained face. 'What's the matter, darling? Is it about Dad still?'

424

'I don't want to go to school,' Luke blurted out with real anguish in his voice.

Tess stroked his hair and heard herself trotting out the usual platitudes. 'Come on, darling, everyone feels like that sometimes. It's just a Monday morning feeling. I don't always want to go to work, but I have to.'

Luke sat up suddenly. 'Mum, is there any chance I could change schools? I mean it'd save you a lot of money, wouldn't it?' The enthusiasm in his voice took her aback. 'I'd go anywhere as long as it wasn't Chelsea Collegiate.'

'Why do you hate it so much suddenly?'

Luke looked for a moment as though he were going to answer, then seemed to change his mind. 'Oh, it doesn't matter,' in a tone of hopeless resignation.

Back in her bedroom Tess decided to go and talk to his teacher and make sure she was keeping an eye on Luke.

'Here you are.' Jacqui plonked yet more files in Tess's in-tray. 'Lots of nice work to take your mind off things.'

Tess looked up at Jacqui suspiciously. 'And what things would they be?'

Jacqui shook her head and tutted, demonstrating both disapproval that Tess hadn't let her into her confidence, and a new haircut. The locks were gone, to be replaced by a shingled bob. It suited her. 'Look, Tess, I've worked for you for nearly five years. I was bound to notice, wasn't I? When Stephen never rings any more and you never ring him?'

Tess looked momentarily stricken. 'I just thought if no one knew it'd be easier to cope.'

'And how are you coping?'

'Fine. Well, not fine actually, but OK. Apart from a

fit of hysterics in a shoe shop in the Arndale Centre. It's Ellie and Luke I'm worried about.'

Jacqui sat down on the edge of Tess's desk so that the eighteen inches of her skirt shrunk to twelve. 'Look, girl, I never had a father, not one who stayed around. And neither did my mum. In fact, there hasn't been a man in our family as far back as anyone can remember. We've forgotten what they're for. Apart from the obvious. And I've turned out all right, haven't I? Not screwed up or into crack? A nice respectable girl who loves her mother. Children are stronger than you think.'

Tess nodded. There was only one problem. She hadn't been telling the whole truth. It wasn't just the children who were missing Stephen so much. She was too.

'Just think. You've got the firm's Twentieth Anniversary bash in a couple of weeks. The social event of the year. And, yes, you do have to come, no excuses allowed, even marriage breakdown. That should give you something to look forward to. Now, do you want a cup of tea?'

Tess settled down to the pile of work Jacqui had left in front of her feeling more cheerful, and even beginning to wonder what she'd wear. Five minutes later Jacqui came back with the cup of tea and a chocolate biscuit. 'You need calories at a time like this. Now, talking of children, Inge's on line two. Something about Luke coming home from school in tears.'

Inge was waiting for her in the hall when she got home. 'Luke came running out crying with his jacket all torn when I picked them up from school. I thought I ought to let you know.'

Behind her, Ellie came bounding down the stairs,

her eyes flaring amber like tiger's eyes. 'He was being teased. Some louts in the fifth form saw him crying and started laughing at him. He wouldn't tell me who or I'd have kicked the shit out of them.'

Tess decided to put this breach of the Queen's English down to sisterly protectiveness. 'Poor Luke. No wonder he's been saying he doesn't want to go to school lately. Where is he?'

'Up in his bedroom.'

She heard the sounds of his computer game even before she opened the door. 'Luke, darling, are you all right? Tell me what happened at school.'

Luke steadfastly ignored her. He'd clearly decided to shut up like a clam and nothing she could say would make him talk about the incident.

She turned his shoulders round towards her, exasperated. 'Luke, I can't help if you won't tell me what happened.'

He turned back to the computer the moment she let him go. 'You can't help anyway. It's all right, Mum, don't go interfering or you'll just make it worse. I shouldn't have been blubbing anyway.' And he retreated once more into his computer world, leaving Tess with the classic mother's dilemma. Was he right? Would she just make things worse if she interfered? On the other hand she couldn't bear the thought of him being picked on because he was crying. She was going to have to think of something.

Josephine smiled to herself as she put away her diary and notebook into the drawer of the polished walnut desk. Stephen had moved his things into her house at lunchtime and this would be their first proper night together. The extraordinary fact was that at the age of forty-one, Josephine had never invited a man to live with her. Even during her relationship with Hugo he had always had his own home. And she realized she was both excited and nervous in equal parts. What if they didn't get on? What if he snored, or picked his toenails? Or worse, what if she felt trapped and that her home was no longer her own?

Oh, for God's sake, she told herself, this is the man you've wanted since the first time you met him. It was going to be a glorious pairing of his talent and her inspiration. Together they'd become one of the legendary couples of the art world. Picasso and Françoise Gilot, Diego Rivera and Frida Kahlo, Duncan Grant and Vanessa Bell, Stephen Gilfillan and Josephine Quinn.

Humming, she locked her door and walked towards the lift. The view from her floor looked out over the whole of the grounds. The lights were still on in the studio, she noticed, and decided to check out what it was Stephen had been working on so furiously.

By the time she got down to the studio Stephen must have already gone because it was in darkness. She snapped on the lights and walked round to the front of the easel he'd been working on.

It was a beach scene in bright sunlight, the sea a brilliant dark blue with small waves, the sand so pale and silky you could almost feel it between your toes. The mood was one of intense physicality, every pore shone on the skin of the protagonists as they glowed with health and pure, animal happiness. As she stood there looking at it Josephine felt an almost overwhelming urge to pick up a knife and slash it from end to end. The main figure in the scene was unmistakably Tess, flanked by Ellie on one side and Luke, with his head in her lap, on the other. And it was undoubtedly the best thing Stephen had ever painted.

On the way to the Lodge Josephine took deep breaths of the clear freezing air until she began to feel calmer. There was no point losing her temper with Stephen over the painting. As with children, confrontation wasn't the answer. Distraction would be more effective. She would just have to offer him other delights tonight that would take his mind off Tess and his family, a feast of the senses that eclipsed domestic pleasures and made them seem dull and disappointing.

As she turned her key in the lock Josephine could already feel the delicious tightening of sexual anticipation.

'Have you heard about Tess Brien?' Patricia Greene whispered to the small knot of partners who were gathered in Kingsmill's boardroom waiting for the rest to arrive for their monthly management meeting. 'Her husband's run off with Josephine Quinn.'

'Who's Josephine Quinn?' asked one of the older partners.

'You know, the perfume millionairess. You must have seen her on television. She's always on. The woman's a genius at self-promotion.'

'Good heavens,' commented another, 'I hope that doesn't mean the firm's name is going to be dragged into disrepute.'

'How do you know?' Lyall Gibson asked Patricia suspiciously. He'd not heard a whisper of this, but then Patricia was always the first to stir up bad blood.

'I saw them having dinner at Drake's in South Ken. They couldn't keep their hands off each other. So I asked around a bit. He left a month ago.'

'Poor Tess,' Lyall threw in staunchly, glaring at Patricia, 'she must be going through hell. I think we should be giving her our fullest support.'

'But then, with the greatest of respect' – Patricia smiled sweetly at him – 'you would say that, wouldn't you?'

This clearly hit Lyall on the raw. 'What exactly do you mean by that remark, Patricia?'

Patricia looked supremely innocent. 'That you're such a perfect gentleman, Lyall. Whatever else would I mean?'

By the day of the Anniversary Party Tess was still in two minds whether to go or not. But Jacqui wouldn't hear of her missing it.

'You haven't got any choice. You're a partner now. It'll look very bad if you don't go. Besides, you'll enjoy it. The secretaries were allowed to organize it instead of Will Kingsmill's old boot of an assistant. Goodbye wine and cheese in the office, hello nightclub fun. The articled clerks are even putting on a cabaret.'

'Oh well, in that case I suppose I'll have to come.'

And to her astonishment, Jacqui was right. It was fun. The small nightclub had been converted by Jacqui & Co's efforts into a mock courtroom with a stage where the dock should have been and small round tables with gilt chairs round them instead of a public gallery. The DJ who came with the disco had correctly identified his market and was playing old Rolling Stones records without even the usual sighs and 'Oh-Jesus-Not-This-Tired-Old-Crap' expression that was traditional on such occasions.

At first Tess stayed distinctly on the sidelines, chatting to the other partners and their wives. But Jacqui wasn't having that. She seemed to be on a one-woman mission to get Tess out of herself, which involved plying her with glasses of wine and sending endless streams of young men to ask her to dance. Exhausted after three strenuous numbers in a row, Tess thanked the current one and started to make her way back to the dignified end of the room. On the way she caught sight of John Finch, the young lawyer who'd been sent to replace her on the Eileen McDonald case. Filled with a sudden devilment, she invited him to dance.

But John, young and pompous and perhaps still smarting from the humiliation of the incident, shook his head. 'I'm sorry, Tess, but I don't dance.'

'I do,' said a voice behind her left shoulder. She turned to find Lyall Gibson standing behind her.

Tess's first instinct was to refuse. Somehow dancing with Lyall was different from horsing about with twenty-year-old articled clerks. But she couldn't think of a polite way of doing so.

Lyall turned out to be a surprisingly good dancer. The long limbs that could at times appear coltish and uncoordinated smoothed themselves out into fluid and sinuous movement with a little bit of help from the music.

Lyall caught the surprise in her eyes. 'My mother forced me into years of ritual humiliation at Miss English's Ballroom Dancing Academy. This is nothing. You should see my *paso doble*.'

Tess laughed at the thought of Lyall tangoing every Tuesday.

'Please, no mockery.' He shook his head in mock disapproval. 'I was Junior Latin American Champion, South-East Region. Before I went to university, that is, and realized ballroom dancing was strictly Lower Class.'

Tess was suddenly conscious that they'd been on the dance floor for longer than anyone else and that every eye was probably upon them. She stopped dancing. 'I think I need a drink before I die of dehydration.'

She turned towards the bar, only to find Lyall's hand on her arm stopping her.

'Don't rush off,' he urged. 'Or at least not for a moment. I've got a proposition to put to you.'

Tess felt a cold blast of panic. She'd heard horror stories of men moving in on you before your husband's side of the bed was cold. But surely not Lyall? She'd always had him down as sensitive.

Lyall smiled, clearly reading her thoughts. 'Don't worry, I'm quite harmless unless encouraged. It's a professional proposition. Now that the divorce laws are being changed, I've been approached to write a book. Not a boring tome full of jargon, but a popular book for ordinary people. And I want you to write it with me. I've even got a title. *The Good Divorce Guide.*'

Tess looked at him, horrified, as though he'd just suggested she co-wrote the Kama Sutra. 'Lyall, I couldn't. Not just at the moment. I'm the last person to write it. There are reasons –' She broke off, not wanting to tell him more, overcome once again by a feeling of failure.

'Tess, don't get upset.' He dropped his voice so that none of the other dancers could hear. 'Look, I know about you and Stephen; everyone does, I'm afraid. But don't you see? It makes you the absolutely perfect person to write the book. You know what it feels like, what other people must be going through. You could use your experience positively.' His voice was low and intense. If this was a sales pitch she had to admit it was an effective one. 'Who knows, you might even find it helpful yourself.'

Still shell-shocked both by the offer and the revelation that everyone knew about the break-up, Tess started to walk away.

'Promise me you'll think about it,' Lyall insisted, 'or I'll force you to dance cheek-to-cheek in front of the senior partner.'

Tess couldn't help returning his smile. 'OK, I promise.' The thought of her roofing bill loomed into her consciousness. She turned back briefly. 'Lyall, will there be any money in it?'

Lyall burst out laughing. 'And this from the incorruptible Tess Brien who wouldn't take Hanover's hundred grand. There might be.'

Tess decided there was no point messing about. Partnership or no partnership she was going to be very short of cash now. 'If there is I'll do it.'

Lyall looked delighted. 'I like a woman who can make up her mind.'

As she made her way back to the bar, Jacqui stopped her, winking knowingly. 'So, what was all that about? Should I be jealous?'

'For heaven's sake, Jacqueline, he's asked me to write a book with him, that's all.'

'Oooh,' Jacqui giggled. She was well into her third vodka and orange. 'What a good excuse for spending lots of time together. All that researching.'

'We'd probably do it separately,' Tess corrected her primly. 'Anyway,' she lied, 'I haven't definitely agreed to it yet.'

'You will, Tess' – Jacqui's voice floated back as she disappeared into a conga-line of noisy legal executives – 'you will.'

It was one o'clock in the morning before Tess got home and the silence was so deep that it was clear everyone had been in bed for hours. She walked into the cold sitting room and leaned on the mantelpiece for a moment. Their wedding photograph stared back at her. She picked it up and examined the two happy faces smiling at each other, so young yet convinced they had a life ahead of love and contentment. She put it back in its place and came to a decision. If she had to feel this anguish and emptiness, she would put it to good use. The book idea was exciting and it would give her a purpose. It was just what she needed.

The next morning Tess overslept and when she finally woke up, it was with a splitting headache. Serves you right, whispered a voice, for thinking you can have fun so soon after the break-up. But Tess ignored it as she mixed herself some Alka-Seltzer, cringing at the deafening buzz of the tablets dissolving. Surely it wasn't beyond the wit of man to invent a silent hangover cure.

She drank it in one gulp, threw on her dressing gown and went downstairs hoping to catch Ellie and Luke before they left for school.

'You look terrible,' accused Ellie with the pitiless eye of youth. 'How much did you have to drink last night?'

'I wasn't counting.' Tess picked up the post and sat down, trying to keep her head level so that it didn't ache so much.

'I can see that. I hope you didn't drive home.'

'Ellie, I'm a lawyer.' Tess tried to remember if she had honed her disapproval of her own parents to such a fine art when she was sixteen. 'Of course I didn't drive home.'

'Good. We wouldn't want another court case in the family, would we?' She handed over a letter with a daunting Metropolitan Police stamp on it.

Tess looked at it, not daring to open the envelope for a good thirty seconds. She knew Luke, sitting the other side of the table, had put down his cereal spoon and was staring at her. It would be the letter telling them whether the police had decided to prosecute Luke or not.

'Come on, Mum,' Ellie encouraged, 'open the box.'

Tess picked up a kitchen knife and slit open the envelope. She read the letter through twice and then grabbed Luke bodily from his chair and waltzed him round the room. 'They're dropping the prosecution! First Foot have decided to make an exception.' She flopped back into the chair. 'I must remember to have hysterics more often. Oh, Luke, it's absolutely brilliant news.'

Luke nodded and gave a small smile of relief. She wondered briefly why he wasn't as over the moon as she was, then decided it was probably the shock.

'Well, this calls for a celebration tonight. I hope you're both in. Pizzas are on me!'

CHAPTER TWENTY-NINE

Stephen held the exquisite painted bottle in his hand, feeling a surge of excitement. The first samples of the perfume were ready! And no matter how down Hugo had been on the packaging, as soon as he saw the finished product he'd have to admit they looked great. Unless all Stephen's instincts were wrong, they were going to have a hit on their hands.

The next step would be to perfect their witty marketing campaign. He got out his lined pad to jot down some ideas before his weekly meeting with Josephine and Hugo.

Next door in Josephine and Hugo's office there was a distinct chill in the air. 'Go on, you may as well tell me.' Josephine tapped her gold pencil on the polished desk. 'What's the gossip? What have those Mesdames Desfarges in distribution been saying about me?'

Hugo crossed his arms and smiled maliciously. He knew how much Josephine loathed having her private life scrutinized, especially by her employees. The disappointing thing was that there was very little to report. One side effect of Josephine's management style, matey on the surface, solid steel underneath, was that people didn't tend to gossip overtly. They were too frightened for their jobs. But he wasn't going to let Jo know that.

'There were a few eyebrows raised at first. After all, Stephen's known to be a family man, but he's popular enough. And all that exhausting enthusiasm of his goes down well on the shopfloor. If you make a big show of keeping business and pleasure apart, no knee-tremblers in the lift or anything' – Josephine looked at him with disgust – 'then I expect they'll come round soon enough. Though whether I will is a different story.'

Whatever objections Hugo felt minded to raise were interrupted by a knock on the door and Stephen's head appearing.

'Ah, Stephen, we were just talking about you. Come in.'

Josephine shot him a warning glance which he deliberately ignored.

'Jo was just asking how all the drones downstairs were taking your relationship with the Queen Bee.'

Stephen masked his shock at Hugo's directness by elaborately removing his suit jacket and folding it neatly. 'And how are they taking it?'

'So far so good. As I was saying, you're a popular chap and of course round here we're all used to the company motto. Whatever Jo-jo wants, Jo-jo gets, isn't that right, my dear?'

Josephine decided she'd had enough of this for one day. 'Hugo, stop behaving like a shit and for God's sake let's get on with the meeting.'

'Yuk, Mum, you got American Hot instead of plain American. I hate chillies.'

'Well, pick them off then. It's exactly the same otherwise. And don't drop them on the duvet.'

All three of them were crowded into her bed eating pizza and watching *The Sound of Music*. Luke had complained it was a girl's film and been overruled two to one. Tess knew pizza in bed was probably the height of indulgence, but too bad. This was the first time since Stephen's departure that they'd felt like a family. A small breath of optimism warmed her. Luke and Ellie really didn't seem too badly affected. Maybe there was life beyond marriage after all.

Maria was just striking up a rousing chorus of 'Doe a Deer' when Tess put her arm round Luke. 'I don't suppose you remember singing that to me when you were little. You were so proud when you got the words all right so I never liked to tell you you were muddling all the actions.' She squeezed him affectionately, but there was something a bit remote about him still. Perhaps he felt all this cuddling was cissy.

'Are you missing Dad? It's all right, you know. It's only natural.'

'No, it's not that.'

'Luke, you're not being bullied still?'

Luke turned his face away and she saw a single tear run down his cheek which he brusquely wiped away.

'Oh, Luke, love, it's not fair!' Tomorrow morning she was going to drop him off and go straight to his teacher to have a serious word.

And then there was no more time to worry because Ellie had jumped out of bed in the black T-shirt Stephen had bought her in Bloomingdale's and was pirouetting round the room serenading them about girls in white dresses with blue satin sashes and snow-flakes that land on your nose and eyelashes.

'Why are you dropping us off instead of Inge?' Ellie asked suspiciously. 'You only usually drop us off on Mondays.'

Tess fought her way through all the Land Rover Discoveries and four-wheel-drive monstrosities that private school parents so favour in the 1990s. No more unsuitable cars could have been designed for taking children to school in the narrow streets of Chelsea, but that seemed to put no one off buying them. She'd once seen two mums, each with a carload of children, refuse to back off and let the other pass for a good twenty minutes, both ignoring the queue of honking cars behind them until the nerve of one of them finally cracked and she reversed, cursing in a most unmaternal manner, a hundred yards up the street. Tess wondered what they said to each other at the next PTA meeting.

This was one of the few occasions when owning an ancient Astra was an advantage and Tess was able to glide into a gap none of the four-wheels could contemplate, even with the benefit of their power-assisted steering.

As soon as they reached the school grounds Ellie was swallowed up by a crowd of friends who were all, Tess was relieved to note, equally outlandishly dressed.

Luke glanced nervously around, then made for the safety of the Assembly Hall. As soon as he was out of sight Tess walked swiftly towards his classroom to explain the situation to his teacher.

She, young and keen and with an under-used degree in child psychology, fell upon the news as though it were the best thing she'd heard all week. At last her skills were going to be called for. Tess listened with only slight misgivings. At least the girl was prepared to *do* something about it.

Tess was halfway across the playground when Mrs Browne, Ellie's teacher, spotted her. 'Mrs Gilfillan, I'm very pleased to catch you. I wanted a word about Eleanor. She tells me you've given your permission for her to drop English A level and change to History of Art. And I wondered if you realized the implications of that?'

Tess listened, astounded. Ellie hadn't even mentioned changing subjects, let alone had her permission to do so. 'Perhaps you could fill me in.'

'Well, as you know, Ellie's very keen to go to Art

439

College. I gather her father paints too. But if she drops English that might be her only option. University would probably be out of the question. I've tried to explain that it would be better to keep her options open, but she's a very determined young lady.'

Tess wished she could lay hands on Ellie and thrash this out now, but it'd have to wait till later. 'Thank you, Mrs Browne, I'll talk to her about it tonight, I can promise you.'

As she drove to work Tess's relief that she'd at least taken some action over Luke was tempered by her fury with Ellie. How dare she go changing A levels without even so much as talking to her about it? For a moment she wondered if Ellie would have had the nerve if Stephen were still there.

The traffic in the King's Road was so bad she cut down a side street and decided to make for Royal Hospital Road. The daffodils were all out in the gardens opposite and a couple of Chelsea Pensioners sat sunning themselves on benches. A few lucky people were playing tennis on the courts opposite Hastings Terrace. Every house in this well-heeled area seemed to have window boxes, dutifully tended no doubt by green-fingered wives. Hyacinths, dwarf tulips and daffs painted every windowsill with spring colour. Easter would be early this year. The first holiday they'd be apart. She found herself dreaming of Cork and their magical time there less than a year ago. Would she go to Killamalooe any more now that they'd split? She thought with a flash of guilt of Stella and Julius. Had Stephen told them? They weren't exactly attentive grandparents but surely they had a right to know? She took a left down towards the river, deciding that they were Stephen's family and it was up to him

440

to break the news. All the same, she smiled at the thought of Julius. He was an old rogue but she was fond of him. And it'd be sad if Luke and Ellie were to lose touch with their grandparents. Especially when they were as colourful as Julius.

During Assembly Luke's teacher came up with a plan. She would send Luke on some errand then tell the class about his home situation. She'd remind them that it was the responsibility of each of them to look out for Luke at a time like this. This was something that could happen to any of them. In fact, she decided, warming to her theme, it would be a great opportunity to discuss the subject of family breakdown in a wider context.

When they got back to class she could hardly wait to send Luke off.

'Luke,' she said eagerly, catching him as he filed back in, 'I wonder if you could take these notes to the School Secretary for me? Don't just leave them outside her office, now. I'd appreciate it if you waited till she was free and handed them to her personally.'

'Now, class.' She gestured for them all to sit down. 'We're having a change of plan. Instead of Geography I want to talk to you about an aspect of Sociology. I asked Luke to go on an errand because his mother came to see me this morning and told me something quite important that I'd like to share with you, because I believe you're mature enough to understand. The fact is that Luke's parents have split up. Luke is very upset about this, so I want you all to be particularly kind to Luke during this difficult period. Remember that one in three marriages now breaks down and this could be something that happens to any of you.'

In the back row of the classroom Luke's tormentor,

Jason Steel, a big boy with close-cropped hair and a double earring, raised an eyebrow. So that was why Luke Gilfillan kept blubbing. What a cissy.

He leaned down to the smaller boy next to him, tapped the side of his nose and winked. 'We'll look after him, won't we, Shane? Take a really personal interest.'

Shane looked back and grinned.

'So, Ms Efficiency, have you done those chapter headings yet?' Lyall asked the moment Tess walked into Kingsmill's reception.

Tess shook her head, smiling. 'I can tell you're single. You only asked me a couple of days ago! I have got a few other things to do, you know.'

'Tell you what. I'll give them to you after Easter. In fact I'll even give you a synopsis by then. Will that be soon enough?'

'Brilliant. Going anywhere nice?'

'Swinging Chelsea.'

'But I thought you lived in Chelsea.'

'I do. We're staying at home. How about you?'

'To my folks in Worthing.'

Tess giggled. 'Lyall, you don't come from Worthing!'

Lyall looked injured. 'Nothing wrong with Worthing. It appears in Oscar Wilde.'

'Only for him to be nasty about it. I didn't think anyone under eighty lived there.'

'They don't. I bring the average down to 79. It's very peaceful. The rattle of wheelchairs. The hum of pacemakers. The crackle of hearing aids. Who could ask for more?'

'Sounds bliss.' Tess picked up her briefcase and headed for her office. She was already late because of the visit to Luke's school. 'Right. I'll get on with the headings straightaway.'

'If you get stuck, just give me a ring.'

'I think I can cope,' Tess replied briskly. 'After all, divorce is my subject.'

Luke, his breath still coming in gasps, hid in the junior toilets clutching his prized Bulk Brogan parka, listening. It was ten to four and he was almost sure that the school yard would be empty by now. He comforted himself with the thought that Ellie and Inge would probably be looking for him already. So even though Jason Steel had 'claimed' him and he'd be breaking the unwritten rules of the playground jungle by not showing up, he wouldn't be completely on his own.

He slipped quietly out of the toilets, deafened by the sound of his own heart thudding. It seemed a very long way to the school gate and safety. Then in the distance he made out the flash of Inge's pale tracksuit next to Ellie's navy greatcoat. He sighed with relief and started towards them. It was going to be all right.

Then he saw them. Jason and Shane, lurking by the corner of the new building, halfway between him and the gate. He'd have no choice but to pass them. He took his courage in his hands and made a mad dash for it. But Jason saw him first. They both barred his path.

'Do you smell something, Jase?' Shane Finnigan, small and wiry, was holding his nose.

'Telling me, Shane. What a disgusting pong. Somebody's definitely got BO. Didn't your best friend tell you, Luke?' Jason grabbed the sleeve of Luke's precious parka. 'So your old man's buggered off, has he, then?'

Shane laughed loudly. 'Bet it's because of his BO.'

Jason laughed. 'Too right.' He pretended to sniff Luke's armpit. 'Bloody hell. I don't blame him. You should wash more often, Gilfillan.'

Luke fought back the tears. He knew that was what they wanted, that then they'd have won. But he couldn't stop one sob.

'Aaaah, listen to that, Shane. Luke here's crying. He should be in Miss Farr's class. Shall we take him back to Nursery?'

And then to Luke's blessed relief he saw Ellie begin to walk towards them. When she saw who was with him she broke into a run. 'Oi! You little shits, leave him alone!'

Shane turned to Jason. 'Fancy hiding behind a girl, Jase.'

But Luke wasn't listening. He wrested his parka out of Jason's hold and bolted towards Ellie as fast as he could, tears blinding his eyes. Shane and Jason melted away before Ellie had any chance of reaching them.

'Ellie,' Luke gasped uncomprehendingly, 'they know about Mum and Dad. How could Jason Steel possibly know about that?'

Tess got home feeling more cheerful than she had for weeks. She'd unexpectedly found herself with a spare half-hour at the end of the afternoon and had used it to work out the chapter headings for *The Good Divorce Guide*. Now all she had to do was write the synopsis. Maybe she'd even impress Lyall by finding time before Easter.

She hummed as she inspected the post on the hall table, not even letting a red council tax reminder spoil her mood. On her way upstairs to change out of her working clothes she was almost knocked over by Ellie.

'Thank God you're back, Luke's in a terrible state.

444

That pig Jason Steel jumped him and told him Dad walked out because he's got BO. And Luke half believes it.'

Tess listened in horror, her mild happiness evaporating at Ellie's words.

'What beats me,' Ellie went on angrily, 'is how that horrible little sod found out. I haven't told a soul. And you couldn't prise it out of Luke no matter what you did. He thinks if he doesn't tell anyone it might not really be true.'

Tess winced. 'That stupid teacher! I only told her because I wanted her to keep an eye on him, not broadcast the split to the whole class.'

'Oh, great. How absolutely bloody brilliant. It was you. The whole of the school will know by now. How could you be so stupid?'

'I thought it was for the best!' Tess felt a flash of anger at Ellie's intolerance. 'And what's all this about you saying I'd given permission for you to chuck English A level? That was a lie.'

Ellie looked at her coldly in the special way she'd refined since Stephen left. 'It's quite simple. I've decided I want to go to Art College. So History of Art'll be more useful. All perfectly straightforward.'

'But you didn't even consult me. And you lied to your teacher. Ellie, this is serious.'

'Looking at the mess you've made over Luke, do you wonder why?' She rushed past her mother to the sitting room, slamming the door. Tess slithered down on to the stairs and put her head in her hands. She'd had countless divorced women sitting opposite her sobbing that their children took it out on them when the marriage broke down, but she'd never guessed how painful that could be. Just when you needed support and comfort yourself your children put the boot in. And you couldn't even get angry with them because you knew it was partly your fault.

Slowly she pulled herself up and went into Luke's bedroom. He was lying on his bed, utterly still, with his face to the wall. She sat down and started to stroke his forehead. His pillow was damp from crying. She turned his face gently round. 'Luke, I'm afraid it was my fault today. It was me who told the teacher. I thought it was better that she knew. I'm so sorry, darling, I had no idea she'd go and tell everyone.'

Luke stared back at her, his eyes wide with disbelief that the one person he'd thought he could trust had betrayed him. Then he turned his head away and she heard a small sigh that tore at her heart.

'We'll do something, darling. We'll find an answer to this. I won't let those boys gang up on you any more. I promise.'

He looked at her again, his face more sad than angry. 'It might be better if you stayed out of it, Mum. Don't worry. I'll be all right. I've always got Ellie.'

Tess walked tiredly downstairs, all her previous energy depleted. The front door banged shut. Ellie, no doubt, refusing to stay in the house in the face of such maternal incompetence. For a few moments she sat on the sofa, feeling a complete failure as a mother. For the first time since Stephen had left she wasn't sure she would cope. Maybe she just didn't have the strength that was required of her. A huge racking sob shook her, leaving her throat sore and her body quivering. She buried her face in the cushions of the sofa they'd chosen together just before they'd got married. The truth was she was no stronger than her poor pathetic clients.

In the end it was a tiny detail, a small niggle of recognition that pulled her back together. Jason Steel's name. She'd heard it somewhere before. Forgetting her misery, she sat up again. There was something at the back of her mind pricking away, the kind of connection that proved so useful to her at work. That name was definitely familiar to her.

She looked at her watch. Just after seven. The library would still be open. She knocked on Inge's door and told her she'd be out for about an hour.

In the library she headed straight for the reference section and asked for back numbers of the *Kensington & Chelsea Post*. The young woman behind the counter, clearly an exponent of social worker chic, glanced up at the clock above the enquiries desk and clucked in disapproval.

After a brief wait she ungraciously thumped a ring-bound pile of newspapers down in front of Tess. 'Twenty minutes till we close,' she reminded Tess helpfully.

Tess sat and thought, trying to ignore the relentless ticking of the clock. If her instincts were right, it should be about a year or so, maybe eighteen months. Thank God the paper was weekly not daily.

At five to eight, ignoring the now overt annoyance of the girl at the desk, she found what she was looking for.

'Could I make a photocopy of this please?'

The girl raised her eyes to heaven as though Tess had just requested she Xerox the entire *Encyclopaedia Britannica* instead of one page of newsprint. She rifled about in her desk, concluding triumphantly that, sorry, she didn't have any change.

'How much is it?' Tess wasn't about to be foiled at this late stage.

'15p a sheet.'

'Here you are.'

To the girl's evident disappointment Tess handed over the exact money.

She shrugged, apathetic now in defeat. 'You have to do it yourself, the copier's over there.'

Tess sprinted over to the machine and inserted the awkward bundle of newspapers. No time to undo them. Besides, she'd probably be tarred and feathered if she tried.

The photocopy was at a crazy angle when it spewed out of the machine, with the bottom right-hand corner missing. But it'd do.

'There you are.' She grinned at the girl, handing back the ring-binder of newspapers, unable to contain her delight at having found what she wanted. 'Thanks for being so helpful.'

'That's all right.' The irony passed the girl by unnoticed. 'Maybe next time you could come in a little earlier?'

'Why did you bring us to school *again*?' Ellie made it sound as though this were little short of the miracle of the loaves and fishes. Luke had run on ahead leaving Ellie and Tess at the school gates.

'It doesn't matter.' Tess took Ellie's arm as nonchalantly as she could. 'Now, perhaps you could point out which one's Jason Steel.'

Ellie turned to her suspiciously. 'What are you up to, Muv?'

'I just want to see what he looks like.'

After a few minutes' searching Ellie pointed out a bruiser of a boy with a crewcut and earrings. He had a much smaller lad, with a pinched ratty face, in tow.

'You're not going to do anything stupid, are you?'

448

Ellie asked anxiously. 'I mean, look what happened last time you tried to help.'

Tess kissed her and turned away, her confidence draining away for a moment. What if Ellie were right and she only ended up making things worse for Luke?

For God's sake, she told herself, *don't be ridiculous. You spend half your professional life fighting for victims of injustice. You can't stand back and not help your own son.*

The bell went for the start of school and all around her children began to melt away from the playground in twos and threes. She glanced nervously to see if Jason had joined them. To her relief, he and his mate were staying on an extra minute to prove their superiority over the petty regulations that bound everyone else.

Putting on her best woman-in-authority manner Tess walked confidently up to them. 'Hello, Jason,' she announced. 'I've got a message from your mother. Come over here a moment, would you?'

CHAPTER THIRTY

'Who are you then?' Jason surveyed her challengingly.

'Just one of the other mums. Yours had to rush off.'

Jason nodded dismissal at Shane and the younger boy slunk off looking sullen at missing the excitement.

'So. What's this message, then?'

Tess hesitated for a moment, wondering whether the reason that neither of his parents had wanted custody of him when they divorced a year earlier was because he was so unpleasant or whether it was the pain of this rejection that had made him so. It had been the strange circumstances of the case that had touched her and made her remember. She'd never heard of a case before where neither mother nor father wanted the child and both fought in court to show their unsuitability as parents.

'Well?' prompted Jason rudely.

Tess turned to him, face on. 'As a matter of fact, I told you a lie because I wanted to talk to you. I'm Luke Gilfillan's mother. You made Luke's life hell yesterday about his father leaving, didn't you?'

Jason looked shifty.

Tess took a breath, knowing that what she was doing was a tad immoral, and probably unethical to boot. 'Why did you do that, Jason? You know how much it hurts when your parents split, don't you, Jason?' Jason had started backing off slightly, putting his chin up aggressively. 'You wouldn't want what happened at *your* parents' divorce to come out, now would you, Jason?' Very slowly she unfolded the copy of the newspaper cutting.

'You cunt,' snarled Jason.

Tess ignored him. 'Just leave Luke alone and no one else'll know. OK?' She tore up the sheet of paper and threw it in a nearby rubbish bin. 'Of course, I can always get another copy, but somehow I don't think I'll need to. Deal?'

'OK.' Jason nodded grudgingly. 'But you won't tell Luke?'

'I won't tell anyone. Unless Luke's bullied again.'

'But what if it isn't me?'

'You'd better keep an eye on him for me.'

Jason turned away and ran towards the door. Half-way across the playground he stopped. 'You're OK,' he shouted. 'Wish my mum gave half a shit like you.'

Tess grinned and waved, weak with relief that her plan seemed to have worked. Jason Steel's repentance was probably about as reliable as the long-range weather forecast – but it was a start.

Half an hour later she ran into Kingsmill's with a broad smile on her face.

'Why didn't you tell me you were going to be late?' Jacqui grabbed her briefcase from her arms, fussing like an old hen. 'Will Kingsmill's come looking for you twice. Where on earth have you been?'

'Being Wonderwoman!' Tess twirled round like Lynda Carter. 'Some kid was bullying Luke and I had to try and sort him out.'

'And you did? Wow!'

'Who knows? I don't think I did any harm anyway.'

'By the way, I told the Old Fart you'd had a puncture. Just so as you know.'

'And blew it back up again with my bare lips,' Tess boasted.

'You *are* in a good mood.'

'Yes. Well, life has been a bit tricky lately, as you recall.' She chucked Jacqui on the cheek. 'It's nice to get a few of the ups as well as the downs.'

On her way to Will Kingsmill's office her elation died down a bit as she wondered what this unexpected meeting was all about. She hoped he wasn't unhappy with her work.

But for once Will Kingsmill was all smiles. 'Sit down, Tess. Cup of coffee?'

'That'd be lovely.'

He left her on tenterhooks as he ordered the coffee from his boot-faced assistant, then settled down in his chair opposite her. 'Now. Lyall Gibson's been telling me about this project of yours, *The Good Divorce Guide*. He says you want to use cases you've worked on here to illustrate it.'

Tess nodded, wondering if he was about to veto the idea on the grounds that it might offend the clients.

'I'm sure you'll use appropriate discretion. What I wanted to say is that I think it's a terrific idea and I'm right behind you. It'll do the firm's image a lot of good. And it goes without saying that if you need a little time off day-to-day work to write it, I'll do what I can to accommodate you.'

Tess almost kissed him. Her only worry about the venture had been that she might end up working through the night and finding herself getting exhausted and grouchy with Ellie and Luke.

'Will, thank you. That's a really kind offer.'

Once outside his office she danced a little jig, ignoring Lilian's look of disapproval. She felt she'd turned some kind of corner. From now on things could only get better.

As soon as she opened the front door that evening,

Tess sensed the atmosphere had lightened. Instead of being slumped in front of the TV or behind their bedroom doors, Luke and Ellie were in the kitchen together. She could hear the usual bickering but, for once, it was good tempered.

'What's this?' she asked, leaning on the door to watch their sudden activity.

'We're making supper,' announced Ellie grandly. 'You go and sit down. Take her a glass of wine, Luke.'

Luke was about to question why it should be him rather than her, but shut his mouth instead. He filled the largest glass he could find and trotted after her.

Tess sank on to the sofa and curled her legs under her luxuriously, sipping her wine and sighing with pleasure.

'Mum,' Luke asked shyly, sitting down next to her, 'did you say anything to Jason Steel today?'

Tess shook her head and smiled as mysteriously as the Sphinx. She owed Jason that much. 'Nothing to do with me, Squire.' But she couldn't resist prying a bit more. 'What makes you ask?'

'It's just that he's been quite nice to me today and I can't think why.'

'Maybe he's realized you and he have got more in common than he thought.'

'I bloody well hope not.' Luke grinned at her cheekily. 'I don't want him trying to be my best friend. He's thick as two short planks for a start.'

'Luke,' Tess reprimanded.

He snuggled against her suddenly, and Tess held him, treasuring the moment. 'Thanks, Mum,' he mumbled into her long hair.

'Anytime.' She stroked his dark head, moved almost to tears by his unexpected gratitude. 'Though I've no idea what you're talking about.'

*

The next stage for the launch of Forever was to design some stunning and eye-catching ads. Stephen sat at his desk flicking through a huge pile of glossy magazines, supposedly looking for inspiration. But the advertisement that lay open in front of him wasn't for perfume. It was for life insurance and it featured a young boy being carried on his father's shoulders. And what had made Stephen forget all about the task in hand was that he had a definite look of Luke. Not Luke now, but at five or six. Wide-eyed and laughing, a mop of dark hair, and the kind of realistic boyishness that didn't usually find its way into the pages of a glossy magazine.

He wondered how Tess would react to him wanting to see them. And would they want to see him? Or would they be too bitter and angry, feeling that he'd abandoned and betrayed them?

Hesitantly he picked up the phone and sat listening to the dialling tone, too nervous to punch in the number, until an electronic voice politely requested him to put back the receiver and try again.

Tess read over the notes she'd made yesterday for her newest custody case. It was such a sad one that she was grateful things were beginning to work out for her own family. Otherwise she didn't think she could have gone ahead. Even in her present cheerful mood the words of the child she'd interviewed came back to haunt her. A rich kid, whose parents had each remarried. She felt her throat tighten uncomfortably as she recalled his matter-of-fact words: 'The thing is, I don't know where to put my posters up any more. Nowhere seems like home.'

The phone on her desk rang, and she picked it up, telling herself she should be more detached. The last person she was expecting it to be was Stephen.

454

'Hello, Tess. How are you?' Hearing his voice temporarily deprived her of speech. 'Is this a bad time?' he added hurriedly, misinterpreting her silence. 'Would you rather I rang back?'

Tess pulled herself together. 'No, it's fine. What can I do for you?'

'I thought if maybe things had settled down a bit, I might be able to see the children.' He paused before asking the question he dreaded. 'How are they?'

Tess wondered if she should tell him about the bullying, then decided it might sound as though she were blaming him. 'They're OK. It was rough on them at first but they seem to be adjusting. Luke's been asked to sing a solo in the Easter recital.'

Stephen jumped on this news. 'Maybe I could come and listen. When is it?'

'On Friday. Three p.m.' She might have mixed feelings but she knew Luke wouldn't.

'Fine. I'll be there. Tess?'

'Yes?'

'Perhaps we could take them for an ice-cream afterwards?'

'They'd like that.' Glad to hide her emotions in the banality of their conversation, she said goodbye and went back to work, willing the afternoon to pass quickly so she could go home and tell them both the news.

'Guess what, Luke? Dad rang today. He's going to come to your concert.' Over his head she noticed Ellie looking at her beadily. 'And then he's taking us all for an ice-cream.'

Luke's face had lit up with pleasure. 'Mum, do you think you could possibly come together?'

The question sliced at her heart. After all they'd

been through he still wanted to pretend everything was all right.

Later that night, as she went up to bed, she heard the sound of muffled crying and pushed open Luke's door. Maybe hearing from Stephen had been harder than he'd let on. But Luke was sleeping peacefully with Ted next to him. The sound was coming from Ellie's room.

'Dad didn't ask to come to any of *my* things, did he? I've got two paintings up in the Assembly Hall. I thought he might at least be interested in those.' As Tess sat down on the bed next to her daughter, she glimpsed the little girl, still jealous of her baby brother, who had just been given the most precious treat of all, her father's interest.

'Don't worry, darling. I'm sure wild horses wouldn't drag him away till he's seen your pictures.'

'I suppose so.' Ellie's face was white and tearstained under her aggressive haircut. 'But he didn't *ask* to, did he?'

'Jo, there's something I wanted to talk to you about.'

Josephine looked up from the arts page of the *Guardian* wondering what was to come. It had to be about Tess or the children.

'If Tess agrees I'd like to take Ellie and Luke to Italy for the Easter weekend. I've tracked down some cheap flights to Naples. There's a little hotel I know in Capri we could go to.'

'Easter's next week. You haven't left much time.' Josephine started to peel an orange, her long red nails suddenly bringing to Stephen's mind the irrelevant information that in certain tribes women were thought to make the best torturers. 'Am I invited?'

For a split second Stephen wondered whether that

would be fair to Tess. But they'd made their decision. 'If you'd like to.'

'I'll think about it.' The truth was Josephine wasn't sure how she was going to take to the role of step-mother. She watched Stephen for a moment over the rim of her coffee cup. He had a happiness and energy about him she hadn't sensed before when he talked about this Italian plan. A subtle smile crossed her lips at the memory of their lovemaking the previous night. It had been the best so far. But she had learned something about Stephen in the last few weeks. Sex wasn't the key to him as it had been to her previous lovers. She knew family was part of it, so maybe she should go along with this Italian trip. And, of course, there was art. She hadn't fully exploited that yet and it was a way of tying him to her that Tess had never possessed. It was time she got some specific dates for that exhibition out of Tad Zora. Then Stephen really might begin to understand how useful she was going to be to his career.

Tess sat in the concert hall, her coat saving the seat next to hers, trying not to admit how incredibly nerv-ous she felt. There was still no sign of Stephen and the concert was due to start in five minutes. Luke's anxious face appeared fleetingly in the wings and she saw the disappointment in it when he took in the empty seat. He was on first and if Stephen didn't get here soon he'd miss it.

With one minute to go Stephen appeared at the back of the hall and pushed his way politely down the row to the seat next to Tess's just as the lights started to dim.

The curtains parted to reveal Luke in the light of a single spotlight, singing William Blake's 'Jerusalem' with flawless perfection. As his voice soared to the crescendo, ' "Till we have built Jerusalem, In England's green and pleasant land",' Tess found tears beginning to well up in her eyes. Without even looking in her direction Stephen reached out and took her hand, making her long to turn and examine his face, until she realized that it was simply a gesture of solidarity and wonder that together they had created a child capable of producing sounds of such pure beauty.

As soon as the concert finished Luke rushed out from behind the scenes and flung himself into his father's arms. Ellie appeared behind him, hanging back shyly until Stephen noticed her and opened his arms to welcome her. She then dragged him off to the Assembly Hall to see her paintings. As soon as they arrived her art teacher came up to join them.

'I gather from Eleanor that you're a painter, Mr Gilfillan. As you see Ellie's clearly inherited your talent.'

Stephen studied both paintings, genuinely impressed. 'These are terrific, Ellie. What talented children I've got.'

The teacher watched with a faint pang of envy as Ellie and Stephen walked off, Stephen with his arm around his daughter. What an attractive man he was, so full of life and enthusiasm. If only she'd had praise like that from her own father things might have been very different.

Tess and Luke were waiting at the school gates and together all four strolled down the King's Road, taking up the whole pavement, to the ice-cream parlour near the corner of Oakley Street where Luke announced he wanted a knickerbocker glory and Ellie, eager to impress Stephen with her sophistication, ordered a cappuccino.

He watched her face fall when Luke's leaning tower of fruit and ice-cream arrived. Unexpectedly the waiter produced a second. 'I thought you'd like one really,' Stephen explained. Ellie beamed with pleasure because he knew her so well.

After they'd finished Ellie and Luke went off to choose some music from the juke box. Neither Tess nor Stephen spoke for a moment, but it was a companionable silence, an echo of their old closeness. Tess wondered if that was where they'd gone wrong when they'd tried to patch their marriage up. You couldn't force closeness. It often came only when you weren't expecting it. Like now. She wondered if he was aware of it too.

As if he were reading her thoughts, Stephen, suddenly serious, started to talk. 'Tess, look, there's something I need to discuss with you.'

Luke, having made his two selections, wanted to go back, but Ellie grabbed him. 'No, leave them alone for a bit. It looks as though he's working up to something.'

Tess remembered the hand that had groped for hers in the concert hall. Then she told herself not to be so bloody stupid. 'Go ahead.'

Instead of looking at her Stephen began to play with the bowl of multicoloured sugar. 'The thing is, I know this is very short notice, but I'd really like to take Luke and Ellie to Capri for Easter.'

Tess felt an irrational kick of disappointment. What had she been expecting?

'Ellie and I could do some painting,' Stephen rushed on, 'and I'm sure Luke'd love Pompei. The wildflowers will be out and there'll hardly be any tourists so early in the season. We'd only go for four or five days, so you'd have the rest of the Easter holidays with them. What do you think?'

Tess tried to swallow her disappointment and look on the bright side. With Ellie and Luke away she'd have all the time in the world to finish her synopsis. And Italy in the spring sounded glorious. There was one question she wanted to ask, but decided it wouldn't be fair. Would Josephine be going too?

Of course she would. And why not? It was all over between her and Stephen.

'It's really up to them. If they want to go, I'm perfectly happy for you to take them.'

'Ellie, Luke,' Stephen called, 'come over here. I was just proposing we all went to Capri for Easter; it's wonderful there just now.'

Ellie looked from one parent to the other in sudden elation. 'What, all of us? You mean Mum too?'

Stephen looked acutely embarrassed at the lack of tact in his wording. 'Well, actually –'

'I'll be far too busy writing the outline for my book to go gadding off to Italy,' cut in Tess. 'You'll be doing me a favour really.'

As they got up to go out Stephen handed Tess an envelope.

'What's this?'

'A cheque. For the roof. I got a bonus because the orders for the new scent are so good.'

Tess smothered any outdated notions of honour and independence. She couldn't afford them any more. She put it in her handbag and thanked him, trying not to think of the sun shining down on the blue Mediterranean.

'OK then.' Josephine stood up and shook Tad Zora's hand. 'We'll try for two weeks at the end of June. That'll give him plenty of time to build on the paint- ings he's already finished. I pay for the cost of mounting and the party, you organize the publicity. One thing, Tad . . .'

'You'd rather Stephen didn't know this was a joint venture. Josephine, I absolutely understand. A young man's pride is an important matter.'

Josephine looked round the gallery with satisfaction. Its rough taupe plaster struck just the right modern note while still providing a perfect backdrop. And Tad's clientele embraced both classic collectors and influential industrialists as well as the two or three owners of private collections who offered just the cachet a young artist needed. This was the perfect place for a début exhibition. 'How delightfully old-fashioned you are, Thaddeus. And thank God for it.'

The following week, after a desperate rush to get swimming things, painting things, passports and money organized, Stephen arrived to pick them up on Maundy Thursday. Luke rushed down to the car, full of excitement, while Ellie had the grace to look a shade guilty.

'You're sure you'll be all right?' she asked Tess.

'All right? I'll be out on the town bopping the night away. I can't remember when I was last single. Have a lovely time. I won't come and wave.'

As Ellie ran off to join the others, Tess glanced out of the window. The car was discreetly parked about fifty yards away, not far in fact from where she'd first seen Stephen kissing Josephine and worked out what was going on. A flash of sunglasses and smart straw hat in the passenger seat told Tess all she needed to know.

And for the very first time she could understand the sentiment uttered by Terry's ghastly wife, Angela, and by so many of her own female clients: 'I'm not letting that cow near my children.'

On Good Friday morning Tess settled down at her desk in the unaccustomed silence – even Inge had gone home to Sweden for a few days – and started work. The level of concentration she was able to build up, uninterrupted by either phone or children, was surprisingly enjoyable, and by the end of the day she was amazed at how much she'd got through.

It was six p.m. before she allowed herself to stop for the day and have a drink. It struck her that three whole days stretched ahead, empty but daunting, in which she was entirely without plans. Suddenly she felt restless. She wanted to do something with her freedom rather than simply have an early night. Her first instinct was to ring Phil, but she was out. Tess left a message on her machine. Looking through her address book she was appalled to realize how many old friends she hadn't been keeping up with. If she rang them now she'd have to start by explaining about the split and she just didn't feel like it. Sympathy wasn't what she wanted, but fun and laughs.

And then Lyall's name leaped out at her. Tess was shocked at herself. As she'd told Jacqui so often, their relationship was purely professional. Maybe she'd just ring him and tell him how well it had gone today. Surely there was nothing sinister in that? She dialled his number. Another bloody answering machine! This time she didn't feel brave enough to leave a message.

She took her glass of wine over to the sofa and flopped. It was obviously going to have to be a night in with the box. At least *Annie Hall* was on. She could settle down with a frozen pizza and sniffle through the scene where the lobster runs away and Woody Allen's too scared to catch it. Funny how love really showed in the ordinary little moments, not in life's Big Scenes.

She'd just settled down with a box of Kleenex when the doorbell rang. In the space of a single day hearing the doorbell had changed from being so common as to amount to a nuisance to an event that made her sit up and start in surprise, spilling her wine on the sofa.

With her luck it was either a double glazing salesman or a Jehovah's Witness, or both.

Standing on the doorstep, clutching a bottle of rather posh champagne, which Tess could see from its delicate frosting was even the right temperature to drink, stood Phil.

'Hi!' She kissed Tess enthusiastically. 'Terry's in Cheltenham and I'm all alone. I got your message so I came right round.'

Tess cheered up immediately. Rarely had she been so pleased to see her friend. An evening with Phil was exactly what she needed. She took Phil's coat and ushered her into the empty sitting room.

'Where is everyone?' Phil asked, surprised. 'It's usually like a scene from *Roseanne* in here.'

'Gone to Capri.'

'With that woman?'

'With that woman.'

Phil pushed her towards the staircase. 'In that case go and get your gladrags on. You and I are going on the pull. And don't worry, I'll open the champagne. You go and make yourself gorgeous.'

Tess woke up the next morning with a crashing hangover and a decided feeling that if that was what being single was like, you could keep it. They said in America you had more chance of being killed by a terrorist than finding a man at forty, and last night she and Phil had

463

gone one further. They'd been picked up by the terrorists. Or maybe they were gangsters. It had been highly entertaining for the first five minutes when they'd pretended to be Elaine and Mary from Liverpool, but not so hilarious when they had to spend the next two hours trying to wriggle out of the consequences.

She sat down at her desk nursing a large mug of black coffee and prayed to God that neither she nor Phil had made the mistake of handing out their phone numbers.

The ideas came slower today because her mind kept lapsing into images of sparkling sea and empty beaches, but each time the vision was spoiled by the sight of a chic straw hat and sunglasses sitting right where she ought to be. And she began to understand why so many of her women clients complained that after the split they were left with the slog while the fathers got all the fun.

By Monday lunchtime she'd finished the entire synopsis and allowed herself to luxuriate in the masochistic glow of having suffered for a cause, then spent an hour scouring the few open shops for the last Easter egg in London. It was filled with mini Mars Bars and she didn't like Mars Bars. But she ate them anyway.

By Tuesday morning she was actually grateful to be getting back to work. It was her last day on her own, thank God, and she swore never to be grouchy or bad tempered with Luke and Ellie again. She'd had no idea how much she was going to miss them. Freedom was wonderfully appealing for about twenty-four hours, and after that it started to feel like tyranny.

She got in to work at eight-forty-five, feeling virtuous, only to find Jacqui, efficient as ever, there before her. She was sporting a dazzling new hair accoutrement, a narrow lock of hair, gelled into submission and plastered on to her forehead like a tiny snake.

'Love the hair.' Tess prodded it, fascinated.

'Don't touch!' squawked Jacqui. 'I've been up since six trying to get it finished.' She brandished the page of *Black is Beautiful* from which she'd copied it.

'Sorry. I didn't realize it was such a work of art.' Tess smiled ingratiatingly. 'I don't suppose that if I bunged you a few quid you could retype my synopsis for me? Then I could give it to Lyall in the next couple of days.'

To her astonishment Jacqui handed her an immaculately typed and bound folder by mid-afternoon. She shook her head, stunned, as ever, by her secretary's ability. 'Why are you burying yourself in a firm of solicitors? You should be running your own business. If not the country.'

Jacqui grinned. 'Too right. Do you know, Tess,' she said, pointing to the synopsis of Tess's book, 'that stuff was really interesting.' And the tone of genuine surprise in her voice was the best compliment Tess could have wished for.

Later that evening Tess flung the front door open almost before the doorbell rang and scooped Ellie and Luke into her arms. 'How was it? Did you eat spaghetti till it was coming out your ears and throw three coins in a fountain?'

'It was great!' enthused Ellie, her pale skin glowing with a light freckly tan. 'Luke lost the batteries for his Nintendo on the plane. Then he got food poisoning from the airline meal so Dad had to stay with him in the room for two days. Then I got bitten by mosquitoes' – she held up a leg covered in ugly red weals – 'and on the last day Josephine had a migraine.'

'I'm not surprised,' said Tess, feeling a faint stirring of satisfaction at the thought of this initiation into reality for someone who was no doubt used to five-star childfree luxury. 'And did she enjoy it?'

'I *think* so. Though she did go on a bit about the air conditioning being too noisy and not having a phone by the bath.'

'Well, one does get used to these things,' Tess grinned. 'Poor Stephen. It sounds as though he's the one who needs a holiday.' She picked up their bags and carried them to the bottom of the stairs. 'So where's he got to?'

'He put us in a taxi and dashed back to Winchester. Some crisis on the perfume front.'

'Do you know, Mum?' Luke riffled in his bag for the music-box paperweight that played 'The Isle of Capri' he'd bought for her. 'I'm not sure Josephine really *likes* children.'

Tess watched him fondly, trying not to laugh out loud. 'Really, darling, whatever gave you that idea?'

'Where's Inge, Mum?' Luke enquired as Tess was brushing her teeth next morning. 'I wanted to give her her present but she's not in her room.'

Tess swooshed her mouthwash and joined him in wondering where Inge had got to. She'd forgotten to ask exactly when the girl was coming back, but had assumed it would be Monday night to start work on Tuesday. Term started next week and Luke needed someone to ferry him from computer club to chess club to French club while she was at work. If Inge hadn't turned up by tonight, Tess would have to chase her up or start looking for someone to replace her. In fact, maybe it'd be for the best. Inge was, after all, something of a mixed blessing.

'Maybe she's been delayed,' she reassured Luke. 'Aren't you lucky? You can be a latchkey kid today and eat peanut butter and honey sandwiches and watch unsuitable videos. Just don't tell me anything about it. Deal?'

'Deal.'

Waiting on her desk at work was a handwritten note from Lyall Gibson, fulsomely praising her synopsis and suggesting lunch so they could sit down and discuss it.

Tess read through the note twice. Lunch. Whyever not? It was strictly professional. Besides, everyone seemed to be having fun but her.

Inge wasn't back that night, or the next, so Tess, beginning to worry, rang her parents where she was supposed to be staying. All she got was an answering machine with, not surprisingly, an incomprehensible message in Swedish. Inge must have decided not to come back after all. Tess had heard endless stories about au pairs leaving you in the lurch, but all the same she was surprised at Inge. She'd shown loyalty way beyond the call of duty. Maybe the atmosphere since Stephen left had got to her too.

The next day she rang an agency who sent round a selection of extremely pricey dragons. Tess was on the point of engaging one when Inge, weighed down with expensive suitcases, suddenly appeared in the hall.

'I nearly stayed at home,' she announced by way of explanation, 'but then I decided we women should stick together.'

Hearing Inge's voice, Luke, who had been surveying the line-up of possible replacements with disapproval, cannonballed down the stairs and into her arms.

Inge's reply was to delve in her bag for the latest in interactive computer games. Tess opened her mouth

467

to remark that Luke didn't really need another computer game when Inge produced a leather-bound set of watercolours for Ellie and a video of *The Lovers' Guide* for Tess.

'What's that, Mum?' enquired Luke as she whipped it behind her back.

'An educational video,' insisted Tess.

'Can we watch it then?'

'Certainly not.'

'I thought it might come in useful,' Inge pointed out, 'when things start to look up.'

Fat chance, thought Tess, but smiled back anyway. Mary Poppins she wasn't, but Tess had got really quite fond of Inge. And Luke needed every friend he could get.

'Owww!' Tess cursed. Every time she used these wretched curling tongs she got her long hair painfully caught in them. How on earth did other women manage to put on a sophisticated soignée appearance and still be at work by nine a.m.?

She pulled the tongs out and looked at herself in the mirror, wondering whether to put on some red lipstick. No. This was a business lunch. As she dusted some creamy powder on to her nose and applied a discreet squirt of perfume she had no idea that, red lipstick or no red lipstick, she looked entirely different from usual.

But Ellie noticed at once. 'Where are *you* going today?'

'As a matter of fact, to a business lunch to discuss this book I'm writing.'

'Who with, Kevin Costner? You should see yourself, Mum. You don't think you're trying a bit too hard?'

Tess bit back the angry answer she was about to

468

give. She knew Ellie was only taking out the hurt she was feeling herself on her mother. But it was hardly fair. Stephen had left her for another woman and she was having to take this flak just for going out to lunch. On the other hand who was a marriage break-up harder for, you or your children? At least you made the choice. They just had to go along with it.

'So where's he taking you?' Jacqui pounced on her as soon as she got in the door.

'Not you too,' Tess barked in irritation. 'I've no idea. Look, this is a business meeting, for God's sake.'

'Sorry I spoke,' Jacqui apologized, obviously nettled. 'And by the way you haven't paid me for the typing yet.'

At one p.m. on the dot Lyall was waiting for her in Reception with a taxi standing by. 'I thought it might be fun to do something a bit different.'

Tess got in the cab. Where on earth were they going? Lunch in Le Touquet? A taverna in Camden Town?

To her surprise the taxi dropped them off at West-minster Pier where they boarded the *River Rover*, a pleasure boat cum restaurant.

'What a lovely idea,' Tess said, touched that he'd given it so much thought.

As they climbed aboard the weather bid them *bon voyage* by changing from warm April sunshine to a fiercely cold wind laced with slanty penetrating rain. Tess shivered involuntarily when they went in to eat. Clearly the management had decided that spring was here and turned off the heating. A small, flickering paraffin stove, which looked like a fire hazard if Tess had ever seen one, provided the only warmth.

'Let's have a drink,' suggested Lyall. 'You look perished.' The idea of white wine seemed too arctic so they opted for red, only to see a waiter remove it from the fridge.

Tess laughed.

'Oh dear,' Lyall apologized, 'maybe this wasn't such a great idea after all.'

'Of course it was.' Tess picked up her menu and pointed out of the window. 'Look, we're moving already.'

Slowly the boat moved into the current and set off downstream towards Greenwich. Which was when they noticed they were the only customers. It soon became apparent why. Tess had had some pretty awful meals in her life, but none as bad as this, not even at her mother's. Her avocado was rock hard, filled with part-defrosted prawns buried under a dayglo pink sauce, the chicken that followed was pre-cut and over-cooked in a watery gravy. It was as much as she could do even to pretend to eat it.

Lyall hadn't eaten any of his meal either. In the end she gave in to the giggles. 'Tell you what,' she suggested, wiping her eyes with a napkin, 'why don't we just admit defeat, order a very large brandy and go and sit on deck.'

It was freezing and blustery upstairs but at least it had some of the atmosphere so signally lacking in the restaurant. Tess hadn't brought her overcoat so they shared Lyall's, sipping their brandies and pointing out to each other landmarks that both of them already knew.

By the time they got back to the pier it was almost four and they were quite sad to arrive.

'Look,' Lyall started apologizing again as he hailed a cab, 'I'm really sorry about this.'

'Don't be!' Tess grinned. 'I enjoyed myself. I really did. It's the most memorable lunch I've had in years.'

'You can say that again.' Lyall started to laugh too.

'There was only one problem.'

'Only one? I could list about six. The food, the drink, the temperature, the atmosphere . . .'

'We didn't talk about the book.'

'Never mind.' Lyall's smile held a touch of engaging smugness. 'We can talk about it next time.'

'How long a delay before they can supply the rest of the bottles?' Stephen could have happily killed the suppliers for doing this to him, now of all times – not least because he'd chosen this firm himself against Hugo's advice to stick to their usual one.

'Two weeks, tops,' replied Glassworks' MD. 'Look, I'm really sorry about this, but that was real Venetian glass you chose, not just some rubbish out of recycled Perrier bottles. We've had to wait for the next shipment.'

Stephen willed himself to keep his temper. What the man was saying was perfectly reasonable. There was no point behaving like one of those shits he'd left behind in advertising. But what was he going to tell the US buyers who were all clamouring for their early samples?

'OK. But you do realize we've got a major launch coming up?'

'Yes, Mr Gilfillan, I do. We've turned the whole factory over to meeting your deadline so you could say we're as dependent on you as you are on us.'

For no apparent reason Tess's words from that stupid quarrel they'd had in the car after getting lost in the Cotswolds drifted back to Stephen. *Typically male reaction. Everything always has to be somebody's fault*. He made himself relax and even smile. 'That sounds like the basis of a good working relationship.'

He tapped on Josephine's office door to tell her that the crisis that had been waiting for them on their return from Italy was now sorted out. She was on the phone but she gestured him that she would only be a moment. He sat down on one of the sofas and watched her. Some men said they could always tell if a woman had just made love, but he defied them to do so with Josephine. He had woken this morning to find her deft fingers caressing him, then she had climbed on top and ridden him like a racehorse, cupping her own breasts as she did so, until she cried out in wild unseeing ecstasy. Usually the dominant partner, he had found the sensation of being taken, used almost, extraordinarily erotic. Yet now, watching the cultivatedly elegant woman in front of him, it was hard to believe it was the same person. She smiled as she put down the phone, with perhaps a hint now of remembered lust. He felt relieved that she couldn't compartmentalize her life completely. 'Good news, the glass suppliers can deliver in two weeks. It shouldn't hold things up much.'

Josephine came and joined him. It was amazing how Stephen complicated her life. She should be worrying far more about the US launch, instead all she was feeling was excitement about having dates for the exhibition. 'I've got some good news too. Tad Zora's just rung. He's giving you two weeks in June.'

Stephen's face split into a huge grin. 'Fantastic! But, Jesus, that's only two months away.'

'I know.' Josephine also knew she should be worrying about the distracting effect it would have on his concentration – what on earth would Hugo say? – but she couldn't see beyond his delighted expression.

'Thanks, Jo!' He put his arms round her despite the fact they were in the office. 'I know what a risk this is for you with the launch coming up, but I guarantee I'll do my best for both.'

'Yes, I know.' She thought for a moment about kissing him, but it would only spoil her lipstick. Besides, Hugo might come in. 'You are going to be a busy boy, aren't you?'

CHAPTER THIRTY-ONE

'Where would you like to have lunch? After cocking it up so royally last time, maybe I'd better leave it to you to decide.' Lyall leaned back in his chair and watched her. It was Saturday and they had both come in to the office to work on the book. Tess looked completely different in her non-working clothes. The leggings and vast jumper made her seem more like a daughter than a mother. And the red hair, loose today except for a narrow hairband, against the pale cream of her skin had an almost Pre-Raphaelite look. There was no sign of the courtroom firebrand. Instead there was a kind of touching vulnerability which he knew was misleading but had still kept distracting him all morning. Despite that the time had been brilliantly productive and they were making real progress with the book.

This was the fourth or fifth session like this they'd had over the last six weeks, as well as working individually, and they were well over halfway to finishing. They'd found they worked perfectly together. He supplied the tough legal mind and Tess added the emotion – the sense of what it was really like to go through a break-up – which was giving the text its readability.

He'd learned a lot about her in the last weeks, and the effect was to make him want to know everything. But he had to be careful. If he played his cards wrong she might back off from him personally and from the project too.

'What about that Chinese restaurant on the barge behind the Zoo? I've always wondered what that's like. We could have a quick walk in Regent's Park after. I need to get outside after all this time cooped up in the office.'

He grinned. 'Are you sure you want to risk another trip on the water?'

Tess stood up and stretched. 'This one doesn't go anywhere. And the smells are glorious when you walk past it.'

'Done.'

It was May now and down by the Regent's Canal the trees were in full leaf. The spring sunshine, startlingly hot after the cool of their offices, filtered through the leaves as they walked down the towpath towards the restaurant. All along the bank Saturday fishermen sat optimistically watching the slightest stir in the water, lovers strolled hand in hand, and from the other side of the bridge they could hear the sound of American voices shouting encouragement in their softball games.

Tess felt the sun warming her shoulders, and a sense of wellbeing spread through her. Life was settling down. Every empty moment no longer felt like an amputation that had taken the limb but left the ache. Like an invalid wheeled out into the warmth, she was recovering at last.

The lunch was delicious. They sat, laughing, folding their tiny pancakes and filling them with aromatic crispy duck, tiny shreds of cucumber and spring onion, spiced with pungent plum sauce, and drinking Wan Fu Chinese wine well into the afternoon. Then they crossed the bridge and strolled in Regent's Park, always the least known and least crowded, and to Tess consequently the loveliest, of all London's parks.

It was after four when she finally looked at her watch and said she must get back. As they turned round Lyall reached out an arm and barred her way for a moment, a sudden intensity in his dark eyes. 'Tess, I have to say this. I may be screwing everything up, but I can't help it. You've had a terrible time, I realize that. You don't talk about it, but it shows in your eyes. You still feel bruised by it all, but I can't stand back and watch. I've tried to wait for the right moment and God alone knows if this is it.' He gently twisted a skein of her long hair as he spoke. 'I want to take care of you. I want to make it hurt less. Tess' – he stepped closer and held both her shoulders – 'please let me look after you. I'm sure I can make you happy.'

Tess stood helplessly for a moment, in a sea of conflicting emotions. Surely it was too soon to get involved? And yet she couldn't go on mourning for ever. It was over between her and Stephen. He was in love with another woman. What was the point of clinging to the past? And then, more than anything, there was the temptation to surrender, to hand over the burdens of loneliness and failure to someone else, to be cherished and valued and wanted. It wasn't as though she and Stephen hadn't tried. They'd probably even tried too hard. With Lyall it could be a new beginning.

She reached out a hand to Lyall's face and touched it gently. He caught it and kissed it.

'Lyall, I'm really flattered . . .' she began.

'Don't say that. That's the beginning of No. You don't have to say anything. We'll see each other, we'll go on working on the book. If it happens, it happens. You don't have to make some big decision.'

Tess smiled gratefully. Maybe that was the best way. They'd wait and see.

'Thank you for a lovely lunch. I really do have to go now.' She turned and began to run, but there was a lightness and freedom in her step that belied her cautious and sensible deliberations.

Lyall watched her sprinting away with the grace of a natural athlete. Had he screwed everything up or planted the seed that with careful nurturing would turn into the bloom he so longed to see unfurl?

'Are you stark, staring bonkers?' Phil stirred her Bloody Mary with her stick of celery so that the pepper didn't sit at the top in a cough-inducing lump. 'He's handsome and rich and potentially very successful and he wants to take care of you. What are you waiting for? Tom Cruise is already spoken for.'

'If you recall,' Tess reminded her, 'you were the one who branded him as dull and boring compared with that human dynamo, Stephen Gilfillan.'

'OK, so he's handsome and rich, dull and boring, and he wants to take care of you. So he'll make an excellent husband. Anyway it may have caught your attention that Stephen's no longer available.'

It was the after-work drinks hour at dell 'Ugo's in Soho. Hundreds of people were squashed into the tiny wine bar under the upstairs restaurant with only one thing on their minds. Finding Somebody. The atmosphere dripped with hope on the female side and lust on the male. The gap between them was so vast that most people here tonight would probably end up falling into it. Did she really want to go through all that again when Lyall was offering her a dignified shortcut to a stable relationship?

'Look, I know it hasn't been that long, and that sometimes it seems a truck has run over you emotionally, but you mustn't keep looking backwards. Why don't you at least undo the wrappings and see what's underneath?'

Tess grinned. She didn't feel quite ready to undo Lyall's wrappings yet, but Phil was right about a new beginning. Maybe she'd give him some gentle encouragement.

'What do you think?' Stephen stood back and surveyed the twenty or so canvases he'd completed over the last year, which lined every inch of floor space in the studio. There were two huge paintings on easels he was still part-way through as well. 'Have I got enough for the exhibition?'

Josephine studied them, fascinated by the variety of subject matter Stephen had covered, from still life to landscape and portrait. He hadn't yet found his own distinctive territory, but that would come. And even though all the paintings varied in content they all shared the hallmarks of a Stephen Gilfillan, the necessary stamp to appeal to a collector, of intense unorthodox colour. 'Almost. Perhaps a couple more would help.'

Stephen nodded. He was on a good run, feeling productive and full of ideas and the imminence of having his own exhibition would give him an extra spur.

'So who do you want to invite to the private view?' Josephine handed him a list she'd drafted. 'It's less than a month away now. We need to get the invitations out.'

Stephen glanced through the list. Everyone he'd ever heard of from the art world was on it, from rich and powerful collectors to the most notable art celebrities, plus the most influential journalists and critics.

'Surely this lot won't want to come to a private view for a complete unknown?'

Josephine's lips twisted slightly. Sometimes she

found the fact that Stephen had no real understanding of her influence sweet and touching, sometimes it annoyed her.

'Oh, they'll come all right. But who do you want to add?'

'My father and mother, I suppose.' He got his address book out almost reluctantly. He had no idea what his father was going to make of all this. 'And Slouch. Plus my old tutor from evening classes. Ted from the agency. He might even buy something since it's tax deductible. Phil and her bloke. Oh, and the children, of course, and Tess if she'll come.'

'Mum, we can go, can't we?' Ellie had just undone her own personalized invitation to the private view and had propped it up against the milk bottle in front of her.

'Of course you can.' Tess removed the bottle from behind the invitation and decanted it into a jug. Dymphna's influence again. 'I'm sure you're both top of your father's guest list.'

'What about you?' Luke asked anxiously. He never liked his parents missing any opportunity to see each other just in case they realized the split had been a ghastly mistake.

'I'm not sure yet. Depends how tied up I am.' A coward's answer and she knew it. But after all she'd been through surely she was entitled to a little self-protection?

'You will try, won't you?'

The pathos in his voice made her guilt-glands start up on overtime. 'Of course I will, darling.' But she didn't add what she was thinking. That she and Stephen weren't going to get back together and that it might be better for him if he could face that.

*

479

'So, Stephen, you are happy at last?'

Stephen, Josephine and Slouch Heyward had spent the last hour following Tad Zora and his assistants, two sylphlike boys, round the three floors of the gallery, arguing fiercely about where each picture should be hung. The first floor was to have the sequence of dramatic seascapes. The really big landscapes would go on the ground floor where they'd have maximum impact. His paintings of people he wanted to go in the basement, with the canvas of Tess and the children getting pride of place on the main wall so that it would hit people as they came down the steps.

'Absolutely.' Stephen shook his hand. 'Thanks for bothering to discuss it at such length. Your expertise has been invaluable.'

'He means you seem to know how to flog a painting, Tad,' translated Slouch.

Tad Zora smiled. 'I certainly hope so. With luck we should flog most of this lot over the two weeks. Don't worry if it's not a sea of red stickers on the first night. Real collectors prefer to come and look again. It's usually the punters who buy on the night.'

Stephen turned to Jo. 'I've got to dash to the framers to pick up the six-by-eight frame. See you later.'

As soon as he'd gone the atmosphere lightened as though now things were back in the hands of the professionals.

'Now, Tad, since I'm sharing the costs I'd like to make a few minor adjustments to the hanging,' Josephine said.

'But Stephen said they were as he wanted them.'

'Don't worry about Stephen. He's only the artist.' She smiled to signify this was a joke. 'I'll handle him. Can you come with me, boys' – she gestured to the blond assistants – 'and bring your notebooks.'

She led them immediately to the basement and made a couple of minor changes. Slouch, trailing suspiciously behind her, was wondering what she was up to when the real point of the exercise became apparent. She pointed nonchalantly to the picture of Tess and the children: 'Oh, and you can move that on to that wall. No, on second thoughts, in here.' She led them into a small ante-room where a lot of people would forget even to have a look. 'It doesn't fit with the tone of the other paintings.'

'Come off it, Jo, you know as well as I do that's his best bloody painting. Why don't you just come out with it and say you don't like it because it's of his wife and kids?'

Josephine turned on him. 'And if you're such a good judge how come you're still a half-arsed tutor in an art college who teaches for beer money so he can get wrecked and bum round Europe in the vacations? Often, I might add, at my expense and staying in my house in France?'

Slouch knew when he was beaten. 'You're absolutely right, Josephine. It's a fucking terrible painting. I think you should hide it away in the annexe where no one will see it.'

'Thank you, Slouch, I couldn't agree more. That's exactly what I'll do with it.'

Driving out to Heathrow to meet his mother and father, Stephen realized he was nervous on two different counts. First because of what his father would think of the exhibition tomorrow, and second because he had to tell them about splitting up with Tess. It seemed inconceivable that he hadn't done it already, but they'd never been a family to unburden themselves emotionally and since he hadn't been over to Cork the opportunity hadn't come up. Now there was no getting away from it.

He waved enthusiastically as they came through the barrier. Julius, as ever, attracted attention even among people who had no idea about art. Fame hung about him like a cloak, making them stare and nudge each other and guess at his identity. Sir John Gielgud, they speculated, or some other theatrical knight. And Stella, in cashmere from head to toe, looked every inch the perfect consort.

Stephen settled them in Josephine's Mercedes. His own car was too unreliable to risk aged parents and their suitcases.

'Nice car,' remarked Julius. 'Things must be looking up for you in the art world.'

Stephen laughed and fed his ticket into the short-stay car park machine. 'It isn't mine. Belongs to a friend.' This was as good a moment as any. 'There's something I need to tell you both. I should have told you already – I'm ashamed that I haven't.'

Julius glanced at him, intrigued. 'Go on then, spit it out.'

'Tess and I split up in February.'

'Good God!' Julius was genuinely horrified. 'Why?'

'Things hadn't been going well for a long time. Ever since I stopped working at the agency really. I don't think Tess trusts art. I kept getting the feeling she saw it as a hobby, not a job. And she found the thought of the financial insecurity hard to deal with.'

Stella, listening in the back, felt her heart go out to Tess. She remembered all too clearly what it was like at the beginning of Julius' and her own marriage, wandering from country to country with no money like the raggle-taggle gypsies-o. It had been fun for a year, but then Stephen had arrived and she'd desperately wanted to have a home, a place of their own, and a normal, ordinary life. The selfishness of men, even the otherwise helpful ones like Stephen, in seeing this basic female instinct as unreasonable, constantly amazed her.

'So you found someone else,' Stella commented tartly from the back. She'd suspected Josephine from the moment she'd seen her at that opening. 'Someone with a nice white Mercedes who can cope with the insecurity of living with an artist because she has plenty of money of her own.'

'The money's beside the point,' Stephen corrected her, nettled. 'Josephine believes in me as a painter and Tess didn't.'

'Are you sure she wasn't just worried about Luke and Ellie and how to pay the school fees and the mortgage?'

Stephen looked uncomfortable. He'd expected his mother to be more sympathetic. After all, she'd been married to a painter herself.

'How are the children taking it?'

'Luke not so well at first, but he seems to be coming round. Ellie seems OK. You'll see them tomorrow.'

He was grateful when they finally turned into Albemarle Street. He installed them in Brown's Hotel, their favourite, handily placed just round the corner from the gallery, and left them to settle in.

Julius, remembering that they did a wonderful dry Martini, disappeared in the direction of the bar. Stella found him there two Martinis later, ensconced in the dark and cosy bar with its stained glass and hovering waiters, regaling some American tourists with the wonders of Cork. She refused all offers of alcohol and ordered afternoon tea instead, insisting it was the best in London.

'Well,' Julius said when his new friends disappeared to rest before dinner, 'what do you think's behind this news about Stephen and Tess?'

'I'd worked it all out already. I suspect Stephen's behaving like a selfish bastard in the sacred name of Art. Just like you did. But unlike me Tess has a temper on her and she wouldn't stand for it.' She considered the array of tiny tempting cakes on the stand and chose one with care, enjoying the look of outrage on Julius's face. 'It's what I should have done to you years ago if I'd had the nerve. But I didn't so I'm still married. And Tess isn't. Which of us came off best, I wonder?'

She was rewarded with the rare satisfaction of seeing Julius choke on the olive in his dry Martini.

'So are you going or not?' Phil tapped a pencil impatiently on her desk as she waited for Tess's answer. 'I really think you should, or that cow Josephine will airbrush you out of Stephen's past and I'll have to throw a glass of wine over her or something to defend your honour, thereby losing a client.'

'You make it sound very tempting.' The truth was Tess had been changing her mind about whether she was up to the challenge all afternoon. Ellie and Luke were going with their grandparents so it didn't really make much odds if she went or not.

'Why don't you come with me and Terry if you need a bit of moral support?'

'I think I'll decide a bit nearer the time,' hedged Tess.

'It *is* nearer the time,' Phil pointed out firmly. 'The show starts in an hour and a half.'

It was only six-fifteen but the Zora Gallery was already

484

filling up with the usual freeloading journalists spiced with one or two minor celebs. Josephine and Tad Zora stood in the thick of it darlinging everyone while Stephen stayed slightly apart trying not to feel so nervous. He didn't give much of a stuff what the critics thought. Of course it would make him richer if he became a pet of the art establishment, but it wouldn't change how he painted. There was only one person's opinion he really cared about. And there was no sign of his presence yet.

The party went on, getting more and more crowded. No one seemed even to be glancing at the paintings but that, Josephine explained, was par for the course. It was considered uncool to go round studying the works through a microscope. Impression was every-thing.

One man, however, was giving them real attention: Terry Worth, who was fighting his way round with Phil carefully checking the pictures against the price list.

'Glorious, dear boy,' enthused a raffish-looking char-acter in a maroon silk shirt which had parted to show his belly button even at this early stage of the evening. 'Absolutely glorious.'

'That's John Bream from *ArtWorld*,' hissed Slouch, who'd just appeared at his elbow, 'but don't let it go to your head. His review may still be a stinker. Just depends on the quality of his hangover tomorrow. I'd insist he sticks to champagne. It gives a better class of morning after.'

Tess looked at herself critically in the mirror and decided she looked as good as she ever had. The midnight-blue silk trouser suit with a hint of white camisole showing underneath was just right, both subtle and sexy. It might not be in Josephine's class but it would certainly do.

The real problem was whether she had the nerve to go at all. Phil was right – not to go seemed cowardly, but she hadn't met Josephine face to face since the split and an art gallery was firmly in Josephine's territory.

For God's sake, she asked herself in the mirror, *what's happened to your nerve? Where's the Tess Brien who's made judges quake and reduced the opposition to jelly with a lash of her tongue?*

She gathered her things together and swept out only to bump into Lyall in the corridor putting on his coat. The appreciative look in his eyes did her no harm at all. 'You look fabulous. You should wear that colour more often. It really suits you. In fact, I'd ask you for a drink if it weren't so obvious you were already doing something.'

'Yes I am,' Tess agreed. And why not ask him too? She would hardly seem like the wronged wife with Lyall on her arm. 'But only for a while. How do you fancy coming to a private view with me?'

'Julius, for God's sake, come.' Stella had been trying to drag him away from Brown's' bar for over an hour now, and had cursed when, just as she thought she was getting somewhere, an old painting chum had walked in and offered him another drink. 'The opening started hours ago. They'll be waiting for us.'

But Julius, who was busy attacking the technical dexterity of Augustus John, proved immovable.

'Ellie, darling, you'd better go on ahead with Luke. I'll bring Grampa in a minute.'

Ellie jumped up, drawing astonished glances from the rich and restrained guests of Brown's Hotel. They

486

weren't, on the whole, used to seeing young women in ravishing tea dresses teamed with torn fishnet tights, bovver boots and tattoos that read 'DIE IN ECSTASY'.

Thankfully, because Ellie didn't feel as sophisticated as she looked, the first person she and Luke saw inside the gallery was their father, who hugged them and gave them both a glass of champagne with the instructions not to tell anyone, especially Tess. 'By the way, what's happened to Julius and Stella?'

'Stella's been trying to winkle Grampa out of the bar at Brown's for hours,' said Ellie. Then, noticing her father's disappointment, she added brightly: 'I'm sure they'll be here soon.'

Josephine, who had just come over with a photographer in tow to capture the moment when world-famous artist father and aspiring artist son were finally together, clucked with irritation and wondered if she should send Slouch round to get him. But Slouch was in such a strange mood he might end up staying in Brown's' bar just to spite her. It really was most inconsiderate of Julius not to show up. What was she going to tell Tad Zora?

She sent the photographer away and helped herself to a drink. Ellie stood behind her studying one of her father's still lifes with total absorption; oblivious to the party around her and much more interested in quizzing him about the technique he'd used. It had been the same in Capri. She'd spent hours just watching Stephen painting, and she showed real signs of talent herself. Watching them, Josephine felt a sudden leap of excitement. She'd played a vital role in persuading Stephen to paint, why not Ellie too? She'd been drawn to the girl from the beginning, loving her uncompromising personality and even the outlandish clothes which somehow suited her so well. Unobtrusively she joined the two of them just as Stephen was carried off by Slouch to meet a critic friend.

'So, Ellie, when are you going to go to art school yourself?'

Ellie looked at her warily. Without Josephine she thought her parents might still be together. 'Not for another year at least. Mum says I've got to stay on at Chelsea till after A levels.'

'And you don't want to?'

'The school's OK but the art teacher's out of the ark. She treats us all like children. It's such a waste!'

A plan occurred to Josephine. It might be difficult to carry off but it was worth a try. 'Tell you what. A friend of mine runs a private art college in Winchester. Maybe you should think of doing a foundation year there. At least they'd treat you like an adult.'

Josephine saw enthusiasm leap into Ellie's eyes. The more she thought about it the better the idea was. Having Ellie near would do Stephen the world of good – and it would greatly annoy Tess.

The same thought clearly struck Ellie. 'Mum would never agree.'

'Wouldn't she? Then we'll have to get to work on your father, won't we?'

Ellie felt a sudden wave of disloyalty at even talking like this to Josephine and made an excuse to go and look for her mother. Watching her go, Josephine realized what it was she responded to so strongly in the girl. She reminded Josephine of herself when she'd first gone off to art school, full of white-hot enthusiasm and a touching innocence that had disappeared a long time ago. How lovely to have a daughter like that, someone pretty and artistic really to share things with. And for a mad moment she wondered if maybe it wasn't too late for her and Stephen to have a daughter of their own.

She looked through the crowd for Stephen and spotted him near the door subtly looking at his watch. She could guess the reason for his agitation. Seven-forty-five and still no sign of Julius. Really, the man was a bastard. She decided to try and distract him. 'Stephen, darling, have you seen all the lovely red stickers? And there's still plenty of time to go.'

A slight hush at the doorway made her glance round to find that Julius, Stella, and a dubious-looking person who was so scruffily dressed he had to be an artist or a tramp, had finally made their entrance.

Stephen fought his way over to them eagerly, only to find that Julius, a drink in each hand, had already settled down to greet reams of old friends, showing no interest whatsoever in the pictures.

Stella, however, kissed him on both cheeks. 'Hello, darling, how's it all going? What a throng! And so many sold signs. You must be thrilled.'

'I'd be even more thrilled if I could get Father to have a look.'

'I should let him chat for a minute. You know him. He's such a social animal. I won't let him leave without looking, I promise.'

Stephen kissed his mother again, grateful that she understood.

And then he saw her. She must have just arrived. She was standing on the threshold of the noisy party looking beautiful and slightly stranded in an outfit he'd never seen before.

Josephine had seen her too, but made no move to welcome her.

Stephen started towards her, smiling. And then

489

stopped. A tall, handsome man whom he recognized vaguely from her office stepped out of the press and took her arm. To his shame, Stephen felt a flash of annoyance.

In the end it was Julius who came to their rescue. He handed them both a drink with a flourish, for all the world as though this were his party, and drew them into his ebullient group. After a few moments Lyall disappeared to have a look at the paintings and Stella drew Tess aside. 'Tess, darling, why didn't you tell us about you and Stephen?' she asked in a low voice.

'It hadn't happened last time I saw you,' Tess said carefully, immediately assuming Stella would take Stephen's part.

'This probably isn't the moment. But I just wanted to say how sorry we are. And that I hope you'll still come and stay as often as you like. With or without the children. Julius won't say anything because he's hopeless with emotion but he absolutely agrees.'

The unexpectedness of her generosity was almost too much for Tess. And then she saw Josephine bearing down on them, holding out her hand regally. 'Tess, how nice you could come. Hasn't Stephen accomplished a lot since . . .' She trailed off delicately.

'Since he left me and came to live with you?' Tess looked her in the eye. 'Yes. You must hardly have seen him.'

Josephine smiled. 'We've had our moments. A painter has to be free to paint. Now if you'd excuse me, the press are fighting each other to take Stephen's photograph with his father.'

'What an unpleasant woman,' Stella remarked a shade too loudly. 'I wonder why men are so blind when it comes to sex?'

Tess stifled a giggle. Strange that it took losing Stephen to gain his mother's affection.

Ten minutes later Lyall pushed his way through the noisy crowd, looking delighted with himself. 'Guess what? I've just bought a painting.' He took Tess downstairs to the basement to show her. Ellie and Luke followed.

Stella grabbed Julius's arm firmly. 'Come on. Time you and I went off with Stephen to see the show.'

The party was thinning out so they started on the ground floor with the landscapes, Julius in the lead, with Stella next, keeping up a flow of bright conversation, and Stephen last, nervously waiting for his father's comments. Julius walked briskly, dropping the odd casual remark. Then they went upstairs to the seascapes of Cork. Surely Julius would have some kind of reaction to this place he loved so much and in which he had spent most of his adult life? But he stood wordlessly contemplating the paintings for almost a minute until Ellie suddenly rushed in and took his hand.

'Grampa, come and see the painting Lyall's just bought for two thousand pounds!'

Stephen followed on silently, so hurt by his father's non-reaction that he hadn't taken in a word Ellie said. Julius hadn't liked his paintings, not one of them. But what had he expected? He knew his father well enough to understand that he wouldn't pretend to feel something he didn't. He should never have invited him.

In the basement Tess stood in front of the canvas of herself on the beach with Ellie and Luke. It was wonderful, yet she'd never seen it before. When exactly had Stephen painted it? It had to be after he'd left, and yet love seemed to illuminate every brushstroke. It was the most emotional painting in the whole exhibition and she felt utterly thrown by it. Behind her she heard Ellie's excited voice counterpointed by Julius's restraining one.

'There.' Ellie almost dragged Julius down the last couple of steps. 'What do you think of that?'

Julius considered it for a long moment then turned to Stephen, the beginnings of a smile lighting up his face. 'Now that's what I call a picture.'

'But you don't like any of the others?' Stephen knew he was picking at a scab but couldn't help himself.

Julius shrugged. 'You don't need my good opinion, surely? Look at all these red stickers. You're a hit. You'll be written up everywhere, from the arts mags to the *FT*.'

Tess listened, feeling for Stephen, amazed that Julius could be so obtuse. Unconsciously she touched Stephen's elbow in support. For a split second his eyes held hers, thanking her for understanding. And then he seemed to take in what was happening for the first time.

He turned to Lyall. 'I'm sorry,' he said softly, 'but I'm afraid there must have been some misunderstanding. That painting's not for sale.'

CHAPTER THIRTY-TWO

'But the woman with the dark hair who's running the exhibition's just taken a cheque,' protested Lyall.

'Then she was wrong. That painting was simply an experiment in style. It's not for sale.'

Tess flashed a look at Stephen, more confused than ever.

Stephen avoided her glance. 'Now if you'd all like to come upstairs, I think the gallery's closing.'

Back on the ground floor only the hard-core drinkers remained. Ellie and Luke dashed up to Tess. 'Mum, Mum, can we go out to dinner? Everyone's going to Ley-ons!'

Julius turned to her. 'But you're coming too, Tess, surely?'

'No,' lied Tess quickly. She'd had enough emotion for one evening. 'We've got a booking at Quaglino's.'

'How very chic,' Josephine said drily, 'while we're slumming it in Chinatown. But probably just as well. The table's only for eight and we're already thirteen.'

Stella agreed to drop the children home by taxi afterwards and they departed in the direction of Soho, a big boisterous group laughing on their way to share dim sum and shark fin soup in Ellie's favourite restaurant. Just as Tess had always imagined her family doing. She tried not to think of the last time they were there.

Lyall watched her curiously. 'Are you sure you didn't want to join them?'

Tess shook her head. She felt far too confused to want to spend an evening in that company.

'So, what's all this about a booking at Quaglino's?'

Tess blushed, feeling ridiculous, wondering whether to bluff. 'I made it up.'

'Good thing I've just booked a table at the Criterion then,' he said.

Tess laughed.

'That's better.' Lyall took her hand and tucked it into his arm. 'We'd better hurry, we're already ten minutes late.'

The evening turned out to be just what Tess needed after the volcano of emotion at the private view. Lyall was like a fine wine to Stephen's champagne, less fizz and charm but steadier and more reliable. Throughout the evening, he behaved like a perfect gentleman and referred neither to Stephen's strange behaviour nor to his own proposal. All the same when he dropped her home she found herself wondering if he was going to kiss her. He didn't. Another of the differences between him and Stephen, she was fast learning, was that Lyall always behaved well. Tess was shocked to find she was disappointed.

She closed her eyes as she sat waiting on the sofa for Ellie and Luke to come back, thinking again of the painting of the beach. There seemed to be so much love and tenderness in it. *Stop being so naïve*, she told herself firmly. It was the skill of the artist to draw on emotions remembered or even imagined, but not necessarily felt at the time.

She heard the sound of laughter and the front door opened. Luke ran into the sitting room and flung himself on to the sofa next to her, boiling over with the news that he'd had duck's feet and octopus and little dumplings that came in baskets and funny Chinese wine.

494

Ellie took in the wistfulness on Tess's face and grinned. 'And Gramma wasn't talking to Gramps and Dad wasn't talking to Josephine . . .'

Tess held out her arms, loving Ellie for having read her mind. 'You mean I didn't miss such a brilliant evening after all?'

'For God's sake, Julius' – Stella threw her bag and coat on to the bed – 'do you have to be such a mean old sod? Couldn't you see what your approval meant to Stephen?'

'Stephen doesn't need my approval,' Julius growled. 'He's never had the courtesy to tell me why he's taken up painting. He didn't even bother to turn up, you'll recall, when I went to meet him at the bloody airport in the summer.'

Stella snapped on the lights in the adjoining bathroom. 'Can't you see, you infuriating man, that that's because of how much he *does* need your approval? He's given up his job and lost his marriage all for painting and you couldn't even say what he needed you to say.'

'I praised the picture of Tess on the beach,' Julius insisted grouchily.

'Only at the expense of the rest of his work. Heavens, I've lied about enough of your paintings over the years! Anyway, maybe the reason you don't like his work is because you're too narrow. Hasn't it struck you that it's a while since you had a commission? Perhaps the truth is you're yesterday's man and you're frightened of your own son's talent. Some of those paintings were brilliant.' She slammed the door shut and retreated into a jungle of steam.

Angrily Julius helped himself from the mini-bar, despite the fact that he knew he'd had quite enough already, and turned the TV up very loud. Stupid old cow. What did she know about painting anyway? Of course he wasn't selfish. And as for being threatened, that was ridiculous.

Julius woke hung over and repentant the next morning but refused to count the number of miniatures, all empty, he'd lined up on top of the television last night. '*Mea culpa, mea culpa*,' he chanted, doing his best to look appealing.

Stella wasn't taken in for a moment. 'I should bloody well think so, and forget the boyish charm. You're nearly eighty, Julius. If you're sorry there's plenty of practical ways you could show it.'

'Like what?' Julius asked suspiciously. He didn't like the way the conversation was going.

'By taking another look at Stephen's paintings.' She got up to answer the knock on their door which with any luck would be breakfast. 'Or taking Tess on a tour of the galleries. All this nonsense about her "not understanding art" Stephen was wittering on about while that snob Josephine sets herself up as some kind of expert . . . it drives me mad! If someone had bothered to explain a few basic principles to me, my life with you would have been a lot easier. I wouldn't have had to spend years feeling inferior.'

Julius looked at her in astonishment. 'I didn't know you felt inferior.'

'No, but then there's a lot of things you don't know about me, Julius. But I think I may start telling you some of them. Now, which is it to be: Stephen's paintings or galleries with Tess?'

The latter option sounded infinitely preferable to Julius. A positive delight in fact. 'All right, you old boot. Galleries it is.'

She handed him a boiled egg, not weakening. 'I

knew you'd say that, but don't fool yourself. We're not going home till you've done the other too.'

Unusually for her, Tess was staring out of the window when Julius's call came through. Her face lit up as Jacqui told her who was on the line.

'Julius! How lovely to hear from you.'

'Tess, my dear, I don't suppose you'd like to make an old man very happy?'

'That depends on what it takes,' Tess replied warily. Julius was clearly up to something.

'I want you to spend the day with me. Highly irresponsible. I know, but I'd like to buy some pictures and I need a fresh eye.'

'Hardly mine. As Ellie'll tell you, I don't know my van Gogh from my Dürer.'

'All the more reason to come with me, then. I'll pick you up in fifteen minutes.'

'Julius, I really can't just drop everything . . .' she protested. But he'd gone. Tess looked at the piles of papers on her desk, and the text from *The Good Divorce Guide* she'd promised Lyall she'd read through. Suddenly the thought of an irresponsible day with Julius seemed wholly delightful. She buzzed Jacqui and asked her to move the one meeting she had this afternoon to another day, put on her jacket, brushed her hair and waited outside the front of their offices for Julius to arrive.

On the way out she bumped into Lyall. 'Where are you going, my pretty maid?' he asked archly. 'It can't be to court. You look far too carefree for a day of Inner London Sessions.'

'Bunking off with my father-in-law to go round galleries, but don't tell anyone.'

Lyall watched and waved as a cab bowled up and

Julius emerged to open the door for her. She really was full of surprises. Lyall just hoped this wasn't clandestine lobbying on behalf of his son. But then last night Lyall had got the distinct impression there wasn't much love lost between them. His father would be an unlikely emissary.

Julius, in his usual summer uniform of ancient cricket whites and Panama hat, raised a bushy eyebrow in Lyall's direction. 'That's the chap who came with you last night. Exact status please?'

Tess realized she didn't quite know the answer to this herself. 'He's a colleague. We're writing a book together.'

'And he'd like it to end happily ever after?'

'Hardly.' Tess was being deliberately obtuse. 'It's called *The Good Divorce Guide*.'

'Not the book. Life.'

'Don't we all?'

'OK. OK. No more personal questions, I promise.' He glanced at Tess briefly. Lyall had struck him as a very determined young man. He just hoped Stephen was sure he'd done the right thing, because with Lyall on the scene there might not be any going back.

'So,' Tess leaned back in the cab enjoying her escape – 'why me? Why not Stella?'

Julius laughed. 'She wouldn't dream of coming. Besides, I told you, I want a fresh eye.'

'But I don't have an eye at all.'

'Nonsense.' He took off his hat and put it on the back window ledge. It was a glorious June morning which even the depressing urban landscape they passed through heading eastwards away from the centre couldn't quite diminish. 'Here beginneth the lesson. Art is about *seeing*. You have a perfect right not to like what you see, but you owe it to the artist to look. It helps if you can forget your preconceptions and try and understand what he's really trying to do.'

'Now I understand what this is all about. This is a crash course in Art Appreciation so that I'll have more in common with my about-to-be-ex-husband. Isn't it a little late? Whose idea was this anyway?'

'Stella's,' admitted Julius disloyally. 'I told her it was interfering. But she just can't bear the idea of you being intimidated by That Woman. She wishes some-one had taken her aside when we were first married and told her a few basic truths. She's only trying to be helpful, you know. May I go on?'

Tess found it impossible to be angry. She nodded her head meekly. 'Please do.'

'Have you ever bought a painting?'

Tess shook her head.

'Posters?'

Tess looked slightly embarrassed. 'The usual. Sun-flowers in my room at college. Klimt during my Roman-tic Period. Oh, and a Hockney bum and pool.'

'Quite a range.'

'Oh yes, my ignorance is quite extensive.'

'Right. Uncle Julius's Rule One: Stop putting your-self down. You're entitled to like what you like.'

'Sorry. It's just that Stella's right. I find art and art criticism a bit bewildering.'

'So do I. That's why I don't have much to do with it. Just remember Julius's Rule Two: Art Criticism is Bollocks. Whenever you read any remind yourself what Braque said: You can explain everything about art except the little bit that counts. It's an industry, Tess! Like any other. It exists to sustain itself. Ignore it. Learn to look at art for yourself.'

By now the taxi was halfway down the Mile End Road. It slowed down and stopped a few yards from a white-fronted art gallery called Art East. 'Here you are, guv,' said the taxi driver. 'London's Left Bank.'

Tess got out. 'So what are we doing here? I thought Cork Street was the centre of the universe for artists.'

'Only when they're too old to be interesting. This is where it starts.' He paid the cab and handed her a brown envelope.

'What's this?'

'A thousand pounds. Rule Three. You have to spend it today.'

'Julius, is this some kind of joke?' Tess was appalled, thinking of the things she could do with a thousand pounds. 'Stephen and I have two sets of school fees and a leaky roof! I can't spend this on paintings.'

Julius smiled at her scandalized tone, while at the same time storing away the useful information about their finances. Clearly he'd have to find a way of helping out.

'Ah,' he corrected her, 'but it isn't your money, is it? It's mine. I just want you to spend it for me.'

Tess was silent for a moment, at a loss what to say next. 'But you may hate what I choose.'

'I'll take that risk. I have a suspicion that under all this protest you've got a good eye. Look, Tess, I'm a rich man. This is the most fun I've had in years. Humour me. Please.'

Tess shook her head, laughing. 'OK. You're on.'

'Atta girl.' Julius opened the door of the gallery for her. 'This gallery's cheap because she does the round of the art school degree shows and snaps up the cream. This afternoon I'll take you to a warehouse full of artist's studios. You can buy direct there without the gallery's commission. Don't wait to buy though. Follow your instincts. If you really like it, buy it. Now I'm off for a cup of tea. I'll see you later.'

With utter disregard for the oddity of his appearance in the middle of London's East End, Julius strolled into a workman's caff, ordered a fry-up and a pint of tea, and struck up a heated conversation with his immediate neighbour, a council dustcart driver, about the racing results from Sandown Park.

Tess felt a heady excitement begin to take her over as she went into the gallery and picked up a price list. This really was an adventure. She looked round. The range of paintings was enormous, from somewhat forbidding abstracts to eyecatching colourism, with one or two highly detailed figurative works. One painting caught her eye at once, but instead of giving in to its lure she walked slowly round the gallery twice. Julius was right. Knowing you were actually choosing something to have for your own made you look at the paintings with a completely different eye. Tess found herself warming to a couple of small paintings whose subtle appeal grew on you the more you studied them. But her eye still kept being drawn to her original choice.

Finally, she gave in. It was quite a large painting, perhaps three feet by three feet with the rich jewel-like colours and faintly exotic feel of a Matisse.

The gallery was empty apart from her but she heard steps behind her. 'Glorious, isn't it?' She turned to find a woman of about forty-five, dressed entirely in black, watching the painting with her. 'Utterly unfashionable of course. I thought it was the best thing at the degree shows, but the unfortunate girl who painted it had been given a rough old time by her tutors. They were into abstract expressionism and they loathed her work. Poor kid. You'd think they'd take the blinkers off and encourage an original, wouldn't you?'

Tess found herself warming as much to the sound of

the artist as to the painting. She'd never thought of pictures in terms of the person who'd produced them. She glanced at the price list. Three hundred and fifty pounds. With an extraordinary lurch of excitement she turned to the gallery owner. 'Thanks very much. I'll take it.'

'Good choice. I think she'll be very big one day and I'm not often wrong.' She stared at Tess in astonishment as Tess took out the brown envelope and counted out the money in cash. 'I'm sorry,' she apologized, realizing how rude she must appear. 'These days you get more used to Visa. By the way, there's a small picture in that corner that might interest you. Quite different in style, but in my view it's got something too.'

It turned out to be a landscape full of the haunting blues of a Tuscan dusk, and Tess loved it immediately. It was £175 and she found herself instantly dipping into her envelope again like a frenzied shopper at the January sales. At this rate she'd be broke by lunchtime. She stopped a moment and decided to think about it.

Julius was waiting outside already, a copy of the *Racing Post* under his arm. Tess's glow of excitement told him everything. He took her hand. 'So, beginning to see? Beginning to realize art isn't something you have to distrust? What did you buy?' He gestured towards her package.

'A woman sitting on a bed. The colours are glorious and jewelly, very Matisse. I adore it.'

'And?'

'I nearly bought a Tuscan landscape, all blues at dusk. But I wasn't quite so sure.'

'Are you sad you didn't buy it? Are you missing it already? Will you kick yourself when you get home?'

Tess thought for a moment. 'Yes.'

'In you go, then. Follow your instincts, remember?'

The gallery owner held it out to her, already wrapped. 'I knew you'd come back,' she smiled. 'After twenty-five years I know the symptoms. I hope you go on loving them.' She took the money from Tess and gave her a receipt. 'I'll take either of them back any time you change your mind.'

Tess thanked her. They obviously shared the same instincts, so maybe her own weren't so bad after all.

After introducing Tess to the delights of jellied eels and pie and mash served with lurid green liquor at an emporium in the Old Kent Road Julius took her to a warren of artists' studios in the Isle of Dogs where she bought another painting, this time so big they could hardly get it in the cab, and also a small sculpture of a man holding a baby, with one hand outstretched as though warding off some danger. A thought hit her as they tied the vast canvas to the taxi roof. 'Where on earth am I going to put it?'

'Ah.' Julius raised an eyebrow. 'I didn't tell you the one catch about today, did I?'

Tess stared at him, devastated. Surely he wasn't about to say this had all been some monstrous joke and she had to take them all back?

'They're coming with me to Ireland. It's the only way Stella and I can make sure you come and visit. To see the pictures if not us.' He squeezed her hand affectionately. 'In fact, why don't you come and visit them this summer? Make us your summer holiday again? The children love it and you'd get a bit of freedom.'

Tess thanked him, touched that they still wanted her to be part of their life as well as their grandchildren. 'You shouldn't throw offers like that around. I might just take you up on it.'

He dropped her off at her office and went on to the hotel to leave the paintings. Stella wasn't back yet. He was about to head for the familiar comfort of the bar when he remembered his second labour. A tougher one altogether, this.

At almost five, the Zora Gallery was deserted, with just one of the two blond assistants inside. Julius nodded to him and went straight upstairs to the sea-scapes. The truth was he hadn't felt neutral about them, as Stephen thought. He had actively disliked them.

He stood in front of one and stared at it. Maybe he should try taking a dose of his own medicine? He'd told Tess to drop her preconceptions and *look*. Try and see what it was the artist was trying to do.

He stood, still and concentrated, staring at the paint-ing, trying to see through its outlandish colours to the familiar scene beneath. Gradually the impact and force of the work, its almost frightening sense of the power of the sea began to take hold of him until he could hear it pounding in his ears and almost taste the fear of the fishermen as they prayed to get home safe to port. And the words filtered into his brain: a Turner for our times.

After the intensity and even confusion of feelings he'd been through in the gallery, Julius didn't feel like being quizzed by Stella. He wandered down towards Piccadilly Circus and up Shaftesbury Avenue heading vaguely for the French pub. Then he had a thought. Muriel's. The alma mater of artistic rascals. He hadn't been there for years. He made for Dean Street and slipped down into the basement of the Colony Club, as it was officially known. Sad that Francis Bacon would no longer be propping up the bar as he had done for so many years, or Muriel herself, made up like a chorus girl. She had long since stopped bellowing orders to her staff, gammy leg up on a bar stool, stick in hand, but there would be other familiar faces there.

'Julius!' shrieked a voice as soon as he walked in. 'I thought you were dead!' Julius smiled. It felt like coming home.

He headed in the direction of the voice, nodding at people he recognized on his way to the other end of the bar. A lot of them were painters. His sort of painters. The kind who were happier talking about the winner of the Grand National than of this year's Turner Prize.

The owner of the voice turned out to be an Irish artist called McDade who Julius had known thirty years ago and hardly seen since. His long hair, stained at the ends by nicotine, a theme picked up by the coordinating yellow of his fingertips, was not a pretty sight. But he wasn't a bad painter. Julius persuaded him off his barstool with the promise of a double Jameson's and carried him off to a dark corner of the club.

'What's this, Julius?' the Irishman cackled. 'Not trying to seduce me, I hope?' He guffawed at his own joke, bringing on a violent attack of smoker's coughing.

'Sorry, McDade, you're not my type. But I do have a favour to ask. There'll be a drink in it for you. Quite a big drink as it happens, provided you keep your mouth shut. I want you to buy some pictures for me. But I don't want anyone to know I bought them.'

McDade shook his head at the wonder of the scheme. 'And who would these pictures be by?'

Julius knocked back his Irish whiskey. 'One Stephen Gilfillan. A new painter.'

'Stephen Gilfillan? Now where have I read about

that name . . . I have it. Today, In *The Times*, no less.'
He looked puzzled, clearly dredging around in the
drink-damaged recesses of his mental retrieval system.
'Now wait a minute. Isn't Stephen Gilfillan . . .'

'. . . My son. He is indeed, McDade. That's why
I don't want him to know. He might think it's
nepotism.'

'And is it?'

Julius considered this proposition briefly. 'No. It'd
be nepotism if I bought them without liking them.
But I do like them, so it's simply anonymous art
collection.'

'Done,' said McDade. 'Which gallery did you say it
was?'

'I didn't. It's the Zora Gallery in Cork Street. You
could go tomorrow morning. I'll get you a banker's
draft. Then you can arrange for them to be sent when
the exhibition ends.'

Stephen looked at the pile of faxes that had come in
from the US overnight almost with relief. It meant a
lot of work but at least it would take his mind off his
anger with his father. He'd been neglecting the perfume launch for weeks in his hurry to get ready for the
exhibition and now it was all over. The reaction in the
press had been terrific. And though a lot of papers
carried photographs of him and Julius, there were
surprisingly few snide pieces suggesting it was the
father–son connection that explained Stephen's sudden
emergence. People actually seemed to like his work.
Everyone except Julius.

Refusing to give in to the bitterness that beckoned
seductively to him, Stephen got down to his correspondence. He'd only just started when Josephine appeared smiling smugly.

'Guess what? You've got a collector. Tad rang to say someone came back this morning and bought five seascapes at three thousand each.'

'Bloody hell! That's incredible! So who's my new patron?'

'Well, that's the mystery. Tad's assistant says he'd never seen him before. And they were all paid for by banker's draft so we can't work it out from that either.' She broke away and sat down in the chair opposite his desk. 'What's it matter, anyway. Do you know how much you've made so far? Twenty-five thousand! Not bad for a new artist. And another week to run.'

'Thank God for that. Now I can pay more of Ellie and Luke's school fees. They must have been crippling Tess.'

'Now that you mention it,' Josephine threw in casually, 'Ellie tells me she wants to leave that school because they treat art so childishly. She'd like to do a foundation year at art college instead. As a matter of fact, I've been looking into a few. There's a very good one here in Winchester, and they'll take her now if her portfolio's any good. She could live here during term times and you'd be able to see her again.'

'Tess would never agree. She wants Ellie to get a rounded education.'

'But Ellie's desperate to leave and if she's talented I take her point. The school's clearly doing nothing for her. Surely you can see that.'

'She's never mentioned it to me.'

'Then why don't you talk to her about it?'

Deftly Stephen changed the subject. There was nothing he'd love more than being able to see Ellie. But he also knew how tough it would be on Tess.

*

'Right. That's the legal stuff sorted out, but what about the emotional advice.' Lyall leaned back in his chair watching her eagerly. It was ten o'clock at night and all around them lay the debris of an Indian take-away. 'You've been living it after all. What makes it easier?'

Tess winced. He was right, of course. She ought to know. Could anything make this awful experience less painful? Was there really such a thing as a good divorce if either of you still cared? She looked away, not wanting him to see the pain in her eyes. 'Not blaming each other, I suppose, even if only for the sake of your kids.' She paused, realizing this was probably true of her too. 'Recognizing there was prob-ably wrong on both sides. Not using the children as emotional footballs.' At least she knew better than to do that. 'Or,' she added, knowing this was nearer home, 'as confidants because you're so unhappy.'

'Sounds marvellous,' Lyall agreed, 'but a bit unrealis-tic, don't you think? People who get divorced are hurt and angry. Especially if one of them goes off with someone else.'

Tess knew at once Lyall was referring to her but she refused to take the bait. 'Certainly. And they want it to be someone's *fault*. Usually not theirs.'

Lyall chewed his pencil thoughtfully. If she wasn't going to take the hint he'd have to be more direct. 'Have you thought about it yourself at all?'

She looked horrified. 'Divorce? No, not really. It hasn't been long enough.'

'Five months. You split at the beginning of February and it's the end of June.' She was astonished at his accuracy. 'Don't you think you ought to think about it? Wouldn't it be better for the children if you did? Then they'd know where they stood. And that time could be counting towards your mutual separation. Unless you want to go for adultery.'

One glance at Tess's face told him he'd gone too far.

'OK, then,' he said lightly, 'if you won't agree to divorce Stephen, what about letting me cook you dinner on Friday instead?'

She laughed at the absurdity of the comparison, realizing he was trying to retrieve the situation. She'd never been to his flat and she was quite curious to see it. It might fill in some of the gaps she found puzzling about Lyall's lack of personal life. 'All right, it's a deal.'

When she got home she was surprised to find Ellie waiting up for her in the sitting room.

'Hello, darling.' Tess sank into the feathery embrace of the sofa never wanting to move again. 'I thought you'd be in bed by now. It's almost eleven.'

'I stayed up because I wanted to talk to you. About school.'

Tess felt her spirits plummet. She didn't feel up to this. 'What's the matter with school?'

'It's my art teacher. She treats painting like it's flower arranging or some other irrelevant hobby no one in their right mind would choose over History or Physics. She's just so narrow. You'd think she was deliberately setting out to discourage us.'

Tess listened, feeling the faint stirrings of guilt. The teacher did seem, as Ellie said, rather limited. 'But if you left now that might mean the end of any chance of university.'

'Mum, you know I don't want to go to university. I want to go to art school! Not that I've got a chance in hell with Mrs Browne. She's hardly even *heard* of Picasso!' This was clearly the final nail in the teacher's coffin in Ellie's eyes.

'Look, Ellie . . .' Tess hated herself for coming out with this. 'Think how awful it would be for Luke if you left and went off to art college.'

'Mum, that's blackmail!'

She was right of course. Was it Luke or her who needed Ellie to be around?

'Anyway, you're too young to get into art college. You'd need A levels.'

'Not a private art college. Providing they think I'm good enough I could start right away. After all, I'm seventeen now.'

'Ellie, darling, I couldn't afford it. I can barely scrape together the school fees now, let alone fees for a private art college.'

'OK.' Ellie retreated under her Walkman with the air of complete dejection so well known to parents of teenagers. 'But if I fail art A level we'll know whose fault it was.'

'You know you really ought to get things sorted out on a proper footing with Tess now that you've got some money.'

Josephine had been thinking about having this conversation with Stephen for weeks and had finally dared to start it in the relaxed atmosphere of their favourite restaurant. 'For the children's sake if not for your own. They need proper provision.'

'You mean getting divorced?'

'Well, at least going and talking to someone about it. Tess obviously has the advantage of you here. It's her job.'

Stephen put down his knife and fork. 'For God's sake, Jo. Tess wouldn't take advantage.'

'I should hope not. But why don't you go and talk to someone? There's a marvellous man a lot of my friends use. He could at least tell you the parameters. You know what they say? Till you get divorced it's hard on the children because they dream of you getting back together all the time.'

Stephen thought about Josephine's suggestion. It made a lot of sense at least to be aware what might face them. He pushed his slight feeling of reluctance to one side. 'OK, give me his name and I'll have a talk. Just to find out the lie of the land.'

The rest of the week passed in a flurry of work and by Friday and the date with Lyall, Tess realized she was quite nervous. She dressed carefully, laying out her smartest black suit. There wouldn't be time to come home and change after work. Tonight would just be a quiet dinner. Nothing untoward was going to happen. All the same she put on her matching underwear, convincing herself it was just for her confidence. Every woman knew you felt better about yourself if your knickers matched your bra.

Downstairs Ellie stared at her, forgetting her intention to give her mother the cold shoulder in her surprise at how glam Tess looked. 'Aye aye,' she asked rudely, 'is the faithful Lyall about to get his reward on earth tonight? I suppose he's earned it.'

'What are you on about, Ellie?' Tess switched the kettle off before it turned the kitchen into a jungle of steam.

'Oh, Mum.' Ellie shook her head. 'You'd be absolutely useless at having an affair. Since when do you wear sheer black tights and high heels to the office and smother yourself in Paloma Picasso? With all that perfume on at least he'll be able to tell where you are in the dark.'

At this, Luke abandoned his breakfast and ran out

of the kitchen. 'Even in Sweden,' Inge corrected Ellie severely, 'we do not talk about our parents having affairs in front of the children.'

Fortunately Tess had a very busy day and forgot all about dinner until Lyall buzzed her.

'What time will you be ready?'

'Not for a while. Why don't you go on ahead?' She was relieved to see Jacqui putting on her coat. She didn't want an audience tonight. 'I'll come along in half an hour or so.' Although they'd been out together often she still preferred leaving separately.

A quarter of an hour later she went to the Ladies to freshen up and check her appearance, feeling pleased with herself that she'd managed to keep their friendship secret so far. She'd just sprayed on some more perfume and brushed her hair and was about to leave.

'Be gentle with him,' counselled a voice from one of the loos. 'I get the impression he's more innocent than he looks.'

It was Jacqui.

By the time she rang Lyall's bell Tess was feeling like a silly sixteen-year-old. This was ridiculous. Then she realized it had been nearly twenty years since her last date. No wonder she was a little nervous.

Lyall answered the door almost immediately. As soon as she stepped inside his flat Tess felt disconcerted by it. The building was smart and select but the interior was utterly impersonal, rather like a dentist's waiting room. She'd always known Lyall threw a lot into his work, yet it was amazing how little of himself he seemed to have put into his home. There were no flowers, no personal knick-knacks, no photos, no trophies. If *Through the Keyhole* came here they'd go away none the wiser.

How strange, she thought as he took the bottle of wine she held out, for Lyall to have so much confidence at work, and so little in his own taste. One thing was absolutely certain. There was no sense of a woman's touch here. Lyall was a classic bachelor. He would probably be able to live happily in a hotel providing there was room service and his shirts were ironed.

He showed her into the kitchen and here, to her relief, there was a little warmth and atmosphere. He had laid the table with a checked tablecloth and Vivaldi was playing on the cassette deck.

'Do you have any candles?' she asked. Eventually he found a Christmas one, which he stuck in a bottle. As he did so she noticed his hands were shaking and realized that he was at least as nervous as she was. At once she felt more relaxed. There would be no question, she thought almost wistfully, of who would be the one in control tonight.

To her horror a memory swam into her consciousness: of the first time she'd walked into Stephen's chaotic house at college, so brimming with personality it had overawed her. Her own room had been far more like Lyall's. In Stephen's hall there had been a life-size statue of Marilyn Monroe, skirt billowing, which served as a coat-rack, and an ancient 'What The Butler Saw' slot machine with a pile of old pennies next to it. Even though it had been the seventies his sitting room contained no Habitat junk like every other student had, but antique bergère sofas, so old the cane was coming undone, covered in piles of balding velvet cushions in glorious faded colours. And everywhere, books. From ancient orange Penguin editions of George Orwell, poets she'd never heard of like Pablo Neruda, to a well-thumbed copy of *Catch 22*. Coming from a household where they hadn't owned a single bookcase, Tess had been staggered.

For God's sake stop comparing them, she told herself. Stephen and Lyall were completely different. And what's more Stephen had left her.

'Glass of wine?' asked Lyall, bringing her gratefully back to the present.

The meal was surprisingly good – Lyall turned out to be a keen cook – and it passed very companionably. Then there was delicious fresh-ground coffee with cognac and Lyall had bought some extravagant Belgian chocolates.

Afterwards they sat on the ugly sofa in his unprepossessing sitting room and listened to more music.

'Another brandy?' Tess shook her head and they smiled at each other. Very slowly he reached out and touched her face. Tess studied him for a moment, the springy dark hair which often looked so untidy, the serious brown eyes, the naturally fit body. And she saw what it was that made him so distinctive. Lyall was handsome without the usual trappings of good looks. He had a solitary air of never having quite fitted in which she found both touching and appealing. They had both grown away from their backgrounds, and she understood him.

Her marriage to Stephen was over and it was time she admitted it. Fantasies like that at the gallery the other night were simply that. Fantasies. What she needed was someone real, someone to hold her, someone she could trust who cared about her. And she knew Lyall did. She'd once asked her friend Catherine what she wanted in a man. Catherine had said: 'When I look up from the fire I want him to be there.' Lyall was that kind of man. He had already offered, with passion and intensity, to take care of her. Sitting here tonight she felt it was far too seductive an offer to refuse.

She put her glass down carefully on the table next to her and took his hand. 'Why don't we go to bed?' she asked, realizing it was the first time in her life that she'd ever said those words to anyone but Stephen.

Chapter Thirty-three

Tess was grateful that the light in the bedroom was dim. She'd thought for an awful moment there might be a hundred-watt bulb to contend with.

Gently they undid each other's clothes and lay on the bed. Lyall had a kind of innocence about him, almost an air of gratitude, not pathetic but open and vulnerable, as though he were offering his whole self to her, that was utterly different from Stephen's laughing passion but which affected her deeply all the same. She slipped under the bedclothes and held out her arms to him and they made love.

If the earth didn't exactly move for her, she felt safe and comforted, like a refugee who has come to a warm place after a long, cold walk and is suddenly treated like a princess.

And she knew, in one swift moment, that Lyall would want to marry her. Not now perhaps, but later. That if she accepted, there would never be a question of divorce or infidelity. There would be complete security and she would never, ever, have to worry about money again.

For a brief second a question flashed into her mind: Why can't we love people who think we're wonderful? And then she dismissed it and folded herself into Lyall's protective arms.

At work the next day Tess was determined to keep the change in her relationship with Lyall as quiet as possible. Thank God he wasn't the boasting in the locker-room type. She knew she could rely on him not to go spreading tales about notches on his bed.

But her case wasn't helped by the large bunch of red roses that arrived for her mid-morning. Jacqui eyed them, wickedly.

'From a grateful client, I expect,' Tess said primly.

'Ah,' Jacqui nodded, 'would that be the same grateful client who put his head round the door five minutes ago and asked if his flowers had arrived?'

Tess rattled her papers loudly and busied herself with some quite unnecessary work. Maybe Lyall wasn't quite the soul of discretion she'd taken him for.

Although she'd spent part of the last two nights with Lyall, Tess had been careful to slip away in the early hours so that she'd be there in the morning for Ellie and Luke.

The sun had only just started filtering through her curtains and her alarm hadn't gone off when Ellie arrived, already dressed for school, carrying a pot of tea and Tess's mail, plus a white vellum envelope addressed to herself.

'What a treat. A cup of tea *and* a visit from my daughter.' She eyed the tray. 'That's a very posh letter. Who's it from? Or shouldn't I ask?'

'Actually, it's an offer of a place at the Crane School of Art in Winchester. Oh, Mum, please let me go! It's a really good school, I've asked lots of people. After all, you don't need me any longer' – she glanced at her mother slyly – 'now that you've got Lyall.'

Tess ignored this, trying not to show her hurt that Ellie wanted to leave so badly. 'And just how do you propose I pay for it? I'd have to pay your fees at Chelsea as well. I just don't have the money, Ellie.'

Then the blow fell. 'Josephine says she'll pay and I can stay there during the term so I'd see Dad all the time and it won't cost any board and lodging. Please, Mum . . .'

Tess was stunned. Until today this had been a wild idea. Now it was suddenly a concrete proposal. Bloody Josephine. First Stephen. Now Ellie.

'And what does Dad have to say about all this?' She couldn't believe Stephen would have sanctioned it behind her back.

At which Ellie, sensing victory, told a lie. 'Oh, Dad says it'll be great to see more of me.'

And with that low blow she carried the day. Tess knew she of all people couldn't commit the cardinal sin of fighting over Ellie. 'Are you sure this is what you really want to do?'

'Yes,' Ellie nodded enthusiastically, 'I'm absolutely sure this is what I really want to do.'

'I suppose you'd better do it then.' Hearing the sad resignation in her mother's voice Ellie began to feel hideously guilty, but a soaring sense of excitement at the thought of going to art school took over, drowning every other feeling and filling her with joy.

Stephen walked down Cork Street towards the Zora Gallery wondering if he'd taken leave of his senses. What did it matter who'd bought his seascapes? And yet, apart from the painting of Tess, they were the pictures of which he felt proudest, and not knowing who had them felt like giving away your children without finding out if they were going to a good home first. So far his efforts to track down the buyer had failed dismally and the only option left was to quiz the people who'd been working in the gallery.

He knocked on the glass door and a young man looked up. The exhibition was over now but by a stroke of luck the right assistant was in the gallery. But he had no idea who the man was, beyond the fact that he was Irish. However, at least he was able to give Stephen a description.

Blond Adonis no. 2, who was restocking the fridge, a task that seemed to strike him as far more vital than selling Stephen's pictures, paused between stacking bottles of Pouilly Fumé. 'Did he have gross yellow hair and fingers to match?' he enquired.

His friend considered this proposition. 'I don't know about the hair, but the fingers ring a bell. He offered me an untipped Caporal, full strength.' Even the thought of such an abomination made him cough. 'And me with my asthma!'

'Try the Colony Club in Dean Street. I think I've seen him in there propping up the bar.'

'Thanks very much.' Stephen was beginning to feel like Sam Spade on the track of a loan shark. He had to admit it was rather fun. 'You've been a great help.' He delicately placed a tenner on the counter. 'Have a drink on me.'

The first assistant looked disdainful. 'I don't touch stimulants since I've been on the programme.'

'The programme?'

'At the Detox clinic. And he's a vegan.'

'Ah. Well, perhaps a vegetarian pizza on me then?'

Stephen finally found the Colony Club sitting oddly amongst the refurbished eateries and smart clothes shops that were taking over Soho, pushing out the Walk-Up-and-Wait tarts' flats thanks to the higher rents they were prepared to pay. A prostitute in Soho these days was about as rare a sight as a nun in Raymond's Revuebar.

It was almost four in the afternoon, when even the most hardened expense-account luncher was thinking about getting back to work, but Muriel's was still crowded. The Colony's success had historically been as an afternoon drinking club, a refuge for those lost souls who had nowhere to go between pub chucking-out time at three p.m. and five-thirty when they opened again. Now the licensing laws had been changed so that many pubs never closed, but amongst Muriel's customers the habit had stuck.

Stephen spotted the yellow-haired man at once. He was sitting behind a large Bells, thin as a bag of bones against the incongruous red plush, snoring gently. Stephen asked the barman his name.

'One Sean McDade, gentleman painter,' supplied the barman, 'who's asking?'

'Just an acquaintance. What's his usual?'

'Anything as long as someone else is paying.'

'Make it a large whisky, just to keep his other one company. And something for yourself.'

The barman poured himself an orange juice and put some of Stephen's change in a jar.

Stephen made his way through the crowd of drinkers and sat down opposite Sean McDade. McDade sat up with a start and eyed the newly arrived whisky as though he had finally witnessed a miracle.

'Hello, there,' Stephen greeted him. 'Didn't I see you at the Stephen Gilfillan opening?'

McDade sat up and addressed himself to his whisky. 'Well, now. Funny you should say that. You see, I don't know Stephen Gilfillan from Adam yet I was asked to go in, brazen as bejasus, and slap a banker's draft for fifteen grand down on the counter to buy five of his paintings. And I got a drink meself out of it.' McDade rocked with laughter at this stroke of good fortune.

'And who was this generous benefactor of the arts?' A look of low cunning crossed McDade's face. Maybe he'd said too much already. 'Well now, I can't tell you that. That was part of the bargain.'

Stephen ordered another large whisky for him. 'Come on, now. It's such a good story. I'm very discreet and I don't really move in the art world as such.'

'Oh, it gets better, believe me.'

'I won't mention it to a soul.'

This time the Irishman dissolved into a paroxysm of laughter so intense that Stephen had to get him a glass of water.

'Well, the queerest thing of all is that I hardly know him except by reputation of course.'

'Who?'

'The chap who got me to buy them.'

For one moment Stephen wondered whether it could be the black-caped grandee he'd met at the Chelsea Arts Club. The one who'd admired his work. But it seemed highly unlikely.

'And who was that?' Stephen tried not to let his exasperation show.

The old painter looked over his shoulder dramatically, as though a spy might be listening who would whip away his commission. 'Julius Gilfillan. You see that's the funny thing. He's Stephen Gilfillan's father. Now what do you make of that?'

Stephen stared at the man, thinking he must have got it wrong. But how could he? Everyone knew Julius's face. And this man was a painter. He had to be telling the truth.

Stephen got to his feet abruptly, leaving Sean McDade still chuckling and admonishing him not to tell anyone. He walked along Oxford Street, then turned left down Regent Street towards the Aer Lingus booking office.

There was a flight in an hour and a half. Back out on the street the evening rush hour had begun so he ran down Regent Street towards Piccadilly Underground to get the tube instead.

What the hell, he'd like to know, did his father think he was up to?

It was after ten by the time he ran up the imposing steps of Killamalooe House and rang the bell. Hardly any lights were on in the house. For a mad moment he realized he should have checked Brown's Hotel. Maybe they were still in London. And then, after two or perhaps three minutes, a bolt was drawn back and his mother stood before him in her dressing gown, looking startled.

'Good heavens, Stephen darling! What a lovely surprise. What is it that brings you here?'

'I just wanted to know, Father,' Stephen demanded, 'what you meant by buying my paintings in this hole-in-corner way when we both know you loathe them? I suppose you thought at least you could hide them away so they couldn't besmirch the great Julius Gilfillan's reputation?'

Julius, also in his dressing gown, looked across the kitchen table at his son, silent and angry, making no attempt to deny the accusation which he clearly thought beneath consideration.

Stephen couldn't help noticing how thin and frail he seemed without his jaunty clothes and he felt a pang of pity. Until he remembered how often Julius had hurt him over the years. Was hurting him still.

Finally Stella, losing patience with both of them, weighed in. 'Come with me please, Stephen.' She swept along the corridor to the main drawing room and threw open the doors.

There, in the room Julius loved most, all the paintings Stephen had grown up with – Augustus John, Duncan Grant, even a tiny Picasso drawing – had been rearranged. And right in the centre of the wall in the most favoured position of all, were his own five seascapes.

Stephen was speechless. These weren't locked away in some attic to protect the family name. They were displayed in pride of place.

He turned to Julius, aware that his father had followed.

'But I don't understand. You hated them. The only one you liked was of Tess and the children.'

'Your mother had a go at me the night of the show. Said I was a selfish bastard.' He half smiled at her. 'Can't think where she got that idea. And that I was threatened by you. That any fool could see your paintings were good. So I went back. I stayed an hour just looking at these five. And she was right. I did feel threatened by them. They were so different from anything of mine. I suppose I realized I was the past and you were the future. So I bought them.' He grinned his devilish grin. 'Just as an investment, you understand.'

There was a moment's silence as Stephen took in the fact that what he had wanted all his life had finally happened. His father thought that something he'd done was good. He stood, overcome by emotion, unable to move or to find any words.

In the end it was Julius who spoke first. 'Forgive me, Stephen, I haven't always been the best of fathers.' To Stephen's astonishment he heard the catch of strong emotion in his father's voice.

'Maybe not the best.' He wanted to reach out a hand. His father had never been one for admissions or apologies. 'But certainly the most entertaining.'

Julius opened his arms and Stephen fell into them. For the first time in his life he could feel the warmth of his father's breath and the tickle of his beard. Ordinary sensations that were known to every child but were completely new to Stephen. To his horror he had to choke back a sob.

'All I can say is you're both very lucky,' rang out Stella's voice from behind them, brisk to hide the tears. 'You got the chance to make up while you're living. Most people end up waiting till one of them's dead.'

'Nonsense, woman.' Julius was instantly back on his old form. 'Stephen has no intention of dying, have you, Stephen?'

Standing there among the paintings Stephen laughed out loud. And his laugh echoed down the wide corridors, reminding him that though he couldn't forget the pain of the past in one single moment, it might still be possible for them to put it behind them and to start again.

Josephine looked at her watch for the sixth time. It was well after eleven p.m. and she had no idea where Stephen was. The only clue she had was that he'd disappeared this morning on the track of his mysterious buyer. He wasn't the type suddenly to take off on a pub or nightclub crawl. She only hoped to God this sudden departure wasn't connected with the conversation she'd started on divorce. Maybe she'd jumped the gun? It was so difficult to know how to predict his reactions. He'd seemed, at the time, to take it in reasonable part, but what if she'd scared him? She pushed from her mind the crazy idea that he could have gone to see Tess and that one thing had led to another.

She was in bed, with one eye on the television and one on the clock, when the phone finally rang and Stephen announced that he was calling from Ireland and that he'd found out the identity of the buyer. It had been Julius, for Christ's sake! Pleasure sang out from his voice, so that she couldn't help smiling in unison, no matter how irritated she felt at his disappearance and at Julius's infuriating behaviour. Why couldn't he have behaved like anyone else and just bought the paintings in the conventional way?

She said goodnight, angry with herself at her silly imaginings about Tess. She really should have more confidence in her power over Stephen. As she lay trying to get to sleep, Julius's sardonic face kept appearing in front of her, his watery blue eyes, mocking as ever, seemed to train themselves on her, stripping away the layers of wealth and sophistication to the person beneath. Bloody man. There was something about Julius she didn't trust. Underneath all that crap about the artistic temperament and the kind of licence it had to be given, she sensed a mind at least as acute and manipulative as her own. And she had this unshakable feeling that it was ranged against her.

At first, watching the sunlight fighting its way into the grand bedroom with its shuttered windows and ornate fading drapes. Stephen couldn't recall where he was. Then, as it came back to him, he leaped out of bed, feeling like he had when he was a small boy on the first day of the holidays, knowing the fields were beckoning to him. He threw open the shutters and the windows behind and looked out at the glorious sight before him. June had turned into July but the heat still held an early summer freshness. The garden, under Stella's watchful eye, bloomed riotously with a million old-fashioned roses stretching down through almost an acre towards the sea.

Stephen grabbed a towel from the bathroom, put yesterday's shirt over his boxer shorts and ran down to the beach. After one quick look to make sure he was alone, he stripped off and dived into the sea, relishing the shock of the clear blue water. He swam in a straight and concentrated line out towards the horizon, then flipped on to his back to watch the sun slowly climbing in the sky. It was probably about ten. Feeling suddenly ravenous he turned back and swam to shore, towelling himself vigorously dry then tramping across the shingle towards the house. He stopped to remove a pebble from his shoe and caught sight of the guest cottage and the path to Cowrie Beach, and a brief but sharp sense of waste pierced his contentment as he remembered how they'd made love there. It seemed like a lifetime ago, yet it was only a year.

Without intending it, he found his steps heading out along the narrow path. The beach was empty and silent, covered as usual with its carpet of shells. He stooped and sifted a handful through his fingers. A tiny, perfect cowrie embedded itself between his second and third fingers, obstinately refusing to be dropped back among the thousands of others. Stephen put it in his pocket and turned towards the house.

The front door of Killamalooe stood open as it usually did and once in the hall he caught the smell of Irish bacon, always the best in the world to him, and the aroma of soda bread toasting. He followed his nose. Stella stood by the Aga making potato cakes and to his amazement Julius was sitting at the table.

Stephen sat down opposite his father with a smile, dripping slightly on to the stone-flagged floor, and reached for the coffee pot. 'I thought you never ate breakfast.'

'Not if I can help it,' Julius agreed. 'If I do she tries to kill me with cholesterol.'

'You've survived plenty of other threats in your lifetime. Drink. Syphilis. God knows what else,' Stella pointed out tartly. 'I think you can handle a little animal fat.'

Julius ignored her. 'Anyway, what I came down to say was that if you wanted to come over here some time to paint I expect I could find some room in my studio.'

Stephen stopped mid-pour, remembering how sacred Julius's studio had always been, and how angry he got with Stella for even tidying it. 'You know, Father,' he said, holding Julius's gaze for a brief moment, 'I might well take you up on that. It really is almost paradise here.'

'Right.' Stella plonked a groaning plate down in front of him. 'That's enough emotion for one day or you'll both end up with indigestion.'

After breakfast Stephen went for a long walk out towards the tower, only returning for a late lunch. There was a mid-afternoon flight to London he could get if he hurried. As he ran upstairs for his jacket a flash of colour caught his eye in a corner of the panelled hall. He retraced his steps. It was a large oil painting of a woman sitting on a bed, with a slight suggestion of Matisse, but a strong individual style of its own. It didn't seem to be Julius's taste, but then, as he'd just discovered, Julius's taste was broadening to include all sorts of dangerous and subversive styles of painting. Even his. Next to it was a small landscape in blue tones, charming rather than arresting, but with a discreet and evocative appeal. In front of it on a small plinth was a stone statue of a naked man holding a baby which reminded him faintly of the works of the Norwegian sculptor Vigelund, who had filled a whole park in Oslo with tender and wonderful nudes of people at different moments in the life cycle. But this work, while sharing his humanity, was more delicate than a Vigelund. And then the final canvas caught his eye. It was enormous, perhaps five by six feet, an abstract landscape of what looked like an Irish bog in pale yellows and shades of purple. Stephen loved it. He squinted hard at the signature, which serpented illegibly in the right-hand corner.

'Haunting, isn't it?' came Julius's voice from behind him.

'Wonderful. I love the abstraction of the pattern. And those brilliantly concrete colours. Who's the artist?'

'I don't know.' Julius leaned down casually to inspect the signature, so that Stephen couldn't see his face when he spoke again. 'Tess bought it. These are all hers. I'm just caretaking them for a while.'

'Tess?' The squawk of surprise made Julius smile, but he was subtle enough to disguise it.

'Absolutely. Her instincts are unbeatable. She just gets impatient with the theory. And who could blame her? There's so much crap talked by the critics.'

'Since when have you and Tess swapped tales of art criticism?' Stephen asked suspiciously.

'Oh, we spent a happy day browsing round galleries together when I was over for your opening. I wanted someone to advise me about broadening out. And Tess has a wonderfully fresh eye.'

'But she's not interested in painting. That was one of our problems. She treated it like a rather irritating hobby.'

'Maybe you didn't take the trouble to help her over the hurdles. For someone of her background it must have been difficult. Art clearly didn't feature much. It was more "The Green Lady" above the mantelpiece. You know, the other day she said something I think'd interest you. That she'd always thought art was about beauty so she distrusted it when it wasn't beautiful. Now she realizes it's about ways of seeing. I thought that was very perceptive.' Tactful, for once, Julius took himself off, leaving Stephen staring at the paintings.

'Tess, there you are,' Jacqui shouted as Tess emerged from a dreary management meeting which had dragged on most of the morning instead of the ninety minutes that had been scheduled for it. There seemed to be nothing but meetings since Patricia had had such a stake in the running of the firm. 'I've got Leonard Savoury's secretary on the line. He wonders if you could spare him an hour?'

Tess raised an eyebrow, intrigued to know what Savoury felt he had to discuss with her. The Eileen McDonald case was firmly over in her book. Maybe there was some new development she hadn't been expecting.

'OK. Book him in some time next week, would you?'

Jacqui relayed this to the girl on the other end of the phone. 'Could it be at his office, then? He's in court all next week apparently.'

How typical of Leonard Savoury. He was the kind of man who tried to get one over on you even when you were doing *him* a favour. But she wasn't going to get into game-playing over status. That was men's stuff. 'Make it first thing then. I'll drop in on my way to work.'

As Jacqui booked the meeting into the diary Tess smiled in satisfaction at the memory of the last time she'd seen Savoury, soaked in Eileen's champagne. God, she loathed the man. He was everything she despised about the law. No trick would be too low, no one too vulnerable for him to attack. How she'd enjoyed beating him!

Stephen looked out of the aeroplane window at the magical view of cotton-wool clouds infused by the late afternoon sunshine. A feeling of unaccustomed peace and wellbeing flowed through him which he recognized with surprise as happiness. For the first time in his life everything seemed to be falling into place. His painting, his troubled relationship with his father . . . but there was still one thing that wasn't. His feelings for Tess. What Julius had said about not taking the trouble to help her understand art had tolled a giant bell of recognition in his brain. Perhaps the gap between them had been more his fault than hers.

The stewardess arrived at that moment and offered him a drink. He accepted a little bottle of red wine, smiling in content as the sun lit it up a jewel-like red. The stewardess smiled back. You rarely got anyone half as attractive as him on this flight. Involuntarily she glanced down at his ring finger. Married. Always the same story.

At Heathrow Stephen, luggage-free, walked straight through the barrier before all the other passengers and headed for the tube station to Waterloo. It was only six and there'd be plenty of commuter trains to Winchester.

At Waterloo everything was chaos. The station had only just been re-opened after a bomb scare and people were rushing everywhere. Stephen decided to head for one of the cafés to get a cup of tea when he noticed a long line of black cabs and it struck him that he was only a short taxi-ride from home. Home. Funny that that was how he still thought of it even though he'd moved out months ago.

Before he thought better of it he ran towards the rank and hailed a cab to take him to the New King's Road.

Tess heaved a sigh of relief that it was Friday. This week had turned out to be unexpectedly wearing and she was still smarting from the conversation with Ellie about art school.

She packed up her briefcase, deliberately leaving the pile of work she could have brought home on her desk. This was a weekend for relaxing. Tonight Luke was staying the night with Ben and tomorrow Ben would be coming to them. They might even have a barbecue if the weather held. Luke adored barbecues and she sometimes let him and Ben sleep in a tent in the garden afterwards. But tonight she had nothing more demanding than a relaxing bath while Lyall cooked dinner.

Halfway across reception she heard Patricia calling her. 'Tess, do you think I could have a quick word? It won't take a moment.'

Tess felt deeply irritated. Just because she had no personal life of her own Patricia thought it perfectly fine to start discussions at six-thirty on a Friday. 'I'm in a bit of a hurry. Surely it can wait till Monday?'

'No, it can't, actually. I'm coming in all day tomorrow to sort out payments.' Reluctantly Tess followed her. 'The thing is, Tess, you still aren't following the tariff system we've agreed on.'

'Look, Patricia' – Tess didn't try too hard to keep

the irritation out of her voice – 'it's quarter to seven on Friday night. I have good reasons for when I don't stick to the tariff but I'm not sitting down and going through them now. I'll be more than happy to do so next week' – she stood up ignoring Patricia's sour face – 'during working hours.'

Stephen paid the taxi and glanced up at his ex-home. It looked reassuringly the same: scruffy compared with the smartly painted houses at the far end of the street, where gentrification was at its most concentrated, and smart compared with the unmodernized and often tenanted row at the main road end.

Luke's wrestler stickers lined the bottom of his window with savage ferocity, like tomb guardians keeping out grave robbers from the pyramids. If he leaned back he could see the U2 poster in Ellie's room. The lights were on in the ground floor sitting room which led to the kitchen at the back. He waited a moment, imagining the scene. Tess, just changed out of working clothes, chopping on a wooden board. He smiled at the memory. She was a pretty terrible cook but she chopped immaculately, rarely even getting the work surface dirty.

Luke would be watching TV and battling with Tess over homework – she suggesting he got it out of the way now, he insisting he'd be fresher and brighter if he left it till tomorrow. Ellie would be busy transforming herself from schoolgirl to outrageous scene-stopper.

Smiling in anticipation, he pressed the bell and waited. Despite his excitement he could feel the sweat damp in his palms as he rehearsed the apology for having misjudged her and the words he would use to ask her forgiveness.

CHAPTER THIRTY-FOUR

The door opened. Stephen's smile froze. It wasn't Tess but Lyall Gibson wearing the striped butcher's apron he'd worn himself so many times. Lyall was carrying one of the small knives Tess always bought in French supermarkets and his face wore the guardedly hostile expression of someone expecting to find an unsolicited life insurance salesman on his doorstep. The finishing touch was his bare feet. He couldn't have looked more at home if his name were on the mortgage agreement.

'Stephen, hello.' Lyall's face changed from suspicion to affable hospitality. 'I'm afraid Tess isn't back yet. Would you like to come in and have a drink?'

Stephen eyed the knife, far more tempted to wrest it from his grasp and do something appalling with it than to sit at his own kitchen table being poured his own whisky by his wife's lover. How ludicrous his little fantasy had been.

'No thanks. I'll catch her another time. At work. It wasn't important.' He almost ran down the steps under Lyall's thoughtful gaze. What the hell had he been thinking of? It was too late for him and Tess. Josephine was right. He should be talking to a divorce lawyer.

Ten minutes later Tess arrived and, for some reason that Lyall didn't want to examine too deeply, it completely slipped his mind to tell her about Stephen's visit.

As was her habit, Tess turned up five minutes early for her meeting with Savoury the following week. It gave you those vital few seconds to get lost on your way from the tube, or read your notes or – if you'd been efficient enough to need to do neither – touch up your lipstick and comb your hair. Today was a lipstick-applying day. Funny, thought Tess as she looked in the mirror, how the more you dislike someone the better you want to look.

Suitably freshened, she went and reported to the receptionist, discreetly placed at a desk round the corner off the main hall. The girl asked her to sit down while she informed Mr Savoury's secretary.

A couple of minutes later his secretary appeared looking deeply apologetic. 'Miss Brien? I'm really sorry, but I'm afraid there's been a mistake and it's all my fault. I wrote down the meeting in my pad but not in the diary. So Mr Savoury's double booked.' It was so typical of Leonard Savoury's technique that Tess wondered for a moment if he'd put the girl up to it, but her concern seemed genuine enough. 'What would you like to do? You could sit in the boardroom with a cup of coffee or if you prefer we'll reorganize for another day.'

Tess tried to do a quick calculation of waiting versus coming back. 'How long's he going to be, do you think?'

The girl shrugged apologetically. 'I really don't know. First consultation for a divorce. Could be in and out; on the other hand you know what it's like, it might be tissue-time. First ones often are, aren't they?'

Tess nodded. You often felt more like a psychotherapist or a marriage guidance counsellor at the first session, especially with women. It never failed to amaze her how many wives, as soon as they'd finished listing their husband's many faults, would turn to her in complete seriousness and ask, 'So, do you think we should get a divorce?' And she'd have to explain very gently that it had to be their decision. She was only there to advise them whether they had the technical grounds to do so.

Tess looked at her watch. 'Is Mr Savoury free after the session?'

The girl nodded. 'Nothing till twelve.'

'OK then, I'll stay.'

She looked relieved that Tess hadn't hit the roof and showed her into the boardroom, then went off to get her a coffee. As she put it down next to Tess she asked hesitantly if Tess would be mentioning the situation to Mr Savoury.

Tess smiled. Working for that shit was clearly punishment enough in itself without her adding to it. 'I don't see why I'll need to.'

The relief in the girl's face was thanks enough.

The artificial smile on the face of the receptionist had become almost natural when Stephen had approached the desk and announced that he had a nine-thirty appointment with Mr Savoury. She even broke the habit of a lifetime and took him upstairs to Leonard Savoury's office herself.

The first impression Stephen took in of London's top society divorce lawyer was that he was supremely disinterested in the case of Stephen Gilfillan and that in an odd sort of way this was a relief. Stephen had been dreading this meeting, the spilling of secrets, the finger pointing and attributing blame to things that were probably nobody's fault. So he welcomed the fact that Savoury gave him only the briefest of glances when he walked in and without further preliminaries picked up a yellow legal pad and began to ask questions matter-of-factly about his marriage and whether it had irretrievably broken down.

'And the spouse from whom you are separated is Mrs Theresa Gilfillan?' Savoury asked, pen poised.

'Yes. Although she operates under her single name of Brien.' He paused, wondering whether this information was strictly necessary. 'She's a solicitor.'

Stephen sensed a sudden awakening of interest in the man sitting opposite him. 'Not Tess Brien, surely?'

Stephen nodded.

Leonard Savoury could hardly believe his luck. This was only Tess Brien's husband coming innocently into his office to seek advice. He almost smiled before he pulled himself together. Undiluted glee was hardly an appropriate response. All the same, visions of taking that cow to the cleaners, as she had taken his client, and maybe even depriving her of her children flitted pleasurably through his mind. That would be the perfect revenge for the way she'd humiliated him in the Eileen McDonald case.

Just about containing his excitement he explained the different grounds for divorce to Stephen.

'To be frank, Mr Gilfillan,' Savoury advised, 'most people go for adultery. Much the quickest and most reliable. Is your wife involved with another man?'

'I haven't the slightest idea,' lied Stephen, banishing the image of Lyall Gibson wearing his apron from his mind's eye, 'and I don't see how it's relevant. I'm the one who was unfaithful.'

Savoury smiled indulgently. 'Sadly you cannot bring a petition based on your own adultery or life would be a lot simpler for all of us. Could you persuade her to say she's committed adultery just to speed things up? Otherwise we're left with unreasonable behaviour which is always a tricky one, unless you're prepared to wait two years. Are there any children of the marriage?'

Stephen, who was disliking Savoury more with every moment, gave him the details.

'And would you want residence – what used to be called custody of the children?' Savoury smiled wolfishly. 'Miss Brien works very hard, doesn't she? We might be able to prove she's a bad mother because she never sees them. The mother usually gets custody – but not always nowadays – and never if she's a lesbian. I suppose that's too much to hope?' Stephen was about to protest when he realized this was Savoury's idea of a joke.

'For God's sake, Mr Savoury, Tess is a much better parent than I am. She wasn't the one who ran out on her children.'

'Mr Gilfillan,' Leonard Savoury pointed out tartly, seeing his chances of getting his own back on Tess slipping away through her husband's wimpish attitude, 'I think perhaps before you go any further you'd better go away and think about what you want out of this divorce petition.'

'Yes,' Stephen agreed. 'Maybe I had.'

Downstairs in the boardroom Tess was getting restless. She'd already been there an hour and unless she saw him soon it really wouldn't be worth waiting. The scenario was pure Savoury. She'd come at his behest and ended up being the one who had to make all the concessions. God, what a loathsome creature he was.

Eager to assert herself she marched out into the Reception area to find the girl putting on mascara and doing her hair. Was she expecting Prince Andrew to walk through the door for a quick consultation with the king of divorces?

'Look, I haven't got all the time in the world. Will you kindly buzz Mr Savoury's secretary and find out how much longer his meeting is going to go on?' She sat on the edge of the receptionist's desk to make sure she did it now rather than when her makeover was complete.

Grudgingly the receptionist picked up her phone. Career women. They were always the worst. They really got up your nose.

Savoury's secretary had just picked up the phone when Stephen half ran down the stairs, eager to be out of the building and away from the revolting lawyer as soon as possible.

Tess turned, just in time to see Stephen's departing back disappear through the swing doors. She sat rooted to the spot, feeling as though someone had kicked her in the pit of her stomach. Stephen had been the person consulting Leonard Savoury!

'Miss Brien,' said a voice at her elbow, 'Mr Savoury will see you now.'

But Tess didn't hear her. Why would Stephen need to consult Savoury unless he was planning something unpleasant? She didn't want alimony. Surely he wasn't going to fight her for the children?

'Miss Brien, are you all right? Mr Savoury's free now. Would you like to follow me?'

Tess froze. Savoury had just been talking to Stephen. He must know exactly who she was by now. The thought of giving him the satisfaction of seeing her like this was just too much.

'I'm sorry,' she blurted to the girl, 'but I can't stay after all. I'm needed urgently at the office. I'll call Mr Savoury later. I'm sure it's something we can sort out on the phone.'

And she ran out of the building into the sunshine of Lincoln's Inn Fields, blinded by tears, while the two girls watched in astonishment. 'It's the stress,' one remarked to the other. 'I've seen it over and over. These career woman just can't hack it, can they?'

As she fought her way to the tube station Tess felt more miserable than she had done since they'd split up. She'd thought they were doing well, that at least they wanted to treat each other as human beings. And look who Stephen was consulting! It was time she stopped being sentimental and got her own lawyer. And it had better be someone who could stand up to Savoury.

Self-pity wasn't one of Tess's usual faults, but when she got home that night to find Ellie positively glowing with joy at the thought of starting art school and moving in with Stephen and Josephine, it was almost too much to take.

She had hardly walked in the door when Ellie descended on her, full of reminders that she'd be starting the Crane summer school in two weeks, and handing Tess a long list of things she was going to need.

Tess glanced at the list and smiled despite her gloomy mood. Among the conventional demands like brushes and a portable easel was a Swatch watch with a Mona Lisa face, two pairs of Doctor Marten boots and some new underwear. She could just picture Ellie wearing them all together. It reminded her of the day when Ellie took her father shopping for painting clothes and they came to drag her to lunch. It had been a day that had felt like a beginning. Instead it had turned out simply to be the beginning of the end.

How dead the house would be without Ellie. And then the thought struck her for the first time: if she and Stephen were getting divorced the house would probably have to be sold anyway. Maybe that would be for the best. It had been such a happy house. And now it was only a house of memories.

Josephine picked a bunch of pale-pink scented roses and arranged them in a pretty jug, singing. She was surprised at how excited she felt at the thought of Ellie's arrival today. She'd spent the morning making Ellie's bedroom look as inviting as possible and now she was wondering what kind of things Ellie liked to eat. Maybe they'd go shopping together. Like mother and daughter. The thought brought with it an unexpected stab of guilt at what it must be like for Tess to lose her. But wasn't it just as important for Ellie to see her father? And the place at art college was a great opportunity. Her old school had been stifling her talent and Tess should have seen it. Besides, Tess still had Luke.

'You're very busy,' Stephen said, putting his arms round her waist as she stood at the kitchen worktop. 'Is that for Ellie?' He felt touched by her enthusiasm. This was a side of Josephine he hadn't seen. He wondered for a moment if she'd feel the same about Luke, who could be so difficult, so prickly. The truth about Josephine was that she preferred promising material. Like him.

Tess, Ellie and Luke all sat in the open-air Italian café at Waterloo Station trying to make bright conversation. Tess had promised herself one thing: that no matter how much she was going to miss Ellie, she wasn't going to cry. Sipping her cappuccino, she realized the extent to which she'd come to lean on Ellie in the last few months – but that was hardly a good thing. She'd seen it happen to countless of her clients. They turned their children into confidants, telling them things about their parents' marriage children should never have to know. Maybe for Ellie's sake it was better that she got away.

But the hardest thing of all was seeing how much Ellie obviously wanted to go. Although she was trying to play it down Tess could tell that the lure of starting a new life far outweighed the pain of leaving home. When it was time to go, Ellie picked up her new backpack and got matter-of-factly on to the train as though she left home every day of the week. Tess watched numbly from the platform with Luke. Then, just as the train was about to leave, Ellie flung open the door again and threw herself into Tess's arms.

'Oh Mum, I am going to miss you!'

Tess held her, knowing that now the parting would be so much easier. Ellie loved her.

Finally, as the guard started to slam all the open doors, Ellie extricated herself and kissed Luke. 'Look after Mum, squirt.'

Despite her promise Tess found herself crying and waving at the same time as Ellie ran on to the train and pushed down the window to lean out. As the train departed she felt Luke's hand slip into hers – a real treat because he didn't approve of soppy stuff any more. He patted her protectively. 'Don't worry, you've still got me.'

And to his enormous embarrassment Tess swept him into a huge hug. 'Yes,' she agreed, squeezing the breath out of him, 'I have, haven't I?'

Stephen was already standing on the platform when Ellie's train drew in. She ran down the platform towards him and he caught her and twirled her round, backpack and all.

'Oh, Dad,' she breathed, the emotion in her voice muffled by his jacket, 'it's so great to see you. It hasn't been the same without you.'

He held her even tighter. 'I've missed you too. My firstborn.'

He helped her take off her backpack and carried it for her, then asked the question that had been worrying him all morning. 'How did Mum take it?'

A flash of guilt crossed Ellie's happy face. 'OK, I think. After all, she's got Luke.' She cast her father a sideways glance. 'And Lyall.'

Stephen pretended to fuss with the car keys. 'What's he like?'

'All right. He's been trying very hard with us, but I don't think he likes kids much. He'd rather whisk Mum off to the opera than takes us to Pizza Express. He likes football on telly, which keeps Luke happy. But he isn't fun like you.'

Stephen grinned and ruffled her short hair. 'Hey, this is the beginning of a great adventure!'

Ellie eased herself into the passenger seat. 'I know,' she said. And the happiness in her eyes chased away all his doubts that it might not be fair to Tess to have Ellie come to stay.

Lyall had been watching Tess moping for days now. 'What you need,' he announced, 'is an absolutely fabulous holiday in a wisteria-covered villa with its own private pool.'

Tess reached up her arms to him and smiled. '*I* might. But Luke would loathe it. No other children. He'd be bored out of his brain. As a matter of fact . . .' She hesitated before telling him about Julius's offer,

542

not sure what his reaction would be: 'We've already been offered a holiday and Luke really wants to go.'

'Where's that?' Lyall was fast learning that life with children was very different from the carefree existence of the single man, and wasn't sure he liked it.

'Julius and Stella invited us to Ireland and Luke's been living for the moment.'

'Couldn't he go alone? They are his grandparents, after all.'

'They couldn't cope. Luke's much too much of a handful. Julius is nearly eighty, remember.'

'Well' – Lyall failed to keep an edge of annoyance out of his voice – 'we can't let Luke down, can we?'

Catching the secret smile that passed between Tess and Lyall across the meeting-room table during a particularly dull session on the company's new billing system reminded the senior partner that he must have a word with Tess. Why Tess and not Lyall he wasn't sure, but it somehow seemed more appropriate to talk to her. Even in these liberated days women had to be more careful than men and people were beginning to talk. Patricia Greene, in particular. But he'd also been asked a question about Tess's marriage by another lawyer completely outside the firm. It was a tricky situation. In a way, divorce lawyers, like politicians, were expected to pronounce on other people's morality without besmirching their own. The fact that Tess had chosen, or perhaps just happened, to fall for a colleague who also worked for Kingsmill's made the whole thing doubly delicate. It should be sorted out soon. The fact that they were writing a book about divorce together meant that should the press get hold of the story they'd have a field day. It was time he spoke up. He just hoped she wasn't going to stalk out of the meeting early. Patricia had missed no opportunity to rap her over the knuckles about her unorthodox billing methods and Tess was clearly irritated.

But the rest of the meeting passed without incident so Will was able, as he'd hoped, to catch Tess on the way out and ask her to stay behind for a moment.

Tess, wary, simply raised an eyebrow in Lyall's direction as he filed out, and sat down again. When the last of the partners had left Will discreetly closed the door.

'Thanks for staying, Tess. I think we ought to have a discussion about your marital situation. I know this is personal, but it affects the firm too.'

Tess's first instinct was to tell him to mind his own business, but she knew that Lyall's involvement made things more complicated.

'The thing is, Tess, I don't think in your position you can allow things to remain – how shall I put it – muddled. People are gossiping. Perhaps you could tell me how you see the future developing?'

Tess made a steeple out of her hands to play for time. It was amazing how many people seemed to want her to get divorced just to make things neat and tidy, without thinking that it was emotion which confused everything and that the law had no control over emotion. 'As a matter of fact,' she said finally, admitting that really there wasn't much alternative, 'I'm thinking of getting a divorce.'

Will Kingsmill's expression of solemn concern transfigured itself into beaming approval. 'I think that would be for the best. It would make things so much clearer. Who are you thinking of getting to act for you?'

Tess realized this was a question she hadn't resolved yet. She didn't want any of the main players in the divorce field. She knew them all too well. And she knew that she wanted a woman. 'I'm not sure yet. I'm considering a number of people.' She racked her brains for the name of the woman who had done Phil's divorce. Phil had sung alleluias to her for months after. Diana someone. She'd have to ring Phil when the Old Fart let her go.

Will Kingsmill stood up. 'If you need any advice, you know I'm always here.'

'Thank you, Will. I expect I'll manage. It is my field, after all.'

He held open the door and she walked out of the room ahead of him. With all this talk of divorce it struck her how curious it was that she'd heard nothing from Leonard Savoury on behalf of Stephen.

Back in her office she phoned Phil straight away.

'Diana Adams,' enthused Phil, 'my lifesaver. Works for a firm called Wentworth's. Are you free for lunch? Meet me at one and I'll tell you all about her.'

Of course, Diana Adams. She'd won a tricky custody case recently and was making quite a name for herself as being tough but human. She sounded distinctly promising.

Phil sat at a window table in the Italian restaurant round the corner from her office and ogled the waiters shamelessly till Tess arrived, by which time they were already abandoning their male customers and falling over each other to take Phil's order.

Tess hardly had time to sit down before Phil handed her a Bellini. 'To divorce!' The waiters clapped delightedly, hoping it was Phil who was celebrating this most contemporary of sacraments.

Tess smiled wearily. Another supporter for the alimony club. It was beginning to feel like a conspiracy. 'So tell me about Diana Adams.'

'Likeable. Straightforward. Deadly. Greg thought I should have custody of the children and he should have custody of the money. She soon put him right. So you've finally decided to take the plunge. About time too.'

The waiter arrived with their pasta and offered them Parmesan cheese. 'Thanks!' Phil smiled at him flirtatiously. 'Is that a pepper mill in your hand or are you pleased to see me?'

The waiter guffawed with delight and went off to tell his fellow-waiters about the subtlety of the signorina's wit at table number ten.

'You seem on good form,' said Tess. 'Quite the old Philomena.'

Phil immediately looked gloomy. 'The truth is it's all a front. I'm actually worried as hell about Terry. Angela's promised to let him take the kids to Sherwood Park – you know, that bubble in the middle of Sherwood Forest full of chalets and children, my idea of hell. And if she lets him down this time I think he might do something stupid.'

'Like what?'

'I'm not sure. But he's started going to this fathers' rights group twice a week and God knows what they hatch there.'

'I'm sure it's perfectly harmless,' Tess reassured her. 'There are lots of these groups. Why don't you get him to take you along one night and you can see for yourself?'

'That's a great idea. Why didn't I think of that myself?' She immediately perked up. 'That is if they'll let any women in. This particular group are weirdoes. They broke away from the mainstream because they weren't radical enough. Honestly, Tessie, they see us as the enemy. Really.'

'I'm sure you're making too much of this. It's probably just therapy. A lot of fathers feel they've lost out. Talking probably helps.'

'As long as it is just talking.'

'Come on, Phil, cheer up. It probably does Terry good. By the way, what about this wedding you were promising?'

'What indeed?' echoed Phil gloomily. 'And how about you and Lyall? Maybe if we wait six months we could make it a double.'

That night, at Lyall's flat, Tess told him that she'd decided to start divorce proceedings. Without saying a word he folded her into his arms and held her.

'Tess, thank God,' he finally muttered into her hair. 'I so want to make things better for you. You've had such a terrible time. I'd never leave you for another woman, no matter what went wrong between us. Promise when it's over that you'll marry me.'

Tess buried her face in his shoulder for a second longer. It was so tempting to be able to offer your problems to someone else to carry. She even knew that was what Lyall wanted. And she believed him about never leaving her even if things didn't work out. Yet there was something chilling too in that offer, the shadow of a sentence as well as a promise of protection. What the hell did she want? She was hardly going to get a better chance than this. Think of all those single women out there not able to find a halfway decent man, while Lyall was offering her so much. So why did she feel this sense of panic?

Eventually she made herself look at him. Lyall would be a good husband and Luke was at the stage where he needed some male influence. She could do a lot worse. All the same, something was holding her back. No doubt it was just a question of getting used to the idea. At the moment marriage still seemed too frightening.

She touched his face tenderly. 'Let's just get through the divorce first, shall we?'

'Well, Ms Brien,' Diana Adams sat across the other side of a polished mahogany desk piled high with briefs, 'I obviously don't need to tell *you* the grounds for divorce!'

Tess decided she liked the woman at once. She was entirely unthreatening in her down-to-earth M&S clothes, her face free of make-up, laughter lines around her eyes. She seemed simply friendly. And Tess was doubly grateful to her for taking the sting out of a potentially embarrassing situation. There was a reassuring briskness about her. She was neither hard-bitten like Patricia nor uncomfortably pally. 'Please, call me Tess. The most important thing is that I want it to be as amicable as possible.'

'Fine then, Tess. Obviously mutual agreement would be best. But as you know it's a two-year wait. Most people want to get things tidied up sooner than that.'

'Of course, but that probably means going for adultery.'

'And you don't want to? You wouldn't have to name her, as you're aware.'

'No. Tempting though, isn't it? She'd be in all the papers.'

'That's why I wouldn't advise it. The lower key the better.'

'I know. I wouldn't name her. For the kids' sake. But I'd still rather not go for adultery.'

'That's up to you, of course.'

'Yes.' She knew she was being impractical, that any

divorce lawyer worth their fee would advise adultery – after all he was living with another woman. But it bothered her all the same. 'Maybe I'd better talk it through with Stephen.'

'Maybe you had,' agreed Diana. 'It would certainly simplify things if you agreed on the grounds in advance. We can get the petition in hand next week. And of course if you went for adultery you'd be free in six months or so. Otherwise obviously the full two years.' Tess thought of Lyall and his proposal. Would he be willing to wait two years? It was a lot to ask.

'By the way, what's the position with your husband? Has he been taking any legal advice himself?'

'Well, that's the strange thing. I saw him coming out of Leonard Savoury's office almost three weeks ago and yet I've heard nothing from him.'

The reaction on Diana Adams' face was instantaneous, but her voice was warm and sympathetic. 'Leonard Savoury's hardly the type to recommend him to stay married, is he? Tell me, have you any idea why he'd have gone to Savoury? I mean there's nothing nasty in the woodshed he could bring out against you that you haven't told me about?'

Tess felt the anxiety flooding back again. 'No. Except that I'm involved with a colleague, a fellow partner from Kingsmill's. But that only happened after he left.'

'Hmmm. Savoury's a bit of a curious choice then.'

'I know,' said Tess. 'To tell you the truth I can't work it out myself.'

Once she was back at work Tess sat at her desk trying to work up the courage to call Stephen. It was ludicrous how difficult it felt. After all, she had all the proof she needed that he was interested in divorce too. It was possible that Savoury might not want Stephen to meet her, but even that would be useful information. So what was holding her back?

Finally she willed herself to pick up the phone and dial Richmond & Quinn's number. The bright normality of his secretary's manner was reassuring. What had she been expecting? That he'd told the girl on no account did he want to speak to his wife?

And then Stephen was on the line. 'Tess, hello. How nice to hear from you.' He even sounded sincere. 'There isn't anything wrong, is there, nothing's happened to Luke or anything?'

'No, no, nothing like that. How's Ellie?'

'Loving every moment. I have to say, I was worried about this art school idea too. She's so young. But she's positively blossoming. Brings home something new she's learned every day. It's a joy to watch. Is that why you rang? Naughty girl, hasn't she been in touch? I'll get her to call you tonight.'

'Don't worry. I expect it's a good sign. She'll probably ring in her own good time.' She paused fractionally, psyching herself up. 'Actually, I'm ringing about something quite different. I've been taking advice about divorce.'

'I see.'

Tess felt a dryness in her mouth which she recognized as fear. That had been the perfect opening for him to tell her he'd been consulting a lawyer too. But he hadn't taken it.

'And the conclusion I and my lawyer came to was that it made a lot of sense for you and me to sit down and talk about it first. I mean we're both civilized enough to do that, surely?'

'Of course.' There was a deadness in his voice Tess hadn't heard before, but then she probably sounded pretty strange too. 'Where do you want to meet?'

It was such an ordinary predictable question and Tess had absolutely no answer for it. Where did people go to discuss the end of marriage as long as theirs? It couldn't be at home for obvious reasons. Crazy places like the zoo, where couples in the movies meet for such things, flashed into her mind.

'The bar at the Waldorf,' she tossed out randomly, realizing she had to say somewhere. 'Beyond the Palm Court right through at the back. If we go about five there won't be anyone there.'

'When?'

'This Saturday?'

'Saturday at five then. Tess?'

'Yes?'

'I wish it didn't have to be in such sad circumstances.'

'No. Well.' What the hell did he mean by that? She felt like snapping, *You should have thought about that before*. But the truth was they'd both had plenty of time to think and this was where it had brought them.

Phil sat on a hard chair pressed up against the wall of the featureless sitting room where Terry's fathers' group was holding its weekly meeting. This week it was at Steve's, in his one-bedroom flat above a news-agent's in Rainham. Steve had made an effort, buying beer and crisps, but it didn't seem to be doing much to dissipate the atmosphere of bitterness and resentment that seemed to Phil to characterize these sessions.

Last week's meeting, according to Terry, had largely been taken up with a discussion of whether she should be allowed to come. Once they'd agreed to let her she had to admit they'd been trying hard to make her welcome, even offering her a seat in the middle of the group. But Phil knew enough about market research to decline. She had sat in on countless groups giving their views on everything from baked beans to TV soap operas, and she knew she'd learn far more if she blended into the background. It was only when everyone in the room had forgotten she was there that anything truthful would start to emerge.

And she was right. The meeting had started gently enough, but slowly the anger had been building up. Phil found herself shocked at how these perfectly ordinary-looking, rather henpecked men felt towards their ex-wives. But then, if they'd all been treated like Terry maybe that was no surprise. She'd read the statistics about how many men lost contact with their children and realized, listening to this group, that it might not always be their fault. They certainly didn't think so.

'How about you, Tel?' Steve asked. 'How's it been going with Angela?'

'She's agreed to let me take the kids to Sherwood Park for a week, and really I'm just living for the moment.' The excitement in his voice both touched and worried Phil.

'How do you know it isn't just another wind-up?' asked Steve.

'Yeah. Look how often she's let you down in the past. She's having you on, Terry,' another of the group chipped in.

'This is her last chance, if she screws me up this time . . . I'll . . .'

'You'll what, Terry? What will you do?' asked another, egging him on. 'I mean isn't this exactly our problem? What *can* we bloody well do?'

'I'll think of something. I'm not taking any more of her screwing me around.'

From her seat on the sidelines Phil felt frightened.

She could see why these men had been expelled from conventional groups. This was the territory of obsession. They may have been driven to it, but it was still dangerous.

'Well, if you need any help when the time comes,' offered Steve, 'I'm always here.'

Phil sneaked out to the kitchen, deeply disturbed. Sometimes she wished she'd taken Tess's advice and left Terry well alone. But he was a good man at heart. The irony struck her of the difference between Greg, her own ex, who hadn't given a toss for his kids, and Terry who cared too much.

She bustled noisily back into the sitting room, breezily implying she'd heard none of this. She had to get out before she screamed at them all that they were unhealthy and inward-looking and that they should try and cope with reality. 'Come on, Terry love,' she said as he looked at her as though she were an apparition, he'd forgotten her so completely, 'time we hit the road.'

'No,' Josephine snapped angrily at Stephen, 'I don't bloody well see why you have to go and have a drink at the Waldorf with Tess to discuss it.' She poured herself another breakfast cup of coffee without offering him one. 'I don't see why you don't just leave the whole thing to Leonard Savoury to sort out.'

'Because Leonard Savoury is an unpleasant shit who specializes in taking people to the cleaners and I don't want him involved.'

'Oh Stephen, don't be ridiculous. He's the best there is.'

Stephen watched her over his cup with a faint glimmering of dislike. Josephine always wanted the best there was whether it was china or paintings or divorce lawyers. He'd thought she was softening now that Ellie had come, but the subject of divorce brought out the worst in her. She seemed to want to punish Tess for having ever been married to him.

At that moment Ellie skipped down the stairs. She was about to come into the room to say goodbye, but sensed the atmosphere and decided against it. When she'd first come it had been great. She'd loved seeing Dad so much and the art school was brilliant. But lately, if she was honest with herself, it had all been getting a bit much. Bloody adults. They told you what to do then happily screwed up their own lives. You'd think they'd learn. Quietly she slipped out of the front door.

Tess put on the marvellous Lycra underwear Phil had recommended that miraculously pulled in your thighs and tummy so that you looked half a stone lighter. It really worked too. The brown linen dress with the halter neck she'd always thought was too clingy looked just right.

She opened the door of her bedroom to call up to Ellie for a second opinion, before she remembered that Ellie wasn't there. It was extraordinary how she missed her, how many times she thought of things she wanted to say to her, jokes to share, soundings to make. She'd always felt cynical about mothers who went round saying their daughters were their best friends, in fact she'd felt faintly sorry for the poor deluded women, so bereft of grown-up comradeship that they turned their own daughters into buddies. Yet now she felt just like one of them! She could always ask Inge, who was downstairs watching TV with Luke, but it wasn't the same.

Then it struck her that even if Ellie were here she

wouldn't have been able to ask her – unless she wanted the truth. She could just hear it now. *For God's sake, Ma, why are you getting all togged up to meet Dad as though it's a date?*

It was a very good question and one that Tess didn't at this precise moment feel like answering.

She found a parking space round the back of the hotel with ease. Most of the shoppers raiding the boutiques in nearby Covent Garden had tired themselves out with the joys of getting and spending, and the theatre crowd hadn't yet descended from the suburbs.

She went in the side entrance of the Waldorf, admiring its lovely art deco Palm Court with the lights twinkling on its balcony and a pianist playing 'A Nightingale Sang in Berkeley Square'. Only a few tables were filled with couples having tea and no one was daring to dance. One of the waiters watched her admiringly as she walked across the marble floor and up the steps towards the main part of the hotel.

The bar, as she'd hoped, was virtually deserted. Almost the only person there was Stephen, looking ludicrously attractive in a loose-fitting summer suit, sipping a beer from the bottle with a slice of lime in the neck. Then she noticed the young woman two tables away who was following Stephen's every movement with her eyes. She made a moue of irritation when Tess appeared. No doubt, if she knew what they'd come here to talk about, she'd look a bit more cheerful.

'Tess, you look great!' Stephen stood up and kissed her on the cheek.

She was about to tell him about the slimming Lycra, then realized that kind of intimacy between them was no longer possible. 'So do you.'

The waiter arrived just as she was sitting down and, without thinking, Stephen ordered her a glass of white wine, then turned to her apologetically and asked if that was what she wanted.

Tess couldn't help smiling. 'White wine would be fine.'

'How's Luke?' Stephen asked in the ensuing silence.

'Rather enjoying being an only child, I think.'

'Good. I was worried he might be missing Ellie.'

'Not as much as I am.' She saw the guilty look cross his face. 'But I'm glad she's loving summer school.'

The waiter brought her wine. Neither of them, Tess noticed, seemed to want to get round to the subject they were meant to be discussing. Finally she made herself do so. 'Look, Stephen, about the divorce. I've taken on a lawyer called Diana Adams and I went to see her for the first time this week. We discussed possible grounds. We could opt for two years' separation, but obviously that leaves us both in limbo.' She plucked up courage to go on. 'Or we could make it adultery and it'd only take six months.'

There was a beat of silence before Stephen spoke. 'And what do you *want* to do?'

'Any good lawyer would advise adultery.'

Stephen thought of Leonard Savoury. He'd said exactly the same, but in spite of that Stephen didn't want to be represented by him. He didn't trust the man. He'd find someone else.

Tess was speaking again. 'Adultery would be by far the simplest. And I wouldn't have to name Josephine. Just saying "with a party unknown" is fine.'

'Adultery it is then. It's the truth, after all.' He leaned towards her. 'I know you're not being vindictive, Tess. That's not your style.'

'I wouldn't be too sure about that. I have been

tempted, you know. To drag you both through the mud. Then fortunately I remembered what it'd do to Luke and Ellie.'

'You always put them first, don't you?'

Suddenly his assumptions annoyed her. 'Come off it, Stephen, I'm not some sainted madonna. I was bloody hurt and bloody angry.'

Stephen knew it was the truth and reached for her hand, wanting to say how truly sorry he was, and that he had come round the other day to see her, but Lyall had been there.

He was holding it between both of his when Josephine spotted them from across the room. He'd told her where he was coming and she'd been debating for two hours whether to just turn up. Clearly she'd been right to do so. She sat down in an elegant wing chair opposite them both. 'Well, this is a touching scene.'

'We've decided to go for adultery,' Tess told Diana Adams the next day. The truth was she was still confused about her strange meeting with Stephen and needed more than ever to get things sorted out between them. This toing and froing was just emotional masochism. Part of Stephen might still be looking back towards their marriage but his commitment to Josephine was clearly just as solid. Look how he'd gone off with her like a lamb when she'd turned up at the Waldorf. The truth was he probably wanted both of them, and that was one game she wasn't prepared to play.

Diana interrupted her thoughts, 'Good. I think you've definitely made the right decision. After all, in your case the claim's more than justified. So. We'll file the petition at once and serve it on your husband's lawyers. If they haven't got anything to say we can go for the nisi next month. That'll take about six weeks to come through. Then we apply for the absolute and by January it should all be over. It ought not to be too painful.'

Diana sounded just like a hearty nurse telling her patient to take the nasty medicine and she'd soon feel better. Divorce. Just what the doctor ordered. All the same, a healing sense of relief came over Tess. The one thing she couldn't stand was uncertainty and now, finally, the process was in motion.

Her mind drifted off to Cork and their plans to go there next month. Was she mad to go somewhere so full of memories? Probably, but Luke loved it and so did she. Maybe they'd even be able to talk Ellie into coming after her summer school finished. There must be a gap before the new term began and Killamalooe was the perfect place for a painter.

Feeling a kind of peace at last, Tess said goodbye to Diana Adams and picked up her briefcase. It had been an exhausting day and she was looking forward to flopping in front of the television and sharing a pizza with Luke.

Diana Adams saw her out. She was glad Tess had come to an amicable decision with her husband. It was always much more upsetting when a fellow professional was faced with their marriage on the rocks. You couldn't help identifying so much more. Especially when you liked them, and Diana had warmed to Tess at once. Down the other end of the corridor she caught sight of Sandi, the new temp, and decided there was no time like the present to get Tess's case under way. Besides, it was only five p.m. and though the girl was supposed to work till five-thirty, she had an irritating habit – on which Diana intended to put the lid – of quietly disappearing half an hour early. The one thing

Diana loathed was people who didn't pull their weight.

'Sandi,' she called, 'I'd like you to type up a few case notes for me so I can draft some important documents tomorrow morning.'

Under her breath, Sandi cursed. She'd been hoping to get off extra early tonight. Bloody Mrs Adams. Sandi had caught the woman watching her lately. 'Of course, Mrs Adams,' she said, taking the file Diana held out to her, and disappeared into the windowless corner she shared with the other girls in the typing pool. She glanced at the notes. They weren't too long and she prided herself on her speeds.

Sandi sat down heavily and turned on her machine. The trouble with word processors, she thought as she tapped away on autopilot, was that you couldn't beat the hell out of them and let your employer know you were pissed off like you could with old-fashioned typewriters.

Twenty minutes later, feeling proud that she'd typed fast even for her, she printed the notes and stood up to give them to Mrs Adams. Reluctantly she thought better of it. She'd better read them through for typos. Normally she didn't bother but Adams was the type who'd make her stay and do it all again if she'd made any mistakes. Honestly, it was like being back at school. She'd much preferred her last job, temping on a tabloid newspaper. That had been really good fun. But being a temp was a dog's life. You were always last in and first out. No one ever had any loyalty to you no matter how hard you tried.

She sat back for a moment, fantasizing about the great atmosphere in that office, everything buzzing, people all round her shouting and teasing each other. Not like this boring dump. How anyone could be a lawyer was beyond her. It was such a drag the paper hadn't had anything permanent.

She read through the notes at breakneck speed, one eye on the clock noting that she could still catch the six-fifteen and beat her younger sister to the bathroom before they both went out later tonight, when a name leaped out of the page at her. Josephine Quinn. Wasn't she that glamorous businesswoman who was always in the gossip columns?

Co-respondent: Josephine Quinn but petitioner does not want to name her.

Co-respondent. That meant the person someone was knocking off, didn't it? Sandi, a bright girl who'd lacked the application to make anything of her brains, put two and two together. She checked through the notes for the names of the other people involved. She had to get her facts straight before she made the call.

If she got caught the agency would refuse to use her again, but there were plenty of other agencies. Anyway after this maybe the paper would want her back for good and she wouldn't need to be a dogsbody any more. She reached for the phone and asked for the editor of the gossip column, a man who'd always treated her like shit, but who was about to change his ways.

CHAPTER THIRTY-FIVE

'Josephine, I think you'd better look at this.' Hugo put down the gossip page of Britain's most popular daily on her desk, neatly folded in half so as to show the headline to its fullest advantage. It read 'NASTY SMELL FOR MILLIONAIRESS JO' and underneath it was a large and rather unflattering picture of her.

She snatched up the article and read about how Josephine Quinn, co-owner of Richmond & Quinn, the multinational perfume company, was about to be cited as the other woman in a divorce case between artist Stephen Gilfillan, son of the world-famous painter Julius Gilfillan, and his lawyer wife Theresa.

'Somebody's been a bit indiscreet, haven't they?' Hugo pointed out sarcastically. 'I wonder who?'

Josephine ignored him and stormed out of her office to look for Stephen, too furious to notice Hugo's smile of self-satisfaction. The saintly Stephen was about to have his balls put through the mincer.

On her train in from Lewisham, Jacqui flicked through her paper and stopped dead at the gossip column. Jesus, poor Tess! She'd known all of this already but it somehow seemed more lurid when you read it in the paper. When she got to the station she decided against the tube and grabbed a cab. Tess might not have even seen the story. Journalists were supposed to ring everyone they named and get a quote but very often they didn't. And she knew Tess would want to see this before anyone else at the office got wind of it. Will was going to hit the roof.

Stephen was on the phone when Josephine appeared in his office. One look at her face made him hastily extricate himself from the conversation.

She flung the paper at him and Stephen read the headline, appalled.

'Jesus Christ. Where did they get this rubbish from?'

'From the lady herself, I assume,' snapped Josephine. 'I certainly haven't talked to any journalists and it's remarkably accurate.'

'What nonsense. She assured me she wasn't going to name you in the petition.'

'And you assumed that dear, honest Tess, champion of the underdog, would keep her word?' Josephine's words splattered over him like machine-gun fire.

'But this just isn't Tess's style. She wouldn't tell me she wasn't naming you then splash it across the papers.'

Josephine eyed him coldly. 'Don't be so naïve, Stephen. She just wants to get her own back on me and this was the most effective way.' It annoyed the hell out of her that Stephen persisted in seeing Tess as Mother Teresa crossed with Joan of Arc. 'Look, by tomorrow this story's going to be everywhere. And it won't be you they'll accuse. It'll be me. I'll be the scarlet woman, the marriage breaker.'

'And isn't there just a touch of truth in that?' Stephen flashed at her, his anger beginning to match her own.

'Oh I see. You were the poor innocent led down the primrose path to ruin, were you?'

'No. I didn't have to make love to you that night. I wanted to.' He watched her face, hard and unrelenting in its fury, and wondered how that desire could have been so all-consuming that he'd forgotten everything

562

except how much he wanted to feel her under him crying out in pleasure. Today her self-obsession, her incapacity ever to see anything from other people's points of view, her need to get what she and she alone, Josephine Quinn, wanted, infuriated him.

'Has it never occurred to you,' he asked coldly, 'that this story might hurt other people as much as it hurts you?'

'And has it not occurred to you what brilliant publicity all this will be for Tess's book? Anyway, I don't give a stuff about other people. I've spent twenty years building my business and I'm not going to see it damaged by some tabloid rag. So no matter what you think of the man you'd better bloody well get Leonard Savoury on the case to sort it out.' She picked up the paper angrily. 'And if you don't, I will.'

Tess read the article Jacqui handed her with mounting horror. Where had they got the story from? Not from Diana Adams, certainly. Phil? She was hardly the soul of discretion, but she'd never discussed the grounds for the divorce with Phil. Of course dozens of people knew that Stephen was living with Josephine, but how would that explain that they'd got the story wrong and said she was naming her as co-respondent when she wasn't?

Her thoughts were interrupted by the phone ringing. It was Diana Adams. 'Tess? Look, I can't apologize enough. I'm devastated. We've found out where the story came from. A temp who's been working here. She took it from my notes and told the paper. Saying you were citing Josephine was simply a better story than the truth, so they ran it. When I threatened to sue them, they told me who'd given it to them. So much for journalists going to the stake for their sources. Needless to say the girl's been fired, but I can't tell you how sorry I am.'

Tess put down the phone and took in for the first time who would really be hurt by the story. Not Josephine or her, but Ellie and Luke.

Lyall Gibson stared out of the window wondering what the impact of this article was likely to be. Patricia Greene had brought it in to him five minutes ago and told him the whole office was buzzing with it. On the whole he suspected its impact would be positive, at least for him. Tess would loathe it, of course, and he was sorry about that, but looking on the bright side it was likely to drive a wedge further between her and Stephen and he found that reassuring. Deep down, he suspected, Tess still had some lingering doubts about divorcing him and this was just the kind of thing to create bitterness and harden attitudes all round. His first instinct had been to go in and comfort her, but now he was thinking better of it. It would be painful for her to face everyone knowing the humiliating details of her marriage break-up, but once it was public property it would also make it harder for anyone to back down.

He folded the newspaper carefully and tucked it into the zipped compartment of his briefcase. As he snapped it shut the thought occurred to him that it might not be long before he, the lover, were brought into the story too. He had better make up his mind quickly whether he wanted to take calls from the press or not.

On the floor below so many calls from the papers got through to Tess during the day that she decided to go home early. Jacqui expertly fielded any that came via the switchboard, but a lot of press seemed to have her direct line. Anyway, she was worried that the reporters, who seemed to sink to any lengths once they were on the scent of a story, might start bothering Luke at his school.

'Just say, "No comment",' she instructed Jacqui grimly on her way out.

'Is that all?' Jacqui grinned. 'Can't I be just a little bit ruder? Tell them I fart in their general direction or that I hope their little todgers will fall off if they print any more lies about you?'

Tess smiled faintly. 'Better just stick to "No comment", eh?'

Tess was five minutes early for picking up Luke and she glanced round to see if there were any suspicious characters lurking. Most of the pupils made their way home by bus or tube but a few mothers or nannies – rarely fathers – still picked up the younger ones. She scanned the first group to come out, recognizing a few of them as Luke's classmates, but no Luke. After fifteen minutes the whole school had emptied and the grounds were deserted. But there was still no sign of Luke. Could she have missed him? She was hurrying towards Luke's classroom when a crew-cutted figure cannonballed in her direction from the area where the dustbins were kept, tossing what appeared to be a small tape recorder in the air. An irate man in a buff raincoat, even though it was high summer, was chasing him shouting obscenities. She recognized the boy as Jason Steel.

'I heard him asking some juniors where Luke was,' Jason explained, tossing the machine higher and higher. 'He's either a perv or a hack. Or maybe both.' He threw the tape recorder higher than ever and then deliberately failed to catch it. It fell with a devastating crunch on to the gravel of the playground. 'Oh dearie, dearie me!' Jason admonished himself. 'What a butterfingers. No wonder I never made the first fifteen at rugby.'

The man bent and picked up his smashed equipment. 'You horrible little fucker,' he screamed, 'I bet you're the product of a one-parent family, aren'tcha? No bloody discipline these days.'

'At least my father married my mother!' Jason taunted. 'And if you're the product of the good old days thank God I wasn't born earlier.'

The man looked as though he might like to wallop Jason but given Tess's presence went off muttering instead. As soon as he'd gone Luke appeared, looking white-faced and shaken. He ran over to her. 'Don't worry, darling,' she comforted him, 'it's just some stupid reporter.'

'Some of the kids were being horrible to him,' Jason said proudly, 'but I kept an eye on him.'

Tess smiled gratefully at him. 'Thanks, Jase. Can we offer you a lift home? We might even stop off for an ice-cream?'

'Done,' said Jason. 'I'd no idea what a laugh it is being a guardian angel or I'd have started doing it sooner.'

Stephen tried to get hold of Leonard Savoury all day but his office simply said he was away on a case in Manchester and they'd try to get a message to him. Josephine was still behaving like a prima donna and Tess's bloody office wouldn't believe he wasn't a member of the press just pretending to be her husband and refused to put him through to her.

In the end he rang their home number. Naturally it was an answering machine and he left a message saying

566

he was coming round this evening to talk. He at least needed to know where Tess thought the leak had come from. He was as convinced as ever it wouldn't be from her.

He set out at six, knowing the rush hour would slow him down, just as Tess opened the front door after dropping Jason back at his block of flats. She dumped her coat on the banisters, feeling utterly drained, and Luke went off to make her a cup of tea. When he came back she took it gratefully and patted the seat next to her.

'I'm sorry about that, darling. The thing is, Dad and I have decided we ought to get divorced and there was a silly article in the newspaper about it. So a few reporters have been nosing round and one came to your school.'

Luke looked up at her, his eyes filling with tears. 'Why? Why do you have to get divorced? Why can't things stay as they are? At least then you could change your mind.'

Tess took his hand. 'We tried to change our minds. You know we did and it was ghastly for everyone. Look how you reacted. Dad and I think it'd be better if it were definite, then we can all start again.' She realized as she said it this might not be exactly tactful.

'With Lyall, you mean?'

In a way Tess was grateful this had come up. Luke usually pretended Lyall didn't exist. 'Don't you like Lyall?'

'He's all right. I just feel a bit as though he's putting up with me, making a big effort to be matey, you know, but that he'd really rather I were out of the way.'

Tess tried to deny this, but the fact that there was some truth in it made it harder.

'He's OK, I s'pose, but he doesn't know any jokes, and he isn't fun like Dad.'

Tess decided it was probably best to change the subject. 'Come on, let's go and find Inge. Then you can go with her and get a video out. And maybe she'll take you to J. J. Dean's for a burger.' She didn't add, And I can have an early night, but she'd been fantasizing about the cool embrace of her bed for hours now. Today's emotion had wiped her out.

Luke and Inge had just skipped off down the front steps when the phone rang. Tess looked at it suspiciously then sat reluctantly down on the bottom stair and picked it up.

It was Phil. And she was almost hysterical. 'Terry's taken the kids. Angela let him down again so he hung round till she went out and got them to come with him. Oh, Tess, I *knew* something like this was going to happen. That bloody group of his. They've been egging him on to try and act like Rambo. And now he has.'

Tess sat up, taking in at once how serious this could be for Terry. He might be arrested. And he could easily lose access to his children altogether.

'Phil, calm down. I'm going to need your help. Have you any idea where he's taken them?'

'You won't believe this.' Phil's laugh got more shrill. 'Where he was always taking them. To Sherwood Park. He's just rung me.'

Even in her anxiety Tess smiled. Only Terry would ever think of kidnapping his children and taking them where they were going anyway, to a public place full of hundreds of visitors. Still, it would help convince the police that his motives hadn't been suspect.

'OK, Phil, get in the car and come and get me.

We're going to find Terry and talk him into returning them.'

She took a last longing look up towards the bedroom and went to make herself a strong black coffee and a sandwich. It was going to be a heavy night.

Fifteen minutes later the doorbell went. Tess was amazed how little time it'd taken Phil to get here. Maybe she hadn't rung from home but from a callbox on the way. She gulped her coffee and put the note she'd just written to Inge on the hall table. Then she opened the front door.

But it wasn't Phil standing there. It was Stephen.

'My God, Stephen, what are you doing here?'

Laughing at her astonished face, Stephen pushed her gently back into the house. As she sat on the bottom stair again too surprised by the turn of events to offer any resistance, he looked around. It was all so achingly familiar. Luke's bike in the hall next to Tess's briefcase; her smart work jacket, which she always took off the moment she got in, draped over the banisters. Seeing it all again, he felt an overwhelming sense of loss. Josephine's house had never really felt like home.

'Didn't you get my message?' he asked. 'I left it on the machine.'

Tess realized she hadn't picked up any of her messages. A red light was flashing to tell her they were still waiting for her.

'I haven't checked it yet. I suppose Josephine sent you to find out about the story in the paper?'

Stephen flinched at the sudden sarcasm in her tone, then sat down next to her. 'As a matter of fact that's not why I came at all. I almost said this the other day but Josephine turned up and I couldn't. Are you convinced we're doing the right thing in going ahead with the divorce?'

Tess felt completely thrown. 'What are you getting at? That we should wait longer? Or just stay separated rather than divorced?'

He looked at her steadily. 'Or sit and talk about whether we were right to split up in the first place.'

And then the doorbell rang.

This time it really had to be Phil arriving to collect her.

It went on ringing as Tess struggled with her conflicting emotions. She didn't know what to make of Stephen's words, except that they couldn't have come at a worse time. Exhausted, yearning for sleep and nervous about her capacity really to talk Terry out of his crazy behaviour, she just couldn't cope with any more demands.

'Look, Stephen, I can't talk about this now. That'll be Phil. Terry's kidnapped his children and we've got to drive to Nottinghamshire and make him give them back before he gets arrested. I've got to go.'

Stephen stood up. The insistent buzzing was getting to him too. 'How stupid of me to think anything had really changed. Tess Brien, who always puts everyone else before herself and her family.' He knew he was lashing out unfairly but couldn't help himself. This was such a different outcome from the one he'd been fantasizing about as he drove here. 'Your precious job still comes first with you, doesn't it, Tess? And of course you always did have a soft spot for Terry.' He walked towards the front door and threw it open. Phil was standing there, and looked at him as though he were a being from another planet. He turned back to Tess. 'Just forget any of this happened, will you? I must have been mad anyway. From now on we'll just do it all through the lawyers.' And he almost ran past Phil down the front steps to his car.

Tess watched him, suddenly furious. Hadn't it been him putting painting first that had really wrecked their marriage?

'Wow,' said Phil, staring at his retreating back, 'what was that all about?'

CHAPTER THIRTY-SIX

It was just after eleven when they arrived, exhausted and tense, at Sherwood Park's Reception and asked for Terry Worth. The girl on the desk needed a lot of persuading to let visitors in at this late hour, and only buzzed for someone to take them to Terry's cottage when Tess said she was a solicitor and that if she didn't the police would have to be called.

The walk through the dark forest illuminated by mock-Victorian street lights was one of the oddest in Tess's life. To her amazement there was a complete village scattered amongst the Norwegian pines, each house with its own path and garden. Hansel and Gretel in a Barrett home. When they got to Terry's, Tess knocked on the door.

There was a beat of silence before Terry's suspicious voice asked who it was.

'Me, you bloody idiot,' shouted Phil, 'and we've just driven all the way from bloody London so you'd better damn well let us in!'

At the sound of Phil's voice Terry opened the door, his haggard face lit by the ghost of a smile. 'Philomena Doyle, you rowdy piece, what the hell are you doing here?'

Phil's anger dissipated at the sight of Terry. Clearly the implications of his actions were beginning to hit him.

'Oh, Terry, how could you?' Phil threw herself into his arms. 'Angela went to the police. Everyone's looking for you.'

'Terry,' Tess butted in urgently, 'how are the kids?'

Terry gestured to Lianne and Johnny behind him on the sofa eating popcorn and calmly watching a video.

'Look,' Tess, went on, in a low, urgent voice so that the children couldn't hear, 'you've got to take this seriously or you could lose them altogether. I'll go and phone Angela and then the police. If you take them home first thing in the morning we might be able to pass this off as a misunderstanding.' She glanced at the two children, who both seemed perfectly happy and unaware of any irregularity in the circumstances. 'Have they stayed willingly? They didn't make a fuss?'

'No,' Terry shook his head. 'But they will when you send them back to Colditz. Tess. I want to apply for custody. Their mother's a nutter. And now that Phil and me are together . . .' He looked at Phil. 'You'd move in with me, wouldn't you?'

'So you could get your kids back?' asked Phil, hurt.

'No,' he insisted, 'not just to get the kids back. Because we love each other and we're going to get married. Remember?'

Tess turned her back on this tender scene. He'd never get custody. But if they took the kids straight back she might be able to talk Angela into dropping the charges. Everything might still be OK.

More bone tired than she could ever remember, she wandered back through the forest in search of Reception and a phone.

It took a long time to pacify Angela, because as Tess recognized from the moment she picked up the phone, Angela didn't want to be pacified. She wanted to make Terry pay.

The desk sergeant Tess finally got hold of at Cheltenham police station was considerably more sympathetic. He had parted from his wife himself and could easily

573

see how such a misunderstanding could happen. Terry thought everything was settled and simply took the kids where it had been agreed he'd take them. Angela, the overprotective mother, panicked and called in the police when she should have just checked with Sherwood Park. Simple.

'Between you and me,' the sergeant opined, 'she sounds a bit of a neurotic, this one. I'll see what I can do to sort things out this end.' Tess could have kissed him. She promised the children would be back with their mother first thing tomorrow morning and trudged back to Terry and Phil.

Most of the way back to London on the train the next day Tess dozed. It had been a very wearing day and it taken all her – and the police's – powers of persuasion to get Angela to withdraw her charges. When she wasn't sleeping, Tess thought about Stephen's visit. All it had achieved was to make her angry. How dare he blame her? OK, so she worked hard but that was nothing compared to him chucking in his job when they'd needed the money so badly and then betraying her with Josephine. And why hadn't he even said he was sorry for the pain he'd caused her?

As the train got to Watford she realized that now that InterCity carried phones she could call Lyall and he would come and fetch her from the station. But she didn't feel like it. It would be simpler to get the tube. And yet what was there waiting for her? Luke would probably have gone to Ben's after school as he often did. An empty house.

What the hell was the matter with her? She didn't usually wallow in self-pity like this. Outside Euston Station she looked longingly at a passing taxi, knowing she ought to go home by tube. A taxi would cost about ten times as much and Patricia's new tariff only allowed taxis in extremis. But she was so tired. She stood on the corner and told herself that if a cab came round in the next two minutes it was a sign that she was supposed to take it. Otherwise it was back to the tube station.

In the end it was five minutes before one appeared but Tess was prepared to stretch the proposition. As soon as she got into it she fell fast asleep. She was startled when the cabbie informed her they were outside her house and gave him too big a tip. He smiled graciously. Women were usually terrible tippers.

Someone was sitting on the top step, asleep, leaning on an enormous backpack. Oh God, don't let it be some homeless druggie asking for a handout. She just didn't feel up to it. The owner of the backpack raised its head and smiled. It was Ellie.

'Hiya, Mum.' She lobbed herself down two steps and into her mother's arms. 'I'm back. Couldn't stand the atmosphere in Winchester any longer. So I decided to come home. Is that OK?'

'Ellie, darling,' Tess sighed with relief that she could finally come out and admit the truth, 'you have no idea how much I've missed you!'

'I've drafted the petition,' Diana Adams said, handing her a standard printed document. 'Perhaps you could check through it for me?' Her tone was even more sympathetic than usual. Clearly she understood the significance of this moment.

The paper outlined the barest minimum details of their marriage. The fact that she, Theresa Bernadette – God, that awful name her mother had insisted on saddling her with – Gilfillan was lawfully married to the respondent, Stephen Gilfillan; the address where they'd lived; their jobs; where Stephen lived now; the names of their two children. It stated baldly that the marriage had broken down irretrievably, that the respondent had committed adultery with a woman whose name was not known to the petitioner on the 4th of April that year and that the adultery was continuing; and that the petitioner found it intolerable to live with the respondent. Then came the crucial words: 'the petitioner therefore prays that the said marriage be dissolved', and it was signed by Diana on behalf of Wentworth's. Tess didn't even have to sign it herself.

The beginning and end of their marriage encapsulated in two sheets of paper. The irony was that Tess had drafted thousands of petitions like this and never before had the full tragedy of each one hit her. Reduced like this there seemed so little to show for eighteen years of marriage. She'd expected to feel relief now that the deed was finally done. Instead she felt a great sweep of sadness and waste.

Diana noticed her distress and very subtly left the room for a moment. Tess knew she was being given the space to cry, but tears wouldn't come. Only a kind of numbness that spread through her whole body. If she'd had to get up and walk, she couldn't have done so.

'That's fine,' she said when Diana eventually came back into the room carrying a cup of tea for her. 'I'm glad really. Limbo's the worst. It's funny suddenly to know how your clients feel.'

Diana smiled, 'It must be, though I'm sure you empathize with yours a lot anyway.' She paused as though wondering whether to go on.

Tess was intrigued. Was she itching to deliver some homily? Some piece of homespun advice gleaned from years of officiating at divorces?

'Yes?' Tess prompted. 'What were you going to say?'

To Tess's surprise, Diana actually looked embarrassed. 'It hardly seems appropriate to mention it at the moment. But I've been thinking of starting a very small practice with two or three other specialists, and if you ever felt like moving from Kingsmill's and starting up on your own we'd love to talk to you about it.' She smiled at Tess almost shyly. 'We're so fed up with endless bloody meetings and having to answer to bosses. Think how much more enjoyable it'd be only to answer to oneself!'

Tess remembered how Mr Justice Martin had asked her if she'd ever thought of starting up on her own; clearly he'd thought she was ripe for change. But then, so soon after Stephen losing his job, the idea had just made her nervous. Oddly enough now, when her life was lying around her in pieces, she found the prospect much less frightening.

She thought about it all the way back to Kingsmill's. Of course she'd need to find out much more about the idea. A lot would depend on how she got on with the other prospective partners and what their aims for the firm would be. But she really liked Diana Adams, and that was a start. Of course the whole thing was hugely risky and Tess was shocked at herself for being so drawn to it.

She was still turning the thought over in her mind, her excitement growing as she did so, when she sat down at her desk. Jacqui was ready to pounce. 'Patricia's on the war path again. Apparently you're behind in filling in your legal-aid forms. She issued some declaration that says they have to be filled in week by week now. Plus, you naughty girl, you've been undercharging the poor and indigent again. No brownie points for you this week.'

'Oh, for God's sake!' With Diana Adams's proposition fresh in her mind she had even less patience than usual with Patricia's schemes. She'd definitely find out more about Diana's proposal.

Stephen was drafting a memo suggesting they finally nominate the launch date of the new perfume for October 15 when the call from Savoury's office came through, summoning him in to read Tess's petition.

As he put down the phone he suddenly wondered how on earth had Tess known that Savoury was representing him? The legal grapevine must be pretty damn effective.

'The petition's very straightforward,' Savoury told him as he handed it over the next day. 'Despite this stupid hoo-ha in the press, your wife isn't naming the co-respondent.'

'I didn't ever think she would.'

'No, well Miss Quinn clearly did. I've had her on the phone several times asking for advice on how to stop her.'

Stephen clicked in irritation. He'd no idea Jo had been bypassing him.

'What you might think about,' Savoury continued silkily, 'is the financial settlement. You'll want to sell the family home, of course. And your wife's clearly an adequate earner so you shouldn't need to pay much maintenance.' His tone had such relish in it, imagining Tess reduced to making sacrifices, that Stephen loathed the man even more.

'I'm sure my wife wouldn't ask for it. And as for the family home, I'd rather they stayed there for as long as they want. And naturally I don't intend to make an issue of maintenance. Whatever Tess thinks they need.'

Savoury sighed. Stephen Gilfillan was proving to be a great disappointment to him. When Stephen had first walked into his office, he'd seemed like the perfect chance of getting back at Tess, revenge gift wrapped. Instead he was handing her everything on a plate. Savoury was more used to clients who hid everything they owned, including the plates, from their wives. To Savoury that seemed much more the natural order of things. What a waste of his considerable talents.

Josephine seemed almost disappointed when Stephen told her that she wasn't named in the petition, as though she'd been cheated of a fight she'd been looking forward to. She'd been about to point out that this didn't necessarily mean Tess hadn't tipped off the papers, but one look at Stephen's face told her such speculation might not be wise.

Besides, Josephine had realized lately that attacking Tess was counterproductive. It drove a wedge between them just at the time when the end was finally in sight. In six months he'd be free to marry again. What she needed was to find ways of bringing them closer together. She wandered into the room that had been Ellie's until she'd just upped and left the other day. Josephine sat down on the windowseat. She'd been surprised at how much she'd minded Ellie's sudden departure. She spotted a hairbrush on the cushion. It was Ellie's Mason Pearson covered in Lynx stickers, the one she'd told Jo she'd had since childhood. To her astonishment the sight of it almost made her want to cry. Ellie had only been with them a few weeks and yet the house seemed empty and echoey without her. She'd been such fun, always so eager to soak up everything Josephine could tell her about the art world and about painting. For the first time Josephine had felt like a big sister – or even, God help her, a mother.

And sitting here, she'd come to a decision. She wanted a child of her own. After all forty-one wasn't old these days. She was always reading about career women in New York having babies in their forties. It wasn't creepy like doing it in your sixties. It was all a question of good medical care. Tests made sure you didn't produce a monster and fitness classes for mothers-to-be meant you didn't even have to lose your figure. She didn't think she'd tell Stephen just yet. He had enough to think about just for the moment. She'd be careful to choose the right moment. He might well need softening up.

Seized by a sudden spurt of excitement Josephine couldn't resist half running down the deep-piled hallway to the dressing room attached to one of the spare bedrooms. It had a large window overlooking the grounds running down to the river, a basin and vanity unit, and being south-facing it never seemed cold whatever the season. With some new wallpaper and one of those friezes she'd noticed with teddy bears on it, plus some pretty painted furniture, it'd make a perfect nursery.

Josephine smiled to herself. All she had to get now was one of those books on how to choose the sex of your baby. She definitely wanted a girl. Boys were noisy and messy and the clothes weren't nearly as pretty. Besides, girls loved their mothers. And Josephine was sure about one thing. If she was about to turn her life upside down to have a baby, she wanted something back in return.

Tess waved to Lyall as he eased his long body through the tightly packed tables of her local bistro to join her.

Tonight had been her idea. A night away from any interruptions from Luke, Ellie or Inge so that she could fill him in about the divorce proceedings and also plan the holiday.

He leaned down and kissed her. 'I didn't think this was your kind of place. What are they going for? The Clochemerle award for corniness?' He looked round at the checked tablecloths, candles in wine bottles, menu on the blackboard. There was even taped accordion music.

'That's why I love it! You wait till you taste the Steak Frites. They're the best you'll ever have outside France. Forget warm pigeon breast in redcurrant coulis, surrender yourself to steak Béarnaise and crème brûlée!'

'So.' Lyall raised the glass of red wine she'd poured him. 'Are we celebrating something?'

'In a manner of speaking. My petition's gone off to Stephen's solicitors. The divorce is finally under way.'

'Tess, that's brilliant. So you should get the absolute in January or February.'

She smiled at his enthusiasm. He sounded like a little boy counting the days till Christmas.

'What are you planning to do about Ellie and Luke? Will they go to Stephen at weekends?'

Tess realized she hadn't, perhaps deliberately, got as far as thinking that through. But of course they'd have to come to some arrangement like that. It was funny how she viewed the prospect with alarm and Lyall with delight. Surrogate fatherhood didn't come easily to Lyall.

There was something she wanted his advice about. Something she'd been thinking about a lot lately.

She decided to raise the subject. 'While I was there Diana Adams came up with quite an intriguing proposition. Of course it's early days yet and it might be too problematic but it's tempting all the same.'

'And are you going to tell me what it is?'

'She's thinking of going into partnership with a couple of other family lawyers and she asked if I'd be interested in coming in on it.'

Lyall looked appalled. 'But Tess, it'd be sheer madness! Setting up any small business is a risk at the moment – look at how many of them are going down the pan. And these new laws they're proposing may well mean less work for divorce lawyers. You can't be serious.'

'Oh, I don't know. I can't ever see a day when there'd be less work for divorce lawyers. And think. No Will Kingsmill. No Patricia. No endless battles to do what I believe in. It's very tempting.'

'And probably no income either. Honestly, Tess, you must be mad. Unless you're expecting some vast beano out of your divorce.'

Tess shook her head. 'I'll probably be broker. Women always are, no matter what they think. But I could move somewhere smaller.'

Lyall shook his head in amazement. 'Tess, I can't believe I'm hearing this. You're usually so sensible.'

'I know. But I feel now that I've screwed up my marriage I want to make sure I don't feel the same about the rest of my life. Can you understand that?'

Lyall shook his head again.

Tess realized there was no point arguing. One thing she'd learned about Lyall was that he didn't approve of taking risks. The irony was that with Stephen she'd been the same way. Then she hadn't been strong enough to risk change. Now, six months later, she was. In fact the challenge of something new was bringing her an extraordinary heady excitement. This must be how Stephen had felt when he'd discovered he wanted to become a painter.

Their food arrived and Tess decided the discussion would be better left. 'So,' she said, helping herself to rather too much Béarnaise sauce, 'what do you think we should do about Ireland? Fly-drive is more comfortable. Taking the car would be cheaper.'

'For God's sake, Tess' – Lyall laid off his words with a smile – 'you don't think I'm driving all the way to Holyhead with Sonic the Hedgehog beeping in the back, do you?'

'Oh, I forgot to tell you. Some good news. Ellie's coming too.'

'Terrific. Fly-drive it is, kiddo. That is if you want me to come.'

'OK, OK. I get the picture. I'll book the tickets.'

Tess sat between Ellie and Luke on the flight to Cork feeling an almost schoolgirlish excitement at the thought of two weeks at Killamalooe. Somehow the place had taken over her heart so that she felt every inch belonged to her from its tiny hidden coves to its wide sweep of beach and the fields that stretched almost down to the shoreline. Luke and Ellie were both absorbed in their own interests and Lyall, who had sensibly managed to get himself a seat separated from them across the aisle, was deep in *The Times*' law report.

They touched down by mid-afternoon, and were in their hire car half an hour later. By five they were driving up to Killamalooe House's imposing iron gates, and as usual Stella stood on the front steps, between the two flower-filled urns, waving.

'Can we swim, Gramma?' Luke demanded, kissing her.

'Well, I was going to suggest tea. But why not? You have to grab the weather while it's here,' she explained to Lyall, shaking his hand. 'We met at the exhibition, didn't we? Do you want to go too?' she asked Tess.

'As a matter of fact,' Tess confessed, 'I've been dreaming about this moment for weeks. Just try and keep me out!'

So they all searched through their luggage for swimming costumes while Stella went to look for towels. Then they raced through the house, fragrant with the smell of cut flowers, out through the open French windows and down the narrow path, surrounded by marram grass, towards the sea. Dumping their things on the empty beach they ran headlong into the waves, ducking and diving like dolphins released from captivity. Even Ellie, normally conscious of looking cool, disappeared under the water and swam through Tess's legs pulling her over as she did so till they both lay giggling helplessly in the shallows while Lyall surprised them all by waving goodbye and taking off for the horizon.

Luke, who still had a secret fear of going out of his depth, watched admiringly. 'I didn't know Lyall was an Olympic swimmer.'

'No,' agreed Tess, fighting an edge of anxiety at quite how far out he appeared to be heading, 'neither did I.'

They watched till he was a distant speck then climbed out of the water and dried themselves. Ellie lay prone on her towel, her eyes tightly closed against the sun. Every pore of her body seemed to be drinking it greedily in. Tess perched on a rock looking out towards Lyall, relieved when at last he turned and began to head back towards the shore.

★

It was halfway through dinner when Julius decided he didn't like Lyall. There was an innate conservatism about him which hadn't been so noticeable during their brief meeting at Stephen's opening. And Julius saw conservatism in all its forms as anti-life. In Lyall's case it showed through his obvious disapproval that Luke was allowed to join them for dinner. Tess clearly hadn't noticed the way every time Luke raised a subject of conversation, Lyall swiftly changed it to something else the moment Luke closed his mouth. Eventually Luke gave up and asked to get down from the table. Ellie, who had been watching exactly what was going on, followed him in solidarity.

'So, Tess,' Julius asked, 'what arrangements are you and Stephen making over the children in the long term?'

Tess went on peeling her orange. 'I don't know yet, to be frank. I need to sit down and talk to them both about it, especially Ellie. She was staying with Stephen and Josephine but now she says she wants to get a flat with two other girls from college.'

Lyall looked shocked. 'Really, Tess, you can't be taking that seriously. She's only seventeen. You give her far too much freedom as it is.'

'The reason I give her freedom,' Tess pointed out frostily, 'is because she's very sensible. I treat her like an adult because she's never let me down.'

'But surely it's up to you to decide what's best for her and tell her. Surely that's what being a parent's all about.'

'It may be when they're little, even at Luke's age perhaps. But in the end you have to let them make their own decisions, and just hope you've done a good enough job and given them the right tools.'

Lyall shook his head. 'I don't understand all this liberal parenting. Thank God we're not going to have any of our own.'

Tess looked at him thoughtfully. 'You may be right. But as a matter of fact that isn't something we've talked about.'

'No . . . er, well, I suppose I just assumed . . .'

Watching them Julius found himself wondering what Lyall would be like in twenty, or even ten years' time. There was no doubt he would make a reliable husband. He just hoped Tess wasn't paying too high a price for the promise of security.

After dinner they strolled in the garden. Stella, ever watchful, tactfully took Lyall on a tour of the greenhouses.

When they were out of sight Tess began, 'Julius, I wanted to ask a word of advice.'

'Fire away. Though I'm hardly a wise old greybeard.'

'Maybe I don't want wise old greybeard advice. I've had an intriguing offer from another woman lawyer, asking me to consider starting our own firm.'

'Do you want to?'

'In some ways, yes. In others no.'

'Which yes and which no?'

'Well, no one in their right mind would want to start a business in a recession. On the other hand I really like the idea of being my own boss.'

'So you're tempted then?'

'Very tempted . . .' She held on to his arm as they walked down the steps to the bottom lawn, breathing in the night-scented stocks and honeysuckle. 'But then I think I'm mad. Lyall thinks I'm mad too.'

'I'm afraid I'd tend to see that as a recommendation.'

'You don't like him, do you? I noticed at dinner.'

'I'm more worried about what he's going to become. You can almost see his attitudes hardening like fat on arteries.'

Tess smiled at the image. 'He's not as liberal as you. That comes of having had to fight to get where he is. But then I admire that in some ways.' She picked a bloom and breathed in its scent deeply. 'And he says he wants to look after me.'

'You don't need looking after.' Somehow the dark made it easier to talk about such personal things. 'Shrinks' couches are jammed with people fantasizing about someone who'll look after them. It's an illusion, Tess, a way of staying a child. Besides, you're growing out of security. Listen to you. You're thinking of taking a big risk when your rational brain is shouting that you'd be mad.'

'I know. Odd, isn't it? I was furious with Stephen for doing the same thing.'

'What would Stephen tell you to do?'

'To go ahead!'

Julius left a beat to allow this observation to sink in before he went on. 'You know, Tess, I'm a very rich man with almost no commitments. This place is paid for, my cellar's full, we stay with friends when we travel. I've nothing to spend it on.'

'Julius, I wouldn't dream of letting you invest in my law firm.'

Julius grinned. 'And I wouldn't dream of offering. It sounds far too risky. On the other hand I would like to be allowed to pay for my grandchildren's education, and make sure they have a roof over their head so that my daughter-in-law whom I love very much has a chance to make the kind of choices *she* wants to make. One thing I've learned in life is that money only has one single importance. To let you do what you want to do.'

It was too dark now for her to see Julius's face but she reached up and kissed his cheek anyway.

'You've changed, Tess. You're ready to spread your wings. And not just financially. Think of the paintings you bought. Don't settle for security. Security kills.'

Stephen threw open the French windows of the studio and let the early morning sunshine flood in. There was a slight mist still hanging over the river which would probably be gone in half an hour, and he wanted to try and capture it before it disappeared. A couple of swans meandered lazily through it, like elegant liners picking their way through fog. An unaccompanied dog ran along the far bank barking at the male swan, who superciliously ignored it until, pushed too far by its insolence, it suddenly flashed three feet of angry wing, making the dog yelp in fright and turn tail to look for its owner.

His hand moving swiftly, Stephen painted the wispy outline of the scene in watery black instead of sketching it, making the drawing almost Japanese in appearance, to try out the technique. At first he was pleased with the effect, so much softer than charcoal, until he made a mistake and couldn't easily rub it out. Furious with himself, he threw it across the room, where it knocked over a jar holding brushes and turps and was ruined.

Stephen closed his eyes. What on earth was the matter with him? Ever since the exhibition he hadn't wanted to paint, and now when at last he'd actually felt like doing so he was reacting as though the slightest irritation was enough to make him snap.

He picked up the drawing and placed it on the work surface, drying it off with some kitchen roll. Then he abandoned it and headed out over the watermeadows. Maybe a walk would do him good. Perhaps he'd been overdoing it working on the perfume launch, and what with the divorce finally going ahead, it was too much strain. He needed a holiday and some new inspiration. The fresh greenness of Ireland filled his mind's eye. The hidden bays and coves of West Cork. The beauty of Galway and Kerry. Not to his father's. He wanted absolute freedom to roam without the hint of a social obligation. Just walking and painting and staying in small hotels where they'd fill you up with an Irish breakfast of fry-up and potato cakes and turn you out for a satisfying day in the open, then give you a good dinner before you fell into your bed at night and slept the sleep of the just.

He'd try and talk Josephine into it tonight. He just hoped she hadn't been laying plans for jet-setting locations like Positano or Sardinia.

He ambushed her that evening as she chopped basil for a tomato salad in the kitchen. She'd spent the day in London and picked up some glorious picnic food from Camisa's in Soho. Olives dressed in herbs, wind-dried tomatoes, peppery salami and crispy ciabatta bread.

He put his arms round her waist. 'Why don't we eat outside, down by the river?'

'All right,' She took a bottle of Frascati out of the fridge and two glasses and started loading up a basket, 'Except that we'll be eaten alive by midges.'

'Come on, you optimist, I'm prepared to suffer for beauty. And so should you be.' He picked up the long-handled basket and slung it over his shoulder.

As they reached the river bank the sunlight was just beginning to fade into that twilight time film people call magic hour. The burghers of Winchester were mostly home watering their geraniums and the towpath was deserted. Stephen and Josephine sat on a rug and watched a string of Canada geese fly cornily up against the sun, honking, as though they were joined together by an invisible chain.

'They can't be off already,' Stephen said, putting his hand up to shield his eyes as he looked into the sunset, 'there's still plenty of summer left. In fact I was wondering whether we might take off for a couple of weeks.' He poured her another glass of the pale wine. 'I was thinking of Ireland. I'd love to do a bit of painting there.'

Objections flooded into Josephine's mind. Ireland was so provincial, and if he thought they were going to stay with his parents where she'd have to face the steely disapproval she'd seen in Stella's eyes, he had to be kidding. But there were pluses. It was only an hour away if any crisis came up in the business, and it might just be the place to broach the subject of a child. One conceived in Ireland had to mean a lot to Stephen.

'All right,' she conceded – to Stephen's surprise – 'as long as we stay in a hotel. Your parents are too exotic for me.'

Stephen laughed, swatting the first of the midges, 'I know exactly what you mean. Killamalooe is a bit of an everyday story of Bloomsbury folk. A hotel it is, then. How about being mad and unpredictable and going next week?'

Ellie was in seventh heaven. For the first time in her life, Julius had noticed she might have inherited the family talent and was taking an interest in her painting. Every day he suggested a different location and by the end of the first week they'd painted everything from cornfields covered in poppies to rockpools teeming with subaquatic life. The sight of Julius in his cricket whites and battered panama was already a familiar one nearby in the small town of Skibbereen. But his granddaughter wearing a flowery frock and straw hat tied under her chin plus what appeared to the local populace to be hobnailed boots – Fragonard in grunge as the owner of the local craft shop put it – was a new and captivating one.

For his part, Julius too had rarely felt happier. When Stephen had been a similar age, Julius had been too busy building his brilliant career, not to mention carousing with his artistic chums, staying up all night trying to pin down the butterfly of art with the glue of rather pompous perception, to pay his son any attention. He'd had no time for children. That had been Stella's domain. But with Ellie it was different. He found he could treat her opinions with respect in a way that he had never been able to treat Stephen's. He had seen Stephen's every contribution, he now saw with shame, as a challenge to be routed and ruthlessly crushed. It took another generation, and some tentative wisdom of age, to see that the ideas of youth were really flowers to be watered.

As they packed up their easels after an afternoon spent quietly painting together, Julius suddenly turned to her. 'Do you know, Eleanor, I so wish I could have loved your father as easily as I love you. So many years I wasted and it's taken me until now to see it.'

Ellie saw the pain in his eyes and ran to hug him. 'But you love him now. And you think he's talented. That means everything to him.'

'Does it?' Julius asked helplessly. 'Does it really?'

'Yes,' Ellie nodded firmly, 'it does.'

'I wish he and Tess hadn't parted.'

Now it was Ellie's turn to feel the pain. 'So do I, Gramps. More than anything.' It was something she didn't allow herself to think about. She buried her head in his jumper just in case she cried.

Josephine had to admit that the hotel overlooking the bay was pleasant enough even by her exacting standards. A plain grey square Georgian building, buried in creeper and blue with wisteria, it was fronted by a circular gravel drive, and had lawns that ran down behind to a clifftop, from where a lift took you down to the beach below.

The problem started when you went into the nearby town. It was the kind of place Josephine found utterly ghastly. Small and provincial, trapped somewhere in the 1950s with its little drapers' shops where they still kept goods in glass cabinets and had one of those metal tubes that whizzed your money to some hidden cashier, a chemist that still didn't stock condoms, and a small hotel whose idea of a smart lunch was overcooked roast chicken and yellow cabbage.

And yet these were exactly the things Stephen seemed to love about the place. He wandered round the streets for hours, wallowing, she supposed, in memories of childhood. He kept buying toffee apples and ninety-nines and those little glass tubes with different coloured sand in them. And she'd actually had to stop him getting one of those paperweights you shook to start a sandstorm on the beach inside for their secretary Lucy.

It had only taken a day or two for Josephine to realize how much she distrusted Irish charm. People here were incapable of straightforwardness. Everything came cloaked in blarney which, in her view, was simply to disguise a lazy, feckless turn of mind. The incident they were witnessing now was typical. They'd just come out of the gents' outfitters where Stephen had bought some new bathing trunks to find that, far in the distance, a funeral procession was coming down the road. Already, as a supposed mark of respect, the roadmenders who were digging a hole in the town square had downed tools and taken their caps off, watching respectfully for what turned out to be a full fifteen minutes before the procession arrived and another ten as it passed and wended its way out of sight again to the cemetery by the sea shore.

'What a country.' Stephen shook his head in pure pleasure at this ritual of taking half an hour off work to honour the passing of a fellow-citizen.

'What a country indeed,' reinforced Josephine, appalled at the sheer waste of manpower she'd just witnessed.

Back at the hotel, after a stroll round the gardens watching the lights of the town below, they went up to their room to change for dinner. Stephen decided to have a bath in the wonderfully deep claw-foot bath, regally placed right in the middle of the room with views of the sea beyond.

He felt Josephine's arm slip round his neck as he stared out. 'Stephen . . .' For once Josephine's voice lacked its usual confidence. 'There's something I wanted to talk to you about. I know it's early days in our relationship but at my age it's something I can't just put off. I want to have our baby. I'm forty-one,' she rushed on, before he had time to answer, 'old, but not too old. Irish women have babies at my age all the time. Oh, Stephen, it would be so wonderful to have our child.'

CHAPTER THIRTY-SEVEN

Stephen turned to her, the bathwater seeming colder than it had before. He knew he had to be gentle but the truth was he felt appalled. 'Jo love' – he took her hand and held it to his damp cheek – 'I'm staggered. I always thought you loathed children.'

Josephine smiled faintly. 'Other people's. Ours would be different.' She handed him a towel. 'It was having Ellie to stay that changed my mind. She was such a joy and I've really missed her. It made me realize how much I'd like a daughter of our own.'

'What if it were a son?'

'Oh, it wouldn't be a son,' Josephine insisted. 'I'm sure about that. Come on, let me dry you.'

Stephen stepped out of the bath. But this ritual, half-teasing, half-sexy, didn't hold its usual appeal. He'd never intended having any more children. The truth was he still loved Luke and Ellie so much another family would seem like ultimate betrayal. But then he'd always assumed Jo was the last person who'd want one. What the hell was he going to do?

He considered Josephine for a moment as she hung the damp towel back on the towel rail. Every inch of her was chic and soignée. He couldn't imagine her lying on the floor playing dead lions or putting up with a baby being sick on her shoulder. Josephine noticed his gaze and came towards him.

'Look, Jo,' he stalled, 'this is a big decision. We can't just rush into it. Besides' – he grinned, trying to distract her with humour – 'if we did it now we'd miss dinner and it's already paid for.'

*

Tess and Lyall were ten days into their holiday at Killamalooe when the weather broke, reminding residents and tourists alike that the bright blue sky and unbroken sunshine they'd come to expect as their due were happy diversions from the grey palette of Irish normality.

Ellie and Tess dug out their raincoats and wellies and tramped along the beach looking for shells, while Luke and Lyall played chess in the drawing room adjoining Julius's studio. As was his habit, Julius shut the door to keep out any possible distraction. But he soon found that the deepest distraction was the silence itself. God help him, he seemed to be getting used to having people around.

He opened the door to the drawing room and watched the progress of the chess game for a moment. Luke wasn't a bad little player, but Lyall was clearly giving no quarter, just as he himself had never done when he'd played with Stephen at the same age. To his amazement Julius found himself wanting to come out and say, *Let him win occasionally, it's only a game*. But Lyall, he suspected, was the kind who would say that was bad for him, Luke had to win on equal terms. And once, Julius told himself, turning back to the studio, I would have agreed with him. But the funny thing is, I don't any more.

As Tess trudged up the cliff path, carrying a bucket full of shells, it struck her that they only had four more days left in this magical place. She loved the sunshine and the swimming but the rain brought out another, gentler face. This was what people round here called a 'fine, soft day': rain as misty as though it came through an atomizer and only the occasional glimpse of pale sunshine. But already the earth smelled as though it were breathing the rain in deeply, taking great lungfuls of it then exhaling that woody, peaty fragrance that told you more clearly than any roadmap that you were in the country.

'I'd like to stay here for ever.' Ellie pushed a strand of damp hair out of her eyes and threw her arms open expansively to take in the wide view of sea and fields.

'Me too,' echoed Tess, 'it really is paradise on earth, isn't it?'

Together they walked along the clifftop path to the ruined tower, eating the first hard early blackberries, their brambles twisted and turned round the base of the tower like something from a fairy tale. Why were towers such magical places? Rapunzel's, Yeats's, Vita Sackville-West's.

Ellie got out the case of watercolours Inge had given her and began to sketch Tess sitting in the window looking out to sea.

By the end of the week Josephine didn't know how she'd survived the boredom. She'd never liked beaches anyway; she much preferred the Hockney blue of pools, preferably with a waiter hovering by to bring you drinks. Besides the water here was freezing, only the crazy would seriously swim in it, and the rocky beach was slippery and narrow. It reminded her of childhood days huddled at their beach-hut in Devon, sentenced to spend the whole day there, buried under rugs, brewing endless cups of tea to keep themselves warm, waiting for the sun to come out. People always said the summers of childhood had been sunnier, but hers hadn't.

It was only the desire to talk to Stephen about having a child that carried her through to rise victoriously above the drab provinciality around her. She looked at her watch. Only three-thirty. Stephen would be out painting for hours yet. She packed up her basket and took the lift back up to the hotel.

Bored at the thought of heading back to their room alone, she made for the conservatory where they would be serving tea. She sat at a corner table with splendid views of the sea and ordered Lapsang Souchong, relishing the fact that she was the only person in here. She loathed sitting crushed up against other people, with their ghastly dull conversation forcing itself into your peace even when it was the last thing you wanted to listen to.

To her horror a young mother in a lurid shell suit with two snivelly children had come into the conservatory and was being led in her direction. The young woman's buggy, loaded down with supermarket bags and packs of nappies, bumped into the elegant tables and chairs as she made her way across the room, finally settling at the table next to Josephine's.

There was then the usual disruption as the woman asked for a high chair and the furniture had to be rearranged to accommodate it. Josephine watched surreptitiously as she installed the baby in it. The child, she noted, bore more than a slight resemblance to Gran in the Giles cartoons, only marginally less pretty. His mother handed him a rattle which he flung on to the floor and smugly waited for her to retrieve it. A green blob snaked tantalizingly in and out of one nostril as he breathed heavily, dribble cascading down his chin.

'He's teething, poor lamb,' explained his mother proudly, showing no sign of blowing the repulsive child's nose.

His sister, meanwhile, had grabbed the sugar bowl and was happily decanting it on to the lace tablecloth.

In the midst of this chaos the young woman's tea arrived. Josephine caught the delicious aroma of toasted teacake, wafting her back to childhood teas at Debenham's with her grandmother and making her wish she'd ordered some herself. With immaculate timing just as the waiter lifted the lid of the silver chafing dish the baby let out an ear-shattering yell.

'I'd better feed his royal highness first, or there'll be no peace for anyone.' She produced a half-empty jar of Heinz Spaghetti Bolognese and attempted to shovel it down him, cold. Not an easy process as the baby, having sabotaged his mother's tea, instantly lost interest in his own.

Fifteen minutes later, with more spaghetti on the infant's face than in his mouth, his exhausted mother reached for a cold, unappetizing teacake. After one bite, she wisely abandoned it. She cast a wry smile at Josephine, assuming she understood. 'Ah well, t' was a mad idea anyway. Trying to take these two somewhere posh for tea.'

But Josephine didn't understand. She'd seen this cheerful self-sacrifice in mothers before, noticed how they let their food get cold, gave up all their own personal time, never got the chance to finish a conversation. They seemed happy to forget any needs of their own to satisfy those of their demanding children.

Josephine sipped her tea and surveyed the debris of the adjoining table, a brutal truth dawning on her. Perhaps she was being unrealistic. Not everyone was the maternal type. What if this miracle of selflessness didn't happen to her and she simply resented it? After all, it was young adults like Ellie she really responded to. Why not surround herself with them instead of having a baby? Start a summer school, perhaps? There was plenty of room at the Lodge.

As she sat watching the family depart the idea took root in her. She was looking for things to hold Stephen, and he might well enjoy something like that. Slouch could do the real work and Stephen could simply be a guest lecturer, presiding over suppers attended by admiring young people. To be honest she'd seen the look of panic that had crossed his face when she'd mentioned a baby. This would be altogether better. And, unlike a baby, if it didn't work out she could simply change her mind. She closed her book and hurried up to their room to make plans. It would give her something to do in this ghastly dump.

When Stephen got back he found her buried in a notebook looking happier than she had for days.

'What're you hatching now?' he asked, knowing her. 'School fees plans? The job description for a nanny?'

Josephine shut her notebook. 'As a matter of fact I've seen sense. I'm not the maternal type. You were kind not to point it out. I've decided to run a summer school instead. If you like the idea, that is.'

Stephen smiled at this attempt at consultation, deeply relieved. 'Sounds a brilliant scheme to me. Why stop there? What about an art festival? A mini-Aldeburgh for the art world? You'd be brilliant at organizing it.' Josephine's face lit up with plans and possibilities. Stephen realized how bored she'd been in the last week and felt guilty. 'Look, Jo, you can't stand it here, can you? Would you like to go home?

Josephine's spirits leaped but she hid her excitement behind one of the small, sad smiles that suited her so. 'But you love it here. I don't want to spoil your holiday.'

'Come on. I've had a wonderful week's painting and plenty of ideas to get me going again. There is one thing, though. I'd like to go back from Cork and take

599

my parents out to dinner. They'll be hurt if they find I've been over and not contacted them.'

'Of course,' she conceded magnanimously, 'why don't we leave tomorrow morning and spend the week-end in Cork. It's supposed to be packed with wonderful restaurants.'

After lunch the following day, installed in a delightful waterside hotel in Cork, Stephen picked up the phone.

Julius was in the studio when it rang and he ignored it for the first minute or so. Surely someone must be in the blasted house who could answer the instrument rather than him? Eventually he put down his palette and opened the door to the sitting room. He hated interruptions, but what he hated even more was deciding to answer the phone and then not getting to it in time. He broke into a comical trot, convinced the ring had taken on a dying fall, indicating that the caller was about to give up.

'Yes!' he barked down the receiver, making Stephen, who had indeed been on the point of giving up, jump.

'Fa, hello, it's Stephen.'

Julius grinned with delight. 'Stephen! How's city life treating you?'

Even down the line he could sense his father's pleasure at hearing from him, 'Well, as a matter of fact I'm at the Greystones Hotel in Cork. I came over to paint. We've been travelling round a lot so we didn't want to trouble you and Ma, but we're sailing home tomorrow and wondered if you were free for dinner tonight?'

Julius knew the rough translation of this was that Josephine hadn't wanted to stay with them. ''Fraid not. Guests of our own.' He felt relieved that the excuse was true. He didn't fancy an evening of preten-tious art talk with that over-refined girlfriend of

Stephen's. And then a thought came to him. A wicked, manipulative thought. The kind that drove Stella mad. He decided to give in to it. 'Tell you what, when are you sailing tomorrow?'

'Not till midnight.'

'Then why not come over to lunch?'

'We'd like that. It'll make a pleasant final day.' Not how Josephine would see it, but too bad. He was giving up his holiday so she could make a few concessions. 'What sort of time?'

'About twelve? Then we'll have time for a drink first. Do you still like Black Velvet?'

'Father!' Stephen realized this was a reminder of their Golden Wedding when Stephen had had rather too much of the stuff and made his speech. 'What about Dubonnet with tangerine peel like you used to have at Northumberland Wharf?'

'My God.' Julius was impressed. 'What a memory you must have! You couldn't have been more than five or six.'

'I wasn't. Your friends used to slip me the occasional glass. That's why I can remember it.'

'Dubonnet and tangerine peel it is, then.' Julius put down the phone, still smiling. It was delightful to know there were some happy memories he shared with his son.

Without mentioning it to Stella he rang and ordered a large salmon from the fish shop in Skibbereen. 'And throw in some decent prawns and monkfish,' he commanded. 'I might even make a fish soup.'

'Julius, what's going on?' Stella watched him suspiciously as he ignored the Sunday papers and donned a pinny. 'First a salmon arrives, then you put on an apron and turn into Fanny Craddock.'

'Johnny Craddock, please,' Julius corrected. 'Why don't you join me? We could be in that great tradition of creative couples. Fanny and Johnny, Armand and Michaela, Hans and Lotte.'

'Hitler and Eva. Anyway, don't change the subject. I know you. You're definitely up to something.'

'Nonsense, woman. There may be a couple of extra guests for lunch, that's all. Don't make so much fuss. Shoo. Go and leave me in peace in my own kitchen.'

Stella shook her head. Anyone would think Julius spent his whole life bent over a hot stove, instead of which he sometimes didn't cross the kitchen threshold from one month to the next.

'Fine. I'll leave the lunch to you, shall I?' Stella asked gleefully.

'If the alternative is standing there criticizing, why don't you do that?'

Stella shut the door, confident he'd be screaming for her assistance in ten seconds flat. Well, too bad. It was a beautiful day again and she was going for a swim.

In the hall, Ellie was trying to talk her mother into another trip to the tower so that she could finish her sketch. Tess clearly wanted to go to the beach. In the end Tess capitulated, blackmailed by Ellie's argument that she should be encouraging her daughter's studies, not selfishly lounging in the dunes reading bad novels.

Down on the beach, Stella found Luke and Lyall about to go in swimming. 'Where's Tess?' Lyall asked her.

'Walking over to the tower so that Ellie can finish drawing her. Not very enthusiastically.'

'Poor Tess. Tell you what' – he turned to Luke – 'why don't we swim over and give them a surprise?'

Luke looked out across the bay, horrified. 'But it's miles.'

'No, it isn't. It's an optical illusion. Swimming in a straight line it'd only take fifteen or twenty minutes.'

'I'd rather not,' Luke mumbled. The truth was the sea scared him. Even on blue days like this it was freezing and he was terrified he might get cramp.

'Wimp!' teased Lyall, pinching Luke's arm. 'You'll never be a big strong boy if you don't push yourself.'

Stella glared at him. Who did he think he was? Not the boy's father, for one thing. And the boy's own father would never be stupid enough to goad him like that. 'You stay here and come for a sedate swim with your grandmother. You never know when I'll need help at my age.'

Luke smiled at her gratefully as Lyall ran towards the water and dived in showily, then cut a straight fast furrow through the water in the direction of the ruined tower.

Stella and Luke were horsing happily about in the shallows when Julius, still in his stripey apron and bearing an ancient toasting fork, which gave him an air of Neptune on the rampage, appeared on the path down to the beach. 'Where've you hidden the bloody fish kettle, woman?'

Stella came out of the sea, laughing. 'And how long were you going to cook it for when you found the kettle?'

Julius waved his toasting fork, annoyed at being bogged down with such minor details. 'I really don't know. About an hour?'

'If you want it flaky and disgusting. You bring it to the boil then turn off the heat. By the time the water's cold it's cooked.'

'Nonsense. It'll be raw. Like that Japanese fish that poisons you. I'm sure it needs an hour.'

'Would you like me to do it?'

'As long as I can still blame you if it's raw.'

'You can blame me if it's raw.'

He handed her the apron and toasting fork as though they were the sceptre and ermine robe of royal office. 'I think I'll stay down here with Luke for a bit.' He picked up some flat stones and skimmed them brilliantly, so that they skipped fifteen or twenty times.

'Sign of a misspent youth,' Stella observed, 'like playing pool too well. Or, in your case, a misspent adulthood too.'

'Hadn't you better get on with salmon?' he enquired. Stella patted his head. She had no idea what he was up to but she knew something was going on. As she'd said to Stephen at the anniversary party, life with Julius was never dull.

Julius held out a big towel for Luke and they sat side by side for a few minutes looking out to sea. 'Where's Lyall?' Julius asked.

'He's swum over to the tower to surprise Mum.'

'Showing off again,' muttered Julius. 'How're you coping with all this emotional stuff, old son?'

Luke suddenly crumpled against Julius's shoulder. What a crass, damn-fool question. Julius could have kicked himself. Had he no tact? And what did he think he was doing, playing God by inviting Stephen here today? The whole thing could easily backfire and hurt Luke badly.

Julius rubbed his thin shoulders with the towel, trying to comfort him.

It was too late to put them off now. They'd be here any minute.

Stella had just taken the salmon out of the fish kettle and was garnishing it with thin slices of cucumber and sprigs of parsley when she heard a car drawing up outside the front steps. This must be Julius's mysterious guests. She had a good mind to ignore them and let Julius deal with them himself but couldn't resist a peep through the drawing-room windows. To her horror she saw Stephen and Josephine climbing out of a white sports car. How could he! How could Julius do this to Tess and the children without even warning them? She would have to do her best to try and smooth things over.

Wiping her hands on her Liberty apron, she ran to the front door, quickly patting her hair in the hall mirror.

'Stephen, darling! Josephine! How lovely to see you,' she breathed, kissing Stephen and, in deliberate contrast, shaking Josephine's hand, giving not the slightest inkling of surprise that they were here or even in the country at all. 'Come into the garden and I'll get you a drink.'

She led them through the drawing room and out on to the lawn where she sat them down in the swinging sofa and disappeared to get a tray of drinks.

At the other end of the garden, from the cliff path, Ellie appeared with Tess in hot pursuit, both red-faced and laughing from their exertion.

From her palanquin-like seat, half hidden from sight, Josephine watched them with a pang of jealousy. She'd been crazy to imagine she could have a relationship like that with a daughter of her own. She'd be almost sixty by the time the child was Ellie's age, for heaven's sake.

They were almost parallel with the swing-chair when Stephen stood up. 'Hello, girls, you look as though you've been having an adventure!'

'Dad!' shrieked Ellie, dumping her watercolours on

the lawn and running into his arms. 'What on earth are you doing here?'

Stephen was about to answer when Julius appeared from the beach, dressed in monstrous white shorts that looked as though they'd been made for James Robertson Justice in *Doctor at Sea*. 'Ah, you're here. I thought it'd be much more fun to keep your visit a surprise. And it is a lovely surprise, isn't it, girls?'

'Lovely,' agreed Tess faintly, wishing she looked just a little less pink and sweaty beside Josephine's emerald wild silk and gold strappy sandals.

'Brilliant!' endorsed Ellie, sitting down next to her father on the swing-chair.

Thankfully, in the beat of silence that followed Stella arrived carrying a tray of drinks with a surprised Lyall in tow.

'Julius was saving Josephine and Stephen's visit as a surprise,' Tess explained in an ironic tone. 'And it certainly is.'

Fortunately the embarrassment of the next few minutes was filled with the fetching of chairs and pouring of drinks and with Julius demanding Dubonnet and tangerine peel for him and Stephen.

Stella looked at him beadily. 'Julius, I have no idea whether we have any of either. Go and look yourself.'

Julius disappeared for a couple of minutes then returned with a dusty bottle and an orange. 'No tangerine, so we'll have to improvise.' He poured two large tumblers of the stuff.

'Julius,' Stella hissed under her breath, 'are you going completely mad?'

But Julius was looking disgracefully pleased with himself. 'So, Stephen, have you heard Tess's exciting news? She's going to start her own firm with some other lawyers.'

Now it was Stephen's turn to look amazed. 'Really, Tess? I always thought you hated risky ventures.'

'She should do if she had any sense,' cut in Lyall. 'The whole idea's commercially crazy.'

Tess looked embarrassed, the irony not lost on her of how she'd reacted when Stephen took a risk. 'I thought maybe it was time I stuck my neck out a bit.'

'Good for you!' Stephen congratulated her. He looked round. 'Where's Luke, by the way?'

'Messing about down on the beach,' said Julius.

'I'll go and find him,' Ellie offered. 'He won't want to miss you!'

'Tess,' Julius suggested innocently, 'why don't you show Stephen your art collection. I'm sure he'd be fascinated.'

'What a good idea,' agreed Lyall, standing up, 'I'd love to see it too.'

Julius tutted. 'What a pity, Stella was only saying a moment ago that she wanted to show you and Josephine her orchids. I can't stand the things, but people in the know think they're quite spectacular.'

'I adore orchids,' murmured Josephine, 'all that sinister beauty.'

'Let's go and see them, then.' Stella shook her head as the direction of Julius's plans became more obvious. The poor man was clearly losing his reason. She only hoped it wasn't early Alzheimer's.

'What brought on the idea of starting your own firm?' Stephen asked as he and Tess headed back towards the house. 'I thought you were a strictly PAYE and pension person?'

Tess stepped inside the cool of the drawing room. 'What you really mean is, How dare I throw security to the winds and risk going bust when I gave you such a bloody awful time when you did it?'

Stephen laughed. 'Something like that.'

Tess decided she had nothing to lose from honesty. 'I suppose I started to see that my obsession with security was one of the things that mucked up our marriage. I just didn't want to make the same mistake with my whole life. Besides' – she returned his smile – 'I can't take much more of Patricia Greene. But you haven't heard the best bit yet. Do you know who it is who's asked me to go into partnership?'

Stephen shook his head.

'My divorce lawyer.'

The smile slipped from Stephen's face and he was suddenly serious. But before he got the chance to speak again there was a commotion on the lawn. They turned to see Ellie, looking frantic, running towards them.

'Dad,' she half sobbed, ignoring everyone else there, 'it's Luke. He's miles out. He must be trying to swim over to the tower.'

'That won't do him any harm,' Lyall threw in, returning with Stella to see what all the fuss was about. 'It's not nearly as far as it looks. I swam over there this morning.'

Ellie grabbed Stephen's arm. 'I think he's in trouble.' Stephen turned to Lyall. 'Did you put him up to this, you stupid bastard?' he demanded. 'It's far more dangerous when the tide's changing, and Luke's never been a strong swimmer.'

Not waiting for an answer Stephen ran down towards the beach path with Tess and Ellie close behind. He scanned the horizon. 'Where is he? I can't even see him.'

'There he is!' Ellie pointed to a speck far out to sea. 'Oh God, he's nowhere near the tower! The current must be pulling him away. Dad, what are we going to do?' Her voice teetered on the edge of hysteria.

Stephen fought off panic, knowing everyone was

depending on him. The weather had cleared briefly but now it was looking threatening again. He could feel a bitter wind blowing in his face. He tried not to think how cold the water must be. 'Tess, does Feargal still keep his boat down in the boathouse?'

Tess nodded, fighting to suppress the shivering that had taken hold of her.

'Ellie, tell Julius to phone the air–sea rescue and get them down here.' He grabbed Tess's wrist and they started running towards the dilapidated structure a few yards down the beach. As she ran she wondered where Lyall was. He was a much stronger swimmer than Stephen and they could do with his help. After all, this was his doing. She cursed as she caught sight of him still up on the lawn determined not to see this as any kind of real emergency.

The boat wasn't in the boathouse but sitting on the beach. They started to push it towards the water when they saw the old man waving behind them.

'Feargal, it's Luke,' Stephen shouted. 'He's swum out to sea and he's in trouble.'

Feargal began pushing with them. 'The tide's on the turn. It's a nasty time. You'd better be quick. But careful – she's low on fuel.' As soon as the boat hit the water Stephen and Tess jumped in while Feargal pulled the starter on the outboard. The motor span, then stopped. 'Drat the thing!' he swore. Feargal pulled the cord again and finally on the fourth try it choked reluctantly into life. He gave them a last push and shouted that he'd go for more fuel.

Tess looked out to sea again. Luke was just visible but clearly struggling. She pushed from her mind the terrible thoughts that tried to invade it. If she concentrated her entire being on that distant figure, maybe she could keep him afloat by sheer willpower.

609

Not daring to speak, they ploughed through the cold blue water, the boat rising and falling with the waves. Each time Luke's slight figure disappeared from sight Tess felt her chest contract with fear.

They were nearer now and she could see that Luke had stopped swimming and was treading water. 'Come on!' she yelled at the outboard, leaning forward as though that alone could make the boat move faster.

Twenty feet away from him the motor suddenly stopped. Tess and Stephen exchanged a look of desperation. No more fuel. Stephen grabbed the oars and pulled the last few yards towards him. It was going to be all right.

Tess knelt up in the boat shouting that they were coming, hope leaping in her heart. As she did so a wave, not huge, but a little bigger than the others, buffeted Luke and he slipped below the water.

'Stephen,' shouted Tess, hysteria making her voice as shrill as a seabird's call, 'he's gone under!'

CHAPTER THIRTY-EIGHT

'Here, take the oars!' Stephen yelled back. Tess grabbed them as Stephen, tearing off his sweater, dived over the side.

She tried to hold the boat straight as the current swept them further away from the tower, terrified she'd lose sight of where Luke had gone down. Staring into the waves, the memory came back to her of Luke as a child of two or three. He'd fallen into a swimming pool and she'd seen his face under the water as she'd dived in to rescue him, his eyes wide open and terrified, seeming to ask her how she had let this happen. Oh God – anxiety closed up her throat until she could hardly breathe – let him live. All around her the silence was huge and malevolent.

And then she heard splashing and Stephen appeared a couple of yards away with Luke in his arms.

She leant to the side, her heart beating wildly, and held out an oar to Stephen. He grabbed it and she hauled Luke aboard. Then Stephen climbed back in, exhausted.

She laid Luke's body in the bottom of the boat, white and motionless, and heard a scream. She was about to turn in fright when she realized it was her own voice. She crouched down, holding him, sobbing.

Stephen shook the water from his clothes. 'Try and get him breathing again, for God's sake!'

Tess turned him on his back, wishing to God she'd taken up the offer on countless tube ads to learn first aid. But to her eternal relief, Stephen knew what to do. He tipped Luke's head gently back, pinched his nostrils and breathed lifegiving air into his still-blue mouth.

Nothing happened. Tess sat watching helplessly as Stephen tried again, alternating breathing with powerful thumps to his thin chest. Anything. She'd give anything, her own life even, for Luke to breathe again. But his body remained as pale and lifeless as a China doll's. Then, at last, there was a sudden convulsion and Luke began to spew up water.

Relief sang through Tess as she watched the life slowly returning to him.

'I think he's going to be all right,' whispered Stephen, knowing, as no one else could, what she'd just been going through. 'Do you want to hold him?'

Tess ducked down and took his slight body out of Stephen's arms. As she did so their hands touched. Stephen's was icy and she longed to warm it for him.

Behind them they heard the faint chug of an outboard. It was Feargal with fuel and blankets.

Ten minutes later, wrapped in an ancient tartan rug, Luke opened his eyes. 'Sorry, Mum. It was dumb of me. I should have known I couldn't do it.'

Tess locked him into a tight embrace. 'And Lyall shouldn't have goaded you into it.' She felt a wave of fury against Lyall, who had no inkling of the fierce passion that was parental love. But Stephen did. From the other side of the boat she felt his presence, listening and watching as Luke fell into an exhausted sleep.

Tess and Stephen sat either side of the large white-quilted bed while Luke, less doll-like by the moment, slept peacefully between them. Neither wanted to lose him from their sight, as though without their constant vigilance disaster might overtake him again at any moment. And to both of them this irrational feeling made perfect sense.

The doctor had come and declared him well on the road to recovery. The house was beginning to stop holding its breath. Downstairs Josephine had the wit to bide her time and wait. Lyall was less sensible. He went upstairs to look for Tess.

When she heard the knock on the door, Tess assumed it was Stella with the Lucozade she'd promised. Her face closed over at the sight of Lyall.

'Look, Tess' – he clearly wanted to come into the room, but Tess stepped outside and quickly shut the door behind her – 'I'm really sorry about all this,' he offered. 'It was stupid of me. But I'd no idea the silly idiot would go off on his own. He'd have been fine with me.'

Tess listened to him coldly. He seemed to feel no real remorse at the near-tragedy, simply an eagerness to set out the facts. A lawyer to the last. Tess saw that he would never love Luke as she did, or even begin to understand the nature of her love.

'I'm sorry, Lyall.' Her greeny-blue eyes told him that he had not been forgiven. 'I'm too angry with you to be able to talk about this now. Let's just leave it, shall we?'

Julius, emerging from his studio, almost felt sorry for the man when he saw him slink back downstairs. Almost, but not quite. Things were going really quite well.

When Tess went back into Luke's bedroom the slanting rays of late afternoon sunshine were making patterns on the high ceiling above them. Already they held in them the promise of autumn, but Tess didn't mind the thought of the year's end. It hadn't been a year she wanted to hold on to. Across the bed, divided from or united with her by the sleeping Luke, Stephen dozed, his head on the quilt cover.

Without him Luke would be dead. Tess felt a surge of tenderness and reached out a hand, gently stroking a stray lock of hair, almost black against the blinding white of the linen. Stephen didn't wake.

To her astonishment, sitting there with disaster still so close, she felt an extraordinary sense of wellbeing, as though having lost the template of content, she had suddenly found it again.

When Stephen stirred he looked around him, seeming not to know quite where he was. Then he saw her and his face lit up, as if her presence here were entirely natural.

Finally it was Tess who broke the silence. 'Stephen . . .' She reached a hand across the quilt for his. 'Life's so precious. Maybe we should be grabbing it with both hands, not throwing it away.'

Stephen's heart leaped and he returned her grip so tightly it almost hurt. Then a shadow crossed his face. She was probably still in shock.

'Look, Tess, what you're feeling is probably just relief.' He thought of Josephine and Lyall waiting for them downstairs. 'It may have nothing to do with reality. I expect it's a reaction to what we've both been through.'

'Is it?' Tess knew he was trying to be fair to her, but she didn't need protecting. 'Then why did I feel it last week, and the week before? It took Luke nearly drowning to make me face up to it. I think we're making a mistake. A healthy marriage should let people change. I tried to stop you because I needed security so much. Now I don't.'

'Stop it, Tess.' Stephen jumped to his feet and came to her. 'I'm the one who should apologize. For

Josephine. For thinking I had the divine right to paint no matter what it cost you. Just like my father. Oh, God, Tess, I missed you all so much.' She saw the pain in his eyes and knew he spoke from the heart.

The truth was they'd both tried to wipe the slate clean. But turning your back on eighteen years of marriage wasn't as simple as that. It was a history. A patchwork of small moments that bound you together. Of friends made, memories shared, crises survived, happiness savoured more because of the presence of the other. And nothing – not even sex or excitement or success – could easily replace it. Tess saw that now. But did Stephen?

He was still holding her hand. 'Do you really think we could make it work?'

'Yes.' Tess lifted his hand and kissed it. 'I really think we could. But now that I've learned to take risks you might even have to support me this time.'

'Done,' promised Stephen, and he kissed her so hard and long that she could hardly breathe.

Neither of them noticed when the door opened and Ellie's head appeared only to disappear again with the speed of a conjuror's baton.

'Gramps!' she squawked. 'They're kissing!' She looked round at her grandfather, eyes alight with excitement. 'Do you think they're going to get back together?'

'I wouldn't be at all surprised; I've been to enough trouble to encourage them.'

Julius knocked discreetly then went into the room.

'Is this a private reconciliation?' he asked. 'Or can anyone join in?'

Instantly Luke sat up in bed. 'Are you two going to stop getting divorced now?' he demanded.

Stephen laughed, suspecting that Luke might not

have been asleep as long as he'd pretended. 'What is this, a conspiracy?'

'Let's just say,' Julius intoned, 'that we've all got your best interests at heart.'

'And ours,' added Ellie.

Tess took Stephen's hand again. 'I think we've wanted this to happen for a long time, but we needed something to convince us.'

'So it was me who got you to make up your minds then, was it?' Luke asked smugly.

'Yes, you little shit.' Stephen touched his son's pale face. 'Just don't make a habit of drowning yourself to bring people back together.'

'We were just wondering,' Ellie asked cautiously, 'you're not doing this for the sake of the children, are you?'

'No,' answered Stephen truthfully, 'I'm afraid it's more selfish than that. This time we're doing it because of us.'

'Thank God for that.' Julius put an arm around each grandchild and hugged them. 'Then at least there's some chance it might bloody well work.'